Fractured Sky

THE TATTERED & TORN SERIES

CATHERINE COWLES

Cover Designer: TRC Designs
Editors: Susan Barnes & Margo Lipschultz
Copy Editor: Chelle Olson
Proofreading: Julie Deaton and Jaime Ryter
Paperback Formatting: Stacey Blake, Champagne Book Design

Dedication

For Buckley.

So much of this story is about the bond between animals and people. And when I lost my little soulmate during the writing of this book, I knew there was only one 'person' it could be dedicated to.

My life was all the richer for having his love, his epic snores, and his stalker tendencies. He was there with me through all the hardest moments of my life, and I will miss him every day for the rest of mine.

Love you to the moon and back, Bucks. Until we meet again.

Fractured Sky

Prologue

Shiloh

PAST, AGE TEN

THE WIND HOWLED THROUGH THE CRACKS IN THE SHED, and I pulled the blanket tighter around my shoulders. The fabric felt like sandpaper. Nothing like the blankets at home.

I closed my eyes and imagined running my hand over the quilt on my bed. It was just the right kind of worn. My mom had made it herself. She'd asked me what colors I wanted, and I'd watched as she pieced the fabric together and then stitched the shapes with her sewing machine. She'd quilted big stars across the covering. And every time I pulled it up to my chin, I felt as if I were sleeping under a blanket made of sky.

A door banged in the distance, and my eyes flew open. My hands trembled as I pulled the blanket tighter—as if that could protect me from whatever might come.

I couldn't tell anymore if the tremors rocking through me were from cold or fear. Probably both. My dad had always told me that fear was natural. It was what you did with it that mattered. Somehow, I didn't think he'd thought of this scenario when he mentioned it.

I listened carefully, but I couldn't hear much above the howling wind. My tongue stuck to the roof of my mouth, and I swore I felt cracks in it.

I looked longingly at the bottles of water next to the flimsy mattress. The man who wanted me to call him *Dad* had left them. But he wasn't my dad. And I'd watched some thriller movies with my big brothers, Beckett and Hayes. I knew someone could put drugs in those bottles.

My stomach cramped as I took in the sandwich the man had placed beside the bottles. Bugs crawled over it now. My hands fisted in the blanket's rough fabric. It was my fault—all of it.

I could still hear the sounds of the fair—carnival rides, music, and laughter. I hadn't wanted to go. Had pouted and complained, wanting to go riding instead. But I'd been overruled. Maybe the man had gotten me because I'd been sulking. He'd said something about pony rides. I wanted to know where.

We had plenty of horses at the ranch, but I'd never ridden a pony. They were so cute. I'd turned to look and felt a pain in my side. The world had gone sideways then. I could see the people walking by, but I couldn't say anything. Couldn't wave my hands or scream for help. There was just…nothing.

Nothing until I'd woken up in this shed. How long ago had that been? One day? Two? More? It was all a hazy blur.

My nose stung, and tears burned my eyes. I wanted my room. Our ranch. Even my tagalong little sister. I would've given anything to see Hadley's face poking in and asking what I was doing.

A tear slid down my cheek, falling off my chin and landing on the blanket. Would I ever hear her voice begging to come riding with me again? Taste my mom's homemade lemon meringue pie? Help my dad feed and groom the horses? Go riding on the four-wheelers with Beck and Hayes?

The tears came faster, sobs racking my body so hard I didn't hear the man coming. The door to the shed crashed open.

The man filled the doorway, his broad shoulders and angry face making me skitter back towards the wall.

"What's all the racket?"

My noise was nothing compared to the brewing storm. Lightning lit the sky, illuminating the man in front of me. I only shook harder.

"I-I-I want to go home. I won't tell. Just please let me go home."

The man's face twisted like the trees behind him, contorting in the wind. "You *are* home. Your family were sinners. Evil. I saved you. You need to show a little gratitude."

My stomach clenched. He said the same things, over and over. Everything was *evil* or out to corrupt. My parents. The fair. School. The government. "They love me."

"They don't. I saw them not paying close enough attention. They pawned you off on your brothers, but they couldn't even be bothered to watch you. You needed to get away from them. You'll be safer with us. Protected from all the evil and worldliness."

He glanced at the uneaten sandwich and stormed towards it, snatching it up. "This is perfectly good food, now wasted." He threw it at me, his face morphing yet again. It was like he was different people at different times, and each one was more terrifying than the last. "Maybe you were a mistake. Maybe you have evil in you, too."

"I-I don't." I didn't think I did, anyway. But maybe I was wrong. I snapped at Hadley sometimes. Tattled on Beckett. I'd stolen Hayes' favorite sweatshirt because I loved how soft it was.

The man's eyes narrowed on me as he leaned forward. He studied me how my dad examined a broken water pump, looking for the leak. "I sense evil. The others might not see it, but I can."

He moved in closer, and I shuddered, huddling against the wall. His hands gripped my shoulders tight enough to leave bruises. "I know when the evil slips in. I know the only choice is to beat it out of you."

"I swear. There's no evil in me. Please." Tears streamed down my face.

The man wiped one away with his thumb and straightened, studying the liquid. He stared at it and sniffed. "You're lucky they didn't taint you. It's a miracle. I saved you just in time. You'll be a good match for my Ian one day."

"Match?" The question was out before I could stop it.

The man grinned. "Meant to be. Never see worldly girls who are free of evil. But you knew that fair was bad. *Knew* you should stay away. I had to protect you. Get my son a good wife, too."

"I can't get married. I'm not old enough." The words came out in a croak. Some foreign fear made my muscles quake. This was wrong. A voice inside told me to run. To fight with everything I had.

The man chuckled. "Of course, you aren't old enough." The amusement fled his face. "But I wasn't going to leave you with your devil family to be tainted and ruined. We'll keep an eye on you here. You'll stay pure."

Pure. It didn't make sense, not like that. I'd only heard it used when it came to water. Dad would check the stream to make sure it was clean enough for the horses and cattle to drink from. It couldn't get stagnant—too full of dirt and algae. It had to keep moving. That meant nothing when it came to describing a human being.

The man picked up one of the water bottles and tossed it at me. "Drink that water."

I said nothing, still frozen, but the urge to run was so strong.

"I said drink it. This is my family, and what I say goes."

I pulled the blanket tighter around me, covering my mouth as if that might protect me. All I could think about was being poisoned—or worse. He'd given me drugs at the fair. I knew it. I wouldn't let that happen again.

The man grabbed the bottle of water. "You will drink this, or you will pay the price."

"Dad?" It was a girl's voice. I could just make out a figure in the dark by the trees. They looked about my age. Had she been taken, too?

"Get back to your room, Everly. This isn't your concern."

She didn't move.

I pleaded with my eyes. Then, I let the words fly. Maybe she would hear my truth. Maybe she would see. "Please, let me go home. Please." I didn't want to be here. Didn't want this man's crazed world to be real. I just wanted my mom and my dad and my room. I wanted to go where nothing could hurt me.

"Everly, go back to the house. *Now*," the man barked.

The girl still didn't move. "She didn't do anything wrong. I can take her back to town and—"

"Ian!" the man bellowed.

"Yeah?"

I jolted at the new voice. It was younger than the man's—much younger. A figure stepped into the light on the outside of the shed. He was older than me but still a boy. Maybe my brother Hayes' age.

His face wasn't twisted in rage the way his father's was. It was almost...gentle. But something about it made my insides feel funny, a little sick. Like I might throw up. But there was nothing in there to empty.

"Take Everly to her room and make sure she stays there."

The boy nodded and stalked towards the girl. She stiffened, but when he got close, she turned and ran for the house. The man watched as they went, so focused that I knew it was my only chance.

I launched myself from the mattress and ran for the door. Even though I was tall for my age, I was slender. I just needed to duck under his side. I tasted the fresh air and the scent of pine. A hand fisted in my t-shirt, yanking me back. Hard.

I slammed into the mattress as hands tightened around my throat. The man shook me, his face a mottled red. "I'm trying to save you! You will obey!"

Spittle landed on my face as my vision went dark around the edges. He shook me harder, and all I could think was that this was the end. There were so many things I wanted to do, and now, I wouldn't get to do a single one. But most of all, I wanted to tell my family that I loved them. To make sure they knew.

Just as the darkness was about to claim me, the man released his hold on my throat. "I won't let the evil take hold." He stormed out, the door slamming in his wake. Even through the howling wind, I heard the lock clicking into place. Then, I was alone.

I shook violently against the flimsy, stained mattress. Every part of me trembled so viciously it rattled my bones. I was going to die here. And no one would ever know.

I shook harder as the rain started to fall. The roof of the shed was cracked in places. A spiderweb that I could see flashes of lightning through. Splashes of wetness hit my skin.

My teeth chattered violently, but I wasn't any colder than I had been moments ago. Raindrops hit my lips. Water. I forced my mouth open, taking in all the liquid I could—water that couldn't be poisoned because it came from the Heavens above.

I stared up at that fractured sky, my only salvation. The faintest glimmer of hope took root in my chest. I opened my mouth wider and prayed for home.

Chapter One

Shiloh

SEVENTEEN YEARS LATER

THE SUN LIT THE FIELDS IN A WAY THAT SAID IT WAS showing off. There wasn't a cloud in the sky, just that dazzling sun. I pulled my flat-brim hat lower to shade my eyes as I scanned the pasture, looking for a telltale speckled coat.

There were a number of horses that I rode on my family's ranch, nestled in the mountains of eastern Oregon. Far more that I trained myself. I tried to give them all love and attention—long rides as often as possible and plenty of treats. But only one was truly *mine*.

She was the first horse I'd bought with the money I'd made working the ranch. It was a little piece of independence when every sliver was hard-won. I didn't take any for granted: each first and bit of freedom. Paycheck. Bank account. Post office box. My apartment over the barn.

They wouldn't seem like much to most people, but *most people* didn't have a family who had been through what mine had. It was impossible not to hold on too tightly when you almost lost someone. So, I'd had to fight for each little freedom. And every one represented a carefully fought battle.

I unlatched the gate to the pasture, my gaze moving across the dips and rolls of the field. It caught on that familiar coat. The mare's markings had called me to her ten years ago. She'd been just two years old, and I knew it was meant to be.

Most of her coloring was that of dark bay, but the pattern across her hind end revealed her true heritage: Appaloosa, through and through. That white with dark spots had been a sucker punch to the gut. A reminder of the darkest moments of my life. But more than that, a remembrance of the one piece of hope I'd had.

That fractured sky. The rain that had given me the water I'd so desperately needed. After I'd been rescued and was in the hospital, I'd overheard the doctor talking to my parents. She'd said that she didn't think I would've made it another twenty-four hours. And that was when I knew the truth: The sky had saved me.

And Everly. The daughter of the man who had taken me. She'd snuck out and ridden through the night to the sheriff's station to help me make my way home. I'd never be able to repay her for what they'd given me—her or the sky. But now, Ev was a part of our family, something that would be official in a matter of months when she married Hayes.

I did what I could to show my gratitude. Helped her at the animal sanctuary she'd built on the land that had once been her family's. Tried to say yes when she and Hayes invited me for dinner. It wasn't much, but it was what I could give.

I had no way of repaying the sky. I tipped my face up to it, letting the sun warm my skin. I felt the vibrations of hooves against the ground but kept my eyes closed, soaking in the heat. A muzzle nosed my shoulder.

My hand found the mare's cheek before I opened my eyes. Pulling off my hat, I dropped my head to hers, our foreheads touching. "Hey, Sky."

She blew air out of her nostrils in greeting.

"How would you feel about a ride?"

I swore her eyes sparked in excitement, and I couldn't help my smile. Hooking the lead rope to her halter, I started for the gate. "You're gonna need a good groom."

Sky looked as if she'd taken a roll in a patch of mud. Those patches were too plentiful to avoid this time of year. Spring in Wolf Gap could be unpredictable. You could have sun like this one day and snow the next. It made for mud city anywhere the snow or rain gathered. But that made Sky as happy as could be.

Movement caught my eye. My mom unhooked the gate and held it open for us. "Where are you two headed?"

I didn't miss the lines of tension around her mouth as she asked. Most would've, but I'd become an expert in human behavior. In reading their movements and expressions. It was my first line of defense. I never wanted to miss the mean or unstable again.

That awareness was both a blessing and a curse. I felt safer, but I never missed just how much my kidnapping affected the people I loved. How much it weighed on their shoulders, even after all this time.

That familiar gnawing sensation took root in my belly, and I focused on the ground instead of my mother. "Just for a trail ride."

Mom shut the gate behind Sky and me, latching it back into place. "Want some company?"

She always offered—every single time. My skin itched as if it were too tight for my body. "Maybe next time."

My mom worried her bottom lip. "How long will you be gone?"

Annoyance flickered to life as my grip on the lead rope tightened. "Not sure." I started walking towards the barn. If I didn't move, the panic that came with the feeling of being hemmed in would grab hold. Even now, my fingers fluttered against my thigh. Stretching and flexing, then taking up a rapid tapping.

The staccato movement helped to keep things in check. I'd learned to hold tight to the things that helped. But the greatest balm for everything churning inside me was the thing I didn't have nearly enough of—solitude.

"Did you have lunch?"

My mom's voice cut through my swirling thoughts. I let out a breath as I kept walking. "In my saddlebags."

Her gaze went sharp, and that telltale furrow appeared between her brows. "I don't think you should be riding without eating. The sun's bright today. You could faint. Fall off Sky, and we'd have no idea where you were."

The movement of my fingers picked up its pace. I clenched and flexed my hand to keep from screaming. As if at twenty-seven years old, I didn't know when I needed to eat. I knew hunger better than she ever would. Instead of biting her head off, though, I stayed quiet.

So often, silence was the best gift I could give my family. Biting my tongue and staying out of the way. Erasing the reminder of the thing that had marked each of them in such different ways.

"Shiloh—"

I cut her off by stepping into the barn.

"Hey, Mom."

Hayes' voice brought a wash of relief. Mom turned, focusing on her youngest son, and I hightailed it to the crossties. If I were quick, I might get out of here before she finished talking wedding plans with him.

I led Sky into the grooming space. The truth was, I didn't even need the lead rope. She would've followed me anywhere. It was the kind of trust I knew I'd only ever have with animals. They didn't have the same kind of agendas that humans did.

They also didn't push for conversation. I hooked Sky to the crossties and bent to grab the curry comb from my grooming kit. I took the brush to her back, working at the worst of the mud. "Did you take a bath in it? This is ridiculous, even for you."

She lifted her head up and down as if nodding, but it was just because she loved the sensation of the curry comb against her coat. It was like one of those little massagers that dug into all the right muscles.

I worked my way around her, getting every speck of caked-on

dirt. Then I moved to the hard brush to clear it all away. Grooming was a silent meditation, in and of itself—for both Sky and me. I could get lost in whatever I needed to puzzle through or let go of.

Today, it was my frustration with my mom's overprotectiveness. With each swipe of the brush, I reminded myself why she was the way she was. And as the frustration melted away, guilt took its place. No matter how many times I told myself just to be the daughter Mom needed, I couldn't do it. Every time I tried, I ended up with panic attacks so bad I nearly passed out.

Footsteps sounded on the stone aisle. The first steps had me stiffening, but by the third and fourth, my muscles loosened some. The tread was too heavy for Mom. It had to be Hayes.

I kept moving through my process, switching the hard brush for the soft. As I did, Hayes stepped forward to give Sky a rub. He wasn't in his sheriff's uniform, so it was either a day off, or he'd taken off early to help Everly with something.

"Where are you headed?"

Hayes played the game better than Mom did. His tone was casual. The question thrown out like a simple one you'd ask anyone. But I knew it wasn't how he'd meant it. If he had his way, he'd have me mapping out my exact route and implanted with a tracker before I left.

I ran the brush down Sky's leg. "Not sure."

His mouth thinned, the dark stubble surrounding it twitching with the movement. "Can't you at least give a destination? Just in case there's an accident?"

I'd lived my entire life after the kidnapping as one big *just in case*. Mom hadn't let me go back to school for the rest of the year. There was no more hide-and-seek on our property. Or riding our bikes around town without one of my parents present. Slowly but surely, every piece of freedom I'd taken for granted had disappeared. On the dark days, I wondered if returning home had made much difference at all. Because in so many ways, I was still a hostage.

I'd slowly gotten some of those pieces back, and I wouldn't let anyone steal them from me now. "Do you tell Everly exactly where you're going when you go on a trail run with Koda?"

Hayes frowned. "She has a general idea."

"Fine. I'm heading that way." I pointed west. It was the truth. But I'd never tell Hayes exactly where I was going. Because if I did, he'd likely lock me up and throw away the key.

Chapter Two

Ramsey

MY PHONE VIBRATED AS I HEADED TOWARDS THE ROUND pen. The gelding inside pawed at the ground the moment he caught sight of me. A wildness in his eyes spoke of a mixture of fear and fire.

I grimaced as the vibrations continued, finally pulling the device out of my pocket. An alert for the front gate signaled, and my frown deepened. I slid my thumb across the screen and opened the security app. The camera showed a delivery truck and a man with a ballcap pulled down low.

My gut tightened as I scanned as much of his face as I could see. He wasn't familiar. My jaw worked back and forth as I tapped an icon for the intercom. "Yeah?"

The man jolted at the bite in the single word. "I've got a delivery for a Ramsey Bishop."

"From who?"

"Uh, no clue."

I was silent, watching the man squirm. He sighed. "Hold on, let me check."

He moved into the back of his truck. I didn't take my eyes off the screen, watching the play of shadows for any hint of more than one person in the vehicle. A few moments later, the man reappeared. "It's from Western Saddlery."

"Leave it at the gate."

The man twisted in his seat. "Requires a signature. Guess it's insured."

I muttered a curse. "What happened to Dale?"

"Dale?"

"The usual driver." The one I'd run background checks on. I knew he spent far too much of his paycheck on his bar tab, but I also knew he was harmless. This guy was an unknown.

"No idea. Must be sick or something because I'm covering this route. Look, they time us, so are you going to open the gate or not?"

Like hell I'd let someone onto my property that I didn't know and hadn't fully vetted. "Stay there. I'll come get the package."

"You've got two minutes."

My back molars ground together as I hopped into the ranch truck. I was at the front gate in just over two minutes, but the guy was still waiting. He'd carted the large package out of the back of the truck and had it balanced on the gate.

He eyed me carefully as I came to a stop and climbed out of the truck. His gaze swept over me and then behind me, trying to see what my property might house. He'd never be able to tell from here. Tall pines lined the road and hid everything. I'd planted more than enough of them to create a wall.

"You're not gonna shoot me, are you? Heard you chased off one guy with a shotgun."

I fought the urge to roll my eyes as I motioned for the tablet to sign for my package. It was a toss-up which I hated more: going to town for supplies or ordering them online and dealing with whoever brought them.

"Asshole," the delivery guy muttered under his breath as he handed me the pen to sign.

I scrawled something illegible across the screen and grabbed the box. I was used to people thinking I was an asshole—and a hell of a lot worse. If their opinions bothered me, I never would've made it through the past twenty years alive. You learned to silence the noise.

I set the box in the truck's bed and climbed behind the wheel. I shook off the annoyance as I drove back towards the round pen. Whatever I was dealing with had no place there.

It was something I'd learned along the way. You had to shed everything that clung to you before you climbed between those fence rails. I eased to a stop and put the truck in park as the gelding eyed me. There was so much intelligence in that gaze.

My mouth curved the barest amount. If someone were watching, they wouldn't have even seen it. But I felt it. That trickle of excitement. The feeling that this horse had a world of potential.

Turning off the engine, I tossed the keys back into the console and slid out of the truck. I shut the door but was careful to keep my movements slow and easy—no jarring sounds or flashes of speed.

I walked towards the pen and bent to pick up the training flag: a square piece of fabric attached to a pole not much thicker than a wire hanger. The gelding let out a whinny and charged the fence at the flicker of color.

I didn't let his flash of temper halt my progress. I ducked between the fence rails and climbed into the pen. The horse pawed at the ground, throwing his head back in warning. I didn't move.

The gelding gave a healthy buck and kicked his hind legs in my direction. I simply flicked the long-handled training flag at his outburst. He could throw his tantrum all he wanted, but he couldn't invade my personal space. Yet I understood why.

He'd been through hell and back, and it would take time for him to trust that I wouldn't put him through more. Boundaries and empathy. You needed them both in equal measure. That, and patience.

No matter what a horse threw your way, you couldn't let your emotions bleed into the work. And this gelding looked as if he were going to give it the ol' college try. He reared up on his hind legs, pawing the air. I flicked the flag again when he got close to me.

He would learn that the flag wouldn't hurt him. It was simply a visual aid to mark a boundary. To tell him where he needed to go. He landed back on his hooves, shaking the ground, then raced around the pen. I stayed still and waited.

There was no rush. He had to know that we'd go at his pace. I wouldn't force him.

I waited as the horse tired himself out. The gallop slowed to a trot. Then a walk. Finally, he stilled and stared at me dead-on. I didn't move. I just let him take my measure.

I kept my gaze even with his but made sure to blink. I wasn't trying to challenge him, just let him know that I wasn't going anywhere. After a few minutes, I took two steps.

The horse's muscles quivered. I stopped and gave him a chance to get used to the new normal. I repeated the process over and over until I was just a foot away.

The gelding sniffed the air. He didn't have a name yet. I couldn't name them until I got to know them. And that took time. Who the horse really was at its core was usually buried beneath layers of self-protection—at least, the horses who came to me.

I raised my hand slowly, letting him get a good sniff. Once he had my scent, I moved my hand to his cheek and stroked. I kept the movements nice and slow. He had to know that touch didn't always have to hurt. I knew better than most that it was a hard lesson to learn.

I brushed at the dirt on his cheek. I wanted to give him a good grooming but knew we were a ways off from that yet. Instead, I moved my hand to his forehead, giving him a good scratch. Different sensation, still no pain. The horse's ears twitched in response.

Movement flickered in the corner of my eye. My dog, Kai, had taken off across the field towards the ridge in the distance. He'd seen her before I had. Over the years, we'd both become attuned to her presence like heat-seeking missiles, but he had that sense of smell on his side.

Shiloh's hair caught on the breeze, that mix of gold and brown. I didn't blame my damn dog for chasing after her. She was the kind of beautiful that lit a fire in your veins. That kind of beauty was dangerous.

Kai leapt, and Shiloh caught him in a sort of hug that ended with them rolling on the ground. Her horse looked on warily. I understood the reaction. Kai was half wolf, half...some other undiscernible breed. Undiscernible because the wolf half had taken over so thoroughly.

The first time Shiloh had shown up here, I hadn't a clue who she was. She'd sat on that same ridge, not approaching. I'd started in her direction to tell her to get the hell off my land before I shot her for trespassing when a miraculous thing happened.

Kai, who was suspicious of every human besides me, had charged. For a split second, I'd thought he was going to attack her. But Shiloh hadn't shown even an ounce of fear. She'd simply opened her arms to the beast, and they'd fallen into a tumble like old friends.

I hadn't had it in me to break them apart. Instead, I'd gone back to work. I'd expected her to approach the pen, but she'd never moved from her spot on the ridge. Sometimes, she came daily. Other times, I didn't see her for a week or two. But somewhere along the line, I'd started to think of that spot as hers.

The idea irked me. This was *my* property. I could count on one hand the number of people I'd let cross its borders. And yet, here she was, making herself at home. But then I remembered what she'd been through.

It had all clicked on her second visit. Something about the pain in those blue eyes had triggered a memory of the countless articles I'd seen in the local paper—ones that revealed far more details than I was sure Shiloh wanted out in the world.

The horse pushed against my hand, and I turned my focus back to him. "Already getting demanding, huh?"

He let out a huff of air.

I moved my scratching to behind his ears. His lips wiggled in a dance of their own.

"I guess that's your spot."

Slowly, without stopping my scratching, I lifted the flag. The gelding shied away three feet. He was there one second and gone the next.

I stilled as he pawed at the ground.

"Not gonna hurt you." I gave him a few minutes to let the panic ease and then closed the distance between us again. I raised a hand to pet his neck. After a few more minutes of that, I lifted the flag again. He didn't shy away this time, but his muscles tensed beneath my hands.

I palmed the flag and rubbed his neck with it. His muscles were still tensed, hard as stone, but he didn't move. I used my hand and the flag to scratch and stroke, showing him that nothing about the item would cause him pain.

It didn't happen quickly, but over time, his tension eased. Each slight give was a gift. A grain of trust. It would take hundreds of moments like these to set a solid foundation, but we were on our way.

When I eased back, I ducked between the rails on the pen and slid a bucket of feed inside. The gelding let out a whinny as he slowly started towards it. After a couple of sniffs, he began to eat.

I lifted my gaze to the field. Those blue eyes locked with mine, searing me to the spot. The tightening of my rib cage had me fighting more of that damned annoyance, but I refused to look away.

Shiloh's hand sifted through Kai's fur, but she didn't look away either. Something passed between us. It was the same phantom ghost of emotion that was always there. The thing that said we understood pain. That we'd seen things no one should have to face, and we'd never be the same because of it.

My boots echoed against the porch steps as I climbed them. Lor looked up from her rocker and inclined her head towards the railing. "Brought you a beer."

She was the only person welcome on this porch. The only one who dared to make herself at home there. But even she, my friend of twenty years, wouldn't venture inside without explicit invitation.

I swiped the bottle and brought the cap down on the edge of the railing with one swift move, popping it off.

Lor frowned at me, the lines of age in her tanned face deepening. "You're messing up your perfectly good porch rail."

I raised a brow in her direction. "Am I planning on having *Architectural Digest* out here sometime in the near future?"

She snorted. "They'd take one look at your terrifying scowl and run for the hills."

I grinned at her, but it was all teeth.

Lor gave an exaggerated shiver. "How's the chestnut settling in?"

I lowered myself into the rocker and began tipping it back and forth. Something about the motion eased me—the rhythmic feel of the blades against the planks of wood below. "It's a good start. He's got spirit."

"That'll make it interesting."

"It means they didn't break him." And I respected the hell out of him for that.

Lor stared out at the small pasture that I'd let the gelding into. "Any sense of what he'll be good for?"

"Too early to tell for sure, but I have a feeling he'll enjoy chasing down cattle." That was much of the process: figuring out where the horses should go next. What they'd be well-suited for, and what would make them happy. Some would be perfect trail horses. Others were meant to be loved by kids and families. Some were made for ranch work and a daily purpose. And then there were those that cracked my damn heart because they couldn't come back completely from what they'd gone through. Those made their homes here for the rest of their days. Safe and cared for, with no one to hurt them ever again.

"Spirit usually does like a task."

"True." I took a pull from my beer. "I'm going out to Kenny Chambers' place tomorrow."

Lor's rocking halted. "You sure that's a good idea?"

"No harm in offering to buy a man's horses when he's struggling."

"There is when he's an abusive asshole," she muttered. "Let me get the sheriff's department involved. They'll open an investigation—"

"That will take months. Those horses don't have that kind of time."

Somewhere along the line, people had begun to report this kind of thing to Lor, knowing she'd bring it to me. A man had stopped her in the feed store and whispered that he was concerned about Chambers' horses. I'd done my recon, and it was bad. The man's ranch was struggling, and he was taking his frustrations out on the animals around him.

Lor blew out a breath. "You're gettin' yourself caught up in things you shouldn't. One day, it's gonna come back to bite you."

I made a sound that wasn't agreement or disagreement, just an acknowledgment that I'd heard her.

Lor picked up her rocking again. "I saw the girl."

I took another sip of my beer, not meeting Lor's gaze. Shiloh typically had a kind of radar for when Lor was around and stayed away, but Lor had seen her more than once now, and it was making her edgy.

"I'm not sure her being here is a good idea."

I knew that. There was no doubt in my mind that it was a horrible idea to let Shiloh Easton come and go from my property at will. But I couldn't stop myself. Those flashes of understanding had become some of the best parts of my day.

Lor let out a sound of frustration. "You know how protective her family is of her. And given all she's been through, I don't blame them. But her brother's the damn sheriff. How do you think he'll react when he finds out she's making little field trips over here?"

He'd lose his shit. My grip on the bottle tightened, but I forced myself to keep rocking.

Lor sighed. "I'm not saying this to be an ass. I worry about you. You might've been exonerated, but to lots of folks around here, you're still an ex-con."

And, to them, that was all I'd ever be.

Chapter Three

Shiloh

I GRIPPED MY KEYS TIGHTER AS I WALKED TOWARDS THE POST office. The tiny teeth of the metal bit into my palm. But that kept me grounded. Kept me from hurtling back into memories as gazes caught on me and held.

No matter how much time had passed, people were still curious. I knew I didn't help matters given how I behaved, but I needed those coping mechanisms. I pulled the brim of my hat down lower as a woman stared.

I vaguely recognized her. She'd been a few years ahead of me in school. She might've been someone that Hayes or Beck had dated for a hot second. But now, she was just another set of eyes.

Her gaze made my skin itch, and I fought the urge to pull my jacket tighter around me. Instead, I focused on the path ahead of me. The door to the post office opened, and Beck pulled up short. "Hey, Shy."

I struggled to keep my expression relaxed and my breathing even. Beckett saw more than my other siblings did. Maybe it was his time serving as a doctor with Aid International. Or maybe it was because he'd fallen in love and married a woman with her own set of traumatic scars. But I had to guard myself more around him than anyone else.

"Hey."

"Picking up your mail?"

No, I was going to ride an elephant. Of course, I was picking up mail. Instead of saying that, I nodded. "How's Addie?"

"She's good. Getting tired more easily but still determined to keep working at The Gallery for now."

"I'm sure Laiken is keeping an eye on her."

The manager of the art space was one of Addie's closest friends, and I knew she'd never let any harm come to her there.

"You're right, but I still don't like it."

My lips twitched. "No, you'd rather wrap her in Bubble Wrap and confine her to the house until she gives birth."

Beck chuckled and rubbed the back of his neck, the strands of blond in his brown hair catching in the afternoon light. "Is that really so bad?"

"No, it's just not very practical."

And while my brother's heart was in the right place, the feeling could be suffocating. Like you couldn't move or breathe without someone analyzing every detail.

"You've got a point there. Hey, why don't you come over for dinner next week? Just the three of us."

The metal keys dug deeper into my flesh. I wasn't a fan of large groups, but intimate gatherings were worse. And if Beck were there, he'd be using that doctor focus to evaluate everything about me. I swallowed hard. "Sure. Just let me know when."

"Addie or I will text you."

I nodded. "I should go. I need to get back to the ranch."

"Sure." He reached out like he might pat my shoulder and then stopped himself. "Glad I ran into you."

My rib cage constricted, and my eyes burned. I felt like the lowest of the low that I couldn't even stand for my own family to touch me. "You, too."

My words came out choked, and I hurried inside before Beckett had a chance to say anything else. I strode towards my destination. Loosening my stranglehold on my keys, I searched for the one to my mailbox. Specks of red dotted the metal, and I glanced down at my palm.

The new, jagged tears in my skin looked angry under the fluorescent lights. I wiped the worst of it away on my pants and grabbed my mail from the box. Tucking it under my arm, I headed for the door.

I closed my eyes for a moment, bracing myself before stepping back into the sunshine. It was fifty-fifty whether Beck would be waiting with more questions. As I pulled open the door, I breathed a sigh of relief at his absence—and I hated myself a little more for it.

I closed the door to my loft and leaned against the wood surface, finally releasing the air my lungs had been holding hostage. I fought the urge to peek through my curtained windows, sure that I'd see my mom or dad with their gazes firmly affixed to my apartment—too many eyes.

A burn lit the back of my throat, and pressure built behind my eyes. I just wanted to feel free. Not tied to expectations and worry. I wanted to know what it was like to be normal.

Yet, I couldn't make myself take that step to go out on my own—for so many reasons. Fear still dominated so much of my daily life. The ranch, while oppressive, was the Devil I knew. And just when I thought I'd gotten up the courage to look for a place of my own, the guilt would settle in. My mom's worry. Dad's concern. So, I stayed put.

I pushed off the door, letting out a growl of frustration. I tossed my mail onto the counter, and it spread out into a fan. My gaze caught on an envelope. *Oregon State Victims' Rights* had been written in bold as the return address.

My stomach gave a vicious twist, and the world tunneled around me. This wasn't happening. The moment I'd turned eighteen, I'd signed up to receive notifications about Howard Kemper through the organization. It was why I'd gotten my own post office box: to hide the letters from my parents.

I'd gotten used to the rhythm of them. Typically, they showed up once a year. I'd send a victim impact statement, and that was that. Never once had there been a sign that Howard might be released early.

I stared at the envelope as if it were a rattlesnake poised to strike. My hands flexed and clenched at my sides as I tried to stave off the panic attack. As quickly as the fear swamped me, rage followed on its heels—such deep anger. Fury that the man could still affect me so much.

I forced myself to reach for the envelope. My hand trembled as I moved, but I grabbed hold of the paper. It took several tries to get the flap open before I finally succeeded. I tugged the single page free.

The seal for the state of Oregon was at the top, the name and address for the Victims' Rights subsidiary of the parole board underneath. And then, my name.

My entire body shook as I scanned line after line of text. *We are writing to inform you that Howard Kemper is deceased.* The next words blurred together. Something about receiving no additional notifications from Victims' Rights.

All the strength left me. The only thing I could do was lower myself to the floor, clutching the piece of paper like a lifeline. No more letters.

No more what-ifs. No more worrying about what might happen when Howard Kemper got released. I was free.

I scooted towards my bed, not trusting myself to stand. I reached under the frame, feeling around for the box. My hand touched the angled edge, and I grabbed hold.

The shoebox's deep maroon color was faded now, even though it rarely saw the light of day. My hand shook as I lifted the lid.

Dozens upon dozens of letters filled the box that had once housed my favorite pair of boots. So many, I was running out of space. But only a handful were from the state of Oregon.

Nausea swept through me at the sight of Howard's looping scrawl—the handwriting burned into my brain. Almost a decade had faded some of the ink on the paper. I flipped through envelope after envelope. So many, I'd lost count.

I only ever read them once. And that was more than enough. I should've thrown them away without looking at the contents, but I couldn't seem to stop myself. They were a taunt in written form. A silent: *I'm watching.*

Because how else would Howard have known that I'd gotten my own post office box? How could he know where to address the letters? Someone had told him exactly where to send them. I shivered as Ian's face flashed in my mind. The way his eyes lingered on me if I saw him in town. The hatred there.

He's in prison. Howard's son had been sentenced to three years for his part in Everly's kidnapping last year. And I was free.

I stared down at nine years' worth of harassment. Letters that had made me lose sleep or the contents of my stomach. It was done.

I'd never had the guts to ask my parents if they received letters on my behalf. Because then they'd have known what was coming my way. And they'd have made me close my post office box for sure.

But I took it as a point of pride. Howard Kemper had tried to break me, but he hadn't won. I was still here. And now, *he* was gone.

I shoved the letter into the box and slammed the lid closed. Sliding it back under my bed, I pushed to my feet and headed for the door. My footsteps echoed on the steps as I hurried down them.

Horses let out whinnies for attention as I passed, but I didn't stop until I reached Sky's stall. I grabbed the bridle from the hook and slid open the door. She lifted her head, taking my measure.

"Wanna go for a ride?"

I should've spent some time working with the new gelding we'd purchased for the ranch, but I needed a ride more than my next breath—to feel the freedom that was now mine.

Sky moved into my space as if to say: "*Hurry up, already.*"

My mouth curved, and I slid the bridle on. She accepted the bit without complaint. I didn't bother with a saddle. Didn't want to take the time. Instead, I stood on the edge of the trunk outside her stall and hoisted myself onto Sky's back.

We fit each other perfectly. As if we'd always been destined for partnership. I patted her neck and started towards the barn doors. I caught sight of my dad in one of the pastures. His gaze cut straight to me, and that familiar concern lined his face.

I shoved down the annoyance and guilt and steered Sky towards the forest. The path was one we knew by heart. I didn't even have to guide her now. It wasn't a short route. It took us thirty minutes, at least, to get where we were going, but the ride was a beautiful one. The mountains peeked out from between endless forests, and one spot had the perfect view of the lake just outside of town. Each moment of peace and beauty helped ease the worst of my edginess.

Sky's ears twitched at sounds I couldn't yet hear. Sky picked up her pace when Ramsey's back pasture came into view. She loved seeing his horses.

I did, too. They were magnificent. And I'd seen him bring many of them back from a state I'd thought there would be no recovery from. Every single horse had a story. They, themselves, were a blanket of stars—pinpricks of hope on the darkest nights.

The horses greeted us with whinnies. A few trotted along the fence line, following us. But most simply kept grazing. They'd become accustomed to my presence since I'd first shown up here, hoping for a glimpse of the man I'd heard could heal even the most broken horses.

I guided Sky around paddocks and pastures until we reached

our ridge. Ramsey was already in the round pen as if he'd known I would need this today.

I slid off Sky's back, taking him in as I did. He had his long, dark hair tied back in a knot with some sort of leather cord. My fingers itched to pull it free and know what it felt like. It was a ridiculous thought for someone who couldn't bear to feel another person's skin against hers.

Even at ten years my senior, the only signs of his age were slight lines in the tan skin around his eyes. Those eyes locked with mine now—a brown so dark they were almost black. The kind of eyes you could get lost in and never emerge from. Onyx eyes. I swallowed hard as I sat on the lush grass.

Ramsey turned his focus back to the horse. The gelding eyed him warily, even after the progress they'd made yesterday. Ramsey never took it personally, though. He went through the same steps over and over until the horse was ready to move on to its next phase.

I watched him move in slow, easy motions, reintroducing the horse to his hands and the training flag. As he covered more of the gelding, moving to his back and hindquarters, I couldn't help the urge to move closer.

Maybe it was the knowledge that I was finally free that stoked my bravery. But for the first time, I walked towards the round pen.

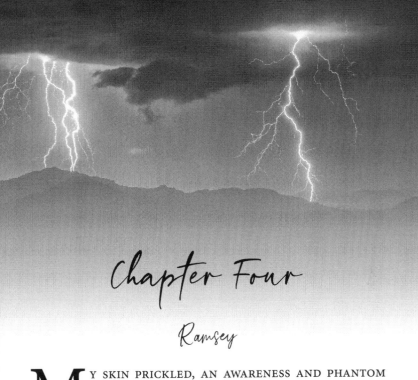

Chapter Four

Ramsey

MY SKIN PRICKLED, AN AWARENESS AND PHANTOM energy washing over me as I stroked the gelding's back. My gaze pulled to the ridge. But Shiloh wasn't there. It was the flash of her long braid in the breeze that cued me into her new location.

My breath caught in my throat at seeing those light blue eyes close-up. They could steal every last semblance of sanity from a man's brain. I froze, standing stock-still.

Shiloh didn't say a word, just watched from her seat on the ground right outside the pen. Her gaze locked on my hand on the horse's back. He twitched in place, and I let a few silent curses fly.

I wasn't easily distracted. I prided myself on my focus and ability to tune out the rest of the world when I worked with the horses. My jaw clenched as I zeroed in on the task at hand. But I was aware of my dog making his way over to her—the traitor.

Sliding my palm across the gelding's back, I gave him a good scratch. He pushed against my hand, wanting more of the contact. That hunger for connection was a good sign. I backed away, reaching for the blanket on the fence rail. The horse shied away from me a few steps.

I stood where I was, rubbing my hand against the fabric. I wanted him to see that he had nothing to fear. I waited for the shift—the one I could feel from across the pen. The one that meant an easing in his energy. As soon as I felt it, I stepped forward.

The gelding's gaze locked on the colorful, woven blanket. It was one of my favorites. Made by a local woman, it reminded me of a sunset—the colors of a brightly painted sky. Slowly, I lifted the blanket and let the horse sniff it. It was freshly laundered, so it didn't have the scent of any other animals.

He inhaled and then huffed out a breath.

"See, nothing to worry about." I lifted the blanket to his neck and rubbed gently.

The horse braced himself at first, muscles locked and seemingly ready to bolt. But as no pain came, he eased a bit. The gelding's acceptance of the *something new* happened in slow shifts. I lost track of time in the dance. There was only him and me.

Finally, he stood in a relaxed posture, the blanket on his back as I scratched behind his ears. "Not so bad, right?"

The gelding's ears twitched.

"All right, enough for today." I pulled the blanket from his back and moved to the fence. My steps hitched a bit as I caught sight of Shiloh again. She didn't move from her seat as I slid between the rails and placed the blanket back on the top.

I waited for her to bolt, but she didn't show any signs of leaving. My pulse beat a rapid rhythm in my neck. Dangerous. Too damn risky. To be this close to her... To see how the gold woven through her light brown hair caught the light. To capture the spark in those blue eyes.

"What's his name?"

Everything in me locked. It was the first time I'd heard Shiloh's voice. It had just a hint of rasp to it. Some huskiness. An edge that I swore I could feel skating across my skin.

"No name yet."

Her gaze turned to me, her eyes glinting in the afternoon light. "Don't you think he deserves a name?"

"He deserves the *right* name. That takes time."

I saw something in Shiloh's expression, a hint of surprise and something that looked a lot like longing. "He does deserve that." Her hand sifted into Kai's fur, and he leaned against her.

Shiloh rested her head atop his, cuddling him to her chest. I'd never seen anything like it. Kai sought me out for affection, but not like this. He was a goner for the woman, and I couldn't blame him.

"You want to meet him?" The words were out of my mouth before I could stop them.

Shiloh's gaze flew to mine. "Really?"

"Sure. It wouldn't be a bad idea to get him used to other people." It was the part of the process my operation lacked since only Lor and I were ever here.

Shiloh nuzzled Kai and got to her feet. "I've worked with plenty of horses, but never one that's been hurt the way he has."

"Calm and steady. Don't let his actions make you react." I ducked between the pen's rails and stepped inside.

She followed, moving slowly and evenly. She kept her gaze on the horse but didn't stare. The gelding pawed at the earth as if marking his territory. Shiloh stilled.

"Breathe through it. He'll feel your tension if it's in you."

She let out a long breath, and I watched hints of unease bleed from her muscles. The horse stopped pawing. His gaze didn't leave us, though. It was two against one, and he wasn't a fan of those odds.

I took a few steps forward, watching for signs of agitation. His muscles were strung tight, but he didn't pin his ears or lower his head to charge. I eased my hand over his face to that spot behind his ears. That seemed to do the trick, relaxing him further.

I shifted my gaze to Shiloh. "Come on up. Nice and easy."

She took a few steps and stopped—halted because she felt the change in the air. The gelding had braced. That kind of instinct was something nearly impossible to teach. It had to be in you. And it usually came from experiencing the dark parts of the world.

My chest constricted at the thought of what Shiloh had faced, but I forced my hands to keep stroking the gelding.

"I don't want to cause him pain," she said softly.

"You're not. You're teaching him that not all hands hurt."

She bit the inside of her cheek and nodded, taking another step. Then another. She found a rhythm that worked for both her and the gelding. And, in a matter of minutes, she was standing next to me. So close, I felt her heat in the early spring air.

"Nice and slow. Raise a hand to pet his neck. Show him what you're doing so he knows."

Shiloh did as I instructed. Her fingers trembled slightly as she moved, and the gelding's eyes locked on that hand. But as soon as it made contact with his neck and started to move in smooth strokes, he let out a breath.

"Feel that?" I asked.

"Like the first taste of air after being underwater for too long."

My mouth curved the barest amount. "Good way to think about it."

Shiloh didn't need any more encouragement. She petted and patted, moving around the gelding until he'd all but turned into a lap dog. I knew the feel of him from working this week, and this was the most relaxed he'd ever been.

"You've got the touch."

Her eyes lifted to mine. "I'm trying to learn—"

I shook my head. "I'm not talking about something you can teach. This is instinct."

Shiloh stroked the gelding's cheeks and then lowered her head to his. "I always did understand horses a lot better than people."

People were overrated. This kind of connection? It was far more precious.

She pressed her lips to the horse's muzzle and then straightened. "I needed that. Thank you for giving it to me, Ramsey."

And with that, she headed for the fence and her grazing horse.

I was stuck, frozen to the spot, trying to take in all the beauty that was Shiloh as the sound of my name on her lips echoed in my head.

⌐

My truck jostled as I drove over Kenny Chambers' cattle guard. I scanned the property as I headed towards the ranch house. Several cattle filled a field that barely had any grass, and more were in a handful of paddocks. I pulled to a stop and parked next to a rusted truck with no wheels.

Sliding out of my vehicle, I searched for any signs of life. As my gaze caught on a few horses, my jaw tightened. Most of them were skin and bones, and many had what appeared to be lash marks on their backs.

Memories flashed. The crack of the belt. The burn on my skin.

I forced the images and sensations from my mind, but my back teeth gnashed together so tightly I might've cracked a molar. The slam of a screen door had me looking up. A teenage boy hurried down the front porch steps with a younger boy on his heels. The older one was probably sixteen or seventeen. His t-shirt hung off him in a way that had me wondering if he was struggling to get food the way the horses were. The little boy couldn't have been more than six, and he held tightly to the teen's hand.

The older boy's gaze bounced around as if looking for someone to jump out. "Can I help you?"

"I'm looking for Kenny Chambers."

The boy swallowed. "He's not here right now. I'm his son, Aidan. Can I help you with something?"

He met my gaze, but there was uncertainty there, a guardedness that prickled the back of my neck. "I wanted to talk to him about buying your horses."

I glanced at the cattle. I should probably see about buying them, too, but I didn't do cows. Maybe I could send them to the animal sanctuary that had opened in the past couple of years. Or give them to a rancher who would treat them decently.

Aidan's eyes widened. "You want to buy our horses?"

I shifted my focus to the five creatures in the paddock. They'd obviously been through hell. Most looked as if they'd given up. But one mare had wild eyes that told me she was still fighting.

"They deserve some peace, don't you think?"

"You should take 'em, mister. Dad isn't nice to them, and now they bite and kick—"

"Elliott," Aidan said in a hushed command.

The little boy looked up at his big brother. "It's true. Maybe he'll be nicer to them." He studied me carefully. "Are you nice?"

My insides twisted violently. "To animals, I am."

The boy frowned. "But not to people?"

"People and I don't get on that well."

He nodded, seeming to accept that. "You should take them."

Aidan shook his head. "He'll never let you."

"I'm willing to offer good money."

His shoulders slumped. "It might work, but I doubt it." He glanced towards the paddock. "And I'm not sure they can come back from this."

I studied the kid in front of me, taking in his hollow cheeks and the circles under his eyes. I had a fiery need to deck his asshole of a father. "You'd be surprised what a horse can come back from. What we can *all* come back from."

"You don't—"

The sound of a truck that clearly needed its muffler replaced cut off his words. The vehicle bounced over the cattle guard and came to a stop in front of our group. The man who climbed out had bloodshot eyes and scruff around his jaw. The paunch at his middle told me only his horses and sons were going without around here.

"Who the hell are you?"

I kept my blank mask firmly in place but didn't miss how Aidan shifted in front of his little brother. "Mr. Chambers, I came by to see if you'd be interested in selling your horses and cattle. I have a horse ranch outside of town and a friend looking for cattle."

The lie slipped out easily. The only friend I had was Lor, and she'd shoot me if I dumped a bunch of cows on her spread.

The man's mouth opened and closed a few times before he answered. "You take my animals, and I got nothing."

"You'll have money in the bank."

"And that'll only last me so long. I need what the animals provide."

By looking at them, that wasn't much.

"Could give you time to look for a new job. I hear the feed store is hiring."

Kenny Chambers sneered at me. "I'm not working for some other asshole. I'm my own boss here. Now, get the hell off my property."

"Mr. Chambers—"

"I said, get the hell off my property!"

Elliott jumped at his father's bellow, and I had the burning desire to end Kenny right there. I pulled a card out of my back pocket and placed it on the hood of Kenny's truck. "You can reach me there if you reconsider. I'm willing to pay top dollar." Anything to get these beautiful creatures out from under his control.

Kenny grabbed the card and ripped it into tiny pieces, scattering them on the ground. "Get out of here before I use my right to shoot your trespassing ass."

I dipped my head. As I did, I caught sight of Aidan. He had his jaw clenched as he glared at his father. Nausea swept through me at the idea of leaving him and his brother here. But I had no choice.

I climbed into my truck and started the engine. My hands locked on the wheel as I pulled onto the dirt road. It took me ten minutes to loosen them enough to hit the hands-free button for my phone. "Call Lor."

It rang twice before she picked up. "How'd it go?"

"He's an abusive asshole who has no business around animals or children."

"Shit. He has two kids, doesn't he?"

"Yeah." It was the only word I could get out.

"We need to get the cops involved."

"Lor—"

"You can't break in there at night and steal all his damn horses and his kids, too. I'm telling you, I know some good people at the sheriff's department. Let me reach out to them."

I ground my molars together as I made the turn towards home. "Fine. They've got one shot."

I wasn't overly optimistic. I knew better than anyone that the cops weren't always on the side of justice. Sometimes, they were on the side of whoever greased their wallets—even if that person was evil incarnate.

Chapter Five

Shiloh

MY FINGERS WOVE DEFTLY THROUGH HAIR STILL DAMP from the shower as I stared down at my phone. The screen glared back at me in the low light of my loft. The sun had set in the time I'd been cleaning up for dinner. And with it, the glow of my time with Ramsey and his newest horse. It had faded, too.

Now, the familiar guilt ate at me again. I tied off my braid with a snap of the elastic and swiped up my phone. "Don't be a coward."

I needed to call Hayes. If I were truly brave, I'd drive over to his and Everly's house to see how she was. She must have received the notification of her father's passing.

My stomach twisted. As much as Everly had distanced herself from most of her family, and as much as she hated what her father had done, he was still the man who had raised her. She would grieve. While I felt freedom, she would be hurting.

I hit Hayes' contact before I could stop myself.

He answered on the third ring. "What's wrong?"

I cringed. "Nothing." I didn't pick up the phone for polite chitchat, but the fact that my brother thought I'd only call him in an emergency only churned the guilt deeper.

"Sorry." He blew out an audible breath. "What did you need?"

My fingers locked around the back of my barstool. "Did, uh, Everly get a letter today?"

Hayes was silent. I counted the beats of my heart in a rapid two-step as I waited. He cleared his throat. "From the penitentiary?"

"Yeah." The single word came out as more of a croak.

"She did. I'm guessing that means you did, too. I was going to come over later and tell Mom, Dad, and you—"

"Don't." It was out before I could stop it. "Don't come over—unless you and Ev need to, of course." I grimaced. "I didn't mean it to come out like that. If you want to be with family, come. I just..." I struggled to find the words.

"You're not ready for everyone to know."

"Does that make me awful?"

"It makes you human."

Slowly, the air that had been locked in my lungs eased out. "How's Ev?"

Hayes sighed. "She's feeding the animals right now. Determined to stay busy."

My mouth curved as I pictured her in the animal sanctuary she had built on the land that had once brought so much pain. I envied how she could take something bad and do good with it. I was envious of her strength and perseverance. "Tell her...I'm thinking about her."

Hadley and Addie would know what to do for Ev. They were so good at comforting those in pain. It was second nature to them. But for me, it was awkward and bumbling.

"What about you? How are you feeling?"

I bit the inside of my cheek. I knew the question came from a place of love, but I'd been the recipient of so much concern over the years, it was hard to hear that through the carefully couched questions. "I'm good. I'm sorry for Ev, but I feel relieved."

"She feels a measure of that relief, too, so don't feel bad there."

It helped to know that. "Can I do anything?"

"Not right now. I'll text you tomorrow and let you know."

"Okay." My fingers tapped out a rhythm on the side of my thigh. "And you didn't say anything to Mom or Dad?"

"No one knows yet. But that won't last, Shy. I have to tell them tomorrow."

"I know. But it's family dinner tonight, and I don't want to deal with…" My words trailed off. I was unsure of a kind way to put it.

"I get it. I do. Get clear tomorrow morning, and I'll tell them then. If you come back after lunch, they'll have had some time to process."

"Thanks, Hayes." My throat burned. My brother was the best. Even amidst everything I'd put him through, he still had my back.

"Anytime. Love you, Shy."

"Love you, too."

I tapped *end* on the screen before he could hear the emotion in my voice. I sank onto the stool. My hand trembled as I set the phone down. One more day.

One day before my mom started hovering. Checking up on me every hour on the hour. I felt the itch to pack my camping gear and simply *go*. Get lost in the mountains for a week with nothing but me, Sky, and that hit of freedom that only came with expansive vistas and winding forest trails.

Instead, I forced myself to stand. I shoved my phone into my front pocket and pulled on my jacket. The sound of laughter hit my ears as I opened the door.

"Not too many carrots," Hadley instructed Birdie.

Birdie grinned up at her. "Treats are the best part of the day, Mom."

Hadley ruffled the little girl's hair, and my heart squeezed.

Calder's twin daughters had officially become hers when they married months ago, and I knew she never took one of those *Mom*s for granted.

At the sound of my footsteps on the stairs, her gaze, so similar to my own, lifted. "Tell Birdie she's going to give River a stomachache."

I smiled at Birdie. "As long as you don't mind cleaning up his poop, you can give him as many as you want."

Birdie scrunched up her nose. "Ew, gross."

Her sister, Sage, laughed softly as she stroked Sky. "Told you."

I moved to the stall, giving my mare a scratch behind the ears. "Taking good care of my girl?"

"I only gave her one carrot," Sage assured me.

"Goody Two-Shoes," Birdie muttered.

"Birds," Hadley said in a warning tone.

"Yeah, yeah. No mean names."

"And?" Hadley prodded.

"Sorry, Sage."

"Apology accepted," Sage answered. "Even if she didn't mean it," she added more softly.

I chuckled.

Hadley simply rolled her eyes heavenward. "Let's get inside. Grandma said dinner's almost ready."

I would've given anything to stay right where I was. Sky seemed to sense it and pushed her face into me, nuzzling my shoulder.

The girls' footsteps echoed on the stone floor as they ran towards the house. Hadley looked my way. "You coming?"

"Sure." I forced myself to step away from Sky but instantly missed her warmth and comfort.

Hadley slowed her steps so I could catch up with her. "How are you?"

I stiffened, glancing at her from the corner of my eye. "Why?"

"Oh, I don't know. Because it's normal to ask someone how they're doing when you haven't seen them in a week."

The tension bled out of my muscles. "I'm fine."

"This is where you ask me how I'm doing."

I scowled in her direction. "Little sisters are damned annoying. You know that, right?"

Hadley grinned. "We're the best. You should all be grateful you got the best little sister around."

We were. She kept us all laughing and had put up with far too much, thanks to me. Those familiar claws of guilt tore at my insides again. Hadley had lost so much of her childhood because our mom had been terrified after my kidnapping. I'd wanted nothing to do with sleepovers and dates, but Hadley had, and she'd missed out on just about everything.

"I'm taking your silence as agreement."

I scoffed, but that only made her laugh.

Calder stepped off the front porch, tickling his girls as they passed. He pulled Hadley into his arms and kissed her soundly. She all but melted into him.

My palms dampened, and I looked away.

"Missed you," he murmured against her mouth.

"I was gone all of ten minutes."

"Too long."

Beckett made a gagging noise as he guided his pregnant wife towards our group.

Calder glared at him. "Like you're one to talk. You practically follow Addie around with body armor."

Addie tried to hide her laugh with a cough. Beckett looked at her with mock affront. "Really?"

She shrugged sheepishly, her shoulder-length, blond hair swaying with the movement. "He does have a point."

Calder held out a hand to Addie for a high-five. She slapped his palm.

"There's no loyalty around here, I swear," Beckett grumbled.

"Where are Hayes and Ev?" Hadley asked, glancing towards the drive.

I shifted on my feet. "I think something was going on at the sanctuary. Hayes said they weren't going to make it."

Beckett's gaze narrowed on me, assessing. Addie looked up at him and then back to me. "I hope everything's okay."

"They probably just got slammed with some extra work," I said quickly. I'd pay for the lies later, but what was one more to add to the pile?

The front door opened, and Birdie popped her head out. "Grandpa says to come and get it."

Our group headed up the front steps to the porch. I hung back, letting the crowd go in front of me. If they noticed, they didn't say a word, but they had all gotten used to my oddities.

I followed them inside, greeted by the smells of steak and potatoes. A massive salad already sat on the dining room table. My dad set down a platter full of meat, fresh off the grill. "Perfect timing."

Calder headed into the kitchen and took a heaping bowl of mashed potatoes from my mom. "I've got these."

"Thank you." She kissed his stubbled cheek. "You always were my favorite for a reason."

"We're right here, Mom," Beckett said with a laugh. "And he's not even your son."

"He is now," she called back.

Dad looked in my direction. I saw the same concern from earlier, but something else was there, too. Or maybe the lines the emotion created were just deeper now.

A wave of anxiety passed through me, and I started for the kitchen. Moving to the sink, I turned on the faucet and washed my hands. I felt heat at my back. My hands fisted in the towel as I turned around.

My mom studied me, her gaze probing. "You okay?"

I nodded slowly. "Yes."

"You're sure?"

"Why wouldn't I be?"

Her lips pursed, and my dad moved in behind her, his hands landing on her shoulders. "Not tonight, Julia."

My muscles locked, and my fingers began to tap, the terry-cloth of the kitchen towel rubbing against them.

Her lips thinned further. "I'm not overstepping. I'm allowed to be worried."

"Of course, you are. I just—"

"What's going on?" Beckett asked, stepping into the space.

Our kitchen was large and open, but it suddenly felt as if I couldn't breathe. Too many people. Not enough room.

Mom looked from Beckett to me. "I got a call from Victims' Rights today. They wanted to make sure we'd both received our letters." Hurt filled her expression as she met my gaze. "Why didn't you say anything about Howard Kemper?"

The room went deathly silent around me.

"What about Howard Kemper?" Fury laced Beckett's tone, and Addie moved in to take his hand. I saw the worry in her eyes, both for her husband and for Everly. Addie loved her cousin like crazy, and as much as she despised Howard, he *had* been her uncle.

"He died in prison this week, and Shiloh knew." My mother's words were accusing. I knew it came from a place of hurt for me not sharing, but that didn't matter. It was just one more cinder-block of pressure.

Addie sucked in an audible breath, her knuckles bleaching white as she gripped Beckett's hand.

"Julia," my dad warned.

"Why didn't you say anything?" Mom prodded.

To avoid the scene we were having now. So I didn't feel everyone's eyes on me the way they were currently. "It wasn't something I wanted to talk about."

Her jaw dropped open.

Dad squeezed her shoulders. "That's understandable. If you *do* want to talk, you know we're here."

"I called Dr. Kensington and left a message. I'm sure she'll make time to see you this week," my mom said.

I dropped the towel onto the counter. The telltale trembling was back. I hated that little show of weakness. I clenched and flexed my fingers, fighting the anger and panic creeping in on me. "I don't need to see Dr. Kensington."

"Of course, you do. This is bound to bring up old trauma. You need someone to process with. I'm not saying you need to talk to me, but you have to talk to *someone*. It has helped me so much—"

"I'm not you," I bit out.

"You may not be, but you still need to talk to someone. At least, once a week."

The walls felt as if they were closing in on me, and I struggled to suck air into my lungs.

"Mom," Hadley said as she crossed to her. "Let's all just take a beat."

She was trying to help, but it was one person too many. They were all too close. I lurched to the side and took off towards the door.

"Shiloh!" my mom called.

But I just kept running. I didn't stop until I reached Sky's stall. I grabbed the bridle with one hand while sliding the door with the other. She opened her mouth for the bit before I even reached her. I tugged everything into place and climbed onto her, bareback.

In a matter of seconds, we were headed for the woods. I didn't miss the sound of my name on the night air, but as soon as Sky had warmed up, I pushed her into a canter. She flew down the worn path. I didn't have a destination in mind. I simply wanted to get *away*. At the sound of the rushing creek, I steered Sky in that direction.

My lungs burned as I struggled to take in air. Each breath hurt. My hands clenched around the reins, my fingers tingling.

That sensation was just one of the warning bells. If I didn't get myself breathing normally soon, I'd pass out.

Sky slowed as we reached the creek, and I slid off her back instantly. She hovered behind me as I took off for the water. My boots submerged in the stream, and I didn't care in the slightest.

I bent to splash the cold water over my face. The fresh snow-melt was so frigid it startled a gasp out of me—my first real breath in minutes. I did it again and again, relishing the bite of pain against my face.

Pressure gathered behind my eyes, but I refused to let the tears fall. I'd never be free. Not completely. I was destined to live in the chains my family had woven around me in a quest to keep me safe.

I splashed more water on my face, trying to drown the pain of that realization. I was so consumed by my spiraling thoughts that I didn't hear the hoofbeats. But the deep voice had me jolting.

"What the hell are you doing?"

Chapter Six

Ramsey

THE WORDS WERE OUT OF MY MOUTH BEFORE I COULD STOP them. It might've been spring, but the sun had disappeared, and it had to be hovering in the low forties. The stream Shiloh was standing in was pure snowmelt. She would get hypothermia.

Those light blue eyes locked with mine, and I froze. She was pale. As if all the blood had drained from her head. And those eyes were too wide, her gaze jumping at each rustle of the wind in the trees.

I slid off Rocky and strode towards Shiloh. "What happened?"

She gave her head a slight shake. "Nothing."

"*Nothing* doesn't send someone into a freezing creek. It doesn't drive the color from their skin."

Shiloh's hands clenched and flexed at her sides in a rapid rhythm. She opened her mouth to speak and then seemed to struggle to get the words out. "I-I—" She let out a growl of frustration when they wouldn't come.

I moved to the creek's edge. When I came within arm's length of her, she stumbled back. I muttered a curse and took two large steps back myself. Of course, she was scared. She was alone in the woods, and I wasn't exactly nonthreatening.

Tears glittered in Shiloh's eyes. "Sorry."

"I'm the one who needs to apologize. I shouldn't have moved into your space like that."

Her hands clenched at her sides again, knuckles going as white as her face. "You didn't do anything wrong. I just—I can't—"

I held up a hand. "You don't owe me any explanations."

Shiloh's jaw clamped tight, but she nodded. Slowly, she started for the shore. Her boots had to be soaked through, but she didn't seem to notice. Instead, she made her way to a fallen log and sat. She hugged her knees to her chest and stared at the swirling water.

She looked so damned lost. Something about the picture she painted made my chest crack wide-open. I would've done anything to fix whatever was wrong.

I lowered myself to a rock near where I stood. I'd wait for as long as it took. Patience was something I was familiar with. This wasn't something I could force out of Shiloh. She had to give it to me when she was ready. Or, maybe she wouldn't give it at all. But the least I could do was sit there while she was in it.

It wasn't how I'd expected to spend my evening, but I couldn't lie to myself. When I'd taken the trail that led between our properties, I'd hoped to catch sight of that long braid swaying in the breeze, a flash of those piercing eyes.

Even now, I lost myself in watching her. In studying the slope of her nose and the curve of her lips. I looked for any hints of the strain around her eyes easing. Her gaze stayed firmly affixed to the water as the deep, blue-green colors swirled.

"Have you ever felt so trapped that you can't breathe?"

Her lips barely moved as she spoke, and the sound was so jarring in the silence that I almost fell off the boulder I sat on. "More than a few times." I battled back the memories trying to break free of the steel box I'd locked them in.

Her gaze lifted to mine, and I saw such deep pain there. "I just want to be free."

"And you're not now?" I knew what it was to have memories that made you feel as though you were still imprisoned, but I wasn't sure that was the whole picture with Shiloh. There was some fresh pain there, and it killed me that she was still suffering after everything she'd been through.

"They love me—my family. I know they do. But they're also suffocating me. I can't breathe. Can't move. Can't do anything without hurting them."

My jaw worked back and forth. "So, you hurt yourself instead."

Her eyes flared. "Yes."

I knew the Eastons were protective of Shiloh. And I understood why. But I could see as clear as day now that Shiloh was dying, piece by piece, to keep them happy. "At some point, you have to choose yourself. It won't do anyone any good if you cease to exist. They may not see that outcome as a possibility now, but it'll happen."

Shiloh's fingers dug into her jeans-clad legs. "No matter what step I take in any direction, I hurt someone. I'm so tired of hurting people."

"If someone gets hurt by you taking care of yourself, that's on them. It sounds to me like it's about damn time you did."

Her lips thinned, pressing together in a hard line. "I don't even know what that looks like."

Hell. I was the last person who should be giving Shiloh advice. I had far better relationships with animals than people, but I found myself wanting to try. To help somehow. "One step. What's one thing that would relieve a little of the pressure? Don't think. First thing that pops into your head."

"Move out." Shiloh's eyes widened at her words. "I can't do that."

"Why not?" My words were gentle, but my heart ached for the woman whose chains were so heavy she couldn't see that no lock kept them in place. So, she simply stayed where she was.

"My parents would freak. They'd never let me—"

"*Let* you? You're an adult. I assume you get paid for the work you do at the ranch?"

She nodded.

"Then you can get a place of your own. Maybe moving out would be good for all of you."

Shiloh's fingers began tapping against her legs in a rapid beat. I had the sudden urge to cover them with mine. To soothe. Her head shook back and forth in tiny movements. "There isn't anywhere that I feel…"

Her voice trailed off, and I searched for the word she was looking for. "Safe?"

She nodded, her cheeks pinking. "I hate it. I don't want to be this way. I'm trapping myself as much as they are."

"What about my place? You feel safe there, don't you?" The words tumbled out as if they had a mind of their own while I cursed them to Hell. It was instinct as much as anything. Shiloh had been showing up for years. She'd been on edge at first, but now, there was none of that. She always seemed relaxed and at peace on the ridge. I wanted that for her.

"Live with *you*?" she squeaked. "We've only ever spoken twice."

My world tilted sideways at that truth. I didn't let people I didn't truly know onto my property, let alone invite them to *live* there. But I kept right on talking. "I've got a guest cabin."

I'd let one other person live there—a friend of someone I'd known from prison. It was a favor I'd only done for the brother who'd watched my back in that hellhole. But Boden had moved out months ago into some fancy lodge with his fiancée, Laiken. The guest cabin was just sitting empty.

I saw Shiloh turn the idea over in her mind. "I don't want to make you do that. I know you don't like people on your property."

I hated it. But Shiloh wasn't people. She was something else altogether. The truth was, she'd become a touchstone over the last several years. And I had a burning urge to help. To protect. Maybe because I knew how it felt to believe there was no way out.

Maybe because I saw those wings of hers that had been so badly clipped. The offer might've been reckless, but I couldn't find it in me to care.

"I've let you onto my property since day one. That's nothing new."

She studied me. "Why didn't you kick me off? I heard you once fired a shotgun at someone who drove down your drive."

I huffed out a breath. "Tall tales."

Shiloh arched a brow.

"I shot at the ground in front of his van. Not at him."

A laugh broke free from Shiloh, and it was the most beautiful sound I'd ever heard. Her eyes glimmered in the low light. "So, why didn't I get shot at?"

My lips twitched. "Kai liked you. He doesn't usually like anyone but me."

Shiloh stilled. "I think animals are the best judge of character, too."

"Just one rule."

"What?"

"Only you. No friends. No boyfriends. No one comes onto my property but you."

She stared intently at me. "I don't have any friends."

Damn, that twisted something somewhere down deep. "Then I guess it won't be a problem. So, what do you say? Want to live in the guest cabin and see how that feels?"

She worried a spot on the inside of her cheek and then nodded. "This is going to blow everything up."

I met her gaze. "Sometimes, a little destruction is a good thing."

The handcuffs cut into my wrists as I walked, and the guard gave me a hard shove. "Pick up your pace."

The guy behind me snickered. "Not in a fuckin' mansion anymore, rich boy."

I pulled the cuffs tighter, using the bite of pain to keep me grounded as we walked towards the detention facility. The tall fencing had barbed wire at the top and cameras every few feet. I swallowed against my dry throat.

Another line of teens exited the building, walking towards us. A man with a shaved head zeroed in on me. He looked larger than the rest, and a tattoo curved around his neck with symbols I didn't recognize. I let out the breath I'd been holding when his gaze moved to the guy behind me.

"Keep moving," the guard ordered.

I tried to move faster but couldn't seem to get my feet to obey. These were my last moments of fresh air—or any hint of freedom. I looked up at the sky, wanting to hold the image in my mind as best I could. That was my first mistake. But it wasn't my last.

Someone grabbed my shoulders and, without warning, leveled a blow to my rib cage. Burning pain bloomed there. I tried to get off a punch to defend myself, but someone held my arms.

The guard shouted something that I couldn't hear.

The man with the buzzed head sneered as he leveled two more hits into my side. "Your stepdad wanted you welcomed proper."

The hold on my arms loosened, and I couldn't keep myself upright. That was my first clue that I hadn't simply been punched. The blood seeping through my tan jumpsuit was my second. The world dimming around me… was the third.

I jolted upright in bed, beads of sweat sliding down my face. I threw back the covers and swung my legs over the side of the mattress. My lungs seized as I tried to pull in air, locking down tight. I focused on the floor in front of me. The rug. The wide floorboards beneath it. The trunk against the wall.

Kai pushed into my side, whining. A tiny bit of oxygen made its way into my lungs. I listened—Kai's breathing, the wind against the windows…

I felt the sheets beneath me, now damp with sweat. Kai's soft fur against my side. The rug under my feet.

More air came now. My lungs loosened just enough for shallow breaths. Then deeper ones.

My fingers sifted through Kai's coat. "I'm okay."

He licked my leg.

Hell. It had been months since I'd had a nightmare like that one. I'd started to think I was past them for good. But memories like the ones I had locked away had a powerful hold.

I pushed to my feet and strode into the bathroom, the first strains of sunrise lighting my way. I turned the water to hot and stepped under the spray. No more freezing showers in a place where I always had to watch my back. When I'd bought the ranch, I'd had extra water heaters put in so I'd never run out. I could stand under the spray for an hour, and the water would still be as hot as it was now.

Those water heaters and the property had been bought with money that shouldn't have been mine for decades to come—my mother's money. A trust fund she should've used to buy her freedom, but one that she'd never found the courage to use.

I rinsed off the sweat from the dream and then shut off the stream and stepped out. Kai eyed me carefully as I toweled off. I gave him a scratch behind the ears as silent reassurance.

I dressed quickly and headed downstairs. I ignored the kitchen and went straight for the front door. Food and coffee could wait. Right now, I needed fresh air. I pulled the pine scent into my lungs. Freedom. It was a smell that had always grounded me. The first thing I'd wanted when I got out of prison was this scent.

Kai leaned into my side, and I stroked his back. "We're good. Let's get the crew fed, and then I'll get you some breakfast."

He panted in agreement.

I worked on autopilot, loading feed into the stalls. The practice helped clear away the worst of the dream and reinforced the locks on that box of memories. By the time I'd let the horses out into the pastures, I was back in control.

I whistled for Kai, and he came running. Just as I was about to motion him towards the house, my phone buzzed. I frowned.

It was a little after seven. The only person who'd call at this time was Lor, but it wasn't her. It was an alert for the gate.

I pulled up the camera. An old truck on its last legs appeared, and I saw a familiar teen behind the wheel. "Aidan?" I greeted.

He jolted slightly. "Uh, hey, Mr. Bishop. Can I talk to you for a minute?"

I studied the camera angles. There was no sign of his father, but his little brother, Elliott, sat in the cab's backseat. I hesitated for a moment, calculating the risk. Images flashed in my mind. Elliott jumping at his father's raised voice. Aidan shielding his little brother with his body. "Sure. Follow the road to the barn."

I hit the button for the gate. It was dumb. Monumentally stupid. But I was doing it anyway. What had gotten into me, inviting Shiloh to live here and now letting a kid I didn't know drive in? Lor had spoken to her contact at the sheriff's office, and, supposedly, they were *investigating* Kenny. I didn't have high hopes.

After a few moments, the rusted, red truck appeared. Aidan slowed to a stop and got out. Then, he opened the back door for his brother. Elliott jumped down, his eyes wide as he took in the property and horses around him. I saw his mouth form a word. *Wow.*

Aidan took his hand and walked towards me. His Adam's apple bobbed as he swallowed. "I hope it's not too early, but I have to get Elliott to school by quarter to eight."

My mouth pulled down in a frown. Why the hell wasn't his dad driving him? "I've been up for a few hours."

He nodded.

"How can I help you?"

Aidan's gaze moved to the pasture where the horses were grazing. "I didn't know who you were when you came to our house, but I pieced together your name on the card my dad ripped up. I, uh, I've heard about what you do with horses. I was wondering if you needed any help."

My eyes narrowed as I studied the boy in front of me. "Your dad send you over here?"

Aidan's gaze snapped back to me. "What? No. He has no idea I'm here."

I read nothing but the truth in his words. And my damn traitorous heart tugged as I took in the skinny kid. "Why do you want to work here?"

He swallowed hard but didn't look away. "I could use the money, and..." His jaw worked back and forth as he struggled to find the words he wanted. "I'd like to learn how to help horses like you do."

Hell. In for a penny, in for a pound. "You know how to muck stalls and groom?"

Aidan nodded.

"Can you show up on time?"

"Yes, sir. I, uh..."

"What?"

He glanced at Elliott. "I watch my brother after school. Is it okay if he hangs out while I work?"

Double hell. This was a horrible idea, yet I found myself saying, "That's fine."

"When should I start?"

"Day after tomorrow." Because Shiloh was moving in today, and one universe-altering event a day was enough for me.

Chapter Seven

Shiloh

Me: *Can you trailer Sky for me today?*

I stared down at my phone, waiting for Hadley to reply. I usually used one of the trailers on the ranch, but I wasn't sure my parents would be keen on letting me borrow it when they found out about my plans.

Hadley: *Sure. When do you need me?*

Me: *How about now?*

Hadley: *On my way.*

God, my little sister was a good one. No questions, just simply here to help. Maybe it was something innate from her years as an EMT. Or because she knew better than anyone how questions and demands for explanations could kill your soul. She'd been far braver in demanding her freedom, though.

I scanned the loft around me. I'd started packing up last night, but it wasn't as if I had a lot of belongings. A duffel bag full of clothes lay on my bed with a box of food next to it. I wasn't really one for mementos—except for one thing.

I lowered myself to my knees and reached under the bed. My

fingers grasped the edge of the old shoebox. I ignored the tightening in my chest as I took it in. *He's gone. You're free.* And for the first time, I was fighting for that freedom.

Shoving the box into my duffel, I zipped it closed, slung the bag over my shoulder, and picked up the container of food. Opening the door, I stepped onto the landing.

The first step was the hardest. The ranch had been my safe place for a long time. In my mind, nothing could touch me here. It was what made leaving so damned hard. Even just short trips into town were always a process: convincing myself that nothing would happen, that I was prepared if it did, and breathing through the anxiety and panic.

My boots echoed on the wood as I descended the stairs. One hand curled tightly around the box, the other clenching and flexing at my side. The familiar scents of hay and horses filled my nose. Would Ramsey's barn smell the same? Or would his be just a bit different?

I shoved down the pang of fear that thought caused. Familiar had always been safe. I knew what to expect here. But that routine was killing me, one day at a time.

I stepped out into the sunshine. There was a bite to the air, but the sun took away the worst of the sting. Pulling open the door to my truck, I slid the box onto the passenger seat and tossed the duffel onto the floorboards.

The sound of tires crunching gravel had me lifting my head. Instead of Hadley's SUV, I saw Hayes' sheriff's department vehicle. I muttered a curse under my breath as I slammed the door to my truck.

Instead of pulling up to the house, Hayes pointed his SUV in my direction. He came to a stop just feet away and slid out. "Hey, Shy."

"Hey. How's Ev?"

Shadows flitted across Hayes' eyes. "She's hanging in there."

More of that ugly guilt clawed at my insides. I'd been rejoicing while Everly was suffering. I didn't feel guilty for being relieved by Howard's death. I felt guilty for not thinking of Ev more. She'd put me before every loyalty she had, simply to do the right thing. She'd snuck out of her home in the dead of night and rode down a mountain in the dark to the sheriff's office to tell them where I was. In many ways, she'd lost her entire family that night. The price for doing the right thing was steep. And now, she was losing them all over again.

I kicked at a piece of gravel. "Do you think she wants to see me? Or should I stay away for a while?"

Hayes ducked down, forcing me to meet his gaze. "She always wants to see you."

"I just…I'm a reminder."

"So am I. But I'm with her every day. She needs her family right now, and that's what we are."

My throat burned, but I nodded. "I'll stop by tomorrow morning."

Hayes' gaze shifted to the truck behind me. "You got plans today?"

My fingers tapped my thighs, and my muscles tensed, bracing for impact. I said the words on one long exhale. "I'm moving out."

Hayes froze. "You're what?"

"I'm moving out. It's time."

He was quiet. I marked the moments in heartbeats—the one-two pulse ringing in my ears. Hayes scrubbed a hand over his stubbled jaw. "There a reason I'm just now hearing about this and only because I caught you in the act?"

Because he would've tried to talk me out of it just like most everyone else in my life would. "I just decided."

Hayes stared at me a beat. "Big step. Have you talked to your therapist about it?"

My fingers curled, my nails digging into my palms. "I don't need to talk to a shrink to know my own mind."

"I'm not saying you do. I just thought it might be good to

have someone to talk to and work through the feelings that come up around the process."

"I'm an adult, Hayes."

He blew out a breath. "I'm not suggesting you aren't. I just…I worry. But I'm so damn proud of you, too."

A little of my annoyance fled at his honesty. I ached to wrap my arms around him, to hug my brother and reassure him. But I couldn't make my arms cooperate. "I'm okay. But I won't be if I don't get out on my own. I can't live like this forever."

Little lines creased Hayes' brow. "I know it's been hard. I just want you happy and safe. Where are you moving? I'll do a walk-through and check the security. We'll get new locks installed, an alarm system if there isn't one already in place."

My stomach dipped as if I'd just taken the plunge on a hellish rollercoaster. "You don't need to do that."

"Of course, I do. It'll make Mom and Dad feel better, too. Where is the place? Apartment in town? Or a house?"

I fought the urge to squirm as Hayes waited.

"Shy?" he prodded.

"I'm renting Ramsey Bishop's guest cabin." We hadn't actually discussed the cost of said rent. I hadn't even asked if I could bring Sky, but I had to assume that he figured I would, and his barn was massive. I was sure he'd have a stall open for her. My brain was spiraling now, anything to distract me from my brother's rapidly reddening face.

"Are you out of your mind?"

He bellowed the words so loudly I felt the vibrations against my skin.

The front door to the ranch house flew open, and my parents appeared. They hurried across the drive towards us. My dad's brows pulled together. "What's all the yelling about?"

Hayes' chest rose and fell in labored breaths. "Shy—she—she thinks she's moving out. Into Ramsey Bishop's guest cabin."

Everyone stilled. My dad's eyes widened a fraction, and my mom's jaw dropped open.

"Moving?" My mom gaped.

"Yes. It's time."

She shook her head in tiny, rapid movements. "This is about Howard Kemper. I knew this would bring up things that were difficult to deal with but running away isn't going to help."

"It's not about that. This is about me. I need some room to breathe."

Dad ran a hand over his head. "And we want you to have that, but I think what your mom is saying is that now doesn't seem like the best time. If you need more privacy, we can build you a cabin on our property—"

"No." It was all I could say. One word that showed there was no room for negotiation or capitulation. I had to stand strong. "I need to do this. And I think it might be good to take a little time off from working here."

The truth was, with as little overhead as I had, I'd saved up years of living expenses, even though my dad rarely utilized my help around the ranch. It was a pity job. And it was time for me to stop taking from them.

"That's ridiculous, Shiloh," my mom clipped.

"He spent years in prison," Hayes gritted out.

"For something he didn't do."

"I know that, but it still changes a person. It hardens them," Hayes pushed. "He's got a short temper. I've had to take him in for a fight or two."

My dad held up a hand. "Ramsey might be hardened, but I don't think he'd ever actually hurt anyone. My dealings with him have always been civil."

"You're buying horses from the man," Hayes snapped. "I'm the one who had to pull him off someone at a bar."

"Probably someone who deserved it," I muttered under my breath. I'd seen Ramsey's patience with his horses. There was no way he'd resort to physical violence unless it was the last option.

Hayes' eyes narrowed. "What did you say?"

I lifted my gaze to his. "He's my friend."

I'd told Ramsey last night that I didn't have any friends. It was pretty much the truth. He was the closest I came to one. However, it wasn't the kind of friendship that most people would understand. Our communication had been a silent one for years. Yet, somehow, he made me feel less alone.

Hayes threw his hands into the air. "The guy doesn't have friends, Shy. He's bad news—a loner. Bites anyone's head off who even tries to say hello. God forbid they show up at his ranch. And you want to go live on his property in the middle of nowhere?"

"I've been going there every week for the last nine years."

The world went deadly still around me.

"What?" my dad croaked.

"I wanted to learn about what he does."

Panic filled my mother's expression. "You've been alone with him? Shiloh, did he take advantage of you? He's so much older than you—"

"STOP!" I yelled so loudly a few of the horses in the barn let out sounds of distress. "I'm not weak. I'm not stupid. No one took advantage of me. I know right from wrong. I know better than any of you when someone has evil in them—because I've seen it up close."

Tears glistened in my mother's eyes, but I didn't let it stop me. I had to get this out. "Ramsey is a good man. He's helping me because of that good in him. He knew I needed a place to go where I felt safe. I feel safe there."

"Then that's where you're going," Hadley said, stepping up to our group.

There was ferocity in my little sister's eyes. She had always had that warrior spirit that I wished I could bottle for myself. Well, maybe today I had.

"You've both lost your damn minds," Hayes said.

"Hayes, don't," Hadley clipped. Then she looked at my mom. "I know this scares you, but you have to let her go."

My mom opened her mouth to say something and then

snapped it closed. She spun on her heel and stalked back to the ranch house. Dad looked at me and then to where Mom had gone. "I'd better go make sure she's okay."

Pain danced along my sternum as he walked away without another word. I'd hurt them. Again. But this time, I was pushing through. I wouldn't let the guilt lock me in place.

"Shy—"

"Please, don't. I can't take any more today. You can yell at me some more tomorrow."

Hayes' jaw hardened. Hadley clapped him on the shoulder and then gave him a little push towards the house. "Go make Mom some tea. She'd like that."

He started walking as if on autopilot. It wasn't until he'd disappeared inside the house that I turned to Hadley. "Am I a horrible person?"

"No."

There was such certainty in her voice that it made my throat burn.

"You're as far from a horrible person as you can get. But it's still going to hurt a little."

"What is?"

Hadley looked towards the house and then back at me. "Whenever things got to be too much, you walked away. But you did it silently. You took a few days, went riding or camping, but you never had a conversation about what you were doing." She paused. "It's a hell of a lot harder when you have to stand up for yourself against someone pushing back."

A smile stretched across her face as she leaned towards me. She didn't touch me, but she was so close, I felt her warmth. "I'm so damn happy for you. It's time. You're ready for this."

My eyes stung with a viciousness that had me swallowing hard. "No one else seems to think so."

Hadley's gaze wandered to the house again. "I was younger when it happened. The rest of them…they were supposed to look out for you. I think, to them, you're frozen at ten. It's going to take some time to make them realize that you aren't that ter-rified little girl anymore."

"I am terrified."

She turned back to me, white-blond hair catching in the breeze. "That just makes you human. It's what you do with that fear that counts."

Chapter Eight

Ramsey

I HELD OUT MY HAND, AND THE GELDING TOOK THE OFFERED peppermint eagerly. His lips danced as he ate the treat, and then he let out what could only be considered sounds of joy. A chuckle escaped me. "I think I've got your name."

My hand rubbed over his face, and the horse didn't even flinch. "What do you think about Pep?" It worked on a few levels. There was an unbreakable spirit to the gelding—a true pep. His love of peppermint just secured it.

Pep wiggled his lips a little more. Whether it was in agreement with his name or to beg for more treats, I wasn't sure. I slid another mint out of my back pocket. "This is your last one. Then we need to introduce you to some new friends."

Pep snatched up the peppermint in a flash, dancing his lips some more. I grinned as I hooked the lead rope to his halter. "We're going together this time."

His ears twitched as I unlocked the gate and led him out of the round pen. His gaze jumped around, taking in the fields and pastures with a new attentiveness.

I patted Pep's neck and began walking. I had him set up with some of my mellowest horses. I called them the welcome wagon because they put up with more than the rest of the herd. They were the perfect test case for socialization.

Pep sniffed the air as we approached the paddock. The mare and two geldings in the field chomped away on lush grass, barely acknowledging us. But Pep's muscles quivered.

I stroked the side of his neck as we stopped at the gate. "It's the next step. Time for some friends. Some community."

It would give him a sense of purpose and belonging. These horses were some of my best teachers, modeling behavior and showing the newcomers the way of things.

I scratched behind Pep's ears. "You've got this."

Unlatching the gate, I pulled it open and unhooked the lead rope from Pep's halter. He took a few tentative steps inside. My mare, Strawberry, lifted her head and let out a soft whinny. Pep answered back and then took off running.

It had been a while since he'd had a chance to truly stretch his legs, and it was a beautiful sight to see. He raced along the fence line, letting loose a few small bucks on the way. But they weren't ones of aggression, they were joyful.

The other horses in the paddock knew it. A few seconds later, they joined him in the run, and four became one—a single force charging around the field.

I couldn't have moved if I tried. It was so damned beautiful to see. After a few minutes, they slowed from gallop to canter to trot and then to a walk. Finally, they halted altogether, finding a spot of especially thick grass and stopping to graze.

Pep's head lifted, his gaze meeting mine. I swore his eyes shined in the morning light. There was joy there. Relief. Peace. It was the greatest gift I'd ever gotten.

My phone buzzed in my pocket, and I slid it out. An alert for the front gate flashed. I opened the app, and Shiloh's face filled the screen.

The surge of heat through my bloodstream set off alarm bells in my head, but I shoved them away and hit the button for the intercom. "Shiloh."

She jumped slightly at my voice. "H-hi."

I hated the slight tremor in her voice, but I understood it. She had never lived anywhere but the ranch. What she was doing now was a huge undertaking.

"The hardest part's over. You're here."

Shiloh let out a huff of air and then bit the inside of her cheek. "You said I couldn't bring anyone here, right?"

I stiffened. "I don't let strangers on my property." Except it seemed I was breaking that rule left and right lately.

"My sister. She brought Sky for me. I don't have my own trailer. I could unload her at the gate if you don't want—"

"It's okay." The words were out before I could stop them, pulled from my mouth by the anxiety coming off Shiloh in waves. "She can help you get settled."

"Thanks," Shiloh said softly.

I hit the button for the gate. "Follow the road to the barn."

She didn't respond, but I saw her drive through the entrance. As she disappeared from camera view, I lifted my gaze to the road and let out a loud whistle. Kai came charging out of the trees and ran to my side.

I sank my hand into his fur and scratched behind his ears. "You're gonna lose your mind in a second." If I wasn't careful, Kai might leave me for Shiloh completely.

Kai's ears twitched, picking up sounds that I couldn't hear yet. My eyes stayed fixed on the road, straining for the first sight of her. It was a bad sign—this *want* buried so deep.

The silver truck rounded the bend, an SUV with a trailer following behind. Kai tensed at my side, bracing. I scratched behind his ears. "You're fine."

Shiloh pulled to a stop in front of me and slid from her vehicle. Those hypnotizing eyes glinted in the morning light, and my blood heated again. Kai let out a sound that was a cross between a howl and a bark, and then he charged.

The smile that split Shiloh's face was a vicious punch to the gut. She sank to her knees, holding out her arms to my dog. Kai launched himself at her, almost knocking her over. Shiloh laughed as he licked her face. "I missed you, too."

That one sentence had my gut twisting in a way that wasn't entirely painful.

Hadley Easton climbed out of her SUV, her gaze firmly affixed to the scene in front of her. "Is that a wolf?"

"Half wolf," I said, my voice tight.

Her focus lifted to me. "Is he going to eat her?"

I scowled at Hadley. "No, but he might eat you."

Hadley's brows lifted but there wasn't fear there. Instead, amusement laced her expression. "Then I guess I should keep my distance." She turned back to her sister. "Where do you want Sky?"

Shiloh pushed to her feet and looked at me. "Is it okay that I brought her?"

"I assumed you would. I've got a stall ready."

Shiloh nodded and climbed into the trailer. She and Hadley worked together in a way that told me they'd done it countless times before—a silent rhythm that spoke of comfort and ease. I was glad she had that, at least one family member who didn't seem to push her into a mold she didn't want to fit into.

I motioned them into the barn, showing Shiloh the stall for Sky. While they settled the mare, I grabbed the trunk and tack from the trailer.

"You don't have to do that," Shiloh said.

I simply shrugged and placed the saddle and bridle in the tack room. When I stepped back out into the barn, I froze. Shiloh had her head bent to Sky's. They were forehead to forehead as she whispered something that no one but the two of them could hear.

"She has a way with them. She always did, but it became more after the kidnapping."

I was never unaware of my surroundings, but I'd been so focused on Shiloh that I hadn't heard Hadley approaching.

She looked up at me. "I think this is going to be really good for her. She could learn a lot from what you do here."

I shot her a sidelong look. "You're not trying to convince her that it's a horrible idea?"

Hadley's lips twitched. "Nope. She knows what she needs." All humor fled her expression. "You might want to watch out for Hayes and my mom, though. They're less keen on the move."

My back teeth ground together. "I don't give a damn about what they think."

"That'll come in handy. And maybe some of it will rub off on Shy." She turned to her sister. "Show me your new place."

Hadley's voice broke the trance between Shiloh and Sky, and I fought the urge to growl at the younger woman. I wanted her gone. She might be Shiloh's younger sister but having her in my space made me twitchy.

Shiloh glanced up at me as she stepped out of the stall. "That okay?"

I grunted and jerked my head, moving in the direction of the guest cabin.

"He's a real Chatty Cathy, that one," Hadley muttered to her sister.

"Enough, Hads."

I moved to the bed of Shiloh's truck but found it empty. "Where's all your stuff?"

She stepped around the passenger side and pulled out a duffel and one box. "Right here."

I took the box from her hands and didn't miss the hitch in her breath as I got close. "This is it?"

She shrugged. "I'm not really a *stuff* person."

I wanted to ask why but shoved that down, heading for the door instead.

Humor danced in Hadley's eyes. "Between the two of you, it'll be a miracle if twenty words get spoken all day around here."

I looked down at Shiloh. "Is it time for your sister to leave yet?"

A small laugh escaped her lips. "As soon as she makes sure you're not sticking me in a hovel. She'll report back to my family, and that'll help."

A foreign feeling slid through me—one I hadn't felt in decades. "Was it bad this morning?"

Shiloh's lips thinned. "It'll be fine."

What she didn't say was that it wasn't now.

Kai moved in beside Shiloh, keeping pace beside her. The damn traitor. I headed up the steps of the front porch to the guest cabin and unlocked the door. Pushing it open, I stepped inside.

I could see that the box contained mostly food, so I moved into the kitchen and set it on the island. Hadley let out a low whistle as she entered. "Definitely not a hovel."

I scanned the space, trying to see it through their eyes. When I'd bought the place, I'd almost had the furnished guest cabin torn down because I knew it would get zero use. But I'd kept it in case I ever found a ranch hand that I trusted enough to live here. That had never happened. I hadn't even found someone I trusted enough to *hire*.

My gaze moved around the open living and dining spaces that transitioned to the kitchen. It was luxury rustic—lots of stone and exposed wood beams. Dark, thick-planked floors. A massive fireplace stood at the opposite end of the room with a television above it. A large sectional made the area welcoming.

Two bedrooms with a bathroom in between were down the hall. The bathroom had a large soaking tub and a walk-in shower. I didn't know what kind of accommodations Shiloh had had back at her parents' ranch, but this had to hold a candle to it, at least.

Shiloh's gaze jumped from one thing to the next. "It's really nice. Thank you."

Hadley focused on her sister. "You need help getting settled? Or for me to go and pick up anything?"

Shiloh shook her head. "I'm good. Thanks for bringing Sky."

Hadley started to move as if she might hug Shiloh but then stopped herself, clasping her hands in front of her instead. "Anytime. Call me if you need me."

Pain flashed across Shiloh's expression as Hadley had started to move. "Thanks."

I tried to put the pieces together of what that could be about—the awkward dance between two women who obviously cared about each other.

Hadley cleared her throat. "I'm gonna head home."

I nodded. "The gate will open automatically when you leave."

We followed Hadley outside and watched as she climbed into her SUV and headed back down the drive.

Shiloh's fingers tapped a rapid beat against her thighs. "We didn't talk about rent. How much did you want a month?"

"I don't need your money."

Heat flared in Shiloh's eyes. "I'm paying you rent."

Hell. "I don't need money, but I could use some help." If Aidan worked out, and Shiloh stuck around, I might be able to bring in more horses. Right now, I was stretched to the limit, even with Lor helping out here and there.

Shiloh shifted as Kai leaned into her side. "I can do that. What do you need?"

"Help with the stalls and feeding. Exercising some of the horses. We might be able to move you into some training, eventually. What do you say to ten hours a week for rent? If you work more on top of that, I'll pay you."

Excitement lit Shiloh's eyes. It was an emotion I only saw when it came to horses. As if they were the only creatures who truly made her come alive. "I'd love to do that. But *twenty* hours a week for rent. That's closer to fair."

My jaw tightened, but I nodded. "You can start tomorrow."

"I can start today."

"Stubborn," I muttered.

She smiled, and the movement lit up her entire face in a way where I couldn't help but stare.

The sound of tires crunching gravel had my head snapping up. It was too fast. Too close. The older truck screeched to a stop in front of us, sending dirt and gravel flying. Kai let out a low growl.

Kenny Chambers jumped out of the truck and charged towards us, his face as red as a tomato. "You piece of shit! I know it was you. You got my goddamned horses taken away."

Chapter Nine

Shiloh

THE URGE TO BOLT WAS SO STRONG MY MUSCLES BEGAN TO twitch. Anger came off the man in waves—hot rushes of energy pulsing in the air. I knew that kind of rage. I'd done everything I could to avoid it since I was ten years old.

The answer had always been the same: Run. Any time voices rose, or arguments began—even between those I loved—I took off. I hid in the barn or took Sky out on the trails. Anything to get away from that feeling.

The one that burned my skin and made my mouth go dry. Transporting me back to that place. The one where my tongue had cracked because I hadn't drunk in too long. Where I huddled in the corner with only the rough blanket to shield me from whatever came. It hadn't been enough.

Ramsey stepped forward, his jaw going hard like granite. "How'd you get onto my property?"

The man sneered. "Just had to wait until someone left. Your gate gives plenty of time to get through."

A muscle fluttered beneath Ramsey's eye. "Leave."

"The hell, I will. I came for payment. For my damn horses. Where are they?"

"Not here." Ramsey gestured to the pasture. "All the horses here are too well fed to be yours."

The man's nostrils flared. "You don't know a damn thing. You're the one who called the cops. I know it."

"I've never once dialed a cop, so I'm afraid you're barking up the wrong tree."

There was a bite to Ramsey's tone, an acidity when he spat the word *cop*. It hit my stomach and sat there like a lead weight.

The other man's hands fisted at his sides, his knuckles losing their color. "It's no coincidence you came sniffing around, and the sheriff's department shows up and seizes all my damn animals three days later."

Ramsey shrugged as if he didn't have a care in the world. "If you'd taken proper care of them, you wouldn't have had a problem."

The man lunged, but Kai stepped forward and bared his teeth in a growl. The man stumbled back a step. "What the hell is that thing?"

"My dog. He's not overly fond of strangers. You might want to make your way back to your truck."

I couldn't help the smile that curved my lips. I'd give Kai an extra treat for that.

The man's gaze shot to me. "What the hell are you laughing at?"

I wasn't laughing, but any traces of humor fled at the snap of his words.

Ramsey stepped between us, cutting off the man's line of sight. "Get in your vehicle and go before I sic my dog on you."

The man's lip curled. "It's not fun when someone threatens what's important to you, is it?"

The muscles in Ramsey's shoulders pulled tight, visibly straining against his flannel shirt. "You come on my property again, and you'll meet my rifle instead of my dog."

The man stepped to the side, his glare cutting to me. There was so much hatred there. My body longed to run. Wanted to put distance between myself and his rage. But I forced my feet to remain planted. I was done running. I'd used it to cope for too long. I was free, but I had to fight to defend that freedom.

Kai snapped his teeth, and the man jolted, letting out a few curses. His gaze narrowed on Ramsey as he backed around his truck. "This isn't over."

My chest burned as he climbed behind the wheel. Gravel and dirt flew as he tore away, headed back towards the front gate. Ramsey pulled a phone out of his pocket and tapped a few things on the screen. After a few moments, his shoulders relaxed a fraction. "He's gone."

My lungs released the air they'd been holding hostage with a whoosh. My next breath was shaky, but I managed a nod.

Ramsey's jaw tightened as he studied me. "I'm sorry. I—"

"Don't." I shook my head, trying to steady my voice. "Don't apologize for him."

"He shouldn't have been able to get in."

"Who is he?"

Ramsey's gaze drifted to where the truck had disappeared. "Kenny Chambers. An abusive asshole, who didn't take me up on my offer to buy his horses."

Nausea swept through me. I could only imagine how that man treated animals. "The sheriff's department took them?"

A muscle below his eye fluttered again. "I guess so."

"If you didn't call them…?"

"Lor did."

A foreign feeling skittered along my rib cage. "Lor?"

"Another trainer. She brings me especially tough cases."

I worried a spot on the inside of my cheek.

Ramsey turned back to me, his gaze sweeping over my face. I felt each point it landed. When he paused on my cheek, I released my hold on the flesh. Something in him eased. "I guess the cops came through for once."

I bristled at that. My brother gave his all to keep the residents of this county safe. "They come through more often than that."

Ramsey didn't say a word, his attention moving to the field opposite us. "I need to get back to work. I'll show you your duties tomorrow. I left a key and the fob that opens the gate in the kitchen. Just remember, no guests."

Before I had a chance to say anything in return, Ramsey walked away. Kai looked at him but stayed put near me. Ramsey let out a whistle. The dog looked woefully at me and then took off after his owner.

And then, I was alone. It was what I'd wanted. No prying eyes or carefully couched questions. But an ache settled deep in my chest. There was a difference between alone and lonely, and right now, I felt a hell of a lot of both.

I sat on the front porch steps, sipping my coffee. I'd need a few more cups to get with the program today. I'd slept horribly, tossing and turning for most of the night.

The sounds were different here. The way the cabin groaned and creaked was different from the barn I'd called home for so many years. I was too far from the stables on Ramsey's property to hear the comforting sounds of the horses here. I did hear other wildlife, though. An owl dipping down over the fields, hunting for its dinner. Possums or some other nocturnal critter scavenging in the brush outside my window.

When I finally dropped off, nothing but terrifying dreams greeted me. I took another sip of my coffee, letting the hot liquid warm the places that had gone cold at the resurgence of old memories. It was understandable. So much had gotten kicked up. Howard dying. Moving away from my childhood home. My family's concern. Kenny Chambers' anger yesterday.

But I refused to believe that the lack of sleep or nightmares meant that this move was a mistake. It wasn't. It was just new.

Anything unknown was hard for me. I simply had to take it one step at a time.

A bark cut through the air, and I caught sight of a blur of fur. I couldn't help my smile as Kai charged towards me. I set my coffee behind me and greeted him with a full hug. As my arms wrapped around his massive form, sinking into his fur, the first sense of peace swept over me.

I burrowed my face in Kai's neck. "Needed this."

He let out a whine and pushed harder against me.

"I missed you, too."

I let myself stay like that for a few moments, soaking in Kai's warmth. Then I forced myself to straighten, scratching behind his ears. As I did, my eyes locked with onyx ones that stole my breath. So much swirled in those depths. Secrets I wanted to know but had no business asking about.

Ramsey didn't say a word for a minute. He simply stared at his dog and me. Then, he nodded. "Lor's bringing a new horse in a few minutes."

The foreign feeling was back. I struggled to identify it. It carried with it a bit of nausea and hints of anger. Jealousy?

"It's one of Kenny Chambers'."

All thoughts of jealousy fled at that. "How did she get it?"

"Lor has a relationship with the sheriff's department and the humane society. I'm approved to take the more difficult cases."

Difficult. Because someone had broken the horse so badly. I swallowed hard and pushed to my feet. "What can I do?"

"Help us get her in the round pen. Then we need to muck out the stalls in the barn."

I nodded, picking up my mug and chugging the contents, then I set it back down on the porch.

Ramsey's lips twitched. "Thirsty?"

"I need the caffeine."

All hints of humor dropped away. "Didn't sleep well?"

"New place. It'll take some time."

Ramsey's jaw worked back and forth. I wasn't sure why my

not sleeping well annoyed him, but it clearly did. "If you're not up for—"

"I'm fine." The words came out a bit more harshly than I'd intended. But the last thing I wanted was to be coddled in my new home. I didn't want to be treated as if I were broken.

Ramsey jerked his head in a nod but didn't say a word. Sounds of an engine cut through the morning quiet, and he started for the round pen. I followed behind. Ramsey unlatched the gate, and I pulled it open. He lifted his gaze to mine. "You'll work the gate once the trailer's in place."

I nodded as a truck with a trailer appeared. It pulled past the round pen and then backed up. The ease with which Lor maneuvered the vehicle told me she'd done this countless times before. As soon as she shifted into park, I moved the gate so it was flush with the trailer. A terrified horse that got loose would be a disaster.

As I moved close to the trailer, the horse inside kicked at the walls. The metal bowed at the contact. The horse let out a loud whinny and kicked again.

"She's not a fan of the trailer," Lor said as she climbed out of the truck.

I'd been expecting young. I didn't know why. This woman was in her sixties or early seventies with gray running through her hair. The relief that swept through me had no roots in logic, but I welcomed the sensation all the same.

Lor's eyes hardened a fraction as she took me in, then she shifted her focus to Ramsey. "New helper?"

"Lor, this is Shiloh. She's going to be working here and living in the guest cabin."

Lor stilled and then swallowed, shaking her head. "Nice to meet you, Shiloh."

"You, too."

She didn't seem all that happy at my presence, which made zero sense. The horse gave the trailer wall another kick.

"Let's get her out of there," Ramsey said, moving to unlatch the door. "She tied?"

"Couldn't even get a halter on her," Lor answered.

Ramsey looked to me. "Be ready. She could try to bolt."

I nodded, tightening my grip on the gate.

Ramsey pulled open the door to the trailer, and the mare leapt out, bucking and whinnying. Ramsey shut the door and latched it back into place. "Move the trailer."

Lor jumped behind the wheel, and I moved the gate closed as she did, looping the chain back into place. Fast hoofbeats had me looking up.

The mare tore around the pen so fast she was a blur. But the snapshots I caught broke my heart. Her ribs stood out against her coat, and the wild look in her eyes spoke of a deep-seated fear.

Ramsey stood in the center of the ring and waited. Like so many times before, he stood by patiently as she tired herself out. It didn't take long. This horse was too malnourished. Her gallop slowed to a trot and then a walk. Finally, she stilled altogether.

I sucked in a sharp breath. Scars crisscrossed her side and the bridge of her nose. The ones on her face spoke of someone fighting her while she had a halter or bridle on. But the ones on her side? Those were punishment.

My throat burned as it constricted. I'd gotten so good at holding the tears back, but they fought to get free. The mare's gaze locked with mine.

My fingers tightened around the fence rail, the wood biting into my palms. There was such despair in those eyes, but there was desperation, too. The combination was one that I knew too well.

I vowed then and there that I'd do anything to help this horse find her freedom.

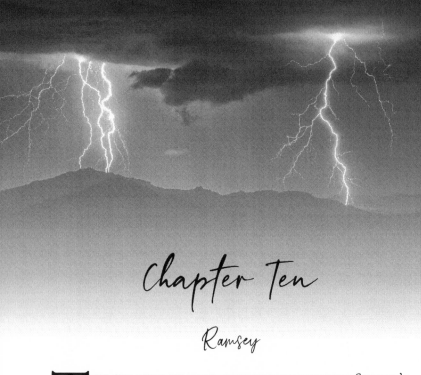

Chapter Ten

Ramsey

THE STRANDS OF GOLD WOVEN THROUGHOUT SHILOH'S braid caught the afternoon light as her head tilted to the side. I traced the little pops of light with my gaze—sparks hidden to most except those really paying attention.

Everything about Shiloh was calm and steady. She sat cross-legged at the side of the round pen with what looked like a small picnic set out in front of her. Everything was arranged just so. A sandwich carefully unwrapped. A water bottle with the lid off. An apple sliced in precise shapes. And my traitor of a dog curled up at her side.

She didn't focus on the mare in the pen; only occasionally lifted her gaze to the horse. But it never stayed. It traveled back to the food in front of her, to Kai, to the mountains and land-scape around us. I stayed hidden in the shadows of my front porch, watching.

I'd spent much of the day yesterday with the mare. I hadn't struggled this much with a horse in years. And this morning had been much the same. She wouldn't let me close and showed no signs of choosing to close the distance between us.

Shiloh had watched silently as I worked with the mare. The only hint of emotion I saw from her had been the purse of her lips. She hadn't said a word, but she had eaten each of her meals beside the pen. I didn't ask why. The one thing I knew about Shiloh was that her heart called out to these creatures. She felt their pain as if it were her own. I was sure she didn't want this mare to feel alone. And this was her small way of reassuring the animal.

Shiloh scratched behind Kai's ears and nuzzled his head. The mare's ears twitched—the first hint of interest I'd seen from her. Shiloh bit into her sandwich and tipped her face up to the sun.

Her braid fell farther down her back as her neck arched. My gut tightened, a stirring of something I hadn't felt in decades. Something I'd never let myself feel. The sun's rays hit the apples of Shiloh's cheeks, showing off the rosy hue that matched her lips.

An image popped into my head of my hand tugging on that braid. Of my mouth taking hers. I swore I could taste her on my tongue.

I gave my head a quick shake. Dumb. So monumentally stupid I didn't even have the words for it.

The mare took two steps in Shiloh's direction, and my breath caught.

Shiloh seemed to sense the movement. She slowly lowered her chin and opened her eyes. The mare halted.

Shiloh didn't show any signs of reaction. Instead, she reached down for a slice of apple and leaned forward. She slid her hand between the rails of the fence and waited.

I didn't move a millimeter as I studied the two. Shiloh had her own gift of patience, it seemed. Her hand didn't waver as she waited.

She tipped her head against Kai's, and he lapped at her face. The faint strains of her laughter caught on the wind. That hint of huskiness from her voice extended to her laughter.

The mare took another two steps, sniffing the air. My fingers tightened on the porch rail.

Shiloh kissed my dog on the top of his head and then smiled up at the horse. The mare bent, stretching out her neck. It would've been so tempting for Shiloh to move her hand to close the distance, but she didn't. She waited.

The horse nipped the slice of apple and darted away. Shiloh didn't react to that either. She simply pulled her hand back and picked up another piece of apple for herself. I couldn't help but grin.

"She's got a way with her," Lor said from the porch steps.

I bit back my smile. "She's made more progress than I have."

"That why you're standing here moonstruck?"

I scowled at my friend of two decades. "I don't get *moonstruck*."

"I was wondering where the hell you were since you went to grab a water twenty minutes ago. Now, I find you oblivious to anything but her and the horse."

My back molars ground together. "I'm worried about the mare." It wasn't a lie. But it wasn't the whole truth either.

"This is a bad idea, Ramsey."

"What is?"

Lor glanced at Shiloh. "How does her sheriff brother feel about her living here?"

My grip on the rail tightened, the wood biting into my palms. "Shiloh's an adult."

It pissed me off how everyone treated her like a child as if she'd been frozen in time when she got kidnapped, never allowed to move on with her life.

"I'm aware. That doesn't mean her family isn't overprotective. We need this community's trust so they'll bring horses in need to us. You piss off brother bear, and he puts the word out? All that could stop."

"I'll deal with it."

My words came out as more of a growl, and Lor held up both

hands. "Fine. Just watch your back because I'm going to be gone for almost a month picking up those horses."

I jerked my head in a nod. I'd watched my back for most of my life. There was no reason for that to change now.

My gaze kept snaking to the side as I worked on cleaning my tack as if Shiloh's movements had some sort of magnetic pull. She worked the sponge over the leather, clearing away the saddle soap. Her fingers moved deftly, trained by years of practice.

It was a basic task, but still, it hypnotized me. That simple fact had my jaw working back and forth as I forced myself to refocus on my saddle. I'd put off doing a full tack clean, but now that I had help, there was time.

"You sure you don't need to help out at your parents'?" The last thing I needed was them being any more pissed off at me.

Shiloh shook her head, a few strands of hair pulling loose from her braid. My fingers itched to tuck them behind her ear.

"They're good with the hands they have right now."

My gaze caught on her mouth as it pulled down. "What?"

Her head lifted as her brows drew together in confusion.

"You frowned. Something bother you about your dad having all the help he needs right now?"

The corners of her lips tipped up the barest amount. "You're annoyingly perceptive."

I chuckled. "Comes from watching the horses I work with."

"That makes sense."

"So..." I prodded. Some need, deep inside me, wanted to understand where that hint of unhappiness came from—something I hadn't felt with anyone else.

Shiloh resumed cleaning the saddle. "They make work for me."

"It's a big ranch. I can't imagine they don't need help with the horses and whatever else you were doing."

She worked over a spot on the saddle that didn't need it. "But they don't need *me* to do it. They don't count on me. It's like a make-believe job. Not one I earned. It makes me feel useless."

"You're far from useless," I said, my voice going gruff. Shiloh had jumped in with both feet here. And for the first time, I wasn't quite so exhausted at the end of the day. "I didn't realize how much I needed the help. And you know what you're doing. I don't say that lightly."

Something that looked a lot like hope lit Shiloh's eyes. A true lightness appeared that I'd only ever seen when she was with animals. "Thank you. I want to help. To earn my keep."

"You are."

Our gazes locked and held. So many silent things passed between us as they always did. Instincts about what we'd both been through. An understanding I didn't think either of us found with anyone else.

My phone buzzed in my pocket, jerking my focus away from Shiloh. I slid it out and pulled up the camera at the front gate. Aidan's truck waited there. I pressed the button to let him in.

"Everything okay?" Shiloh asked.

I nodded. "That's more help. I'm just throwing all the rules out the window now," I grumbled.

Shiloh's lips twitched. "The rules, huh? You gonna give me a copy of those so I don't get detention?"

I shook my head and pushed to my feet. "What good would it do when I'm breaking them all anyway?"

She looked up at me, something swirling behind those ice-blue eyes. "Sometimes, we need to break the rules to get to where we're supposed to be."

Shiloh had broken all the ones she and her family had made for her to get here. I had to hope it was the right move. I stared down at her, trying to see all the things she hid away. "Sometimes, rules are chains that hold us down."

Her throat worked as she swallowed. "Heaviest weight you can wear."

Gravel crunched as Aidan's truck rounded the bend in the

road, and I forced my gaze away from Shiloh. It came to a stop in front of the barn, and Aidan rolled down his window. "Am I okay parked here?"

"Yup."

He climbed out and let Elliott out of the backseat. Kai's head lifted at the newcomers. I snapped my fingers, and he immediately came to my side.

Aidan's eyes widened. "Is that a wolf?"

"A wolf-dog hybrid."

"So freaking cool," Elliott whispered. "Can I pet him?"

Aidan wrapped an arm around his little brother's shoulders, pulling him to his side. "I don't think that's a good idea, El."

"Aidan," Elliott whined. "If I go back to school with this story, I'll be the coolest."

Shiloh's hands tapped at her sides as she studied the boys. I knew that kind of focus. She was registering each and every thing about them. The way Elliott's clothes were just a little too small for him. How Aidan's hung off his form. The dark circles under his eyes, and the protective way he shielded his brother.

She let out a shaky breath. "Kai's a love." Her voice was quiet as she spoke, and then Shiloh let out a low whistle. My dog deserted me in an instant. Shiloh sank to the ground and patted the dirt. Kai lowered to his belly.

Aidan didn't look especially convinced, keeping a hold on his brother.

Shiloh nuzzled the dog, her face burrowing in the fur at his neck. "Kai, these are new friends."

"Elliott," the little boy filled in. "And that's Aidan."

The teen grunted, still not releasing Elliott.

Shiloh smiled, the expression a little shaky around the edges, something that spoke of uneasiness with new people. I didn't think it had anything to do with the boys. It was more the having to hold conversations that she didn't know the outcome of.

"I'm Shiloh."

"The love of Kai's life," I muttered.

Elliott grinned. "I get it. She's really pretty."

For the first time since he'd arrived, Aidan smiled as he ruffled his brother's hair. "Always the Casanova."

Elliott's face scrunched. "The what-a-nova?"

"Good with the ladies."

Elliott's chest puffed up. "Duh."

A more genuine smile played on Shiloh's lips. "I bet Kai will like you just as much. Hold out your hand."

I didn't miss how Shiloh moved hers out of the way so there was no risk of her coming into contact with him. Elliott extended his hand. Kai sniffed it a few times and then lashed out with his tongue, giving the boy a good lick.

Elliott giggled. "That tickles."

"Wait till he licks your face. That *really* tickles."

Aidan sent me a hesitant glance. "Thanks for letting him pet your, uh, dog."

"Sure." I waved them towards the house. "We're breaking for our afternoon snack. We can talk about your responsibilities while we eat."

Shiloh's brows rose at that, knowing that hadn't been in our routine so far. But I should've guessed she'd already have figured out the why for it. Her gaze kept traveling to Aidan, picking up on each piece of his appearance.

"You don't have to feed us, sir," Aidan said.

"Call me Ramsey. And you're working here, so you're getting fed."

Elliott grinned. "I could eat."

Aidan's expression softened as he pulled his brother back to his side. "You can always eat."

"I'm *growing*. You said."

"You are."

We made our way to the front porch. I pointed to a long set of rockers. "Grab a seat. I'll get the food."

I stepped inside before anyone could say a word otherwise. I moved past the entryway and through the open living space with its massive windows. Coming to a stop in the kitchen, I grabbed the sandwiches I'd made this morning, some drinks, and a bag of chips. It would have to do for now. Balancing everything in my arms, I headed back.

As I reached the entryway, the door opened, and I stiffened. Shiloh poked her head in. "Do you need any help?"

"I'm good," I gritted out. Even just having her hover at the door had my pulse quickening. *This is Shiloh*, I reminded myself. Someone whose gentleness seeped out of her pores. It wasn't her that bothered me; it was the crossing of that invisible boundary and the loss of control.

She lowered her voice to a whisper. "Who are they, Ramsey?"

I glanced out the front window, taking in the boys as Aidan pointed to some horses. "Kenny Chambers' kids. Aidan needed a job."

Shiloh's eyes widened, and then anger lit in them. "He's not getting enough food."

I held up the plate of sandwiches. "That's not going to be a problem anymore."

A shadow passed over Shiloh's face as she took the plate from me. "You're a good man, Ramsey."

My chest burned. Each word hit like a physical blow. I hadn't heard words like that in decades. Maybe longer. *Good* wasn't a word someone equated with a man who'd done hard time as a teen, even if it had been expunged from my record. It was too late to make it disappear. It had already carved itself into my bones.

Shiloh didn't wait for my response. She turned around and headed back out to the boys, setting the plate on a small table between their two chairs before unwrapping it.

I cleared my throat. "Wasn't sure what you liked. There's turkey and peanut butter and jelly."

"Turkey!" Elliott cheered.

Shiloh grinned and handed him one while she picked up a PB&J.

"I'll take whatever you don't want," Aidan said to me.

"There's plenty of both. Choose whatever you like."

His hand hovered over the sandwiches before choosing a turkey one. I made a mental note of that.

Elliott bit into his sandwich and then began peppering Shiloh with questions from her favorite color to what she did on the ranch.

Aidan was quiet as he ate but kept glancing my way. He ducked his head closer to me. "My dad's real mad at you. I, uh, he doesn't know I'm working here. But you need to watch your back."

Alarm bells went off in my head, but I kept my expression relaxed—the same way I would with a skittish horse. "I'll be fine."

Aidan stared down at his sandwich, picking at the crust. "He can get real mean, and he holds a grudge."

I stiffened. It was too soon to push, I knew it, but what other choice did I have? I had to try. I ducked my head to meet his gaze. "Are you safe at home?"

His jaw tightened. "I'm fine. He's an asshole, that's all. But I don't want to see him cause trouble for you or your ranch. He'll do it if he can."

I studied the teen in front of me, trying to read between the lines. But Aidan's face was a carefully blank mask. I knew from experience what hid behind masks like that. And it was nothing good.

Chapter Eleven

Shiloh

I COULDN'T STOP THINKING ABOUT AIDAN AND ELLIOTT. They'd stayed for several hours yesterday. Aidan was a hard worker, doing more than his share of mucking stalls and cleaning tack. But worry gnawed at me.

Even as I made the drive towards Hayes and Everly's house, the boys' faces flashed in my mind. I hadn't pushed Ramsey for more information because I could tell that he didn't have it. For now, it would have to be enough to keep an eye on them. Maybe I could ask Hayes to stop by their house.

I turned off the gravel road and onto the private drive. My stomach tightened as a familiar landscape came into view. I kept waiting for the sensation to ease.

With each change to the property, I hoped. But that flash of panic was always the same. It never lessened. Not when the pens for the animals had been constructed. Not when Everly and Hayes had built a new house on the land. Not even when I'd taken down the godforsaken shed. My gut instinct when it came to this place was always to run.

That was why I made myself face it. I refused to let it have power over me. To let *him* have power over me.

The panic always eased after a minute or two. I'd focus on the animals that Everly was helping with her sanctuary. Or on her and my brother's faces. How much they cared about me. This place that had once been the cause of so much pain and misery was now a place of light and healing.

That gave me hope. Things could change. Be transformed. And that meant maybe I could be, too.

I pulled up next to Everly's SUV. Two other vehicles were parked in front of the barn. Employees Everly had hired to help her tend to the animals and take visitors on tours.

I began to second-guess the wisdom of just showing up in the middle of the day. I'd wanted to avoid another scene with Hayes, but I didn't want to have this conversation with others around either. My hand tightened on my keys as I stared at the barn.

Everly stepped out into the sun, her golden-blond hair catching the light. She held up a hand in a wave as she headed towards me.

Too late. I shut off my engine and slid out of my truck.

She smiled as she approached, but I saw the shadows under her eyes. "Hey, Shy."

"Hey." I toyed with my keys, spinning the ring around my finger. I thought about the words I wanted to give Everly, but they stuck in my throat, unable to escape.

"Lemonade?"

"Sure." Lemonade would give me time to find the words again. To grip them better and force them into the air around us.

Everly motioned me towards the house. "Hayes said you moved. How's your new place?"

I glanced over at her as we walked. "Is that how he really put it?"

She chuckled. "He might've been ranting about you living with a dangerous guy."

"Ramsey's not dangerous." Those words came easily and with more force and bite than I'd intended.

Everly slowed, studying me. "No, I don't imagine he is."

I looked back at her, trying to find the reason for her agreement.

Everly pulled open the front door, wiping her feet on the mat. "I know Hayes is overprotective. He's gotten so much better, but it's still a challenge for him. Especially when it comes to you."

I bit back a curse. I was so tired of being seen as the weak one. The one who needed shielding. If anything, my ordeal should've shown them how strong I was.

Everly led the way to the kitchen, pulling out a pitcher of lemonade. "It can make him blind. Working in the animal rescue world, I've heard about Ramsey and the miracles he can work with wounded horses. I don't imagine a man like that has bad in him. The animals would sense it."

She was right. It was what had put me at ease with Ramsey over the years. I'd seen his gentleness and patience. It was the opposite of what I'd seen from those who were evil and cruel. "The things he can do are pretty amazing."

Everly's mouth curved as she poured two glasses of lemonade. "I'd love to see it someday."

I could've told her not to hold her breath. Instead, I took the glass she offered me. "Thanks."

"Want to take it out back?"

"Sure."

We made our way to the back deck that looked out across an extensive garden, and a gazebo butted up to the forest. It was a magical atmosphere, and I couldn't help but be a little envious. I'd never done the nesting thing—settling and making a place mine. Maybe it was time. I could start small. Perhaps some pots on the front deck of the guest cabin.

"The gardens have really come in."

Everly's face lit up as she eased into the Adirondack chair. "It's the perfect backdrop for a wedding, don't you think?"

I sat in the chair next to her, studying the yard. "I don't know if I'm really an expert on weddings, but it is beautiful."

"Who cares about expertise? All that matters is if you like it."

"I do. It's magical."

She beamed at me. "Good. Magic is a quality I can get behind." Her smile wavered a bit. "I actually wanted to ask you something about the wedding."

My mouth went dry. "Sure."

"It would mean a lot to me if you'd be a bridesmaid. Hadley said she'd be one, and Addie's going to be my matron of honor. I'd ask Laiken, too, but she's doing some of the photos."

My fingers curled around the edge of the chair. I gripped it so hard splinters poked into my palm. "You don't have to ask me, Ev."

Her face fell. "I know I don't have to, but I *want* to. I don't mean to force you into it, but you're important to me."

My throat clogged. Everly's and my paths were interwoven in so many ways, but I knew I was a reminder of painful things for her. Of a choice she'd had to make that'd cost her the love of her family—most of them, anyway. "I'm sorry about your dad."

Of course, the words I'd practiced came at the most awkward time imaginable. It was me, after all. I never seemed to manage to say the right thing at the right time.

Instead of shock or confusion, Everly simply rolled with the punches. Something she had always been great at. "Thank you." She leaned back in her chair. "It's a relief, if I'm honest. His life wasn't a happy one. His sickness ate at his mind until he didn't trust anyone."

"Is there evil in you? I'll beat it out."

Howard's voice battered at my skull. The smell of his sweat filled my senses, and I felt the cramps in my stomach from hunger. Other images flashed in my mind, too: his face twisted in rage and the certainty that I was going to die.

"I'm so sorry he hurt you, Shy."

Everly's voice pulled me out of the memories, but the panic had already been set free. It raced through my bloodstream and pulsed in my muscles. I clenched and flexed my hands in my lap, trying to stave off the worst of it.

"But you saved me." It was all I could get out.

"I'm sorry I didn't do it sooner."

"You did it when you could. And just because he did bad things doesn't change that he was your dad."

Everly let out a shaky breath. "No, it doesn't. I think now, more than anything, I'm just thankful that he's free. That we all are."

But in that moment, I didn't feel very free. I felt like Howard Kemper still had a stranglehold on my life, and I wondered if that would ever end.

My hand trembled as I swiped the key fob over the intercom system. Two hours after the onslaught of memories, and I was still shaky. I'd forced myself to stay with Everly for a while. To be her support, even though I was dying inside. Then I'd gone to the grocery store and stopped to pick up my mail.

It pissed me the hell off that I was still rattled. I clenched the wheel as I waited for the gate to open—anything to keep the shakiness at bay. The large, metal gate swung inward. Ramsey had spared no expense with his security setup. It made sense, having gone through what he had. I couldn't imagine spending over a year in prison for a crime I didn't commit.

Or maybe I understood more than I gave myself credit for. We had both lived in prisons of a sort. Mine had just been one of my own making. Now, we both coped however we could. For Ramsey, it was security measures and keeping people at arm's length. For me, it was avoiding people altogether. Maybe neither system was serving us very well.

I pulled to a stop in front of the guest cabin and grabbed my bag of groceries from the passenger seat. I wasn't much of a cook, but I could handle the basics. And I made one hell of a lasagna. Now, I just needed to find a way to pawn some leftovers off on Aidan and Elliott.

I climbed out of my truck and headed for the cabin. Opening the door, I made my way to the kitchen. It didn't take long to unload the contents of my bag. I snagged a Coke from the fridge and headed for the front porch with the mail that had piled up over the last week.

As I stepped outside, a bark sounded. Kai came running from the direction of the barn, and I couldn't help my smile. I lowered myself to the front steps so I could brace for impact. I'd barely set my soda down when he leapt.

I laughed as he landed on me with a woof. "I missed you, too."

Kai licked my cheek.

"I know. I was gone too long."

He let out a chuff.

"I don't like going out in the big, bad world either. But, sometimes, you have to."

Kai settled onto the steps and laid his head in my lap.

"All's forgiven, I guess."

I scratched behind his ears as I picked up my Coke and took a long drink. My gaze caught on Ramsey in the round pen with my mare. I'd started thinking of her as such over the past two days. I wasn't sure how Sky would feel about sharing my affections, but right now, she was too busy enjoying her new home and friends to notice.

Ramsey had pulled off his flannel and was working in only jeans and a white tee. The shirt clung to his broad shoulders and sculpted chest, showing off every dip and ridge. I swallowed hard, forcing my eyes away from him.

I reached for my stack of mail, anything to distract me from the man just fifty yards away. I tossed catalogues and other junk mail into a pile for recycling and began going through the rest. I made another pile of bills. I didn't have many, but the ones I did still came every month like everyone else's.

I slid my finger under the seal of a plain white envelope with no return address, tugging a sheet of paper free. Dirt smudged the stark white, and wrinkles creased the page. As I unfolded it, the first thought that surfaced was that I didn't recognize the handwriting.

The only handwritten letters I received had been the ones from Howard, and his angry scrawl was burned into my brain, etched there in a way I knew I'd never forget. This was blockier. Square shapes and jagged lines, where Howard's had been slanted, harsh loops.

There was no name or greeting, but each word after that empty space had my heart picking up speed.

PURITY. THAT'S WHAT MATTERS. YOU SWORE YOU'D NEVER GO THE WAY OF YOUR TAINTED FAMILY. YET HERE YOU ARE, SHACKED UP WITH A STRANGER. I SHOULD'VE KNOWN YOUR PROMISES WERE NO MORE THAN CAREFULLY CRAFTED LIES. THERE'S EVIL IN YOU. BUT I KNOW HOW TO GET IT FREE.

The can of Coke slipped from my hand, the cola spilling onto the porch steps. My lungs seized. I didn't have a chance to fight off the panic now. It was too strong. It hit with a force that knocked all the air from my body.

The world blurred around me, and I wondered if this was the end. If the panic would finally bring a stroke or heart attack. If I would never truly know what it was to be free.

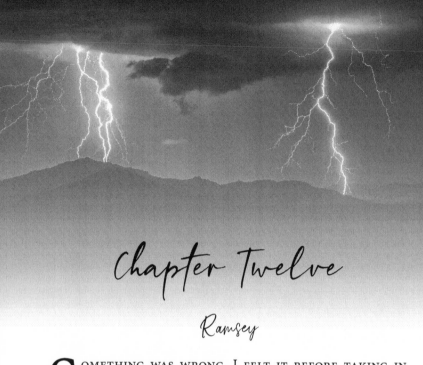

Chapter Twelve

Ramsey

SOMETHING WAS WRONG. I FELT IT BEFORE TAKING IN anything by sight or sound—that subtle change in the air. I'd become attuned to it over the years. Felt the shift in energy, the hair on my arms lifting with it.

I turned my focus from the mare in front of me to the guest cabin porch. I'd known the second she emerged from the house—before Kai had barked in happy glee. Because I had a radar for Shiloh Easton. The existence of it made her dangerous for me, but I'd given up giving a damn.

My gaze zeroed in on her. I could see her trembling from here, a piece of paper fluttering in her hand. I was moving before my brain gave my legs the command—pure instinct.

I ducked between the rails on the fence and picked up to a jog. Kai whined as I approached, nudging into Shiloh's side.

She had her hands clenched into tight fists like the talons of a bird wrapped around a branch. She didn't even seem to register my presence, her chest rising and falling in shallow, rapid pants.

"Shiloh?"

She blinked a few times, but her breathing only came faster. No words came at all.

Hell. I recognized the signs of a full-fledged panic attack.

I lowered myself to my knees in front of her and took her hands in mine. The grip was an iron vise around nothing but air and the corner of a paper. "Focus on one thing. Me. My face."

Her eyes were glassy and unfocused, but I saw the struggle to zero in on me. She blinked rapidly, her breaths still jagged and shallow.

I pressed my fingers against her pulse. Her heart beat in a rapid, chaotic rhythm. Shiloh wavered in place.

My hold on her hands tightened. "It's just you and me. You're safe. You think Kai would let anything happen to you?"

That seemed to register, causing a flare of something in those ice-blue depths.

"That's it. Look at me. Pick one thing."

Her eyes tracked over my face, stopping to lock with mine.

"What color are my eyes?"

Shiloh let out a noise. It wasn't a word, exactly, but it was something.

"Think about that color. What does it remind you of?"

Mud eyes. That was what my stepdad had always called them. But that wasn't the point. I had to get Shiloh thinking about something other than what had sent her into this state.

"Beautiful," she croaked.

The vise around my chest loosened a fraction. I'd never been happier to hear a single word.

I squeezed her hands. "Tell me more."

"Your eyes. They're beautiful."

The kindness of her words burned my gut, but I forced it down. "Careful, that could go to my head. What else do you see?"

"Pain."

That vise around my ribs tightened right back up.

"So much I could drown in it."

I didn't want to take Shiloh into that darkness with me. Didn't want her to even be able to see it. "Didn't think pain could be beautiful."

"It is when it makes you feel not so alone."

She blinked a few times as if coming out of a stupor. Her pulse and breathing slowed. Her gaze traveled from my face to where my hands were locked around hers.

"You're touching me."

There was wonder in her tone that had my brows pulling together. "Would you rather I didn't?"

Shiloh's gaze flew to mine. "Don't let go."

"I promise. I won't let go."

My grip on her tightened a fraction, just to let her know I was still there.

Her eyes glittered with unshed tears, but she shoved them back. I could feel her battle to keep them from falling. In one way, I admired the hell out of that stubborn determination. In another, my heart broke that Shiloh felt as if she couldn't set them free in front of anyone. That kind of bottled-up emotion could eat a person alive.

"It doesn't hurt," she whispered.

"What doesn't?"

"You touching me."

I fought the urge to rear back—only decades with horses kept me from doing so. The training that kept me from reacting strongly when I got knocked sideways. "You thought it would?"

"It always does. Whenever someone touches me. It...it's like it grates against my skin."

I bit back a million different curses. "Tell me if it's too much."

She shook her head back and forth. "It's not."

"Okay." I rested back on my heels, not letting go of her hands even after their death grip had loosened. "Can you tell me what happened?"

A shudder ran through Shiloh that had me kicking myself. She took in a steadying breath. "I'm okay—"

"Bullshit," I snapped.

She jolted and then blushed.

"Shit. I'm sorry. I didn't mean—"

"No. It's not your fault."

"Give me your truth. Please." I hadn't earned her truth. Certainly didn't deserve the right to demand it. But I wanted it so damn bad.

Shiloh searched my eyes, looking for something. Whatever it was, she must've found it or decided I was worth the risk. "I got a letter."

"Okay…"

She looked down at the paper still clenched tightly in her hand.

I released that hand and took the letter while still holding on to her other. I wasn't letting go until she told me to. I scanned the handwritten page, and each word dug into my flesh. By the time I reached the end, I was barely holding on to a control I'd mastered years ago.

I struggled to keep my expression neutral and lifted my eyes to Shiloh. "Who sent this?"

"I don't know. It's Howard, but it's…not."

I reared back at the name—something my years with the horses had trained me not to do. But I couldn't help it. I'd done my research when Shiloh started showing up at my ranch all those years ago, and that name was burned into my brain. "It sounds like things he told you?"

Shiloh had only been ten when Howard Kemper took her, but whatever he'd said when he had her was likely permanently etched in her psyche.

She shifted on the step, and Kai moved in closer. "You can let go," she said softly.

It took me a second. I didn't want to lose the contact—that link between us. I forced my fingers to open, setting her hand free.

She stared down at it as if it held all the answers in the world. "He wrote me letters. I started getting them when I got my own mailbox. I have no idea if he tried to send them before or how he got my address. It's a small town, and I can only guess that his son told him he'd seen me picking up mail at the post office."

Blood roared in my ears. "There's no way letters to a victim should've made it out of prison."

Shiloh shrugged. "I'm guessing he had someone else send them."

"And they were like this one?" The words and tone made me sick. *Purity*? "Shiloh, did he…?" I couldn't even say the words.

She shook her head vigorously. "No. Nothing like that. He told me I was going to marry his son. That I had to stay pure and that my family would taint me. That they were evil." She looked up. "But he's dead. And this handwriting…it's different. Plus, he never would've used words like *carefully crafted*."

I snatched up the envelope from the porch step. "Mailed two days ago." My pulse stuttered. "From Wolf Gap."

Fear blazed brightly in Shiloh's eyes. "Someone *here* sent it?"

"We need to call your brother. He'll know who had the most contact with Howard while he was in prison."

Her hand snaked out to grip mine. "No. Hayes is the last person I want to know about this."

I was far from a fan of law enforcement, but this was one case where we needed it.

"Shiloh."

"No. He finds out about this, and he'll force me to move in with him and Everly. He'll never let me out of his sight."

"He has the resources—"

"He doesn't know about the letters."

I stilled. "You never told anyone about them." It wasn't a question. I knew it with a certainty I couldn't entirely explain.

"What good would it do? Besides freak them out."

"They could've talked to the prison to make it stop."

Shiloh looked towards the horizon, tracing the mountains with her gaze. "I've had so few things that are mine. Even my loft at the ranch wasn't really *mine*. It belonged to my parents. I had Sky and my mailbox, and that's about it. When so little is yours, you're not willing to lose any of it. Even if it would stop something that terrifies you."

A jagged stab lit pain through my chest. "Someone wants to hurt you. And it's someone seriously messed in the head if they're sending fake letters from a dead man."

I ran through the possibilities in my mind, trying to put together a list of names from the articles I'd read about the case. Howard had a son, but he was in jail for his part in a kidnapping. He'd had a brother, but Allen Kemper had been killed in a shootout with the police after kidnapping his daughter, Addie.

Shiloh pulled her knees up to her chest, hugging them tightly. "I don't know who would do something like this. Who would hate me that much? But there were so many letters, Ramsey. Someone could easily copy that tone if they'd seen one."

The vise returned at the forlorn bent to her voice.

"Sometimes, I'd get a packet full of them. Like he'd written every day for a month but hadn't gotten the opportunity to send them." Her knuckles bleached white as her fingers dug into her legs. "Who knows how many there were floating around or who might've seen one?"

That meant she could've been leveled with one at any time, like invisible landmines that could appear in her mailbox without warning. And if they were capable of putting her through what I'd just seen? It was too much.

"I think you need to talk to your brother."

"My life will be over. Everything I've worked so hard for… gone." More unshed tears shone in her eyes. "Howard Kemper doesn't get to win. He stole so much of my life. I don't want to let him keep taking from me after he's gone."

Emotions warred, a back-and-forth battle between keeping Shiloh safe and not clipping her wings. "Promise to tell me if you get another one?"

She swallowed but nodded.

"You need to keep an eye out for anything suspicious. Someone who shows too much interest. Any cars that might be following you."

"Ramsey, I'm always on alert. I have been since I was ten years old. Those days changed me. I haven't trusted the same way since. I feel safe because I know how to handle myself and because I notice *everything*. If someone was tailing me, I'd know."

My jaw worked back and forth. "It's only ever been the letters?"

"That's it. People in town are curious about me, but they mostly steer clear." The corner of her mouth kicked up. "I think they're worried my oddness might be catching."

"You're not odd."

"I am. But I'm okay with it. People are overrated anyway."

The chuckle that escaped me took me by surprise. I never would've thought I could move from threats to laughing so quickly. "I've never been much of a people fan either."

Shiloh's gaze locked with mine. "I know. That's why it means everything that you let me stay here. I'll never forget it. I know I can't repay you—"

I took her hand in mine, weaving our fingers together. Her breath hitched, and I saw her pulse quicken.

"I like having you here. I think I needed it just as much as you did."

The truth of those words hit somewhere deep in my chest, burning. But it was a beautiful kind of pain. One I welcomed. One that belonged only to Shiloh.

Chapter Thirteen

Shiloh

I STUDIED THE HORSE AS SHE SHIFTED, TAKING MY MEASURE. I sent silent messages that I would never hurt her and that I was on her side. But she didn't approach.

Maybe she could still feel the anxiety of my earlier panic attack clinging to me. It sometimes took days for that frenetic energy to clear completely. I didn't blame her for not wanting to approach. Yet, I couldn't turn away.

Elliott scooted closer to the round pen's fence as he looked up at the mare. "Is she gonna be okay?"

My heart clenched at the concern lining his little face. I rolled the words around in my mouth before speaking. I wanted to be cautious of the ones I chose, but I didn't want to be dishonest with him either. Pretty lies only hurt more in the long run.

"She's trying to figure out who she can trust. It's going to take time."

Elliott's mouth thinned. "Dad was real mean to her. He never even let us name her."

Nausea swept through me. "I know."

"You guys will make her better. Aidan says Ramsey can do anything with horses."

My insides warmed at the little boy's certainty. "I've got a lot of faith in this beautiful girl. She's got warrior spirit in her."

The horse swished her tail as if relishing the compliment. I pulled a carrot out of my back pocket, slid my hand through the rails of the fence, and held it out to her.

The mare didn't move. I simply kept my hand still and turned to Elliott. "You wanna go for a ride with me the next time you're here?"

Elliott's eyes brightened and then dimmed. He shuffled his feet. "I've only been once. I'm not that good."

Anger lit in me that he'd never had the chance, despite growing up around the animals. Kenny Chambers' horses had been too abused for Elliott to learn on, and I doubted Kenny would've taken the time to teach his son out of the goodness of his heart.

"We all start somewhere. One time, I didn't check the girth and ended up under my horse. I bet you know enough not to do something silly like that."

Elliott stifled a giggle. "What happened?"

"I had to put my hands on the ground and do a handstand to get down." Thankfully, I'd been riding one of our oldest and calmest horses. He'd barely batted an eye at the ordeal.

Elliott toed a piece of gravel with his boot, and then his gaze traveled to where Ramsey and Aidan were bringing in some of the horses for the night. There was such longing in those eyes. A desire to be a part of it all. "I want to learn."

"Then that's what we'll do." As soon as the words were out of my mouth, I began second-guessing them. I hadn't ever taught anyone anything. My words didn't always come out right. But when I looked down at Elliott, I knew I had to try.

He sucked in a breath. "She's coming."

His words were barely audible, but I couldn't hold in my smile. "She just needed to do things in her own time." I understood that. The sensation of being pushed would only make us lock up.

I slowly turned my focus back to the ring. The mare moved at a snail's pace, her eyes alert. Her coat reminded me of Ramsey's eyes—so dark brown it was almost black. A glimmering onyx in the fading sunlight.

I held my hand steady, waiting.

She eased a little closer. Then a little more. Her lips reached for the carrot, the hairs on her muzzle tickling my palm. This time, she didn't bolt after grabbing the treat. She stayed still as she ate it.

Progress. Hope flickered to life down deep. I slowly pulled my hand back and reached for another carrot. Sliding it through the rails, I waited. I hadn't stretched my arm out as far this time.

The mare took another couple of steps and gobbled up the second carrot. She didn't move away. I held out my hand for her to sniff again. This time, I gave the underside of her chin a gentle scratch.

She jerked her head away as if startled but didn't bolt. I froze. After a few moments, she lowered her head to my hand. I tried the motion again, lightly scratching. Her lips twitched, but she didn't pull away.

"That's it. See? A little massage can feel good."

Elliott giggled. "Her lips are dancing."

They were, indeed, twitching in a rapid movement as I stroked her.

I grinned. "That means we found one of her favorite spots."

"She's starting to see it's good here. She's safe."

Something cracked in me at that—the fact that Elliott could recognize the need for safety at his age. I looked down at him. "I think you're right. This has been my safe place for a long time. Now, it's hers, too."

Elliott looked around at the ranch, a look of longing coming back into his eyes. "You're both really lucky."

We were, and I'd give anything for Elliott and Aidan to have the same thing.

I tipped the rocker back and forth as the sun slipped below the horizon. The mare nestled into the shelter connected to the round pen, but I sensed she watched me, too. I hoped there was a little more understanding. That we were beginning to weave the barest strands of trust.

"You've gotten farther with her than I have."

Kai climbed the porch steps and made a beeline for me as his owner spoke. I lifted my gaze to Ramsey's dark depths as my hands sifted through Kai's fur. "What do you think about the name Onyx?"

He turned to look at the mare, taking her in.

"It's her coloring but more. I looked it up. It means nail or claw in ancient Greek."

Ramsey nodded slightly. "She clawed her way out of Hell and straight to us."

Us. As if we were a team. I liked the idea too much.

Ramsey stepped forward and into the glow of the porch lights. "Onyx, it is. I'll get her name plaque ordered tomorrow."

I took in the man in front of me, seeing how ladened he was with things for the first time. A duffel over one shoulder. Grocery totes over the other. A box in his arms.

I lifted a brow. "Going camping?"

He shook his head.

"Preparing for the apocalypse?"

He grunted.

"I might need more than non-existent charades to help me guess this one."

There wasn't even a flicker of the amusement I could usually drag out of Ramsey.

"I'd like to stay here for a while."

Energy sparked through my nerve endings. "Here?"

The single word came out more high-pitched than I'd intended as if I were a middle school boy going through puberty and unable to control my voice.

Ramsey leaned against the railing, studying everything about my reaction. "I think it's smart to be cautious. Someone knows you're here. That means they've been watching."

My skin itched as if it were too tight for my body, and my fingers picked up a rapid tapping against my thighs. "You have a gate. A security system—"

"One that needs some beefing up. I put a call in to the guy who helped me set it up, but he's on vacation right now. Let me stay here until we get that sorted."

A million different emotions warred inside me. I wanted the solitude and freedom I'd fought so hard for. But after today, my nervous system was shot. I was on edge, and the idea of having someone across the hall? It helped.

Just feeling that need for security in the form of another person made me feel weak. Annoyance flickered through me. "Your house is basically a hundred yards away." There was some tree cover between, but Ramsey would be able to see anyone approaching the front of my cabin.

"More like two hundred." Ramsey's gaze met mine, and there were no walls in that moment. He let me see it all. The concern. The care. "I don't like the idea of you staying alone when someone's messing with you."

A riot of emotions flew through me. Disappointment. Anger. Frustration. Relief.

Of course, Ramsey wasn't here for any other reason than to make sure I was safe. I was so damn tired of only being seen as something to protect. But I was also exhausted. Tired to the bone. And, the truth was, I didn't want to be alone tonight.

Ramsey moved in closer, dropping a box filled with food onto my porch. "Those wounded eyes kill me."

I bristled at that. "They aren't wounded."

"Like I shoved a knife between your shoulder blades."

I dug my fingernails into my palms to keep from saying something I shouldn't. Instead, I kept all emotion from my tone. "I can take care of myself."

"I don't doubt it for a second. But there's something to be said for someone watching your back."

"And who watches yours?"

"Lor. Kai."

The jealousy that hit me was swift and strong. I wanted him to include me in that tight circle. But wasn't that what Ramsey was asking of me? For me to let him in? He was knocking. I just had to open the door.

I let out a huff of air. "You leave the toilet seat up one time, and you're out."

A laugh burst free from Ramsey. Everything about it was uninhibited. For the first time, he wasn't holding himself back from me. I felt the vibrations of the sound skate over my skin, and nothing had ever felt better.

Except maybe Ramsey's hand in mine. The warmth of his palm. Skin that didn't make me want to crawl out of my own. Heat that comforted.

Ramsey held up a hand. "I solemnly swear never to leave the toilet seat up."

I nodded and motioned to the box and bags. "Worried you won't make it back to the main house?"

He looked at me, a bit of hesitancy bleeding into his expression for the first time. "I thought I could make you dinner."

Chapter Fourteen

Ramsey

I'D NEVER FELT MORE LIKE AN IDIOT. I DIDN'T OFFER TO MAKE women dinner. I hadn't cooked for anyone but myself since the day I walked out the prison doors and no longer had kitchen duty. Sandwiches for the kids were one thing. *This* was something else entirely.

Surprise lit Shiloh's expression, and it made the light blue of her eyes sparkle under the porch lights. "You cook?"

"I get by well enough not to poison us."

It was more than that. Cooking had become an outlet—a way to unpack the day. To exercise my freedom. I hadn't chosen what I ate since the age of seven when my mom married that asshole and I lost everything. He dictated every single meal—even what snacks were in the house. Then there was prison, where all I got was food barely fit for rodents.

When I finally got out, free of that man and those walls, food was my first expression of freedom. I ate all the things I'd never been allowed to have. My stepdad had seemed to have a radar for the things I liked and made sure I never had access.

When I got out of prison, I hadn't wanted the feeling of having people's eyes on me. So, I'd slowly learned to make meals for myself. I had that damned kitchen duty to thank for teaching me the basics. I'd built from there.

Shiloh's cheeks pinked. "I'm really only good at lasagna."

"That's a good staple to start with. I could teach you more, if you want."

"I'd like that." She bent and picked up the box. "Tonight, I'll be the sous chef. Because I'm freaking starving."

I followed Shiloh inside, Kai darting in ahead of me. Always trying to steal my girl.

My steps faltered. *My girl?* Alarm bells went off in rapid succession.

I'd always been at peace with the knowledge that I wasn't made for relationships. I couldn't let down my walls enough for that. It wouldn't be fair to the woman.

Yet, here I was, wanting that. Wanting *her*. And not just because of the healthy dose of lust that thrummed through me any time I caught sight of Shiloh. It was more than that. I wanted to be near her. To hear what she thought about things. To see her work with the horses on my ranch or tear across the field on Sky's back as if she could touch the clouds.

"I'm just gonna put my bag in the guest room."

The gruff edge to my voice had Shiloh's brow furrowing. I ignored her confusion as I set down the bags of groceries and then headed for the bedrooms. I couldn't stop my gaze from pulling to the room I knew she'd taken. I swore I could smell a hint of that floral scent that clung to her. I didn't know if it was shampoo or lotion. It could've been perfume, but she didn't strike me as the type.

Whatever it was, it floated through the air in the hallway, just another in a series of temptations that told me that staying in a confined space with Shiloh was a recipe for disaster. Like always, I ignored the warnings and dropped my duffel onto the guest bed.

I twisted my head, cracking my neck. "Get it the hell together."

I took one more lungful of air that wasn't tainted with Shiloh's scent and then headed back towards the kitchen.

"I wasn't sure what you needed," Shiloh said as she pulled items from the box.

"I harvested the last of the winter squash. I was thinking something with that if you're game."

"I'll eat just about anything but liver and onions."

I chuckled and moved to the sink to wash my hands. "Noted."

"Do you mind if I take a quick shower? I'm grody from the day."

My Adam's apple bobbed as I swallowed. "Of course. Take all the time you need. This will be a bit."

Shiloh nodded. "Don't do the dishes. I'll get those when we're done."

"Deal."

Kai looked up at me as Shiloh took off for the bathroom. There was an accusation in his eyes as if it were my fault that she was no longer here.

"The way you moon over her is a little pathetic."

Kai barked, and I swore he was saying: *"Like you're any better."*

Shiloh had her damp hair wound into a knot atop her head. All through dinner, I found myself tracing the kaleidoscope of colors in it: browns and golds and even a hint of red.

Everything about the woman drove me to distraction. But at least it was better than the sounds of the damned shower as I'd cooked. Or worse, the silence that followed, knowing that she was just feet away, all bare, damp skin.

"That was incredible. You could open your own restaurant."

Shiloh's voice cut through my lust, followed quickly by guilt for letting myself idle there. I cleared my throat. "No interest in that."

She pulled a knee up to her chest and rested her chin on it. "I wouldn't be interested either." She was quiet for a moment. "I have to be honest. I wouldn't have pegged your go-to dish as roasted squash with quinoa and pear."

"And what would my go-to dish be?"

Shiloh raised a shoulder in a half shrug, her oversized t-shirt sliding down and exposing smooth, tanned skin. "Some form of meat and potatoes."

I stiffened slightly. That had been my stepdad: meat, potatoes or rice, and one vegetable at every dinner. The sound of plates flying off the table and crashing to the floor filled my mind. Angry words hurled at my mother, one after the other. The crack of a slap.

I shoved the memories down—every last one.

"There's chorizo in there, too."

"Fancy sausage. It just goes to show you shouldn't make assumptions."

I traced a design in the condensation of my glass. "I like playing with different flavors. Things you wouldn't think would go together."

"Salty and sweet."

"Exactly." Images flashed in my mind again, but these were different. My lips on Shiloh's skin. The taste of her on my tongue.

Shit. I needed to get out of this room before I did something stupid.

I shoved back from the table. "I need to send a few emails before I crash."

She blinked a few times, lowering her leg to the floor. "You don't want dessert? I've got some ice cream in the freezer."

"No," I clipped, the single word coming out harsher than I'd intended. I cleared my throat, trying to temper my words. "I'm good. You need any help with the dishes?"

Shiloh's face completely shut down with no hint of any emotion shining through. "No, I'm fine. Do whatever you need to."

I hated everything about this moment: The door she'd cracked open then slammed shut in my face. Knowing her expression of nothingness hid hurt. The desire still thrumming through me. All of it had alarm bells blaring in my mind.

I jerked my head in a nod. "'Night." I was out of the dining area before the word was completely out of my mouth.

I was an asshole. But better that than someone who took advantage. Shiloh had been through so much, and this past week had been a rollercoaster. She needed a friend, not some sleaze making a move on her.

Kai didn't follow me into the bedroom, but I wasn't shocked. I was sure he was in hog heaven at Shiloh's side. And, honestly, I felt better that he stuck close.

But as I closed the door to the guest room, I felt damn lonely—by my own choice. I'd walked away from what I wanted, what I wanted more than anything since I'd prayed for my freedom two decades ago.

I'd gotten it, but there had been a price for that freedom. It was something I needed to remember. There was always a cost.

I pulled my laptop out of my duffel and sank onto the bed. The knot of my hair tugged as I settled against the pillows. I pulled the tie free, and the pressure in my scalp released.

Flipping open the laptop, I tapped a key to wake it up, then opened an internet browser and got to work. Shiloh had been calm all through dinner. Hadn't mentioned the letter once. But *I* hadn't forgotten. I couldn't.

Someone was watching—someone who knew that she was here. That was too close for comfort for me.

I opened a notes app and started a list of everyone with ties to Howard Kemper. It shocked the hell out of me to find out that his daughter, Everly, was now engaged to Hayes. But then again, I'd read an article that had touted Everly as the one who'd saved Shiloh all those years ago.

I found some articles about Everly's brother, Ian, but from everything I could tell, he was still locked up in prison. I moved to other types of connections: Men who had worked for Howard. Those tied up in that off-the-grid world he'd been a part of. His cellmates.

My fingers froze over the keyboard as I scanned the website

on my screen, one that would tell me which of Howard's cell-mates were still in prison, and which had gotten out. He'd only had three in all his time inside. Two had lasted under a year. But the third? They'd obviously been enough of a match to remain paired for the duration.

August Ernst. He'd been sentenced to twenty years for stalking and aggravated assault. But he'd gotten out early—just two weeks before Howard Kemper died. Now, he was walking free.

Maybe he had an urge to terrorize the woman his cellmate had been obsessed with.

Chapter Fifteen

Shiloh

I LEANED AGAINST THE RAILS OF THE ROUND PEN, AND ONYX stared back warily. The session with Ramsey hadn't gone well this morning.

"You're certainly giving him hell."

The mare huffed.

"I get it, more than you know. But I've been here longer than you. He's a good man. You can trust him."

The mare's ears flicked.

I slid half an apple through the fence rails. Onyx started slowly towards me. Her gait wasn't as hesitant as it had once been. She knew only good things came from me. I just hoped she could find that same acceptance of Ramsey.

Onyx took the apple from my hand. As she chewed, I rubbed her cheek—more progress. My gaze caught on the scars crisscrossing her side. I kept my strokes steady. "I'm so sorry he hurt you."

Images flashed in my mind, phantom sensations through my body: The feel of Howard's hands around my neck. The certainty that those were my last moments on Earth.

I squeezed my eyes closed, my hand dropping away from Onyx. The panic zipped through my body. I clenched and flexed my hands, shaking them at my sides, trying desperately to beat it back.

A warm muzzle pushed into my neck. My eyes flew open. Onyx was right there as if she knew everything I was feeling—she probably did. Better than just about any other being on the planet.

I dropped my forehead to hers, resting it there. One single tear slipped free before I forced the rest back. "We're not alone. We have each other. We have Kai."

We had Ramsey, too, but I couldn't seem to find the bravery to say those words out loud. "I won't let anyone hurt you. Never again."

We stayed that way for…I didn't know how long, simply taking comfort in each other and the knowledge that someone understood.

My phone buzzed in my back pocket, and I forced myself to straighten but not before dropping a kiss to Onyx's muzzle. "Thank you."

I slid the phone out as the mare stepped away.

Mom: *How are you doing?*

I let out a breath and attempted to rein in my riot of emotions. I tried to put myself in her shoes, but as soon as I did, the guilt threatened to drown me, and every doubt along with it. Angry voices told me that I was selfish and heartless. Said that if I cared for my parents, I would've simply stayed where I was and done as they asked.

Ramsey's voice filled my head. The one that told me to focus on just one thing. I zeroed in on Onyx's face and those dark eyes that reminded me so much of his—ones that held pain but so much beauty.

The worst of the guilt eased. I lifted my phone and snapped a picture of the mare. I sent it to my mom.

Me: *I'm good. Working on befriending this girl.*

I worried my bottom lip as I waited for her response. It was a new tactic, volunteering information. Usually, I simply responded to questions, but I wanted her to know that I really *was* good. That this place was right for me in so many ways. I didn't have the exact words to tell her that, so I gave her this instead.

Mom: *She's a beauty. Looks a little thin.*

Me: *Ramsey rescued her from a bad situation. We're trying to help her heal.*

There was nothing for a few moments.

Mom: *That sounds like something you'd be great at.*

My nose stung. It was an olive branch. The biggest compliment, too.

Me: *I'm trying. And I'm learning a lot.*

Mom: *I'm glad. Maybe you can stop by sometime and tell me more about it.*

I bit down on the inside of my cheek. I hated the doubt that surfaced at her words. That I was wondering if going home would bring an onslaught of arguments. But I had to try.

Me: *Sure. I can come by towards the end of the week. I've got a few projects around here that I need to wrap up first.*

I was still making my way through the tack and getting the horses on more of a riding schedule. Aidan had proven himself to be more than capable, and having him on the riding roster helped tremendously. But it was a lot. I had no idea how Ramsey had been doing it all on his own for so long.

Mom: *Whenever you have time.*

I blinked at the screen a few times. That wasn't a Julia Easton response. She usually pushed. Couldn't help herself. But this, giving me space… It was new.

Me: *Thanks. Give Dad a hug for me.*

Mom: *Will do. Love you more than words.*

The stinging sensation was back. I locked my phone and shoved it back into my pocket. More guilt pricked at me. All the lies I'd told—the outright untruths *and* the unspoken ones— swirled around me.

It had been going on for so long, there were days that I questioned reality. I simply hadn't wanted to admit the truth. To let those around me know how bad things had gotten. How terrified I was. And then, the letters had started.

I'd shoved it all away as something of mine and mine alone to deal with. And now, there was too much. Even if I'd wanted to lay it all at my mom's feet, to crawl into her lap and have her tell me it would all be okay, I couldn't because I'd built a mountain of lies between us.

So, I'd have to deal with this latest development alone. *Not completely alone*, a voice whispered in my head. Ramsey knew. Not everything, but a lot of it. He knew what haunted me in the here and now, at least. And simply knowing that he was in the room down the hall had helped me sleep. No nightmares or flashbacks, just a pure, dreamless sleep.

It annoyed me that he had the ability to ease me like that, especially after putting an invisible wall between us. I wasn't sure what trigger I'd stepped on at dinner last night, but it was something. He'd slammed the door closed between us with a severity that had me reeling. And by the time I'd gotten up this morning, he was already gone.

I pushed off the round pen railing and started for the barn. He cared enough to want me safe, but that was it. It burned that what he felt for me was born of pity and obligation, but I'd get past that. I'd show him that I was capable of taking care of myself, and then things would go back to how they were before.

Friendship. Understanding. I'd learn from Ramsey. And, eventually, when I was ready, I'd move on.

The burn was back, but it was more intense this time. The idea of leaving this place. Of leaving him… It was too much.

Kai scrambled to his feet and followed me. I scratched his head as I walked to the barn. "You want to come with me?"

He let out a whine. Ramsey had seemed fine with Kai sticking close to me. He had come with me on a couple of rides. None had been quite this long, but I'd bring water for him.

I grabbed my saddle and Sky's bridle and stashed them on the rack near the crossties. I snatched a lead rope and moved to Sky's stall. "Hey, girl."

I slid the door open and hooked the rope to her halter. "How about a ride?"

She let out a whinny and danced her head up and down. A small laugh escaped me, even knowing what we would be en route to do.

I made quick work of grooming and saddling her, then put two bottles of water in my saddlebags and swung onto her back. With a whistle for Kai, I started out the back of the barn.

I forced myself to keep my focus on the trail ahead and not look for onyx eyes that I wanted to get lost in. He was a friend who was helping me, not my person—the one I could lean on and share my load with.

Kai ran ahead on the path but knew enough to check back with me. We wove around national forest land as we made our way towards town. When the trail forked, I veered away from the path that would lead us there. Instead, I took the one headed for a ridge.

The spot I had in mind had plenty of forest cover, and those trees would disguise me from any prying eyes. Not that they'd be looking. No one would expect to see me within a mile of this place.

Sky slowed as I pulled back on the reins and slid off her back. My legs trembled as I hit the ground. I told myself it was because of the ride but knew that was a lie.

My throat closed as I took in the people clad in black. It was a small crowd—ten at most. I saw Everly's blond hair catching in the wind as Hayes wrapped an arm around her shoulders. A minister stood by a glossy coffin.

My hands clenched into fists, nails digging into my palms. He was gone. Whoever was messing with me would lose interest when I didn't react, and my life would go back to normal.

Except I wasn't *normal*. I hadn't been since I was ten years old. I never would be again. I'd gotten too used to walking through life this way.

Hot tears burned my eyes. I'd lost so much, and all because of one man's sickness. Rage clawed at my chest, followed quickly by a grief so intense it was like a sucker punch to the gut.

I struggled to breathe. Fought to hold back the tears—the ones I never let fall.

But it was hopeless. I was drowning all over again.

Strong hands curled around my shoulders. I whirled, pulling my hand back to strike out. I stopped myself just shy of the man's nose.

A whirlwind of emotions swirled through me: Relief, anger, sadness. But I could only get one word out.

"Ramsey."

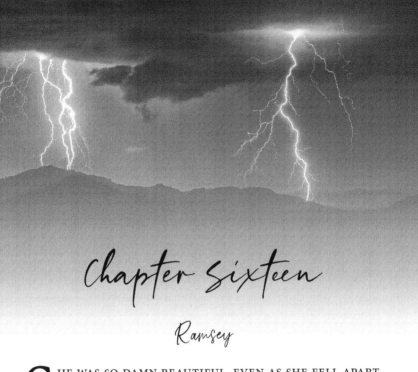

Chapter Sixteen

Ramsey

SHE WAS SO DAMN BEAUTIFUL, EVEN AS SHE FELL APART.
Maybe it was the loss of composure that made her even more
gorgeous, those fiercely guarded walls beginning to crumble.
I'd seen them falter before, but I'd never seen them fall. In all
the years she'd been coming to my ranch, I'd never seen a tear escape those captivating blue eyes. Not once. I'd seen her struggle
for composure. Saw her heart breaking. But tears had never come.

The fact that they came now broke something in me. I moved
on instinct, wrapping my arms around Shiloh. She froze, going
rock-solid. The rigidity beneath my hands was so stark I almost
released her, but then her hands fisted in my shirt.

She gripped the flannel so hard the material pulled taut against
my back. She burrowed into me as if I were the only thing standing
between her and whatever currently wreaked havoc on her system.

My gaze lifted to the sight below, whatever Shiloh had been so
intently watching that she hadn't heard my approach. My spine
went ramrod straight as I took in the mourners. I knew instantly
who they were honoring.

A man who didn't deserve their tears and memories. My back teeth ground together. I knew it wasn't that simple, but I couldn't help the simmering rage. Howard Kemper had done irrevocable damage to Shiloh, and that wasn't something I could forgive.

"Why?" It was the only thing I could think to ask. When I saw her start off alone with Kai, I'd never expected this to be her destination.

Shiloh shuddered against me but pulled back, lifting her gaze to mine. She didn't ask for clarification of my question. Like so many other things that passed between us, she instantly understood. "I needed to see him go into the ground. To know that this is over."

An ache started in my jaw, my molars protesting the tight clench. "Why didn't you tell me? You know I would've gone with you."

Shiloh stepped back out of my hold. She didn't move to wipe the tears from her face, though. She let the evidence of their presence stay just where it was. No apologies, even though I knew she hated to show what some might consider weakness.

She stared at me in a way that had me fighting to squirm. "I didn't think you'd want to go anywhere with me."

The muscles between my shoulder blades tightened. "Why in the world would you think that?"

"You put up a pretty clear boundary last night. And I respect that. I appreciate you giving me a place to stay, looking out for me—"

"Shiloh." Shit. I'd made a mess of things. But what was new? "This isn't about me not wanting to spend time with you."

She arched a brow in question, the movement a graceful way of calling bullshit.

I squeezed the back of my neck. I wouldn't let her hurt because of my screwup. "I want to spend time with you. Too much."

Those ice-blue eyes flared, pleasure followed quickly by uncertainty swirling in their depths.

Hell. I didn't need to see that hint of desire in her—it was the last thing I needed. "I'm not built for relationships. I can't—I wouldn't be the kind of partner anyone needed."

"So, you shut me out?"

There wasn't anger in her tone, more like confusion as if she were trying to understand the *why* behind my actions.

"Didn't want to do something I'd regret. Something that might hurt you in the long run."

Shiloh nodded slowly. "I'm not built for it either. Don't know the first thing about it." She reached down and scratched behind Kai's ears, her cheeks pinking. "I usually can't even handle anyone touching me. I wouldn't be good at…."

Her voice trailed off, but I caught her meaning. She'd mentioned before how touch hurt. I needed to know more. To understand where that came from. "What happens when someone touches you?"

Shiloh's gaze drifted to the funeral below. "It's like it grates against my skin. I feel like I can't breathe. Trapped."

"Like you're still in that shed."

She nodded, her hands clenching at her sides and then picking up a tapping rhythm against her thighs. "He beat me. Told me it was to get the evil out. He wrapped his hands around my throat and squeezed to the point where I thought it was the end. He told me Ian would be my husband and that he would make sure I was a good wife for his son."

Rage lit and blasted through me, burning my insides in its wake. She'd been too young to truly understand what that threat could mean, but some part of her had intuited it. No wonder she balked at touch of any kind. She'd been brutalized and threatened with worse.

I struggled to breathe properly, to get words out. Sadly, when they came, they weren't useful ones. "None of that came out in court. I read the articles—"

Shiloh's head snapped up, her eyes glassy. "I didn't tell anyone. They thought the bruises came from him getting me away from the fair. From the actual kidnapping. But it was after."

I went stock-still. "Why didn't you tell your parents? Someone?"

The tears came again, cascading down her cheeks and falling off her jaw. "I didn't want anyone to know. I was so ashamed. I felt like it was my fault. That I'd done something…"

I wanted to pull her into my arms again so badly, but I wasn't sure if it would cause her pain or trigger her. "This could never be your fault. Not in a million years."

"I know that now. But there were so many years of lies and un-truths. I dug myself a hole and couldn't get out. It only got worse with the letters."

I moved closer, weaving our fingers together and stroking my thumb across the back of her hand. "I'm so damn sorry you've been alone in this. But you're not alone anymore. I'll listen any time you want to unload. And you sure as hell don't have to go to the asshole's funeral by yourself."

A small laugh escaped her, and the vise around my chest released a fraction. She twisted the flannel of my shirt between her fingers. "Sometimes, I feel like I'm the kind of broken that won't ever get put back together right."

Each of Shiloh's words hit me like a physical blow. Because I knew that feeling. "Like your insides got rearranged in a way that would never have you on the right side of normal ever again."

Her gaze lifted to mine. We were close. Too close. That hint of floral…something swirled through me. So close, I could count the freckles dusted across her nose like stars scattered in the sky.

"Sometimes, I know that *normal* isn't anything to strive for. But other times? I want it more than my next breath. I feel like I missed out on so much."

"Then you start fighting to get those pieces back. If there's something you want to do, we'll find a way."

Shiloh's mouth curved, and her perfect, berry pink lips angled with humor. "You've been doing that without even knowing it."

"What do you mean?"

"I wanted to learn about working with horses who had been hurt. You've been teaching me for years. I wanted to move off my family's ranch but was scared to reach for it. You showed me a way."

They were such simple things. Nothing crazy or extreme. But it gave me a deep sense of pride to know that I'd helped in some way.

"It looks like we need to find some new adventures for you to go on."

Shiloh laughed, the sound catching on the air and carrying to my ears, filling them with the sweetest sound. She shook her head. "Let's take it one thing at a time. I'm still learning about the way you work with horses and settling in to living somewhere new."

"Fair enough." But I wanted to give Shiloh more. I wanted to give her *everything*.

Kai let out a whine, and Shiloh turned her attention to him. She rubbed his face and behind his ears. "Feeling neglected?"

"He doesn't like when your attention is elsewhere." The little traitor.

He looked up at me with what I swore was a smile. I just shook my head.

Movement caught my attention. I stepped forward, closer to the ridge line. "It's time."

Shiloh moved to my side as the coffin was lowered into the earth in the cemetery below.

I turned my focus from the sight below to her. Her eyes were locked on that shiny piece of wood as it disappeared into the hole, a ceremonial shovelful of dirt thrown on top of it.

"He's gone."

I heard the desperation in her voice. She so badly wanted this to be the end. I wanted that for her, too. But someone wasn't done torturing her. And all I wanted to do was rip that person limb from limb.

Shiloh froze, her body going rigid.

I wrapped an arm around her instantly. "What is it?"

She lifted a hand, pointing at a man below. "Ian. Howard's son. He's back."

Chapter Seventeen

Shiloh

I LEANED AGAINST THE RAILS OF THE ROUND PEN AS RAMSEY waited Onyx out. She was in a mood today and had made her opinion about Ramsey in her space crystal clear. As if to punctuate my point, she kicked out at him.

I sucked in a sharp breath as her hoof narrowly missed Ramsey's hip. I would've been cursing up a storm, but the only reaction he showed was to flick his training flag in her direction, drawing a boundary on his space.

Onyx let out a huff of air and gave a healthy buck. Ramsey simply held his ground.

"I don't know how he stays so calm," Aidan said softly.

I looked over at the teen. His gaze was riveted on Ramsey, a true case of hero worship in his eyes. While Elliott had given up watching the training, opting to lay in the grass with Kai, Aidan hadn't moved from this spot for an hour.

"He's got more patience than anyone I've ever seen."

Aidan swallowed, his focus not moving from Ramsey and Onyx. "That's a gift. Most people aren't capable of that kind of thing."

He was right, but I hated that he knew that at such a young age. Hated that his father was likely the one who had taught him that lesson. That he'd seen the man hurt these animals.

"You are. You're learning it here every day."

Aidan looked over at me. "You think?"

"I've seen the way you are with the horses here. Gentle but firm. And the longer you work with Ramsey, the more you're finding that balance."

Aidan's cheeks blushed under my praise. "I hope so. If I didn't have school, I could work more hours here. I talked to one of my teachers about maybe getting my GED instead."

I bit the side of my mouth, trying to hold back my strong reaction. "You've got time to work more hours here. You've only got a little over a year left of school."

He deflated, his gaze traveling back to the ring. "A lot can happen in a year."

I searched for the right words. I wasn't good at saying the right thing, but I wanted to with Aidan—he deserved that and more. When nothing came, I decided something was better than nothing: brutal honesty.

"I'm not good at finding the right words."

Aidan's gaze flicked to me.

"But you should know. It seems like where you are now will last forever, but it won't. Even the worst pain isn't forever. It passes. Changes. It might come back now and then, but it never lasts forever. All we can do is make the best of where we're at—finishing school, giving yourself as many options as possible. That seems like making the best of things. At least, to me."

A hint of a smile played on his lips. "Seems like you're pretty good at words to me."

I chuckled and knocked my shoulder against Aidan's. There was no flicker of panic or grating sensation on my skin. There was only the need to let Aidan know that I was here for him if he needed me.

We turned back to the round pen, focusing on Ramsey and

Onyx. He'd closed some of the distance with her. She was tense but allowed it.

"Shiloh," Ramsey said, his voice low, "why don't you come into the ring?"

Excitement hummed under my skin—the first real sense of pleasure since the funeral yesterday. The shock of seeing Ian was free. The rollercoaster of wondering if he was out for good or just on a pass for the funeral.

I ducked between the fence rails. Onyx's nostrils flared. We'd developed a bit of a rapport, but she didn't like two people in her space.

"Walk over to me, nice and easy."

I did as he instructed.

"You're going to take point on this."

My head snapped in his direction. "I don't know if that's a good idea…"

Ramsey's mouth curved. "It's a great idea."

"I don't want to hurt her."

The words were out before I could stop them. It was my greatest fear in all this: that I would do something to cause more pain.

Ramsey's hand lifted to the small of my back. Heat flared at the contact. "Trust yourself. You've built a bond with her already. We're going to strengthen that."

He pressed the training flag into my hand. "This is to mark your space and show her where you want her to go."

He stepped back a few paces. "I'm right here with you. I'm just giving you two some room."

Onyx's ears twitched as she watched Ramsey's retreat.

"What do you feel?" he asked me.

"I'm not sure."

"Bull. You know. Sense it. Sense her."

I watched the mare carefully. Her muscles twitched every so often, a byproduct of the tension running through them.

"She's on edge."

"Good. Now, what can we do to ease that?"

"Wait until she's ready."

"That's a good start. It'll also help to have you as calm as possible."

Calm was easier said than done. I inhaled deeply, filling my nose with the scents of horses and the pine trees surrounding us. As I exhaled, I tried to let it all go. The fear and anxiety of the last couple of weeks. The weight of disappointing my family. I released it all.

I closed my eyes for moment, picturing all those things being carried away on the breeze. I felt it then, a tiny shift in the air.

Opening my eyes, I met deep onyx ones that melded into her coat. She had moved one step closer, her muscles slightly more relaxed.

"Meet her where she is. This is a dance. She comes to you, then you go to her."

I kept the training flag relaxed at my side and took a step.

A frisson of energy flashed through Onyx, and I halted. I focused on keeping everything about me relaxed. I imagined nothing but air filling my body. Light. Free.

I imagined Onyx feeling the same way. I wanted that for her so badly. For her to be able to release the pain of her past and step into this new world at her feet.

My eyes stung with the intensity of the emotion. We were similar in so many ways.

"I know it's terrifying. You've had to defend yourself with everything you had. But you can let that go now."

Onyx took another step.

I matched her, keeping my voice low. "I've got you. I won't let anything happen to you."

Closer.

I kept talking. It turned to nonsensical reassurances. Promises of safety. Sweet nothings—until we were face-to-face.

I slowly lifted my hand to that spot under her chin. "Hey, girl."

She pressed her muzzle into my chest, searching for more.

I rubbed her cheek, her neck. I didn't know how long we stayed like that with Onyx's head resting on my shoulder as I stroked her.

"Nice and easy, now, back away," Ramsey instructed. "Come get the feed bucket and give Onyx her dinner."

I didn't want to leave her, but I also knew she needed routine. Had to trust that I would come and go but always return. And that she would be safe through it all.

Carefully, I pulled back. I moved to Ramsey and took the bucket of grain. When I approached Onyx with it, a hint of wariness returned to her eyes, but she didn't move. I set it at her feet.

As soon as I moved away, she sniffed at the bucket. Seconds later, she started eating.

Ramsey slid through the round pen's rails, a little of his dark hair falling free of the knot it had been tied in as he moved. My fingers twitched at my side, wanting to know what those strands felt like. I shoved that feeling down, Ramsey's words about not being built for relationships echoing in my head.

He grinned as he strode towards me. "Hell of an afternoon with our girl."

I couldn't help the answering smile from forming on my lips. "I've never felt anything like that. What she gave me…"

"Her trust," he finished for me.

I nodded, swallowing hard. "It was the most beautiful gift I've ever been given."

He moved in closer, the heat from his body seeping into mine. "It becomes an addiction, that feeling. Those gifts."

I wanted to lean into him. To lose myself in his warmth and comfort. To know what it was like to disappear entirely into everything that was Ramsey. "I can see how."

"That was amazing." Aidan practically bounced as he walked up to us. "She totally let you in. I can't believe she could still do that with you after everything she's been through."

"She's showing us that it's possible to heal from anything," I said softly.

Something flashed in Aidan's eyes, and he looked down at his watch. "Crap! I have to go. I'm late for chores at home." He yelled for Elliott and started towards his beat-up truck.

"I've got leftovers for you," I called.

"Thanks! I'll get 'em tomorrow." He was already opening the back door for Elliott, who waved, grinning at us. Seconds later, he was behind the wheel and headed towards the gate.

I bit my bottom lip. "I'm worried about them."

"You have a right to be."

"Do you think there's anything else we can do?"

"I'm not sure what that would be just now."

I looked over at Ramsey and saw his gaze locked on where the truck had disappeared. "Maybe we should call Child Protective Services and tell them our concerns."

A muscle in his jaw ticked. "We don't have any proof. If we don't know for sure they'd be removed from the home, we'd only be making things worse for them."

I stared down the drive as Aidan's truck disappeared. "Is their mom in the picture at all?"

Ramsey shook his head. "Aidan told me the other day that she passed away when Elliott was a baby."

My stomach churned. "I hate this."

Ramsey moved in closer, that heat seeping into me again. "I know."

Only two words, but with them, I knew I wasn't in this worry alone. Our eyes locked and held.

A faint buzz sounded, and Ramsey jerked his gaze away from me, pulling his phone from his pocket. He swiped his thumb across the screen and tapped an icon. His jaw went hard as granite.

He tapped another button and held it to his ear. "Yeah."

Ramsey listened and then glanced at me. "Your brother's here. He wants to talk to you."

Chapter Eighteen

Shiloh

CRAP. CRAP. DOUBLE CRAP.

"Which one?"

Like that made a difference. I had made Ramsey a promise that I wouldn't bring other people onto his property. He seemed at ease with me, fairly relaxed with the boys, and Lor was no big deal. But I'd seen reticence or agitation flare when anyone else buzzed the gate.

"Hayes," he bit out.

"I can go to the gate and talk to him—"

Ramsey cut me off with a shake of his head. "No. But if you don't want to talk to him, I can send him away."

That would only make things worse. I'd been ignoring Hayes' calls and texts. It was likely why he'd shown up like this. I hadn't wanted to be subjected to a lecture or his ignorant comments about Ramsey, but it was time to deal with him.

"I should talk to him."

Ramsey put the phone to his ear. "Follow the road to the guest cabin." He hung up without waiting for a response and then motioned me towards the house that we were both staying in.

My cheeks heated at the reminder. If Hayes knew that Ramsey was staying in there with me, he'd lose it.

"You don't have to wait with me. I'll be fine."

Ramsey didn't say a word; he simply whistled for Kai, who came running. As much as the dog loved me, he'd become even more partial to Elliott. He sulked every day after the little boy left.

I bent down, pressing my head to Kai's and scratching behind his ears. I soaked in his warmth and reassurance. "If anyone gets out of line, you can bite 'em."

Ramsey snorted with derision.

My stomach churned as Hayes' sheriff's department SUV came into view. He pulled to a stop in front of the cabin and climbed out of the vehicle. His gaze narrowed on the dog.

I patted Kai's head and rolled my eyes at my brother. "Don't be dramatic."

"It's part wolf. I don't think it's dramatic to be wary."

"You live at an animal sanctuary. I would think you would have a little more understanding and trust of animal behavior."

"*Domesticated* and farm animals."

I let out a sigh. "Don't make me call Everly on you."

His lips twitched. "Fine. How are you?"

"Good."

Hayes' gaze swung to Ramsey. "Can I have a minute alone with my sister?"

Ramsey met his stare dead-on. "Depends on what she wants."

I let loose a million mental curses.

"Hayes, this is my friend, Ramsey."

If I hadn't studied Ramsey for years, I would've missed the slight flinch at the word *friend*. I tried not to let that sting. Ramsey might not want *more* with me, but I at least considered us friends. He'd promised to be there for me whenever I needed him. What was that, if not friendship?

My stomach churned at the thought that he might see me as

an obligation more than anything else—one that he had an unfortunate attraction to.

Hayes nodded at Ramsey. "Bishop."

A muscle in Ramsey's cheek ticked, but he said nothing.

Hayes turned back to me. "This is where you're staying?"

I nodded. "I have a lot more space than at the loft."

"You know Beckett and Addie won't be using my place in town much longer. You can move in there and have even more space."

I felt the shift in Ramsey's energy before I saw it, a crackling in the air as tension radiated through him. "You don't get to force Shiloh into moving."

Hayes' head snapped in Ramsey's direction. "I'm not forcing her into anything. I'm giving her options. A place where she's not living on someone else's property."

"You mean she'll be on *your* property. Somewhere *you'll* have more control over her."

"What the hell are you talking about?"

"Enough!" I barked. "I'm not going anywhere, so both of you can stop acting like I'm a tree stump to pee on."

They both scowled at me. Great.

"Hayes, I'm fine. More than fine. I'm happy here. The work I'm doing with Ramsey means something to me. It's fulfilling in a way I never felt at the ranch. I'm helping horses that need it the most. I'm making a difference. And I'm spreading my wings in the process. This is good for me."

Hayes' jaw fell open, and he stared at me in total silence.

I tried to remember the last time I'd uttered that many words to my brother. Years ago, most likely. And never with that much passion. And maybe that was the problem. In holding all my secrets close, I'd held myself back from my family, too. I hadn't let them see what I wanted or who I truly was.

Hayes cleared his throat. "I'm glad you're happy and that it's working here." He eyed Ramsey carefully. "I've heard about the work you do. Know it's good."

It was an olive branch. Ramsey could take it or crush it beneath his boots.

"I try," Ramsey gritted out.

It wasn't exactly an offer of friendship, but it *was* better than a punch in the face.

I turned to Hayes. "I'll see you at family dinner this weekend. We can talk more then."

Something flashed in Hayes' eyes—something that looked a lot like hope. It shoved a blade of guilt right into my stomach. I'd shut them out for so long. I'd hurt them. It seemed all I was capable of doing.

He nodded. "That will be good. Call me if you need anything. I'm glad..." He struggled to find the words he wanted. "I'm glad you've found a place here."

"I am, too." I toyed with the zipper on my fleece. "Thanks for checking on me."

"Always."

Hayes' words burned my skin as he walked back to his truck and climbed behind the wheel. I didn't look away even after he'd disappeared between the trees. *I'm glad you've found a place here.*

"You okay?"

Ramsey's rough voice broke the spell, and I turned in his direction. "Yeah. But you're not."

It wasn't a question. The tension radiating off Ramsey was enough to power all the electrical outlets in the house behind us.

"I'm fine."

"Don't do that. Don't lie to my face."

Ramsey's nostrils flared. "What do you want me to say? That I hate cops? That I don't trust your brother as far as I can throw him? That's not going to make anything better."

Blood pounded in my ears. "Why?"

Ramsey struggled to get his breathing under control. "It's not rational. I know it. There are men and women in law enforcement who do good work. Your brother is probably one of them. But it doesn't change what I see."

My fingers tingled, and I realized that I wasn't breathing—not the way I needed to. "What do you see?"

"I see the guys who looked the other way because my stepfather donated to the local police department. I see the people who believed every lie he spun and didn't listen to a word that came out of my mouth—not even when I cried and begged and told them that he beat my mother on a regular basis. That he beat *me*."

His breath kept coming quicker as he struggled to keep his voice even. "Instead, they took his lies and ran with them. Said that I pushed my mother down the stairs because I was upset that she told me I couldn't go out with my friends. They locked me up and threw away the key, knowing the place they were sending me was Hell on Earth. All they cared about was the money lining their pockets. And all it took was those two officers promising to look the other way to take that lie and weave it into truth."

Each word tore at my chest. I'd known that Ramsey had been sent to prison for assault and that the conviction had been overturned. Most of the town did. But he hadn't grown up here, and I hadn't known the details. I'd never looked into the man who had captivated me for the last nine years. Hadn't wanted to probe into his past the way others had picked mine apart.

What I'd been through was nothing compared to this. *This* was betrayal on every level. The police officers who had sworn to protect and, instead, did the opposite. A stepfather who should've loved him but chose violence and lies instead. There was one last piece I honestly couldn't fathom, though. "What about your mom?"

Ramsey's onyx eyes blazed brightly with a dark, glittering heat. "She tried to take the brunt of the abuse. When he pushed her down the stairs, she got a concussion so bad she lost her memories from the two days leading up to her fall. She couldn't tell the police anything."

"She should've told them that he hit her. That he hit *you*."

I'd never felt the kind of anger that lit through me at that moment. It burned me from the inside out. Anger for this man who brought broken creatures back to life. Because he knew what it was like to be broken. To have no one. And instead of becoming a monster, he became a savior.

Ramsey's jaw worked back and forth. "She should've said something, but she didn't. And she paid for it with her life."

I froze, everything in me going stock-still, but no words would come.

He looked out at the fields where so many of the horses he'd rescued grazed happily. "He killed her. When they did the autopsy, there was no hiding that it hadn't been the first beating. He finally fessed up to it all. I think he was proud of what he'd done, putting me in jail for his crimes. He tried to walk it back later, but the confession stood up at trial. His sick need to let the world know took him out in the end."

My heart cracked. Splintered into pieces for the man with the gentlest soul I'd ever known.

I moved on instinct, closing the distance between us at a fast clip. I hurled myself at Ramsey, wrapping my arms around him in a vise-like grip—so tight no one would ever be able to pry me loose.

"You're a miracle."

A shudder ran through him.

"A miracle in every way. You took a pain that could've made you bitter and built it into something beautiful. You let that pain connect you with creatures who didn't have anyone. And you made their lives better. You healed them. They wouldn't trust you if they didn't feel a kinship with you."

"Shiloh—"

"It's true. And you're a miracle for me, too. You gave me a place to come when I needed escape. You made me feel safe when I rarely feel that way. You taught me so many things before you ever uttered a word."

"Shiloh—"

"And you're doing the same for Aidan and Elliott. You're giving them an escape. A haven. It's one of the greatest gifts they'll ever receive."

Ramsey's hand slid under my braid and tipped my head back so I met his gaze. There was so much emotion in those eyes, deep pools of feeling you could get lost in forever. "Stop."

"No. You need to hear the truth." He needed to know the depths of his goodness. How much he gave back to a world that had taken so much from him.

He shook his head, but the barest flicker of amusement played on his lips. "You're damn stubborn, you know that?"

"I'm taking that as a compliment."

Ramsey chuckled then, and it warmed the inside of my chest. His thumb swept down the column of my throat, and a wave of sensation cascaded over my skin, unlike anything I'd ever felt.

"I'm sorry I was an ass to your brother."

I swallowed, not breaking our stare. "He's a good man. A good sheriff. He cares about the people in this county. He may not always get it right, but he never stops trying and always admits when he's wrong. What you dealt with? Those were the lowest of the low. Hayes would fry their asses and not think twice."

Ramsey nodded, but there was still so much pain there. Hesitation. He'd been hurt by those cops and at such a formative time of his life. It would take time for him to trust again.

My fingers twisted in his flannel. "You'll see. With time. Just give him a chance."

"I'll try. For you, I'll try."

Chapter Nineteen

Ramsey

SHILOH MOVED WITH A GRACE THAT WAS HYPNOTIZING. Fluid movements that had me leaning forward as she guided the brush over Onyx's neck. I didn't want to miss a moment. I shouldn't have been surprised that she'd made this kind of progress in less than twenty-four hours. She said *I* worked miracles, but the truth was, she was the walking miracle—in every way.

As Shiloh pulled the brush away, she bent to kiss Onyx's nose. She whispered something I couldn't make out, and the mare's ears twitched. The smile that stretched across Shiloh's face as she walked towards the fence was a sucker punch to the solar plexus.

I rubbed a spot on my sternum, trying to alleviate the sensation. It was too much. Everything I experienced around Shiloh was. It was as if I'd been living in perpetual winter, wholly numb and feeling again for the first time. But reemerging from that numbness hurt the way fingers regaining sensation after extreme cold did.

Shiloh slid between the rails on the fence and beamed up at me. "I got her whole neck, back, and face. I wanted to do her belly, too, but I thought that might be pushing it."

"Smart. You don't want to backtrack by going too far, too fast."

She glanced over her shoulder at the mare. "She's incredible. It's like you said. The feeling of that trust…it's addicting."

The best kind of addiction you could find.

"You're doing great with her. Don't even need my help."

Shiloh laughed, the sound catching on the air and swirling around us. "I have a feeling I'm going to need plenty of help when we get to saddling and bridling."

"You caught on pretty well when I was working with Pep this morning."

The gelding was making amazing progress, too. I had a feeling with a few months of work, he could find a home on a cattle ranch somewhere and be as happy as could be, chasing after the steers.

Shiloh shook her head. "Watching is a lot different from doing."

"You've incorporated more than you think by watching over the years. I see it in everything you've done with Onyx. And part of that is just *you*."

She had the same empathy she said I had. The knowledge of what it felt like to be hurt by someone else's hand. It gave her a gift and a way with these creatures. To make good from the bad.

A smile curved her beautiful mouth. "I hope so."

My hands itched at my sides. The urge to pull her to me was so strong. I remembered how she'd thrown herself at me yesterday and the way she'd held on with feral ferocity. I wanted more of that. More of *her*. Needed to feel her body pressed against mine. To inhale her scent. Every little piece of her…I wanted it. Craved it in a way I'd never craved anything.

I was playing with fire, but I couldn't walk away. Not when I'd seen how I'd hurt Shiloh by putting up my walls before. She hid her tender heart from most of the world, but she couldn't hide it from me. She might've mastered the blank-masked, cool exterior where nothing seemed to make her react, but I saw the flickers of pain beneath it, and how she held the weight of the world on her shoulders.

"How was your phone call with Hayes?" My throat tightened

around his name, but I did my best to keep my expression neutral. I knew he cared about his sister, that much was as clear as day. I just couldn't make it all the way to trusting the sheriff.

Shiloh worried that spot on the inside of her cheek. "He called to tell me about Ian. Said he got distracted when he was here yesterday but wanted me to have a heads-up in case I saw Ian in town."

"So, he's out for good?" My throat constricted, making it hard to get the words out. I hated anything that brought those memories back for Shiloh, and I'd seen the way Ian terrified her.

She swallowed hard, nodding. "I guess there was an overcrowding issue, and he was a model prisoner."

I flexed my hands to keep them from clenching at my sides. "You tell Hayes about the letter?" As far as I was concerned, Ian must have sent it. Who else would've had access to Howard Kemper's belongings after he passed? Who would want to scare her that badly?

She flushed, looking out at the field. "If another one comes, I'll tell him. I just…everything comes crashing down if I do."

"Maybe it needs to come crashing down. You can build something better in its place."

Shiloh let her gaze drift back to me. "I've kept so many things hidden. It's going to hurt them more, and I've already caused them so much pain."

I moved in closer, the urge to touch and comfort so strong. I fisted my hands at my sides, forcing them to stay put. "*You* aren't the one who caused them pain. Howard Kemper did. You dealt with things afterwards the best you could."

She swallowed hard, her throat working with the motion as if it required all her effort. "I feel like I handled everything badly. Every choice I made was the wrong one. It's a lot to undo."

"You did the best you could, given where you were at and what you could handle. You need to give yourself a little grace. But you can think about what the next right step is *now*. Focus on that, not whatever comes after it."

Shiloh's fingers tapped out a beat against her thighs. "You've got a lot of Zen wisdom. You know that?"

I chuckled. "It's all the time I spend with the horses."

She grinned.

My phone buzzed in my pocket, and I pulled it out. I tapped on my camera app. At the sight of Aidan's truck, I hit the button to open the gate. "Aidan and Elliott are here."

"Oh! The cookies." She took off running for the guest cabin.

I couldn't help the smile that played on my lips as I followed behind her. She'd gone overboard last night, baking at least three dozen. If we ate all of them, we'd be sick for sure.

I lifted my hand in a wave as Aidan drove by to park near the barn. By the time I reached the guest cabin, Shiloh had reemerged with sandwiches, drinks, and cookies on a tray and a bag of chips under her arm.

My gaze caught on Elliott as the boys walked towards us. His head was downcast, and he barely reacted as Kai ran up to him with a happy bark. A pit formed in my stomach as Aidan wrapped an arm around his brother's shoulders.

"Hey," Aidan greeted, adjusting the bill of his ballcap.

I flashed a grin in hello.

"I've got a world of goodies today. Even made M&M cookies," Shiloh said.

Not even a flicker from Elliott at that.

That pit in my stomach became a boulder.

"That's really kind of you," Aidan said.

As he stepped forward, I caught sight of his face. His eye was swollen and ringed in purple. I froze, everything in me going wired. "What happened?"

Aidan swallowed hard. "I was stupid. The gate was stuck. I yanked too hard and got clocked in the face."

I struggled to keep my voice even, *calm* in the face of the fury coursing through me. "Aidan. Truth. What happened?"

Elliott sniffled. Shiloh was by his side in a flash, dropping to her knees and wrapping her arm around the little boy. There was no glimmer of apprehension at the touch, only the desire to comfort.

Elliott burrowed into her. "I'm sorry! It's my fault. I dropped my milk. Dad was so mad, and Aidan got in his way. I'm sorry."

Shiloh held him to her chest, rocking back and forth. "It's not your fault. None of this is your fault."

"She's right, E. I'm fine. No big thing," Aidan said.

I'd wanted to kill my stepfather so many times. But I'd never felt the call to violence more than in this moment. "He's not going to hurt you again."

Aidan's head snapped in my direction. "There's nothing you can do. One more year, and I'm free. I can file for custody of Elliott. I just need a job and an apartment."

His words shredded my chest, everything becoming clear. I knew now why he'd been so desperate for a job and why he'd told Shiloh that he wanted to get his GED.

Shiloh kept rocking Elliott. "We're going to get you some help now. My brother's the sheriff—"

"No!" Aidan shouted. "They could break up Elliott and me."

"Trust me," she begged, "we won't let that happen. But we can't let you keep getting hurt. I'd never be able to live with myself."

Panic ran wild through Elliott's eyes as he gripped Shiloh harder. "Promise they won't split us up."

"You have my word," Shiloh said. "I'll make sure of it."

It was a risky promise. Child Protective Services didn't always control where openings were available in foster homes. But being in a smaller community, there might be more flexibility.

Elliott sniffed. "Please, A. I don't want to live with him anymore."

Grief swirled in Aidan's eyes, but he nodded slowly. "I'll talk to your brother."

"Thank you." Shiloh lifted her gaze to me. "Can I call him now?"

I moved my head in a jerky nod and hoped it wasn't the biggest mistake I'd ever made.

Chapter Twenty

Shiloh

HAYES PULLED TO A STOP IN FRONT OF THE GUEST CABIN and climbed out of his SUV. Ramsey went rigid. I felt the tension coming off him in waves as he stepped closer to Aidan. Everything about his stance said: *protective*. He wouldn't let anything else happen to Aidan.

The movement made my chest constrict. Even though rough around the edges, goodness oozed from him. I wanted to wrap my arms around him, too. To build a barrier between the world and these boys. Between the world and Ramsey. They'd all been hurt too much.

Elliott pressed deeper against my side, burrowing his face into my stomach. Kai sat protectively in front of us. I rubbed a hand up and down Elliott's arm. "Guys, this is my brother, Hayes. He's going to help."

They both stayed quiet, but Aidan eyed Hayes carefully. He was clearly looking for some sign of whether or not to trust him, and I hoped Hayes would give it to him.

Hayes kept his expression relaxed, but I saw his attention catch on Aidan's black eye. "Hey, Aidan. Elliott. I hear you're friends with my little sister."

Aidan nodded, but Elliott stayed right where he was.

"Did she tell you about the time she locked me in a closet during hide-and-seek?"

I couldn't help the laugh that startled out of me. "Hayes…"

He arched a brow in my direction. "Am I lying?"

My cheeks heated. "It was an accident."

Hayes scoffed. "You were mad that I ate the last chocolate donut that morning."

"I might've been holding a bit of a grudge."

Elliott straightened, looking up at me. "You locked him in a closet? He's so much bigger than you."

I grinned down at him. "Just because we're smaller doesn't mean we can't be trickier."

His lips curved a fraction. "How?"

Hayes chuckled. "She was the seeker, but I'm guessing she peeked when she was supposed to be counting. She knew I was in the closet under the stairs."

"It had an old-fashioned key that always stayed in the lock. It needed to be in there to open it. I pocketed that key and told the rest of our siblings I had no idea where Hayes was," I said.

Elliott's mouth dropped open.

Hayes shook his head. "I was stuck in there until Mom came in to cook dinner and heard me yelling my head off."

"What'd you do to get back at her?" Elliott asked in a hushed whisper.

"I covered her toilet in plastic wrap."

Elliott burst out laughing. Even Aidan let out a small chuckle.

I glared at my brother. "That was not nice."

"You cried, and Mom and Dad grounded me for a week. I'd say you got payback twice."

"Maybe I need to have Mom ground you again."

Hayes grinned. "Sorry, Shy. I'm free of your reign of terror now."

"Yeah, yeah," I muttered.

Hayes shoved his hands into his pockets, looking at the two boys. "I know I'm probably the last person you want to talk to, but I can promise you this… If you're honest with me, I'll do everything I can to keep you both safe. That's all I want. I'm on your team and no one else's."

Aidan toed a piece of gravel with his boot. "Shiloh said you'd keep Elliott and me together."

My brother sent me a sidelong glance.

"We're not letting them get separated," I told him.

He nodded. "I called a social worker friend of mine. She'll be out here soon. But I already asked her only to pull foster placements that could accommodate two children. You have my word."

Aidan looked up at Ramsey, an unspoken question in his eyes. Ramsey squeezed his shoulder. "I know it's scary. But you can tell Hayes."

Aidan's eyes reddened, unshed tears filling them. "I didn't want anyone to know."

Ramsey moved in closer. "I didn't either when it was happening to me. It's one of the things I regret most. If I'd told someone sooner that my stepdad was hurting my mom and me, maybe things would've turned out differently. But you're so much braver than I was."

Aidan swallowed. "It happened to you, too?"

"So many times, I lost count. It says nothing about you and everything about *him*. The moment you tell someone, your dad loses some of that power. Especially when you tell someone who can stop him. That's Hayes."

Pressure built behind my eyes, tears yearning to get free. I knew that Hayes was likely the last person Ramsey wanted to say that in front of or be vulnerable with. But he was doing it for Aidan—to help him.

Aidan lifted his gaze to Hayes. "My dad. He hits me when he gets mad."

The next hour passed in a blur of sickening stories about

physical and emotional abuse. Of withholding food and proper clothing. By the time Aidan had finished talking, I was ready to hunt Kenny Chambers down and kill him myself—but not before a round of torture.

The social worker was a kind woman in her twenties, warm and reassuring. She opened the back door to her SUV for the boys to hop in. Elliott made a beeline for Ramsey, throwing his arms around his legs. "Will you come see us? Make sure we're okay?"

My heart cracked. In the couple of weeks that they'd been coming here, Ramsey had come to mean safety to these boys.

Ramsey ruffled Elliott's hair. "How about I bring burgers for lunch tomorrow?"

The social worker smiled. "I think that would be perfect. I'll let the Millers know you'll be by."

"Just text me when I can be there."

She nodded, motioning the boys to the SUV. Elliott jogged over and climbed in, but Aidan hovered by the door. He looked at Ramsey. "Thank you. For everything."

"You have my number. Call me if you need anything."

Aidan nodded and climbed into the vehicle with his brother. Ramsey, Hayes, and I watched as the SUV drove away. The lump in my throat made it hard to swallow.

Hayes turned in my direction. "You okay?"

"I'm just worried about them."

A muscle in Hayes' jaw ticked. "I've got officers picking up Kenny Chambers now. He's not going to get away with this. Those kids will never be back in his custody."

I nodded. It wasn't enough, but it was a start. All I could think about was what they'd endured, and for years. Ramsey seemed to sense my turmoil because he moved in closer. His thumb reached out and swiped back and forth across my hand. Just that barest touch sent a flood of warmth through me that I couldn't explain.

"They're strong. They're going to bounce back from this," he assured me. "It'll take time, but we'll be there for them along the way."

Hayes locked on Ramsey's and my hands and the point of contact, and then he forced his gaze up to Ramsey. "Thank you for what you've done for Aidan and Elliott. They're lucky to have you."

He reached out a hand to Ramsey for a shake. Ramsey hesitated for the briefest moment and then took it. "Thank you for getting them the help they need."

Hayes nodded. "I need to head back to the station and call the district attorney. I want this thing to move as quickly as possible. I'll have an officer come and pick up Aidan's truck and drop it off at the Millers."

"Thanks, Hayes." My stomach churned, but I forced myself to step forward. My move was quick. I stretched up on my tiptoes and pressed a kiss to his cheek. There was a slightly unsettling feeling at the contact, but mostly, there was relief that I could show my brother that I loved him with a simple touch. "It means a lot that I can always count on you."

He swallowed, his throat working. "I'd do anything for you, Shy. You just have to call."

"I know. That's why I did."

He nodded, ducking his head as he moved to his SUV. A few seconds later, he was heading for the front gate.

So many emotions whirled within me. The familiar guilt was there, but so much more, too. Most importantly, there was hope.

Fingers linked with mine, and I turned to Ramsey. I didn't stop until I'd wrapped my arms around him. I couldn't voice what I wanted to say out loud. Ramsey had made it clear that he didn't want that from me. So, I said it silently, telling the air between us how much I cared for this man.

I burrowed into his chest. "I'm so sorry."

"It's not for you to be sorry about."

"I can still hate that you're hurting. That those boys are hurting. I know this had to bring up a lot of hard memories."

Ramsey rested his chin on the top of my head as his arms came around me. "I could kill him."

"You and me both."

"No. I'm capable of it. I know I am."

"I'm gonna say it again. You and me both." I had that level of rage in me. There was no sense in pretending that I didn't. "If you think that's going to scare me away, you're wrong. Because it's in me, too. And I'm not sorry. It means we can fight back when we have to. That we'll never be victims again."

Ramsey brushed the hair out of my face, his hand cupping my cheek. "You're amazing, you know that? Pure fire."

I looked up into those onyx eyes. "Only for the people who matter." And I burned the brightest for one person. Him.

Chapter Twenty-One

Ramsey

THE STEADY SOUND OF THE SHOWER WAS LIKE TORTURE. Each water droplet that fell brought with it images that had no business being in my brain. Smooth, golden skin. Long hair in a cascade of brown and gold. Face tilted up to the water.

I squeezed my eyes closed, trying to clear the image away. Kai's head landed with a thud on my lap. I slowly opened my eyes. "Don't give me that look."

There was so much judgment in that steely gaze.

"Like you're any better. You follow her around, practically drooling."

Kai let out a low, grumbling sound.

I scratched behind his ears. "I know. We're both hopeless."

He licked my arm as if to say, "*At least we're in it together.*"

The water shut off, and my gut tightened. The sounds of the shower were bad, but the silence was somehow worse. Thoughts of her toweling off, spreading lotion over those long limbs…it was almost more than I could bear.

The thought that I should move back into the main house

swirled in my head. There hadn't been another letter. Not a single sighting of Ian or anyone else lurking around the property. But the idea of heading back to that empty house twisted something deep. I didn't want to leave Shiloh, and it wasn't just because I thought she needed protection.

By the time she emerged a few minutes later, my back molars were nearly ground to nubs. She had a towel wrapped around her hair in one of those twist things. Nothing about her pajamas should've been sexy but, somehow, they were. The flannel bottoms hung off her hips in a way that had me begging for just a glimpse of that golden skin around her waist. The t-shirt she wore was paper-thin and worn in a way that I knew meant comfort but also left little to the imagination when it came to the curves beneath it.

I swallowed hard. "Feel better?"

She nodded, lowering herself to the opposite end of the couch. Kai immediately ditched me and moved to her, dropping his head on her lap. Shiloh stroked his fur, and he practically purred. "How are you doing?"

Her gaze was assessing, a survey that spoke of worry and care. Normally, that kind of attention grated. But from Shiloh? It was a balm. "Just hoping they're settling in okay."

"Hayes said the Millers are good people. They've been foster parents for decades."

Just because you looked good from the outside didn't mean you actually were. My stepdad had been revered in our community. A successful financial planner who donated to local charities and volunteered at the homeless shelter every Thanksgiving. He used that impeccable image to hide the monster within.

Fingers linked with mine on the back of the couch, and Shiloh squeezed tightly. "You'll see for yourself tomorrow afternoon. If you have any concerns, we'll go to Hayes."

I nodded slowly, relishing the contact and the feel of her skin against mine. I swore my heart traveled up my arm and towards my chest. I couldn't remember the last time I'd felt a warmth like that. "He was good today. With Aidan and Elliott."

It burned to let the words free, and I hated myself for that. I didn't want to be the kind of person who judged all by the actions of a few. But I couldn't seem to stop myself. My experiences had been too intense and had made me too guarded.

Shiloh's thumb traced a circle on my palm. "Thanks for giving him a chance to be."

I wasn't going to sign up for any sheriff's department fundraisers, but I could admit that Hayes' heart was probably in the right place. There was no guarantee for the rest of his department, though.

"One at a time," Shiloh said as if she'd read my mind. "All you have to do is give people a chance to show you who they really are."

My gaze burned into hers. "Some people are good at hiding it."

"Some are. But the truth always comes out eventually."

That much was true. But, sometimes, the price to pay for the time it took was too high.

"Your stepfather...he's in jail now?"

I tried to keep my body from going rigid but failed. "Life sentence."

Shiloh kept up those circles, keeping me from falling into the spiral of memories and keeping me in the here and now. "I'm so sorry they didn't believe you and that they let money corrupt them. I'm so sorry you lost your mom."

Her words hurt. Pained me because she couldn't take away the past. But I felt how much she wanted to try. "It was a slow sickness, the way he warped her mind. He got her into this cycle where she didn't know up from down."

"But he didn't pull you into it."

"How do you know that?"

A sad smile played at her lips. "You see the truth too well to have believed the lies."

"I fell for it the first time. He backhanded me for spilling peas on the floor. The next day, I got a brand-new bike. I thought it meant that he was sorry. I thought it was his promise to never do it again."

Shiloh's grip on my hand tightened. "But you were wrong."

"He didn't even hold out another week. Eventually, the presents stopped. Maybe because I never touched them. Maybe because he lost the desire to create the illusion."

"I hope he hurts as bad as he hurt you and your mom."

He likely did. Prison wasn't a kind place for those who hurt children, and his trial had been a very public one.

"I'd never want to go through it all again, but in a lot of ways, it made me who I am."

Shiloh picked up tracing the circles on my palm again. "It gave you that empathy and understanding."

I nodded. "I wouldn't wish that away for anything."

"I think that's the best thing we can do with our pain, mold it into something that can help others in some way. It's why I wanted to learn from you. I'm not good with people, but I thought maybe I could use the hurt inside me to help horses."

An ache flared deep in my chest. "You have a way with them—with every animal I've seen you come across. But you're not bad with people. Elliott went straight to you today when he needed comfort, and you gave it to him."

"That's different—"

"It's not. Maybe you got into a rhythm with your family that kept them at arm's length, but I see you trying to change that. I saw it today with Hayes. And he noticed the change, too."

Shiloh toyed with the seam on the couch cushion. "I hate that I've hurt them so much."

"They hurt you, too. Just because we love someone doesn't mean we never hurt them. It's pretty much a guarantee. Life happens. What matters is how you deal with it. You're changing things, and that takes the most bravery of all."

Shiloh's eyes glittered in the low light. "I'm trying. I want…I want things to be better."

"One foot in front of the other. That's all you can do."

"Just take the next step."

"That's right."

I just hoped like hell it didn't take her away from me.

"Go," Shiloh ordered for the third time. "Kai and I will be fine here. I'm going to exercise a few of the horses in the south paddock and then get cleaned up for dinner with Hadley."

I hated the idea of leaving Shiloh alone. Not because she couldn't handle things but because we'd been through a lot yesterday. I knew we were likely both feeling a little raw. Yet Shiloh had called her sister this morning and made dinner plans, taking that next step. I needed to take mine.

"Okay. I shouldn't be too long. I'm just picking up lunch and going to hang for a little bit."

Shiloh smiled. "Take as much time as you need. And give Aidan and Elliott hugs from me. If they don't want Aidan working here after school, I'll go visit them tomorrow."

I hoped that wasn't a rule the Millers would set. Working here had been good for Aidan. Had given him a sense of accomplishment that he desperately needed.

"You could come with me…" I was sure the boys would love to see Shiloh, a part of me hated the feeling of walking away from her, even just for an afternoon.

She toed a piece of gravel with her boot. "I think they need you right now. You've been where they are, and they know you understand. I don't want to overwhelm them when they're still settling in or ruin a chance for them opening up if they need to talk."

My chest constricted as I stared down at this miracle of a woman, one who put the boys first when I knew she would've given anything to see them this afternoon.

She was close. So much so that I caught a hint of that floral scent that clung to her skin. I blamed it for my stupidity, for leaning in and closing the distance between us and pressing my lips to her forehead. It was the barest touch, and only for the briefest of moments, but the feel of her skin burned through me like a wildfire.

I jerked away, knowing I'd be scarred forever. "They're lucky to have you."

The pink that hit Shiloh's cheeks only made her look more beautiful, and I knew I was screwed. She cleared her throat, staring at her boots. "I'm the lucky one."

I twisted my keys around my finger, gripping them tightly, and then moved towards my truck without another word. I needed a little distance, some space to get my head back on straight before I started panting after her like my dog.

I beeped the locks and climbed behind the wheel. As I drove down the lane, I couldn't resist a glance in my rearview mirror. I saw her bent over Kai, giving him a rubdown.

"Damn lucky dog."

The drive to town didn't take too long, but images of Shiloh played in my mind the whole way. She was a living ghost, haunting my every waking moment. So much for the space helping.

I pulled into the small parking lot outside the burger joint, a favorite of locals and tourists alike. Thankfully, tourist season hadn't hit yet. Once it did, I stayed far away.

I slid out of my truck and shut the door. As I beeped my locks, movement caught my eye. I recognized the swagger, the cocky walk that had an air of anger to it. The expression on his face held nothing but rage.

I braced. The lot had a couple of other cars, but we were just past the usual lunch rush since I wasn't meeting the boys until two. My stance came instantly, memory carved into muscle and bone from the time I'd spent in prison, the year of having to watch my back at all times. Loose. Ready for anything.

"Bishop," Kenny barked.

"What can I help you with?"

"You think I don't know it was you? Heard you convinced

my boy to work for you. Been filling his mind with all kinds of bullshit."

I shrugged. "I gave him a job when he asked. Don't think there's a crime there."

Kenny's nostrils flared. "There's a fuckin' crime, all right. You stole from me." He shoved at my chest.

The man had more strength than I would've thought, but I still barely budged. Instead, I leaned forward and lowered my voice, a growl edging my words. "Careful who you lay hands on. You're used to picking on people smaller than you—those who won't fight back. You know where I've been and what my story is. You don't want to mess with me. I'll end you, and no one will ever know."

Fear bled into Kenny's bloodshot eyes for a moment, but then his jaw hardened. "Fuck off. You don't scare me. You just need to learn some manners. Maybe you need to know what it's like to lose what's yours."

My body locked as my gaze hardened on the worthless waste of space in front of me. "Is that a threat?"

He shrugged, a grin spreading across his face. "More of a question. Do you know what it feels like to be powerless? To lose what belongs to you? Maybe those horses. Maybe something else…"

Chapter Twenty-Two

Shiloh

I OPENED THE DOOR TO THE WOLF GAP BAR & GRILL AND stepped inside. My hands clenched and flexed as I moved through the entryway. It wasn't horribly crowded since tourist season was still a ways off, but it wasn't empty either. I felt eyes on me before I saw them, that grating sensation against my skin.

I looked around and saw at least three different people intently focused on me. A woman who I knew was in my mom's quilt guild bent to whisper to her husband, her gaze fixated on me. The panic started to come—the urge to run fast and far.

Ramsey's voice echoed in my head. *One foot in front of the other.*

I struggled to breathe against the constriction in my chest. What was the next step? Not all of it, simply the thing I needed to do right now. It was just that—a physical step.

I forced my legs to carry me forward towards the hostess stand.

"Shiloh." A bright voice greeted me.

I swallowed hard and lifted my gaze to the familiar face. "Hi, Cammie." My voice trembled as I spoke, and I hated the weakness.

Cammie's smile didn't falter. "Hadley's in a booth in the back. I'll take you to her."

I nodded but couldn't get any other words out, just the next step as I followed Cammie to the table, ignoring the staring people.

Cammie expertly wove through tables, and I kept my gaze pointed directly at her back, not taking anyone else in.

"Here you go. Can I get you a drink while you look at the menu?" Cammie asked.

I shook my head as I slid into the booth.

Hadley's gaze swept over my face, concern filling her expression. As soon as Cammie left, my sister leaned forward. "We can get our food to go and head back to my place."

God, she was the best. I didn't deserve her, but I was grateful for her just the same. "No. I—I want to get better at this stuff."

Hadley arched a brow in question.

"At being normal," I explained.

She scoffed. "Who gives a crap about normal?"

My mouth curved. "I wouldn't mind having their french fries hot out of the fryer for a change."

I only ever got takeout. I didn't stick around at restaurants or anywhere in town, really. I got in, got out, and hightailed it back to my solitude.

Hadley grinned. "They are delicious."

"How are the girls?" I asked, trying to focus on something other than the feeling of being uncomfortable in my skin.

"Birdie is raising hell like always and turning Calder's hair gray. Sage is still obsessing over wildflowers and counting down the days until she can start hunting for them again."

Hadley was the mother the girls had always deserved, and it warmed my heart to see them getting that. "It's been warming up. I bet things will sprout before she knows it."

"It's going to be a gorgeous spring."

I nodded and took a sip of my water.

"So, fill me in. What's the latest with the new place?"

I traced a circle in the condensation on the glass. I didn't have the first clue how to answer that. Yet, I wanted to explain it to my sister, and have her help me sort out the feelings I was struggling with. "It feels like home."

Hadley's ice-blue eyes brightened. "I can't imagine anything better."

"Me, neither." I toyed with the straw wrapper, shredding it into tiny pieces.

"But?" Hadley prodded.

I kept my eyes trained on the tiny bits of paper as if they could give me the words. "I like him."

The words came out as barely a whisper.

Hadley laughed. "Of course, you do. Ramsey's hot as hell. He's got that tortured, broody thing going on. *And,* he obviously cares about you a great deal."

My head snapped up. "Obviously?"

Hadley sighed. "The man only lets people onto his property under great duress. Yet, he jumped all over himself to let you stay."

"He let Aidan and Elliott onto his property."

"Two kids who needed help."

A wave of nausea rolled through me. "*I* needed help. He's a good man."

"Shy." Hadley ducked her head so her eyes met mine. "I see the way he looks at you. It's not with pity."

My stomach twisted. That was what I'd gotten my whole life: pity and morbid fascination. I was so damn sick of it. "I want to hope it's not. I think we're becoming friends. I just…"

"You don't look at him like a friend."

Ramsey's words echoed in my head. "He told me he isn't built for relationships."

A huge grin stretched across Hadley's face.

"Why are you smiling? I just told you he doesn't want to be with me like that."

She shook her head. "Shy, if he's telling you that he's not built for relationships, that means he very much wants to be with you. He's just scared."

I didn't think *scared* was something Ramsey was often—and certainly not of me. "I'm not so sure."

"Be bold. Show him what he's missing. A shirt that shows a little cleavage wouldn't hurt…"

I choked on the sip of water I'd just taken. "Are you crazy?"

Hadley laughed. "Calder would say yes. But I think I'm also incredibly smart. What do you have to lose by flirting a little? If he's not interested, you can cut your losses and move on."

"I could lose everything. He could ask me to move out and not help around the ranch anymore—"

"Shy, Ramsey doesn't strike me as an asshole. I don't think he'd do any of that. At the very worst, he might pull back for a while."

The idea of losing the intimacy I had with Ramsey right now—the brushes of his fingers, the pressure of his arms around me—nearly ripped me to shreds.

"Would you really rather not know?" Hadley prodded.

"I'd rather have these little pieces of him than an entirety of anyone else."

Hadley's eyes glistened in the overhead lights. "Well, maybe all he needs to give you everything is a little push in the right direction."

"How about when Hayes got that M&M stuck up his nose?" Hadley asked through her laughter as we stepped out of the restaurant and into the cool night air.

I couldn't help my snort of laughter. "The M&M had nothing on the time Beckett broke his wrist climbing up to Sally Crenshaw's window."

Hadley's eyes widened. "I completely forgot about that. I don't think I've ever seen Dad so mad at one of us before."

"But it was Mom who threw down the hammer. I think she grounded him for a month. Missed Halloween and everything."

Hadley shook her head, but her smile stayed firmly planted on her face. "This was fun. What do you say we make it a monthly date?"

For the first time since I could remember, I didn't feel dread at being locked into plans with someone or panicked at how I would hide whatever I was feeling from my family. I wanted this kind of time with my sister. "I'd like that."

"Me, too." She looked down the street. "Where are you parked?"

"Around the corner."

Hadley beeped the locks on her SUV. "Want me to drive you?"

"I think I can make it a block."

"All right. Text me what day works for you next month."

I moved on instinct, quickly pulling my sister into a hug and then letting go before she could say a word. "Text you tomorrow."

I started down the sidewalk before I had a chance to take in the shock in Hadley's eyes or give her a chance to respond. I'd hugged her once in the last decade, but that was changing now, too. My chest burned as I rounded the corner and headed for my truck, but it was a good burn, one that pushed me to live my life to its fullest.

The street was dark, but the moon made the path ahead glow. I tipped my face up as I walked, taking in the shining stars in the clear night sky. I smiled up at them. The sky was what it had always been for me: a beacon of hope. But it burned brighter tonight. The hope was even stronger.

Suddenly, a hand clamped over my mouth, and someone jerked me backwards.

I froze. All the time I'd spent honing my instincts and awareness vanished in a flash. All I could remember was how powerless I'd felt all those years ago, how out of control as the fair passed by me.

That memory jerked me out of my frozen state. My arm swung back hard, my elbow landing in my attacker's gut. He grunted, and his hold on me loosened a fraction.

I twisted, bringing my knee up to his groin. His reaction was instantaneous. The blow hit me right in the side of the face. Light flashed, and then I was falling.

Chapter Twenty-Three

Ramsey

AIDAN RINSED A DISH AND HANDED IT TO ME. "THANKS for staying. I think it made Elliott feel better."

I glanced over my shoulder into the living room. Elliott laughed as he bumped Art Miller's game piece off the board. I turned back, placing the plate in the dishwasher. "I'll stay as long as you guys need."

Aidan swallowed hard and grabbed another plate. "They seem nice."

Art and Sandy couldn't have been kinder. They didn't bristle at me for making myself at home all afternoon. Sandy had given me the phone number to the house and told me to call or stop by anytime. They were gentle with Aidan and Elliott, never pushing but inviting them into their lives here. They were older, more like grandparents than parents, but I thought that might help make them seem less threatening.

I turned to Aidan. "You don't like something, call me or just come to the ranch."

Aidan still had his truck since he'd bought it with his own

money. That gave me peace of mind. He had a way out if things ever got bad.

He ran the sponge over the plate again and again, even though it was spotless. "What happens to us after here?"

A burn lit along my sternum at the fear in Aidan's voice. "It's not a short process. Your father will have to be tried."

After our run-in earlier today, I'd called Hayes to see why the hell he was walking free. Kenny had been charged, but he'd also made bail, putting his ranch up as collateral.

"I'll have to testify."

It wasn't a question. And there was a steely resolve to Aidan's words. Still, I had the urge to comfort the boy. "I'll be with you every step." I met his gaze. "I've been there. It isn't easy, but it's worth it."

Giving the world the truth in open court had been more freeing than I could've imagined, even with my stepfather glaring me down.

Aidan's jaw clenched. "I don't want Elliott to have to testify. He's too young."

My chest cracked at Aidan's fierce protectiveness of his brother. He'd taken on the role of father for the boy in every way that counted. I leaned a hip against the counter, shutting off the water. "We can talk to the district attorney. See what can be done to make this as easy on Elliott as possible."

"He shouldn't have to do it at all," Aidan bit out.

"No, he shouldn't. But you and I know that life is rarely fair."

Aidan mumbled something under his breath that I couldn't make out.

"But Elliott has *you*. He knows he isn't alone. That's more than so many kids have. More than you had."

It killed me that Aidan had been alone in this for so long. I knew that battle, and I wouldn't wish it on my worst enemy, let alone a kind, bright kid who deserved the world.

"I didn't protect him enough."

A jolt of pain lanced through me. I leaned forward and gripped

Aidan's shoulder. "You gave everything for him." He'd stepped into the line of fire more times than he could probably count. Yet, he still blamed himself.

Aidan didn't say a word. I squeezed his shoulder, ducking down to meet his gaze. "This isn't your fault. Your father's a sick man."

Aidan's eyes glistened in the bright light of the kitchen. "I kept thinking if I just stayed two steps ahead, it would be okay. I'm usually good at it, seeing what might set him off: Not having dinner done fast enough, not getting the chores finished before he's home, El's toys not being put away. But I couldn't stop spilled milk."

A tear slipped free and slid down Aidan's cheek. "He was going to hit Elliott. I could see it in his eyes."

Rage pumped through my veins as I saw the incident playing out in my mind. "So, you stepped in."

"I set him off, got him focused on me. Told him to get a grip. That it was just a little spilled milk. He usually just backhands me, but he punched me this time. I blacked out for a few seconds. When I came to, Elliott was crying. All I could think was that I'd failed. That I'd let Dad hurt him."

I didn't think. I simply moved, pulling Aidan into my arms in a hard hug. "You didn't fail. You never could."

Aidan's chest heaved as he released it all, the weight he'd been carrying for so long. I held on tightly. "Let it go. I've got you."

His sobs were silent yet powerful enough to shake us both where we stood. I simply kept holding on. I took all the pain and worry and fear. All I could think in the moment was that I needed to show him that it wasn't too much. That *he* wasn't too much.

I didn't know how long we stood there. I didn't have the right words to give to Aidan. All I could give him was my presence and the knowledge that I wouldn't leave him to deal with all this alone.

Aidan pulled back, wiping at his face. "Sorry, I didn't mean to be such a chickenshit."

I gripped his shoulders. "No. Don't brush whatever you're

feeling away. You do that, and it'll eat away at you and slowly blacken your insides."

Aidan's eyes hardened. "I won't be like him."

"Then you have to let yourself feel it all. Turning it off changes you. But if you let yourself feel, you'll never be him. Your heart is too good."

Aidan wiped at his eyes again but nodded.

"I'm here any time you need to let this shit out. You want to scream and punch something? I'll find you a heavy bag. You need to cry? I've got you. You just need to know you're not alone? I'll sit with you all damn night. I'm with you. Every step of the way."

His Adam's apple bobbed as he swallowed. "Thanks." He picked up the plate, his lips twitching. "Think we can finish cleaning up now, or do you have more shrink-like wisdom to impart?"

I choked on a laugh. "Such a smartass."

He shrugged. "I am a teenager. Gotta have a little of that."

And I was damn glad he hadn't lost it. My phone buzzed in my pocket. I pulled it out, expecting to see a text from Shiloh, but it wasn't her name that flashed on my screen.

Lor: *Got space for a gelding at the end of the month?*

I frowned at the screen.

"What's wrong?" Aidan asked.

"Nothing. I just haven't heard from Shiloh."

I'd texted her a couple of hours ago to tell her I was staying for dinner, but she hadn't responded. Shiloh wasn't big on phones, but it wasn't like her to go this long without responding.

"Call her. Sometimes, that text alert is too quiet."

He had a point. Maybe it revealed a little too much, but my thumb slid across the screen to her contact. I held the phone to my ear as it rang. Each reverberation that went unanswered had my gut tightening. Finally, it cut off. There was silence, and then a male voice came across the line that I didn't recognize. "Ramsey?"

"Who's this?" I barked.

"Calder Cruz, Hadley's husband."

"Why the hell are you answering Shiloh's phone?"

I didn't care if I came across like an asshole; my need for information was too strong.

"Shy was attacked tonight."

The world around me slowed, and each beat of my heart shook my entire body. This wasn't happening. Images played on an endless reel in my mind, each one worse than the last. And all of them were my fault. Because I'd known that someone was out to hurt her. And I'd left her alone anyway.

Chapter Twenty-Four

Shiloh

I WINCED AS I ADJUSTED THE ICE PACK ON MY CHEEK. MY entire face throbbed.

"Walk me through it again," Hayes gritted out.

Hadley elbowed him in the stomach. "Tone."

"It's fine," I said. I could feel Hayes' barely restrained rage, but I knew it wasn't pointed at me. "I didn't hear him coming. I was distracted." And I'd be kicking myself for that for the foreseeable future. "He grabbed me from behind. It all happened so fast. I didn't see his face. I think he might've been wearing a hat. It was dark, and when I kneed him in the balls, he punched me. I didn't see anything after that."

Not until a woman helped me sit up. And all she'd seen was a man running away.

"Did you get a sense of his size?" Hayes pressed.

"Taller than me. Strong. That's about it."

A vehicle door slammed somewhere, and then Beckett was jogging towards us, worry lining his face. I sent Hadley a dirty look. "Really?"

She held up both hands. "I'm an EMT, but it doesn't hurt to have a doctor look you over."

"I'm going to have a shiner, that's all."

Beckett moved towards the gurney I sat on. "Let me be the judge of that."

I reluctantly pulled the ice pack away. "See?"

Beck winced. "That's gotta hurt. Hope you gave him a little payback."

"His balls should be black and blue for a while."

He grinned. "That's my girl." The humor fled his face as he studied my cheek. "I need to make sure nothing's broken. It's not going to feel great."

"Just get it over with."

Beckett gently probed my cheek. I sucked in a sharp breath as his fingers moved around my eye. "How bad, on a scale from one to ten?"

"Six?"

"That means eight, at least," Hayes cut in.

"It does not," I shot back.

Calder strode towards us, holding up my phone. "Found this. Screen's not even shattered."

That was a miracle. The device had gone flying when I fell. "Thanks."

"I, uh, answered it because Ramsey was calling."

My muscles locked. "What did you say?"

"He wasn't exactly happy that some guy he didn't know was answering your phone, so I had to explain that you'd been attacked—"

"Seriously, Calder?"

His brows rose. "I'm pretty sure that's accurate information."

But it was the last thing Ramsey needed to hear after everything we'd been through the last few days.

"I think he's headed here now," Calder finished sheepishly.

I tried to sit up on the gurney, but Beck pushed me back down. "Lay still. I'm not done."

"If I broke something, I'd know."

He pulled a penlight from his medical bag. "I need to make sure you don't have a concussion or signs of a brain bleed."

"You're being a little dramatic, don't you think?"

Beckett leveled me with a stare. "It's either this or I call Mom."

My mouth dropped open. "You wouldn't."

He shrugged. "Try me."

I muttered a creative curse under my breath, and Hadley laughed. I glared at her. "This is your fault. You called the drama queen."

She grimaced. "Sorry. Dinner's my treat next month."

"Try for the rest of the year," I mumbled.

Beckett flashed his light in my eyes.

"Shit, a little warning would be nice."

"That was for the drama-queen comment." He studied my eyes. "You might have a mild concussion. You should stay with Addie and me tonight—"

The sound of screeching tires cut off his words as Ramsey's truck jerked to a stop just behind the ambulance. The engine was barely off before his door slammed, and he was running towards us.

Even in the dark and across the distance, I saw the feral edge in his eyes—the panic. I tried to get up to assure him that I was fine, but he was at my side before I had the chance. His hand went to my uninjured cheek as his eyes scanned my body for injuries.

"I'm fine. Just a shiner."

He didn't say a word, simply pulled me into him, holding me close.

Everything in me melted at his embrace. And for the first time since the attack, I felt true relief—as if I could finally admit how terrified I'd been. My body trembled, and he held me closer.

"I've got you." He whispered the words against my hair, his lips brushing the strands.

The world around us disappeared as I sank into him. His strength. His reassurance. His comfort.

A throat cleared, and I forced myself to lift my head. Four sets of eyes stared at us. Even the other officers and EMTs had gone quiet in the background. I fought the urge to squirm.

Ramsey didn't show even a hint of discomfort. "What happened?"

I started speaking before any of my siblings could tell a more dramatic tale. "Someone tried to grab me. I kneed him in the balls, and he punched me in the face."

A muscle along Ramsey's jaw fluttered wildly. "Who?"

I shook my head and immediately regretted the action, pain flashing through my face. "I didn't get a good look. It all happened too fast."

Ramsey pulled me back against him as his gaze moved to Hayes. "Kenny Chambers?"

Hayes' fingers tightened around his phone. "I'll be paying him a visit."

"I thought he was in lockup," I said, looking between the two.

Ramsey's hand trailed up and down my spine. "I had a run-in with him earlier today. It wasn't warm and fuzzy."

"But why would he go after me?"

Ramsey looked down at me, and those onyx eyes held so much I couldn't decipher. "Because he knows you matter to me."

My heart sped up, tripping over itself in a double-time rhythm. "Oh."

It was the only thing I could get out. That single syllable.

He leaned in closer. "You have to tell Hayes about the letters. This could be related to that, too."

My head spun with how quickly Ramsey had jumped from one possibility to another—and with his nearness.

"What letters?" Hayes growled.

He'd always had hearing like a damn cat.

Ramsey straightened but kept his hold on me. He didn't hurry to fill the silence with explanation. He let me find my way, even if I bumbled it.

I bit the inside of my cheek. "I, um, I used to get letters from Howard Kemper."

Everyone around us went dead silent. I could hear the hum of the lights in the ambulance. A vehicle's engine running. The breeze in the leaves.

"What did you say?" Hayes asked slowly.

I swallowed hard, weaving my fingers through Ramsey's. I was facing this myself, but I was leaning on his strength to do it. "He sent me letters from jail once I had my own post office box."

The sheriff's mask was in place as Hayes stared at me—the one that made it impossible to read what he was thinking. "What was in the letters?"

I looked down at our joined hands, studying them as if they could give me the words to say. "Garbage. Sometimes, he just told me about his life in prison. Others were angry."

Hadley glanced between us all. "But what does that have to do with this? He's dead."

"I got one after he died. One similar to what he used to say but…different."

"It was a threat," Ramsey filled in.

Beckett whirled on him. "You knew about this and didn't say anything?"

Ramsey didn't even blink at Beckett's outburst. "It wasn't my story to tell."

"And now my sister's sitting here with a concussion. She could've been killed!"

Most people wouldn't have seen it, the flinching of Ramsey's muscles, but it was more than I could take. I swung my legs over the side of the gurney and stood, giving Beckett a healthy shove. "Shut your mouth. You don't know what you're talking about. If you have a problem with information *I* didn't share, then take that out on me. Don't lash out at the person who has been there for me through all of this."

Beckett's eyes widened, and his jaw went slack. "He should've been looking out for you—"

"He was! In every way. Just because he doesn't use a method you find acceptable doesn't mean it's not everything to me."

A hand curled around my waist, tugging me back to the gurney. "You don't have to defend me."

I looked up at Ramsey, seeing the first hint of amusement in his eyes. But there was pain there, too. Because my brother's words had landed. I scowled. "I do when people are being idiots."

Hadley made a choked sound.

"I'm worried about you," Beckett defended. "Why didn't you tell anyone?"

"Because she was worried that she'd lose the little bit of freedom she had."

It was Hayes who'd spoken, pain and regret lacing his voice.

He moved towards me, taking my hand and squeezing. "I'm so damn sorry, Shy. I'm sorry we made you feel so trapped you felt you couldn't tell us any of this."

"I should've. I was trying to find a way…"

He squeezed my hand. "You told us now. And we're going to figure this out. But I need to see those letters."

Chapter Twenty-Five

Ramsey

THE WALLS OF THE GUEST CABIN SEEMED CLOSER THAN earlier in the day, the air warmer and thicker. I cracked my neck as I took in Hadley and Calder in the kitchen with Shiloh. Hadley handed her a cup of tea, saying something I couldn't hear. Shiloh nodded, and I didn't miss the wince with the action.

She needed rest, but I knew that wouldn't happen anytime soon. The tension between my shoulder blades eased a fraction when she headed towards the couch, Hadley and Calder on her heels. My gaze stayed locked on Shiloh as she eased onto the sectional, Kai lying down on the floor next to her.

Hadley dimmed the lights overhead in the living space, and the lines of strain around Shiloh's eyes lessened the barest amount. Beckett had returned home to his pregnant wife but had given me strict instructions to wake Shiloh every three hours tonight just to be safe.

As Shiloh took a sip of her tea, I turned back to Hayes. He had clearly perfected his mask over his years in law enforcement, but

I saw glimmers of his true emotions beneath it. He was ravaged. Too many letters to count lay across the dining room table, each one placed in an evidence bag. But there were still more in a box that Shiloh had retrieved from her bedroom.

I hated the idea of her sleeping near the container of vileness, and that Howard Kemper's voice was always close. If Hayes hadn't needed them, I would've burned every damn one.

I didn't want to see the words, but they jumped out at me.

KEEP YOURSELF PURE FOR MY BOY. YOU'LL BE HIS ONE DAY.

YOU'LL PAY FOR RUNNING FROM THE FAMILY I TRIED TO GIVE YOU.

I FORGIVE YOU. YOU KNOW NOT WHAT YOU DO.

Each letter oscillated in its level of sanity. Some read as completely unhinged, while others sounded like a pen pal had written them, with Howard sharing what books he'd been reading and how bad the food was in prison.

"How did she live with these and not tell anyone?" Hayes' voice was barely audible.

My hands tightened around the back of the chair where I stood. "Because she has a strength that's otherworldly."

He pulled his focus away from the letters and glanced up at me. "I'm seeing that more and more."

I couldn't help the flare of annoyance at his words. Shiloh's family had mistaken her silence for weakness for too long. I let out a breath, searching for calm. The mistake hadn't been made because they didn't care. Anyone could see how much they loved Shiloh.

I pulled the chair back and lowered myself into it. "You have to let her fight these battles. Trying to shield her from everything isn't helping."

A muscle in Hayes' cheek ticked. "I know."

A little more of the tension along my shoulders bled out of me. "But it can't be easy."

"Do you know what it's like to blame yourself for someone's life being destroyed?"

I sucked in air. He had no idea how well I knew. I could keep that fact to myself, or I could reach out and offer Hayes some understanding. I searched his face. I didn't see any of the callous uncaring the officers who'd sent me away showed.

"Every day after my stepfather murdered my mother. I wondered if it would have been different if I'd just told a teacher what was happening at home. If I could've caught him on camera and gone to the press with the tape. A million different what-ifs haunted me."

"Hell," Hayes muttered. "I'm so damn sorry you went through that." He shook his head. "I guess we all carry wounds."

"It's what we do with them that matters. Shiloh is putting hers to good use."

Hayes' head jerked. "To good use?"

"She has a gift. Reached a horse in a matter of days. One that would've taken me months to build trust with. I'm teaching her some methods, but that piece of magic you need in you to do this work? She has it in spades. And that's because of what she went through. She's taking the bad and turning it into good."

Hayes let out a shaky breath. "Everly does that. Takes the bad and twists it into something so beautiful you wouldn't believe."

"The animal sanctuary."

He nodded. "I never thought I'd be able to see that land as something good. But it is. It's giving back to animals and the community. She healed something in all of us by doing it." His mouth curved. "She bought a bunch of sledgehammers and gave them to us to tear down the shed Shiloh had been kept in."

I felt a tearing sensation deep in my chest. *Shed. Kept.* I struggled to push down the rage straining to get free.

"Shy was the first to take a swing. It was a piece of freeing her."

I could picture it in my mind. Because as much as Shiloh used avoidance as a defense mechanism, she wasn't afraid to fight. And that strength in her was so deep. So powerful.

I scrubbed a hand over my face. "She's finding more and more of those pieces. You just have to let her."

"I want that for her. I really do. But then there's this." He lifted the newest letter, his jaw tensing.

That rage was back, pushing at the walls I used to lock it down. "Can you tell anything?"

"Definitely a different sender. The handwriting tells me that much. But the language is tougher to decipher."

"What do you mean?"

Hayes' finger scanned the lines. "The sentiments are similar to what Howard sent, and even some of the verbiage. But then it diverts, too."

"Shiloh said he never would've used *carefully crafted*."

"She's right. He's more straightforward. Nothing flowery like that."

"So, it has to be someone close to him."

Hayes' jaw worked back and forth. "I need to look into some people. Have a conversation with Ian."

"Kemper had a cellmate who recently got out."

Hayes' gaze shot to mine.

I shrugged. "I can use a computer." And I had some resources that could get me less legally obtained information.

"I'll run him and see if I can find out where he is. Have a conversation with him, too."

I nodded, my gaze finding its way to Shiloh. I understood the urge to shield her. I felt it every damn day. She'd already been through so much. She shouldn't have to take this on, too. But I refused to clip those beautiful wings.

"You care about my sister?"

My head snapped back to Hayes, my eyes narrowing.

"It's an honest question. I'm not trying to be an asshole."

"I care about her." It was so much more than *care*. Words that I hadn't used in decades sprang to mind. And even those didn't do my feelings justice.

Hayes gave a slight nod. "All of this." He gestured at the letters.

"It messed with her head. The shit about purity. Threats forcing her to marry Ian. She never told us any of it. I don't know that she's capable of any sort of a relationship."

"This isn't that." I knew where he was going. And it wasn't that I didn't want that with Shiloh. I wanted her more than my next breath. But I refused to potentially hurt her.

Hayes arched a brow. "I'm just asking you to tread carefully."

"I'd cut off my own arm before I cause her any pain."

Hayes stared down at the sea of letters again. "She's been hurt too much already." He was silent for a moment. "It's why I went to work for the sheriff's department. Maybe it's my way of doing good with the bad, trying to help others who are in those desperate situations."

"I can't think of a better reason to become a cop."

Hayes' lips twitched. "Sheriff."

I scoffed. "Yeah, yeah."

The amusement fled Hayes' expression. "She's let you in more than anyone I've ever seen. Please, take care of my sister."

My chest constricted, air barely making it into my lungs. It scared the hell out of me, but there was no other option. I'd give anything for Shiloh. Because she'd found a way through the walls I'd spent so much time fortifying. And she'd brought light to a place I'd thought would be dark forever.

Chapter Twenty-Six

Shiloh

MY HEAD THRUMMED AS I WAITED FOR EVERYONE TO leave. I did my best to keep the tension out of my expression, but it was a losing battle. "I'll go see Mom and Dad tomorrow. Explain things."

Hadley winced. "Want me to come with you?"

"I think I need to do it alone."

She reached out and squeezed my hand, quickly releasing it. "Call me if you change your mind."

"Thanks."

Hayes balanced the box of letters on his hip. "I'll stop by their place tomorrow morning and give them the lay of the land."

I started to argue, but Hayes held up a hand. "This isn't me thinking you can't handle it. This is a big brother taking one for the team. They're going to lose it, and it'll be better for everyone involved if they let that out before you guys talk."

He had a point there. Trying to talk about the past was

difficult for me on a good day. If Mom was freaking out at the same time, it would be a disaster.

"Thank you."

His lips twitched. "Oh, there will be payback. You're going to say yes to being one of Ev's bridesmaids. And you're going to wear whatever dress she picks out."

Hadley laughed as Calder wrapped an arm around her shoulders. "That's harsh, Bubby."

Hayes grinned. "I know how to play the sibling game."

"A little too well," I muttered.

He leaned forward and pressed a quick kiss to the top of my head. "You'll have fun. I promise."

"Maybe if I didn't have to wear a dress." And if a crowd of people wouldn't be there, watching me. But I'd deal with it for my brother. And for Ev.

Calder opened the front door and held it for Hadley and Hayes. "Call if you need anything."

"I will."

Hayes nodded at Ramsey and sent me one last look as he headed out the door. "We'll talk tomorrow as soon as I have an update."

That wasn't his usual. Typically, Hayes didn't want to share anything with me that he thought might bring on bad memories. "That would be good. Thanks."

He lifted his chin in farewell and pulled the door shut. The second it snicked closed, Ramsey switched off the lights in the dining area and strode towards me. "You're hurting."

Of course, he saw everything I tried to keep hidden.

"Just a little."

"Liar."

He guided me back towards the couch, and I lowered myself to the cushions.

"Do you want some more Tylenol? Something to eat?"

"No, I'm okay. Turning down the light helped."

Ramsey sank onto the couch. His hand found mine on the

back of it, his thumb tracing circles on my skin. "I'd do anything to take it away."

My heart thudded against my ribs. "It really isn't that bad. Just a knock to the head."

His jaw clenched. "It could've been so much worse."

I squeezed Ramsey's hand, bringing his attention to me. "But it wasn't. Because I know how to handle myself."

"I know you do. It's not that. I just…"

"Don't want to see me hurting." I felt the same way about him.

"I hate it."

My lips curved. "Whoever it was is likely hurting a hell of a lot more than I am."

I saw the slightest flicker of movement around Ramsey's mouth. "I hope you burst a ball."

I choked on a laugh. "Brutal."

"Damn straight." He picked up the circles on my hand again. "It was brave. Not just fighting back but sharing everything you did with your family."

I swallowed hard. "It was time." Guilt flared again for keeping everything hidden for so long. "I want a good relationship with them, one where they don't have to worry—something normal."

Ramsey's brows pulled together. "I don't know that any family is normal."

"But I've made ours all sorts of messed up. And I just keep doing it."

"Shiloh—"

"It's true. I felt different after the kidnapping. Like a freak. But no matter how hard I tried, I couldn't get myself to just act normal. None of my siblings could have birthday parties at the house because I couldn't handle big groups of people. Our parents never let them go to sleepovers or high school parties because they were overprotective. Even field trips were a no-go if one of my parents wasn't a chaperone."

Ramsey's rough thumb continued tracing designs on my skin, never ceasing. "You know that's not on you, right?"

My throat burned. "Part of me does. But I was sulking that night. I didn't want to go to the fair. I begged my parents to let me stay home and go riding. They wanted all of us to go together, as a family. Instead, I blew it up."

"You were ten years old. Every kid on this planet pouts when they don't get their way. That doesn't mean they deserve to be kidnapped."

"I know I didn't deserve it, but I could've done some things that would've prevented it. That haunts me. That and the fact that I made things so hard for everyone afterward."

Ramsey was quiet for a moment. "You were hurting. Drowning. Trying to find a way to keep your head above water. You have to give yourself some grace for how you dealt with it."

"I have grace for myself. But what it put my family through? That's harder. I could handle the kids making fun of me, but they gave Hadley such a hard time, too. Mocked her for not being allowed to do all those things."

Ramsey's dark eyes flashed in the low light. "I'm sure it wasn't a picnic for you either."

My free hand tightened around the couch cushion. "It wasn't easy. A part of me wanted normal. But every time I reached for it, things ended in disaster. I'd freak out and run."

I toyed with a loose thread on the seam of the cushion. "Even as I got older, when I knew the socially acceptable things to do, I just…couldn't." The remnants of old frustrations flared to life in my chest, the burn of all the unshed tears gathering behind my eyes. Aggravation for how much I'd wanted things to go back the way they were but knowing they never would.

Ramsey's thumb swept back and forth across my palm. "I'm sure it wasn't as bad as you thought."

"I've never even kissed someone. The one time I tried, I had a panic attack."

The words slipped out before I could stop them. Maybe

some part of me wanted Ramsey to know the truth. Just how much I'd let that experience warp me. Maybe I wanted to hope that he would see the *me* beneath it all.

Nothing but silence greeted me. The longer it went on, the more my skin began to itch. Of course, he didn't know what to say. What did you say to an adult woman who'd just laid that at your feet? I tugged my hand from Ramsey's and moved to stand. "I'm gonna head to bed—"

He moved then, grabbing my hand with a featherlight grip and tugging me forward. "Shiloh."

We were close. So close I smelled the scent of leather and pine clinging to him.

I moved on instinct, closing the distance. Then my lips were on his. So damn soft but still beneath mine. Unmoving. That had me jerking away. "I'm sorry. I shouldn't have—"

He cut me off with his mouth on mine. This time, there were no awkward movements or frozenness. There was only Ramsey and me and a delicious, building heat. I leaned into him, needing more of that phantom warmth.

Ramsey's hand dipped under my hair, tipping my head back. His tongue parted my lips, stroking mine. My head spun with the sensations. That heat spread to my belly. The tingles expanded across my skin. I lost myself in the taste that was only Ramsey. I wanted to drown in it all.

Slowly, he pulled back, his eyes blazing.

I blinked a few times, my fingers lifting to my lips. "That was…"

The corner of Ramsey's mouth kicked up. "Better than the best damn whiskey I've ever tasted."

I blinked a few more times, my hand dropping away from my mouth. "I shouldn't have forced you into that—"

Ramsey grabbed my hand, tugging me closer to him. "You didn't make me do anything."

"I made you feel bad for me. I basically forced a pity kiss out of you."

He barked out a laugh. "Shiloh, the last thing I feel for you is pity." He bent forward, touching his forehead to mine.

"What do you feel for me?"

Ramsey's fingers twined with mine. "I don't think there's a word for it in the English language. But it burns through me. And I don't want to ever let it go."

Chapter Twenty-Seven

Ramsey

KAI'S HEAD LIFTED AS I WALKED INTO THE KITCHEN, but Shiloh's eyes didn't move from the cup of coffee she stared at. She studied it as if it had all the answers in the world. I cleared my throat, and her head shot up.

"How do you feel this morning?" It had been a long night for us both with me waking her up every three hours. Between that and the memory of our kiss playing on repeat in my brain, I'd barely gotten any sleep.

Shiloh worried that spot on the inside of her cheek. "A lot better this morning."

Nothing about her expression told the same story, but I didn't see pain exactly. I studied her as she shifted her weight back and forth on her feet and tapped out a rhythm against her mug.

I moved in closer, watching for any hint of apprehension, but the nearer I got, the more Shiloh seemed to calm. Wrapping an arm around her, I leaned my forehead against hers. "I'm right here. My feelings didn't change with a few hours' sleep."

Shiloh melted into me at those words. "I'm not going to be good at this."

"Me, either, but I think we can fumble through it together. Give each other room to mess up and tell one another how to fix it." Because I couldn't hold back from Shiloh any longer. I'd fought the pull with everything I had in me, so scared I'd hurt her if I gave in. And the truth was, I would hurt her. I'd inevitably screw something up and cause her pain. But I was hurting us both every damn day by not giving this a shot.

She set her coffee mug on the counter and burrowed into me. "I've been scared to want this."

"You and me both."

She smiled against my chest. "Why does that make me feel better?"

I chuckled. "Because you know you're not in this alone. And you never will be." I might not have the tools to be the best in relationships, but I had patience. I didn't give up, and I always found a path through.

I brushed the hair away from her face. It hung in loose waves around her face today, curled from that braid she typically wore. She was so damn beautiful it was like claws digging into my heart. My fingers trailed along her cheek, down her neck, and beneath her hair. "This goes at your speed. You have the reins."

A flash of panic lit her expression. "I don't know the first thing about leading something like this. I—I'll screw something up."

I brushed my lips across hers, a hint of coffee and Shiloh filling my senses. "Just do what feels right. Don't be afraid to ask for what you want or tell me what you don't. That's how this works."

She glared at me. Full-on scowled as if I'd stolen the last donut.

I barked out a laugh.

"Don't laugh. It's not funny."

I kissed her again, unable to help myself. "It's a little funny."

Shiloh huffed. "Then you have to do the same. Tell me what you want and don't."

"That's simple."

She arched a brow in question.

"I want you. Always. Whatever you want to give."

A blush stained her cheeks. "Not scared I'm going to turn into some stage-three clinger?"

I pulled her closer to me. "You can cling all you want."

She grinned up at me. "Well, I'm not clinging today. I need to go see my parents and then stop by the feed store and the grocery. You need anything?"

Everything in me tensed, the events of last night playing in my mind. "Why don't I go with you?"

Shiloh shook her head. "I'm not letting what happened last night scare me out of my life. I have to keep living. I'll be cautious, but I'm not taking up a bodyguard."

"I don't think going places alone right now is smart." A rapid-fire slideshow of all the horrible things that could happen played in my mind.

She pressed a palm to my chest. "It's broad daylight. I have my cell phone. I'm going to public places. This asshole jumped me from behind in the dark. He's not going to attack at ten in the morning on a busy street."

My gut churned, but I forced myself to nod. The more I fell for this woman the greater the pull was to protect her. But I couldn't clip those wings. I'd take myself out before I did. She'd had it happen too many times before.

"Do me a favor and call or text when you head somewhere new?"

It was a compromise—the best I could do.

Shiloh stretched up onto her tiptoes and brushed her lips against mine. "I can do that."

I forced myself to let her go as she tugged out of my arms, but it was the hardest thing I'd done in recent memory.

My phone buzzed, and I pulled it from my pocket. Shiloh should just be getting to her parents', so I didn't think it was her. The alert for the front gate flashed. I pulled up the camera, and Aidan's truck came into view. I hit the button to open the gate and shoved my phone back into my pocket.

I turned back towards Onyx, and she eyed me warily. Slowly, I raised my hand to stroke her neck. "I'll be back. And I promise Shiloh will be, too. I know you like her way better, but we gotta get you used to all sorts. Even ornery bastards like me."

Onyx huffed and turned her head away as if to say, "*Please, don't make me lower myself to that level.*"

I couldn't help but grin as I headed for the fence and ducked between the rails. We were making progress. It was slow and sometimes awkward, but it would all be worth the hardship in the end.

Gravel crunched as Aidan's truck approached. He pulled to a stop in front of the round pen and climbed out.

"Hey, wasn't sure if you were working today."

He shrugged. "The Millers were taking Elliott to the park with a family across the street. They have a kid who's in the same grade."

"Well, I'll be glad to have the extra set of hands."

Aidan shuffled his feet, kicking at a piece of gravel, but his gaze was everywhere. Searching.

"You okay?"

His attention snapped back to me, and I saw the strain in his eyes. "Is Shiloh okay?"

I'd made an excuse for why I'd had to leave last night, not wanting to scare Aidan or Elliott. "What do you mean?"

His jaw clenched. "I heard Sandy on the phone talking to a friend this morning. Someone attacked Shiloh?"

I mentally cursed the gossip mill in our small town. When the police and EMTs responded to a call, it was impossible to stop the news from traveling. But this had to be a record.

I leaned against the fence and met Aidan's stare. "Shiloh's completely fine. Just has a bit of a headache."

"Then where is she?"

"She went to visit her parents. She knew they'd be worried about her and wanted to reassure them."

Aidan nodded, toeing a piece of gravel with his boot. "Someone hit her."

Shit. I gripped Aidan's shoulder. "And she fought right back. Kneed the guy in the balls."

His expression brightened a fraction at that news. "That's good."

"She's fierce. No one is going to take her out."

I had to hope that was the truth. Shiloh was stronger than anyone I'd ever met, but the rest of the world didn't always fight fair.

Aidan swallowed visibly. "Do you think it was my dad?"

His voice shook as he asked the question, showing such bravery in giving voice to his worst nightmares.

I wouldn't lie. That wouldn't help. Not when I wanted Aidan to trust me. "We don't know. It could've been a few people."

"But my dad's one of them."

"Hayes is going to ask him some questions."

Aidan kicked another piece of gravel, this time harder. "He'll just lie. He gets away with everything."

"Not with hurting his horses. Not with hurting you. He's gonna pay for both. And if he hurt Shiloh, he'll pay for that, too. We all know the truth about him now. The sheriff's department knows the truth. They're going to stop him."

The irony that I was placing my hope in law enforcement wasn't lost on me. But I'd seen the determination in Hayes—and also the kindness. He'd do whatever he could to help.

"She'll never forgive me if it was him," Aidan said softly.

My ribs tightened, making it hard to pull in a full breath. "Aidan. Shiloh would never blame you for something your father did. Not in a million years."

"You don't know that."

"I do."

Aidan lifted his stubborn gaze to me. "How?"

"One of Shiloh's best friends. Her name is Everly."

He nodded for me to continue.

"Her father kidnapped Shiloh when she was ten. Shiloh loves her like a sister." I'd seen it in the way she talked about the woman and her willingness to be a part of a wedding that I knew would be a struggle for her.

Aidan's jaw dropped. "Are you for real?"

"Real as it gets. Shiloh sees you for who you are, and that's an incredible young man who gave everything for his little brother. Nothing will ever change that."

Chapter Twenty-Eight

Shiloh

I PULLED INTO A MAKESHIFT SPOT IN FRONT OF MY PARENTS' house, but I didn't turn off the engine or make any move to get out of the vehicle. I simply sat and stared at the home I'd grown up in. The front steps where my brothers, sister, and I had played a game where we had to jump a certain distance to avoid *sharks* in the water. The rockers I'd often escaped to after a particularly bad nightmare, the sky being my one comfort. The front door I knew would always be open for me.

Swallowing hard, I switched off the engine. The only sound as I opened my door was that of the ranch: wind rustling the leaves, the faint strains of the cattle's call, birds overhead.

Both of my parents' cars were here. I looked at the front windows but didn't see any sign of movement. I pulled out my phone and opened my texts.

Hayes: *They're up to date. They're worried but dealing.*

My stomach twisted in a series of intricate knots, the kind you weren't sure could ever be unraveled. I'd brought this on. Me. If

I'd just been honest since the beginning, maybe they wouldn't be hurting so much.

I forced my feet into action, carrying me up the steps and towards the front door. My hand stilled on the knob a few beats before I twisted it open.

"Anyone home?" I called as I stepped inside.

"In here," my dad answered.

I steeled myself as I headed towards the living room and his voice. Normally, he'd be out with the cattle or horses at this time of day. But he wasn't working alongside the ranch hands. He was home. Waiting for me.

As I stepped into the open living and dining space, I took in my parents. They looked older, lines of strain around their eyes and mouths, and I knew I'd been the one to put them there.

I tried my best to get my mouth to curve into a smile but knew it came off as more of an awkward grimace. "Hey."

My dad scanned my face, zeroing in on the deepening bruise around my eye. He stood, making his way to me, but stopped just a foot short. "Shy."

I felt the need in him to touch me, to make sure I was okay, but he held himself back. For me. I stepped closer, wrapping my arms around his waist and squeezing hard. "I'm okay. Really."

His arms were tentative at first, encircling me lightly as if I were made of glass. "I'm sorry this happened."

"It's over. And I'm fine." Except it wasn't over. Not really.

I stepped out of my dad's hold. His eyes shone with unshed tears. My mom looked on with shock and awe filling her expression. I crossed to her on the couch and leaned down. I gave her a quick hug and a kiss on the cheek, then quickly squeezed her hand before I took a seat in one of the overstuffed chairs.

My heart hammered in my chest. I'd been waiting for that sensation to come, the one that grated against my skin with touch. But it didn't come.

My mom blinked a few times. "You're okay?"

I nodded. Better than I'd been since before the kidnapping,

even though things were messier than ever. Even with the threats and the attack and having to spill the truth to my family, I was better than okay. I was *good*. *Happy*. It felt like I was truly living for the first time in years.

"I'm good. And I'm not just saying that."

My mom dabbed at her eyes. "I can see that."

Dad cleared his throat as he sat next to Mom, taking her hand. "Why didn't you tell us?"

I heard the hurt lacing his words. Not being able to protect his family killed something in a man like my father. And my kidnapping had been the worst kind of blow. Knowing that someone had been taunting and terrorizing me years later was almost too much for him to bear.

My fingers tightened around the chair's cushion, digging in deep. "I wanted to deal with it myself. I didn't want to lose what little freedom I had. And if I'd told you…"

"We would've locked everything down again," my mom finished for me. She shook her head, her gaze traveling to the back windows to stare out at the ranch. After a moment, she turned back to me. "I'm so sorry. I know I didn't handle any of this well. I've had a few sessions with my therapist, trying to unpack it all. I could explain my reasons but—"

"I get it. I promise. I know all of this is hard. I should've told you so many things. But I couldn't find the words."

Dad's throat worked as he swallowed. "Did Howard Kemper—did he—?"

"No. I swear on my life, nothing like that happened. He just… he told me he was going to marry me off to his son." I searched for what I wanted to say next—what I had realized through my conversations about it with Ramsey. "I think that messed with my head more than I realized. Made me scared of relationships."

My mom sat up straighter. "Of course, it did. You may not have known everything marriage entailed at ten, but some part of you knew that what he was saying was wrong. And as you got older, you put more of those pieces together." She squeezed my dad's hand tighter. "We should've seen it. Realized there was more to what happened."

"This isn't your fault."

"It's none of our faults," Dad said as he let out a long breath. "All we can do now is be honest with one another going forward. No more secrets, no more locking you away for your protection."

Mom nodded and searched my face. "What do you need, Shy? From us, I mean. I want to help, but I don't want to hurt you in the process of trying to do that."

My eyes and throat burned. She'd never asked that before. She'd always just done what she needed to make herself feel better. Safer. I didn't blame her for it. Losing a child, even just for a few days, changed a person.

I dug my fingers deeper into the chair. "I need you to trust me and my judgment. I need you to let me live."

Tears filled my mom's eyes, but she nodded. "I trust you. It was never about that. I let my fear get the best of me."

"We all did," Dad added.

He was right. I'd done the same, just in different ways. "I'm trying not to live in fear anymore. I don't want it to control me."

"That's good, Shy. Real good."

Mom smiled. It was a little wobbly around the edges, but it was motivated by genuine emotion and not fake in the slightest. "Do you want to tell me about this new life you're building? Hadley said you've befriended a wolf-dog."

I couldn't hold in my laugh. "Kai. He's a total sweetheart. And the horses at Ramsey's are amazing. They've all been through so much, but they're fighting for a new life, too."

My dad looked at me, and I saw so much unspoken emotion in his dark blue eyes. "It sounds like you've found the perfect place for yourself."

"I think I have."

The sun hit my face as I stepped out of the feed store. For the first time, it truly felt like spring—the kind of weather that could bring new blooms. And with them, new beginnings. I hoisted the bag onto my hip. I'd run out of Sky's favorite treats, and she wouldn't be happy with me if she had to go without for very long. I'd gotten a few other kinds to see what Onyx liked best, as well.

A flicker of motion caught my attention. The man's gait, the way he moved, triggered my brain first. He strode across the pavement as if he owned it, his eyes trained directly on me. And they were full of hatred.

My heart pounded against my ribs. I could've run, hurried back into the store, and slipped into the back office until he left. But I wouldn't cower. Not to Ian Kemper.

He stopped just a step away, his nostrils flaring as his gaze swept over me.

I fought the urge to shudder, memories of all those years ago and the recent attack flashing in my mind. But I stood my ground and met his stare. I wouldn't waver.

Ian's jaw worked back and forth. "You killed him. You and my bitch of a sister. He died in that hellhole, thanks to you. Never even made it to the hospital."

I simply stared at him, not saying a word. Nothing I could say would make Ian realize that his father was responsible for his own demise. My words only gave another piece of me away, and Ian and his father already had enough.

Another man snickered as he stepped up next to Ian. "Heard she was messed up in the head. Can't even talk."

My eyes narrowed on him. He was older than Ian, likely in his late forties. Taller and broader, too. But his eyes held a hollow quality. Sunken and lifeless.

Ian leaned forward. "You were never what he thought you were. Not special. The only thing you are is worthless."

Images battered the walls I'd constructed in my mind, memories of sheer terror. I forced them down and stared at Ian. "The only worthless one here is you."

"Not even worth that sandwich he tried to give you to keep you alive. Should've taken you out back and shot you when I had the chance."

Blood roared in my ears. "That chance is past. I fight back now."

The man next to him choked on a laugh. "Damn, girl's got some fire in her. Maybe Howard wasn't wrong about her, after all."

The flare of appreciation I saw in his eyes had me swallowing bile. I needed to get away. Now.

I hurried around them, but Ian lashed out, grabbing my arm. I reacted on instinct. My hand came up in a palm strike straight to his nose.

Ian released me, letting out a curse as blood gushed down his face.

I didn't wait, I just picked up to a jog. I was halfway down the block, not sure where I was going, when I pulled my phone from my pocket. I hit Ramsey's contact before I even knew I'd made the decision.

He picked up on the second ring. "Leaving the feed store?"

"I-I ran into Ian and another guy."

"Where are you? Did they touch you?"

"He grabbed my arm, and I hit him in the face. I'm fine. I just needed…" I needed Ramsey. To hear his voice. To feel his comfort.

"Go to the sheriff's department right now. Don't stop until you're there."

I looked around and realized that I was already headed in that direction. "I'm going."

"I'm on my way. Stay on the phone with me until you get there."

"Okay." My voice cracked on the word, and I hated the show of weakness.

"Shiloh?"

My body started to shake as the adrenaline left my system. "Yeah?"

"You're not alone."

Chapter Twenty-nine

Ramsey

MY TIRES SCREECHED AS I PULLED INTO A PARKING SPACE at the sheriff's department. I yanked the keys out of the ignition, my hands trembling with the movement, but I barely had time to register the fury blasting through my system because I was already running up the front steps.

It was a miracle I'd made it to the station in one piece. I didn't remember most of the drive there. All I knew was that I'd yelled something half-intelligible to Aidan and took off for my truck.

Yanking open the door, I charged inside. "Hayes?"

The question came out as more of a demand, and the young officer behind the desk casually placed a hand on the butt of his holstered service weapon. "Do you have an appointment?"

I wondered if he'd shoot me if I went for the door that likely led to the offices. This all wasted too much time.

The door swung open, and a woman with inky black hair and features that spoke of her indigenous ancestry stepped through. "I've got him, Smith." She inclined her head in an order for me to follow her. I didn't hesitate.

She wove her way through a sea of desks, about two-thirds full. Some officers ignored us, while others stared blatantly.

"Shiloh's fine. Hand might be smarting a little, but that's it."

I didn't say a word, but fury blazed to life again, pumping through my system, heating my blood, and squeezing my heart.

The officer knocked on a door that read *Sheriff Easton*.

"Come in," Hayes said.

She opened the door but didn't enter, stepping aside so that I could pass.

I moved quickly, my gaze immediately going to Shiloh. She turned her head in my direction, and those ice-blue eyes were like a sucker punch to the gut, though not in the usual way that had me fighting attraction—in a way that had me wanting to commit murder.

There was fear—I read it the same way I did in the horses that came to me from the worst circumstances—and Ian Kemper had put it there.

I moved on instinct, not caring that we were in her brother's office. I lifted Shiloh into my arms and deposited her back on my lap. I needed to hold her and make sure she was okay. I thought she'd give me hell for the move, but instead, she curled herself around me, pressing her face into the crook of my neck.

I held her tightly against me. "You're okay."

"I know."

I'd said the words more to reassure myself than her. I rubbed a hand up and down her back, the ridges in her spine pressing against my palm. I closed my eyes for a moment, concentrating on the feel of Shiloh breathing, the rise and fall of her chest against mine. She was here and whole.

When I opened my eyes, Hayes stared back at me, assessing. I didn't look away. I let him read whatever he needed to. I wouldn't hide what I felt for Shiloh. Even if I hadn't given it a name, I knew the burn it left in its wake would change me forever.

After another minute, Shiloh squirmed. I didn't want to let her go, and it took everything in me to loosen my hold and let her slide into the chair next to me. I framed her face in my hands. "You're really okay?"

She dropped her forehead to mine. "It rattled me."

Those three words cracked something deep inside me. Typically, Shiloh wouldn't share something like that, but she was trying—with her brother and me.

I swept my thumbs across her cheeks. "Of course, it did. You're human."

Shiloh straightened, and as my hands fell away from her cheeks, she linked her fingers with mine and squeezed.

Hayes cleared his throat. "Can you walk me through it? I need to get it down for the report."

I bit back the curse I wanted to hurl at him, reminding myself that Hayes was only doing his job.

Shiloh nodded and started talking, slowly at first and then picking up speed. Each revelation had fury burning brighter inside me. I gripped the arm of the chair with my free hand as Shiloh described Ian grabbing her.

Hayes looked up from his notepad, his mask firmly in place. "It could've been him who grabbed you last night. Could you tell if it was the same person?"

Shiloh shook her head, frustration lighting her features. "It could've been him, but I can't say for sure."

Hayes nodded. "And you didn't recognize the other man?"

"I've never seen him before. He was older. Maybe in his forties or fifties. Dead eyes."

A chill ran down my spine.

Hayes' eyes flared. "Hold on." He searched a stack on his desk, pulling out a folder. He thumbed through it and plucked a photo from the pages, turning it around to face Shiloh.

She sucked in air. "That's the guy. How do you have a photo of him?"

Shiloh was right. The man *did* have dead eyes, the kind of hollow that made you wonder if a person had a soul.

Hayes' silence had me glancing up. A look of worry passed over his features before he covered it with the mask again.

"That's August Ernst. Howard Kemper's old cellmate."

⌒

"Are you sure about this?" Shiloh asked, worrying that spot on the inside of her cheek.

I couldn't deny the twitchiness that had taken up residency in my muscles, but that didn't change my resolve. "I'm sure."

She glanced in the direction of the front gate. "It's not like you don't already have security in place."

And that security was decent, but it wasn't the best. Beckett's friend, Holt, had assured him that he worked with someone who could give us the best. "I've been wanting to beef up my system, and I looked up Holt's security company. He's the real deal. And he said he'd bring a friend who knows the technical pieces of security systems, inside and out."

Shiloh was quiet as her gaze traveled around the ranch, landing on Onyx. After her run-in with Ian and August yesterday, she hadn't wanted to talk about it anymore. She'd lost herself in working with the mare, deepening their bond and giving the horse the gift of understanding and the knowledge that she wasn't alone.

I hadn't pushed to talk more last night. I'd simply held her on the couch as we watched the fire dance in the fireplace. I did my best to keep any evidence of worry from my face.

But the fact that I'd agreed to let strangers onto my property was evidence enough that fear had ground its way deep into my gut—terror that someone could get to Shiloh when I wasn't around. She didn't leave my ranch much. And, usually, it was to go and see her family or run to the store. She wouldn't be making those trips alone anymore. And if I could make my property a fortress, whoever was responsible wouldn't have an opportunity to get to Shiloh. Because, after two attacks in twenty-four hours, I wasn't taking any chances.

I moved towards her. The pull to wrap my arms around her was too strong, and I had to give in to it. Shiloh felt so damn small in my hold. Fragile. But I knew that was only an illusion. She was fire and steel, and I had to remind myself of that.

My lips ghosted over her hair. "I'd do anything for you."

She swallowed hard. "But you shouldn't have to. I can go back to my family's place if that's easier—"

My arms tightened around her, cutting off her words. I forced myself to loosen my hold, tipping my head down to take in her face. "Do you want to go back?" I couldn't bring myself to say *home* because, in my mind, *this* was her home. With me.

Emotions warred on her face. "No. But I don't want to be a burden on you either."

I brushed the hair away from Shiloh's face, aching to kiss her. "You could never be a burden."

She stretched up onto her tiptoes and pressed her mouth to mine. It was a featherlight contact, but heat still swept through me, my entire body going taut. Her fingers twisted in my flannel shirt as she lowered herself back to her heels. "Thank you. I know this isn't easy. But I don't want to leave, and this will put my family's minds at rest."

"It'll make me feel better, too."

Shiloh rolled her eyes. "I don't need some fancy security system. I have Kai."

My dog's ears twitched at the sound of his name, and he pushed into her side. He seemed to sense our worry because he'd been sticking close both yesterday and today. There was no roaming around and chasing rabbits. He was locked to Shiloh's side like glue.

"That helps, too."

My phone signaled in my pocket. I opened my security app, and the video screen flared to life. I couldn't fight the tightening in my gut at the three SUVs waiting for entry, mostly full of people I'd never met. My finger hovered over the button to open the gate. For Shiloh, I tapped it.

She pressed against my side. "Beckett said they should only be here for a few hours."

"They can stay as long as they need to." Because I'd meant what I'd said: I'd do anything for Shiloh.

The line of SUVs pulled up to the barn, and six men and two women poured out. I recognized Hayes, but I instantly assessed the rest. Some were built in a way that let me know they'd seen action. It was evident in how they carried themselves and how they assessed everything around them. A couple immediately went for gear bags, and I had to guess they were from the security system company.

Hayes strode towards us. "Thanks again for doing this."

I lifted my chin. "I'm glad you guys know some people who could help."

My gaze caught on a man who strode towards us, a darkness in his eyes that told me that his life hadn't been all sunshine and rainbows. He stretched out a hand. "Holt."

I shook with him. "Ramsey. Thanks for coming."

"Hey, Shy," Holt greeted with a tender smile. "Good to see you."

She pressed harder into my side. "You, too."

Holt gestured to a man with dark hair. "This is my friend, Cain. He owns Halo and is going to have his people beef up your security system."

Cain nodded with a smile. "Wish I was meeting you both under different circumstances." He turned to Hayes. "I've heard great things about you and Calder from the COO of my company, Mason."

Hayes returned his smile, but it didn't reach his eyes. "Tell Mase I said hi and that he needs to get his ass up here."

"We'll all come back for a vacation next time. But you know you're always welcome in Sutter Lake."

"Sounds like a plan."

I cleared my throat. I didn't need polite chitchat. I needed action. "The system I currently have in place is Halo."

Cain nodded. "That will make this go faster. And the plans you emailed helped, too." He inclined his head to a woman and man pulling more gear out of an SUV. "We already have an upgrade laid out. If it's okay with you, we'll get started."

"Have at it." I wanted this place locked down as soon as humanly possible.

"Great. We'll let you know if we run into any problems."

My phone buzzed again. The video view of the gate showed Beckett. I gritted my teeth but hit the command for open.

A few moments later, he pulled to a stop next to the SUVs and climbed out of his truck. He strode towards Holt and pulled him into a back-slapping hug. "It's good to see your ugly mug."

Holt chuckled, and it eased some of the shadows in his eyes. "I'm only here for Shiloh and because you promised me some of your mom's lemon meringue pie."

"Yeah, yeah," Beckett said, slapping his shoulder. "You going to head home for a visit after this?"

Holt's jaw tightened. "Yeah. I'm actually going to stay for a while, too."

Beckett's eyes flared. "No shit?"

Holt shrugged. "Life has a way of forcing you where you don't want to go, I guess."

Beckett studied his friend for a moment. "But, sometimes, it's exactly where you need to be."

"For you, maybe."

"Boss, you want the dossiers?" a woman called from the SUV.

Holt shook his head. "I've got them on my phone." Whatever pain had been in his voice before disappeared as he pulled a cell out of his jeans. "I've got reports on Ian Kemper, August Ernst, and Kenny Chambers. I've been doing a deep dive into Howard Kemper and who he spent time with in prison. I want to check a few people out." He glanced at Hayes. "I sent everything to your email."

Hayes scanned the email on his phone. "This is great. Way more than I've gotten so far."

Holt sent him a mischievous grin. "It helps when you can bend the rules a bit."

"I didn't hear that," Hayes said as he continued reading.

Holt scrolled through the report on his phone. "None of these guys are good dudes. I'm glad you'll have tighter security here and two of my guys shadowing you—"

"Shadowing me?" Shiloh stiffened at my side.

Holt looked up. "I told Beck that I recommended a security detail until you found out who was behind this."

Shiloh glared at her brother. "And I told *him* that I've felt like a prisoner for too long already. I'm not going to have strangers following me around everywhere I go."

"Be reasonable," Beckett argued.

Her eyes narrowed. "How about you try listening? I've made it clear how I feel about this, Beck. I'm done living like I'm still a prisoner in that damn shed. I told you why I felt that way, but you didn't listen. You just did whatever you damn well pleased. But here's the thing, they need *my* permission to guard me because I'm a grown adult—"

"I know you are."

"Do you?" Shiloh pushed. She let out a breath, but I could feel her trembling next to me. It wasn't fear. It was anger. "Then trust me to know what's best for myself. I'm not a little kid anymore."

Beckett ran a hand through his hair, tugging on the strands. "I'm sorry. I just…it would kill me if anything happened to you."

His voice cracked on the words, and it was all he needed to melt Shiloh's anger. She strode towards her brother and wrapped him in a hug. "Something could happen to any of us at any time, but we can't stop living because of it. I'll be as careful as I can be without caging myself. I promise."

Beckett pressed a kiss to the top of her head. "Okay."

Holt glanced over his shoulder at the four people who had obviously been intended as Shiloh's security detail. "Let me regroup and come up with a new plan. We'll figure this out."

Shiloh stepped back towards me. "Thanks, Holt."

"No problem." He grinned at her. "It's good to see your fire."

Shiloh's cheeks reddened. "It's been nice to find it again."

I wrapped an arm around her shoulders and pulled her closer. I was so damn proud of her for speaking her mind and holding her ground. I pressed a kiss to her temple. "I have an idea."

She looked up at me. "Please, tell me it's not one of those chips that will tell you my location at all times."

I barked out a laugh. "No, but that's not a bad thought."

Shiloh smacked my stomach.

"How about we have your family over for a barbeque this afternoon? It might ease everyone's mind to check out the new security and see that you're handling all of this like a champ."

Shiloh's ice-blue eyes widened. "Ramsey…"

I pulled her tighter against me. "I think it'll help." It was the last thing I wanted—more people I didn't really know swarming my home—but I'd do it. For Shiloh.

Chapter Thirty

Shiloh

I POURED THE PASTA SALAD INTO A SERVING BOWL AS RAMSEY slid a platter of marinated chicken into the fridge. I couldn't help but study the space around us. I'd only been in Ramsey's house once, and just the entryway. If I didn't know Ramsey had a way with food, I wouldn't have thought the kitchen fit the man at all. It was light and airy with a massive range, a second oven on the opposite wall, a farm sink, and enough gadgets to sink the Titanic.

Warmth hit my side. "What is it?"

"I'm just picturing you in this space."

Ramsey grinned. "You know I like to cook."

If I'd forgotten, he'd made that abundantly clear when we'd gone to the grocery store earlier. When I suggested getting already prepared foods for the barbeque, he'd looked at me as if I'd suggested shooting him in the chest.

"And you're good at it." I licked the pasta salad dressing from my thumb. "Nothing I make ever turns out this good."

Ramsey wrapped his arms around me and pulled me in close. "I'll cook for you any time you want."

"Careful, I could get used to that kind of treatment."

"I want you to get used to it."

Apprehension and hope battled within me. I wanted that so badly, to rest in everything Ramsey was to me, the comfort he brought, and so much more. But it terrified me, too.

Like always, Ramsey seemed to sense that battle. He dropped his forehead to mine. "You've got the reins, remember? This is your show. Your pace."

"It's *ours*." I didn't want this thing between us to be solely mine. It had to be something we built together.

"Okay, it's ours. But you have to use the brake if you want it."

"I will." What worried me more was that I'd always be too scared to step on the gas. I wanted Ramsey with everything I had in me, but I couldn't seem to get myself to take that first step for more.

A buzz sounded, and Ramsey pulled his phone out of his back pocket. He tapped the screen a few times. "Your family's here."

"How's the five-angle shot of them?"

Ramsey chuckled. "Clear enough to see your mom brought that lemon meringue pie with her."

I simply shook my head. Within a matter of hours, Cain and his team had wired Ramsey's ranch to within an inch of its life. Cameras showed each fence line, and they'd put more on each gate. There were motion detectors around the houses and each of the outbuildings. No one would get onto this property without being seen.

Ramsey draped an arm around my shoulders and guided me towards the front door. "The cameras aren't exactly inconspicuous. That should be enough to keep people away."

I hoped he was right. But whoever was behind my attack wasn't exactly thinking logically. I had to believe that they would at least have some sense of self-preservation.

We stepped out onto the front porch just as four SUVs pulled to a stop in front of the house. "It looks like a presidential motorcade," I muttered.

Ramsey squeezed my arm as he held me close. "It'll be good."

I looked up at him, searching for any signs of regret. There was a hint of tension in his jaw, but that was it. He wanted this for me. Even if having a bunch of people in his space made him twitchy.

Elliott jumped out of Hayes' SUV. "Shiloh!" He charged towards me, hitting my middle with a force far greater than his size should've allowed.

I let out a soft *oomph* and looked up at Ramsey.

He shrugged. "I asked Hayes to pick up Elliott and Aidan, too."

I ruffled Elliott's hair. "I missed you."

"Me, too. I'll come to work with Aidan tomorrow, and we can hang. I missed Onyx, too. How is she? And where's Kai?"

Aidan shook his head, but a grin played on his mouth as he climbed the porch steps. "One question at a time."

Kai bounded out of the house in answer to one of those questions. Elliott dropped to his knees and threw his arms around the dog.

Hayes' eyes flared as he headed towards us. "I'll be damned."

"What a gorgeous dog," Everly said. "Is he a husky?"

"He's half wolf," I explained.

Her jaw went slack. "Well, he's clearly a love."

Ramsey glanced at me. "Shiloh brings that out in him, apparently."

Heat hit my cheeks, and I looked away.

Birdie charged up the steps, and her eyes narrowed on Ramsey. "You whisper to horses?"

His lips twitched. "I do."

"Ones that are wild?"

"Sometimes, they're wild. Other times, they've been in bad situations and need someone to help them heal."

She looked harder at Ramsey as if trying to see beneath the surface to whatever was below. "And you're helping Aunt Shy heal, too."

My heart gave a painful squeeze as Ramsey glanced in my direction. "He is," I said softly. I'd been given so many gifts since I found this place. It was an embarrassment of riches, really. But this healing with Ramsey…it was the greatest.

"I want to meet this famous Kai," my mom said as she headed up to the front porch.

Holt took the pie from her hands. "Don't want you to lose precious cargo if that beast jumps on you."

Mom laughed. "Always thinking with your stomach."

"Isn't that what we should all be doing?"

Mom shook her head and gave me a quick hug. Kai looked up at her, tongue lolling out of his mouth. She bent to give him a scratch. "You're the most gorgeous thing I've ever seen."

"He knows it, too," I said with a laugh.

She straightened and looked at the man next to me. "Thank you for having us, Ramsey. I'm Julia."

Ramsey held out a hand to shake hers. "It's nice to meet you."

My father stepped up behind my mom, squeezing her shoulders. "Good to see you, Ramsey."

"You, too, Gabe. How's Shadow treating you?"

"One of the best-trained horses I've ever had in my barn. In fact, I might be in the market for another horse or two."

"After we eat, I can introduce you to a few more who are ready for homes."

My dad nodded with a smile. "That would be great."

Holt looked down at the plate in his hands. "But we get pie first, right?"

I leaned back in the Adirondack chair on the back porch, taking a long drink of my lemonade. The sun had dipped below the horizon, casting the back lawn in a golden glow.

"He's good with them," Hadley said as she took a sip of her beer.

I watched as Sage let out a squeal of laughter as she ducked around Ramsey. They were playing some form of tag that I didn't completely understand. "It's that same gift he has with horses. That empathy."

"I can see it with those two boys."

My gaze moved to Elliott and Aidan. Elliott had teamed up with Birdie, and they were going after Beckett in a coordinated attack. Aidan watched with a huge grin on his face. They were more at ease tonight than I'd ever seen them. Maybe it was the knowledge that they were safe. Maybe it was being surrounded by a boisterous family that clearly loved one another amidst the chaos. Or maybe it was the haven that Ramsey had given them at the ranch.

I swirled the ice in my glass. "I think those three are bonded for life."

Kai let out a bark as he charged through the crowd, and I laughed. "Or should I say four?"

Hadley looked in my direction. "I think it's more like five. You're a part of it, too. He's different, even since that day I dropped Sky off. You've opened him up to people. To life."

A pang lit along my sternum. "I hope so because he's done the same for me."

"That's the best we can hope for. Making each other better, giving each other a safe place to land."

I looked out at all the people I loved gathered in one spot, laughing and enjoying the moment. This was a place that Ramsey and I had created, and it had come to mean everything to me.

I just hoped I could keep it.

Chapter Thirty-One

Shiloh

I PULLED THE BLANKET TIGHTER AROUND MY SHOULDERS AS the cold sank deeper into my bones. I didn't mind the crisp edge to the air, not when the sky was as clear as it was tonight.

Kai let out a snore as I tipped my rocker back and forth. I didn't once take my eyes off the sky. The stars seemed to glitter in a sea of deep purple.

I wasn't holding on to them for refuge this time. They weren't some desperate grasp at freedom. Because I'd found some of that for myself. They remained what they had always been meant to be: beautiful. A reminder to take a moment and appreciate everything around me.

My phone buzzed in my lap, and I forced my gaze away from the sky and towards my device.

Mom: *Thank you again for today. And you didn't ask, but I like him...;-)*

A smile played at my lips. Since when did my mom make winky-face signs?

Me: *I'm glad you like him. And Kai.*

Mom: *Kai stole everyone's hearts. Bring that boy to visit me next week.*

A full laugh escaped me at that. Kai just snored louder. He had been the star of the show. But Aidan and Elliott hadn't been far behind. My whole family had fallen in love with the boys, and I knew that Aidan and Elliott would have supporters for life. They deserved that and so much more.

I glanced down at the clock on my phone. It was almost eleven. I'd lost track of time, sitting on this precious porch of mine. My numb fingers should've alerted me that I'd been out here for over an hour. Ramsey had excused himself to get cleaned up, and I'd come out here to avoid the sounds of the shower inside. I didn't need the reminder of a naked Ramsey playing around in my brain.

Pushing to my feet, I bent to give Kai a scratch. He startled awake and stared at me, bleary-eyed.

"Went a little too hard today, huh?"

His eyes started to close again.

"Come on. Let's get you inside, and then you can go right back to sleep."

I gave Kai another little nudge, and he clamored to his feet. He made his way towards the front door but walked as if he'd had one too many shots of whiskey. I stifled a laugh as I opened the door.

"Can you make it to your bed, or do you need an escort?"

Kai had taken to sleeping with me, but he made a beeline for his bed by the fireplace tonight as if walking the twenty extra feet to my room was too great a burden. He collapsed onto the bed and started snoring before I even turned the lock on the front door.

I keyed in the alarm code on the fancy new panel and scowled at the device. It had been incredibly kind of Cain to install it, but it pissed me off that it had been necessary. And as much as I knew that Holt was a good guy, I didn't like having him in town either. Not when I knew it was because of me. But as of tomorrow morning, they'd all be gone, back to their homes and lives—and it would give me a chance to get back to mine.

I stood in the entryway and listened but heard nothing but Kai's snores. I moved towards the back hallway. Glancing to the right, I saw Ramsey's closed door. I frowned at it. The sight cut more than it should've. He didn't owe me a goodnight kiss, and he was likely peopled out from the day, but that didn't change that I wanted the brush of his lips on mine.

I forced myself to turn back to my room. I kicked off my boots and changed out of the day's clothes. Slipping into my robe, I headed for the bathroom. Shower and sleep. That would clear away the sting.

Stepping inside, I froze. The bathroom wasn't empty. Ramsey was there. In the bathtub. Bubbles that I was sure had once been plentiful were melting away, leaving that bronze chest on full display. He had his dark brown hair tied up in a knot with that leather cord I wanted to tug free. His muscular shoulders, while relaxed, spanned more than the width of the tub.

My fingers itched to touch. Yet I stood there frozen, unable to move closer or walk away.

Ramsey's eyes popped open, and those onyx depths pierced right through me.

I whirled around, facing the wall. "I'm so sorry. I thought you'd gone to bed."

"Shiloh—"

"I really didn't mean to intrude—"

"Shiloh."

I let out a shaky breath.

"Come here."

My heart hammered in my chest, but I forced myself to turn around.

He grinned at me, and it was devastating. "Hey."

"Hi," I squeaked.

Ramsey held out a hand. I stepped forward, linking my fingers with his.

"I thought you were taking a shower."

He shrugged. "Wanted to soak my muscles."

At that last word, my eyes traveled down to his chest. Then lower. "A-are you usually a fan of baths?"

Ramsey chuckled. "I don't think a few bubbles are going to challenge my manhood."

They definitely weren't. I swallowed hard as I lowered myself to the tile floor next to the bathtub. I swiped a finger through the foam. "I'm a fan of bubbles."

He arched a brow. "You want in here with me?"

There was hope in those dark eyes, but panic seared through me. He reached up and brushed the hair away from my face. "Hey, you don't have to do anything you're not ready for."

There was no judgment, no pressure, simply kindness and understanding. But I wanted more. I lifted my gaze to his. "Can I touch you?"

His eyes flared, a dark heat pooling there. "You touch whatever you damn well please."

My mouth curved. I reached out, going for the hair that my fingers had been itching to touch for years. I found the end of the leather cord and pulled. It came free with just that one tug, Ramsey's dark hair skimming the tops of his shoulders.

I sifted my fingers through the strands. So damn soft, but thick and strong, too. That juxtaposition was so like the man: hard but gentle. Fierce yet kind.

I wanted more. Wanted to know what every part of him felt like under my fingertips. I moved lower, my hand stilling just before I reached his chest. With a deep breath, I closed the distance. It was a riot of sensation, the prickle of chest hair, the smooth skin beneath, and the hard muscle below that.

I lost myself in exploring, tracing invisible designs and

mapping the curves of his body with my fingers. My hand dipped lower, circling a nipple.

Ramsey sucked in a sharp breath, and I froze, my gaze flying to his face. "Did I hurt you?"

"Shiloh, your hands on me? Best kind of pain I've ever felt."

Heat like liquid gold pooled somewhere deep. "Why don't you ever call me Shy? Everyone else does."

He reached out, his rough thumb skating across my cheek. "I don't feel like Shy fits you. It's not who you are to me."

Shy had always felt a little like an attack on my character after the kidnapping, on how I was dealing. "I like that you call me Shiloh." The sound of my full name from his mouth was deep and grounded but also free—everything I wanted to be.

"Good." Ramsey leaned forward, pausing in question. I closed the distance, and his mouth took mine in a long, slow kiss. His tongue stroked, pulling me forward and closer to him.

My hand dipped beneath the water, dancing over the ridges of his abdomen. I pulled my mouth away from Ramsey's, not because I didn't love the feel of his lips on mine but because I wanted to see his face. Wanted to know how my touch affected him.

As my hand moved lower, those onyx eyes burned.

My fingers wrapped around his shaft, and air hissed through Ramsey's teeth. The skin was so smooth, almost delicate. But he was rock-hard beneath that silk.

I didn't look away. "Tell me what to do."

Ramsey swallowed. "Firm grip. You won't hurt me."

I tightened my hold on him a fraction, and he let out a humming noise.

"Move your hand up and down."

I started the motion. It was awkward at first, but I watched Ramsey's face, paying attention to each change in his expression and every hitch of his breath. He didn't have to say a word, and I slowly found what felt good for him. And each stroke of my hand brought with it a surge in my confidence.

Knowing that I turned him on? It had me pressing my thighs together to relieve the ache building there.

"Shiloh," Ramsey whispered as I moved my hand faster.

That golden skin pulled tight across his muscles as I continued stroking. His head tipped back, his hips pushing into my hand. With a grunt and shudder, release flowed through him, and I'd never felt more powerful.

Ramsey's eyes fluttered open. "Best damn bath I've ever taken in my life."

Chapter Thirty-Two

Ramsey

WRAPPING THE TOWEL AROUND MY HIPS, I DIDN'T MISS the way Shiloh's gaze trailed over me. I wanted to touch her more than anything I'd ever wanted in my life. But I would never push. I couldn't bear it if I were the source of her fear. It had to happen in her timeframe.

I pulled the terrycloth taut and folded it over. "Stay with me tonight?"

The words were out before I could stop them. I watched for any sense of hesitancy on her face. Her fingers grasped the tie of her robe tightly, but she nodded. "I need to take a shower first."

Those everyday words were almost painful to hear. I would've given anything to step inside those shower walls with Shiloh and run my hands over that smooth, tanned skin. To feel the weight of her breasts in my palms and grip her hips as I—I gave my head a tiny shake, trying to clear the torturous images from my mind.

"I'll be in my room." I hurried from the bathroom like my ass was on fire. Too much temptation.

I closed the door behind me and sucked in air. Silence greeted me. I could picture Shiloh on the other side of that door, unmoving, both of us trying desperately to right ourselves after our encounter.

Kai's deep snores sounded from the living room, and it had my lips twitching. Leave it to my dog to bring me back to Earth.

I headed down the hall and into the secondary room. Moving to the dresser, I pulled out a pair of flannel sleep pants. I didn't typically bother with them, but since coming to stay in the guest cabin with Shiloh, I'd been donning them.

Tossing the towel into the hamper, I moved to the bed. The shower switched on, and the sound was like a cascade of bullets hitting my chest. I groaned as I slipped between the sheets and collapsed against the pillows.

I listened to the symphony of agony, taking note of every change in tenor. When something interrupted the water. When it switched tempo. And, finally, when it stopped altogether.

A blow-dryer switched on. I pictured that cascade of brown and gold as Shiloh dried her hair. Saw how the fairer strands caught the light as if she were right in front of me.

The hair dryer went silent. My gut tightened as I waited. One minute bled into the next, and I started to wonder if Shiloh had reconsidered when a soft knock sounded on my door.

"Come in."

The door opened, and Shiloh filled the space. She wore navy plaid sleep shorts and that damned t-shirt that hung off her shoulder, the one that was so threadbare I could see the curves beneath it.

"Hi," she said softly.

I pulled back the covers on the other side of the bed.

She paused for a moment and then started towards me. Climbing into the bed, she pulled the covers up to her chin, her hands trembling slightly.

I turned onto my side to face her. "Hey, you don't have to stay in here." It killed me that I might be the source of any kind of distress for her.

Shiloh shook her head and shifted so she was looking at me. "I want to. I just…it's new. I'm not good with new."

My fingers linked with hers. "I'm not always good with new either. I like my routine. Being in control."

She turned so that she fully faced me. "I have that same need for control."

"I think it's a given with what we've been through."

Shiloh's expression softened. In the past, I might've mistaken a look like that for pity, but I knew now that it was empathy, understanding. Her hating that I'd been through something like that. Her thumb traced circles on the back of my hand. "I want to understand better."

I searched her face. "What part?"

I felt a tightening in my chest that I couldn't deny. It wasn't something I'd talked about. I'd testified at my stepfather's trial, but other than that, I didn't go there.

Her thumb kept stroking my skin. "Everything."

"That's a lot of ground to cover."

Shiloh stared down at our joined hands. "Did you have anyone on your side?"

It wasn't a question I'd expected. Usually, people wanted to know the sinister details: How my stepfather had hidden his true nature for all those years. How awful prison had been. But not Shiloh. She still had hope—a prayer that I wasn't alone.

"The first day I was there, I got shivved."

Shiloh let out a soft gasp.

"My stepdad paid the guy to do it. To *welcome me*."

"Ramsey…"

I pressed on, wanting her to understand. "That kind of thing happened a lot in the time I was there. It makes it hard to trust anyone because you never know who might be on the payroll or who would be open to some cold hard cash lining their pockets. It's why I've always had a hard time letting people onto my land."

Shiloh's fingers tightened around mine. "I don't think I've ever hated anyone more than I hate that man."

"Don't bring that into your heart. Not for me."

Her eyes glistened in the low light of the room. "You were totally alone. I hate him for that."

"Not completely. I had a cellmate. Gaines. We had each other's backs."

Something in her eased at that knowledge. "What was he like?"

"Had an obsession with those snack cakes. All of his commissary money went to that. I swear the guy existed on sugar alone while he was inside."

The corner of Shiloh's mouth lifted. "You're not a fan of snack cakes?"

I couldn't hold back my grimace. "They taste like chemicals."

"Delicious chemicals."

I chuckled. "You sound like Gaines."

"I'm glad you guys had each other."

"Me, too. And the second year, we got Lor."

Shiloh pushed up higher on the pillows. "You met Lor in prison?"

"She ran a program where we trained wild horses."

That soft expression returned to Shiloh's face. "She helped you find your gift."

"She did." Those hours with Lor and the horses were my only true refuge during my time in prison. The only time I could let my guard down for a moment. Because with the horses, you had to. They could sense when you had your walls up. You had to let them see everything to gain their trust.

I shifted closer to Shiloh. "I won't lie. It was hell." I felt the crack of my ribs as a guy on our block slammed his foot into my gut. The slice of the shiv on my first day. The swelling of my face from another beating.

Shiloh's grip on my hand tightened. "I'm so sorry."

"I'm not."

Her eyes flared. "Why?"

"Because it led me here. It gave me the horses. Made me see

the truth about life. When you see the darkness, it makes you appreciate the light."

Shiloh stilled. "That's how I feel about the sky."

"The sky?"

She nodded, lifting her gaze to the window. "It always reminds me that there's hope. Those pinpricks of glittering light in a sea of inky black."

I didn't need to turn to follow Shiloh's line of sight. I could see everything reflected in those pale blue eyes. And in the moment, I was no longer alone.

Chapter Thirty-Three

Shiloh

I DREAMT THAT I WAS SWIMMING IN SUNLIGHT, FREE AND weightless and blissfully warm. I couldn't help the moan that slipped from my throat.

Soft lips surrounded by stubble pressed against my neck. "Sounds like that are sweet torture."

My eyes flew open. Not my bedroom. Not alone.

Strong arms tugged me gently against a rock-hard chest. Ramsey. I was drowning in him. His scent. His feel. His very being.

"I was dreaming," I said by way of explanation.

He grinned against my neck. "And what were you dreaming about?"

"I was swimming in the sun."

"Sounds like a good dream to me."

"The best."

Ramsey turned me so I faced him. "How'd you sleep?"

I ran through a mental inventory. "The best I have in years."

His smile widened. "Me, too. No nightmares."

My mouth pulled down in a frown. "Do you usually have them?"

"Every now and then. There've been less lately, though."

I couldn't help but hope I had a little something to do with that—even if the thought was ridiculous.

I heard a scratching sound, and the door to Ramsey's room flew open. Kai let out a happy bark and launched himself at the bed. Ramsey grunted as the dog landed on him, and I couldn't hold in my laughter. Kai licked my face and then his owner's, then rolled between us, burrowing in.

I wrapped my arms around the furry beast. "Morning, Kai."

"He stole my spot."

I looked up to see Ramsey full-on pouting. "Careful, your face could freeze that way."

Ramsey scowled at his dog. "I love you, but you're a damn woman-stealing cockblock."

That had me dissolving into laughter. It might be chaos, but this was the best morning I'd ever had.

"When I said no bodyguards, what did you think I meant?"

Ramsey sent me what could only be described as his attempt at a charming smile. "You don't like my company?"

I scowled at him. "I like your company just fine, but not when you're following me around like a Secret Service agent."

"I needed some stamps."

I arched a brow as I turned the corner from the small grocery store and headed towards the post office. "And I couldn't get them for you?"

"You don't know what options they might have. I need to pick my favorites."

I let out a growl of frustration.

Ramsey caught my elbow. "Shiloh."

I hated that simply saying my name in his low, rumbly tone had me melting.

He pulled me in close. "I don't want to suffocate you, but I *do* want you safe. Can you cut me some slack and let me stick close for a while? When we're on the ranch, I'll give you all the space and alone time you need."

The problem was, I didn't want space and alone time. I wanted Ramsey: the feel of his rough fingertips, the scent that was only him, the comfort of his presence. "Sometimes, it scares me how much I like having you close."

His expression softened, and he moved in even closer. "It scares me, too, but I'm not running. And neither are you."

"You sound sure about that."

"You're not a coward. You don't run just because it might make things easier."

Guilt fluttered in my stomach. "I used to do exactly that."

"You might've avoided hard conversations with your family, but you didn't *run*. You stayed at that ranch. And you're having those hard conversations now."

He was right, and a certain kind of pride came from that, from knowing that I wasn't stuck in the same patterns—I was changing and growing. I stretched up onto my tiptoes and brushed my mouth against Ramsey's. "Thank you."

He grinned against my lips. "That mean you're gonna let me follow you around like a lost puppy?"

"Yeah, yeah. Come on, Fido."

Ramsey chuckled, and we started towards the post office. When we were a few steps away, the door opened, and Kenny Chambers stepped out. The rage that swept through me had me struggling to catch my breath. All I saw was Aidan's black eye and Elliott's tear-filled gaze.

Kenny's eyes narrowed in our direction, but a grin played on his lips as he took in my still-black-and-blue cheek. "Heard you ran into some trouble. That's what happens when you stick your nose where it doesn't belong."

Ramsey's muscles strung tight. "What did you say?"

Kenny's grin spread into a smile. "Just saying your woman got what she deserved. She should've spread her legs for someone else. But maybe she already is."

Ramsey charged forward, but I gripped his arm tightly. "Don't. It's what he wants. Don't give him that power."

Ramsey struggled to get his breathing under control. "I hope you're enjoying your last weeks of freedom because you'll be locked up before you know it."

The humor fled Kenny's face. "A lot can change in a few weeks. You'd best remember that."

He checked Ramsey's shoulder as he stormed past. I tightened my grip on Ramsey's arm. "He's a lot of talk. That's all."

Ramsey looked down at me, a muscle in his cheek ticking wildly. "Unless he's the one who attacked you the other night."

The thought had my stomach cramping. There was no denying the cruelty that lived in Kenny Chambers. Maybe he'd seen me at the restaurant and followed me to my truck, determined to get payback however he could. "That doesn't fit with the letter."

"The two might not be linked."

It made sense. Maybe the letter was Ian playing with me, and the physical attack was Kenny. My head swam. The thought that more than one person might have it out for me made me feel twitchy.

Ramsey wrapped an arm around my shoulders and guided me into the post office. "Let's get your mail. I'll text Hayes when we're back at your truck and let him know what happened."

I nodded, pulling my keys from my pocket and opening my mailbox. I held my breath as I scanned the envelopes. Bill, junk mail, bill. No blocky lettering with no return address. Maybe one last letter was all I would get. Perhaps the change in handwriting and tone was simply an old man in failing health.

We stepped outside and started back to the truck. Heat burned the back of my neck, itchiness skating across my skin. I scanned the space around me, and my steps faltered as I saw Ian staring at me from across the street. So much rage billowed out of him it almost physically hurt to witness it.

Clearly, Hayes' conversation with Ian had done nothing but piss the man off more. That anger reminded me so much of his father's that a shudder ran through me.

"I've got you," Ramsey said quietly.

It was all I needed, the simple knowledge that I didn't have to fight my battles alone. And for the first time, it didn't grate to have someone at my back because I knew I would do the same for Ramsey. We were a team and far stronger together.

I took his hand and squeezed. "Thank you." I wanted to say more, to utter those three little words that said everything, but I held myself back. Instead, I picked up my pace. I wanted to be home with Ramsey in the little haven that now felt like mine, too—because he'd gifted that to me.

I beeped the locks on my truck, pausing as I approached the driver's side door. A pale-yellow piece of paper fluttered in the breeze beneath my windshield wiper. My stomach twisted as I plucked it free.

Jagged letters streaked across the page, each one full of fury.

WHORES PAY. ARE YOU READY TO LEARN THE PRICE?

Chapter Thirty-Four

Ramsey

I PACED BEHIND SHILOH'S CHAIR AS HAYES STUDIED THE letter. I'd tried sitting but couldn't manage it. Everything in me begged me to move. More than that, it clawed at me to end any threat to Shiloh.

"I can't tell straight off if this is the same handwriting as the other letter or different. It's clearly hastily done, and that changes the slant to the lettering." Hayes looked up from the paper. "Did you see anyone near your vehicle?"

Shiloh shook her head. "Not near my truck, but we had a run-in with Kenny Chambers at the post office, and Ian was staring at me from across the street after I left."

Hayes' jaw tightened. "Define run-in."

Shiloh repeated the encounter for Hayes, each word only intensifying the pulse of rage thrumming through me. *Just saying your woman got what she deserved. She should've spread her legs for someone else. But maybe she already is.* His words echoed in my head on an endless loop, and each pass had me clenching my fists tighter.

"It's time for a restraining order. I'll write up an emergency order of protection now. Hopefully, with your and Ramsey's testimony, a judge will make that permanent," Hayes said.

Shiloh glanced over her shoulder at me and then at her brother. "Are you sure that's necessary? Don't get me wrong, I don't want him anywhere near me, but this seems extreme. He's a bitter, angry man, who will be in jail soon."

Hayes leaned forward in his seat. "It's necessary. We have no idea how long a trial will take. If he breaks a restraining order while out on bail, he'll go right into lockup."

She was silent for a moment, so Hayes pushed on. "Right now, my best suspects in your attack are Kenny and Ian. With this incident today, I lean more towards Kenny, but I think it makes sense to get restraining orders on both. It might even be enough to get Ian's bail revoked." He dipped his head to meet Shiloh's gaze. "We need to take every precaution we have right now."

She worried the inside of her cheek for a few moments before lifting her gaze to Hayes'. "Okay."

Hayes reached over and squeezed her hand. "Thank you for not fighting me on this."

"I'm not trying to make things harder for you."

"I know that. I really do. And I know it's hard for you to bring more attention to yourself."

Shiloh stared down at her hands. "I'm sure someone will write an article about this."

He let out a long breath. "It's possible it might only end up in the police blotter at the back."

Shiloh's shoulders tightened as Hayes spoke, visible tension weaving through the muscles.

The local paper had run countless stories on Shiloh's kidnapping over the years, including coverage on each parole hearing after. I moved in behind her, digging my thumbs into the spaces along her spine. "I'm sorry."

"It's not the end of the world."

"They're vultures." And I knew exactly how it felt to have them circling, searching for any morbid detail they could find and not giving a damn that they were slowly destroying you in the process.

Shiloh leaned into my arm, seeking more contact.

Hayes cleared his throat. "I'll do what I can to keep this under wraps, but it'll become a matter of public record at some point."

Shiloh turned to her brother, her expression turning stern. "It's not on you. Don't take any more of this on your shoulders."

His lips twitched. "You sound like Ev."

"I take that as the highest compliment."

"You should." Hayes pushed his chair back and stood. "I'm going to get this dusted for prints. It's on a flyer, so it was obviously a heat-of-the-moment choice. They might've been careless enough not to wear gloves."

I hoped like hell that was the case and that we could finally know for sure who was behind these threats and send them away for good.

Hayes reached out a hand to me, and I shook it. He gripped my palm tighter for a moment. "Thanks for having my sister's back."

"Always." It was a vow, and he heard that loud and clear.

Shiloh stood, giving her brother a quick hug. "Thanks for everything."

"You need anything, just call."

"I will."

He grinned at her. "I'm actually starting to believe that for once."

She gave him a playful shove. "Get out of here and go get some donuts."

Hayes chuckled and headed out the door of the guest cabin.

Kai climbed out of his bed and moved to Shiloh's side, nosing her for some affection. She scratched behind his ears, but her eyes stayed trained on me. "You okay?"

"You get a disgusting letter, have to file a restraining order, figure out that your name might be all over the papers, and you're asking me if *I'm* okay?"

She shrugged. "You were quiet the whole time Hayes was here."

Because it had taken all my focus to keep my rage in check. "Just thinking."

"About how to get away with murder?"

I barked out a laugh. Only Shiloh could make me laugh when it felt as if I were burning alive. "I think you might know me a little too well."

She moved into my space, wrapping her arms around me and pressing her face to my chest. "Don't go murdering anyone just yet. Give Hayes a chance to deal with things the legal way."

"I hate feeling powerless. And feeling that way when you're in danger is a special kind of torture."

Shiloh's hands twisted in my flannel shirt. "You and I have both built this sense of control over things in our lives. But the truth is it's just an illusion. A façade. No one can truly control the world around them."

I rested my chin on Shiloh's head, breathing her in. "I think I've done a pretty good job this past decade or so."

"Because you locked out the world around you. Didn't let anyone in. There are people in your world now—ones you care about." She tipped her head back, searching my face. "Do you regret that?"

My hands went to her face, cupping her cheeks. "I could never regret you. Even when it hurts, I want to feel that pain because you make me remember that I'm alive."

Chapter Thirty-Five

Shiloh

"JUST LIKE THAT. PERFECT," I SAID TO ELLIOTT WITH A SMILE as I patted Sky's neck.

Elliott ran the brush over Sky's belly. "It doesn't hurt her, does it?"

My heart squeezed. Despite growing up in the environment this boy had, there wasn't a mean or cruel bone in his body. He was all goodness and light. It was the same miracle Everly had managed.

"She loves getting groomed. I think it feels like a head scratch to her." I reached over and demonstrated on Elliott.

He giggled. "That feels good." He focused back on Sky and his task. "Can I help with this every time I come?"

I glanced over at Ramsey in question. He and Aidan were bathing another horse. Ramsey squeezed out a sponge. "I've been thinking I could use some extra help with the grooming," he said.

Elliott's entire face lit up. "Really?"

Ramsey nodded. "We've got a lot of horses around here. It takes a lot of hours to keep them looking good."

"I don't think I've even ever counted them all," Elliott said.

Aidan grinned as he rinsed off the bay gelding. "Thanks, Ramsey," he said so quietly I could barely hear.

"It's me who should be thanking you guys. I can basically kick back and relax with all the help you've been giving me."

I couldn't hide my snort. Ramsey would never take it easy. This ranch and the horses on it meant too much to him.

Ramsey raised a brow as he stalked towards me. "You laughing at me?"

My gaze zeroed in on the sponge in his hand. "Ramsey…"

There was a devilish twinkle in his eyes that had me backing towards the open barn doors. "You wouldn't dare."

His lips twitched. "I wouldn't?"

I let out a shriek as he lunged. I dodged the first attempt to fling water at me, but then Ramsey caught me around the waist and squeezed the sponge over my head. The sound that escaped me was enough to send Kai running. He barked and yipped, wanting in on the fun.

"I got him for you," Aidan called.

I pinched Ramsey's side, and he released me with a muttered curse.

"Now!" I yelled.

Aidan aimed the spray nozzle straight at Ramsey and let it fly. Ramsey was soaked in a matter of seconds.

Elliott let out a howl of laughter, dancing through the stream of water with Kai. Ramsey wiped off his face, spluttering. I covered my mouth to try to hold in my own laughter.

Ramsey pointed the sponge at me and then Aidan. "Payback's coming."

I stuck my tongue out at him. "I'd like to see you try."

He moved so fast he was only a blur in my vision. Ramsey hauled me over his shoulder like a sack of potatoes. I squirmed, and he smacked my butt with a light tap. "Aidan, you spray her now, and I won't get you later."

"Get her, A!" Elliott shouted.

"Hey!" I cried. "Don't go traitor on me."

Aidan grimaced. "Sorry, Shiloh. I don't like getting wet."

The water hit me in a shock of cold, and I screeched in Ramsey's ear as he laughed full out. It was such a beautiful sound I didn't even mind the ice bath. I twisted and writhed until Aidan halted the spray.

Ramsey slowly lowered me to my feet, and each inch of friction sent a shiver through me that had nothing to do with the freezing water. Our eyes locked and held, and Ramsey brushed the hair out of my face. Closing the rest of the distance, he brushed his lips against mine. "A little ice bath looks good on you."

I shivered as I ran a hand through his hair. "You don't look half-bad yourself."

Kai barked, and I forced myself out of the hold Ramsey had on me. Elliott stared up at us, looking thoughtful. "She your girlfriend?" he asked.

Ramsey tugged me against his side. "She's more than that, but I guess girlfriend works."

Warmth spread through me at the claiming. I'd never wanted to belong to someone until this moment. The belonging didn't take away any freedom; it only gave me more.

Elliott frowned.

"You don't like that?" Ramsey asked.

"Well, I was gonna ask her to be my girlfriend. You kinda put a crimp in my plans."

I choked on a laugh. Elliott sounded so much the little man. I grinned at him. "I bet Ramsey will still let us go on dates occasionally."

He brightened. "Really?"

Ramsey kissed my temple. "I think I can make it work. But

first, I think we need to put the horses away. Then it's dry clothes and some hot chocolate."

I kissed the underside of his jaw. "Sounds like the perfect plan."

I moved from what the website called cobra pose into downward dog and breathed deeply. Yoga was supposed to clear my head, but it certainly wasn't doing the trick today. The article hadn't been on the front page or anything—it had been on the fifth, somewhere between a play-by-play of the high school baseball team's game and the list of community meetings. But for me, it might as well have been a billboard outlined in neon lights.

It had only been a handful of paragraphs, but the reporter had made sure to recount my kidnapping, Howard Kemper's arrest, and the trial. The subtext was something along the lines of: *Poor girl can't catch a break.* Then they dove into the restraining orders against Kenny and Ian.

Hayes had put them both in place, but it would be a couple of weeks before I had to go in front of a judge in the quest for something more permanent. In the meantime, they'd dredge up everything they could.

Just the thought of it had me feeling twitchy as if even on the safety of the ranch, in my precious cabin, eyes might be on me—ones that wanted to know everything they didn't have a right to know.

I pushed deeper into downward dog, feeling the burn of the stretch in my legs and back. I relished that bite. Chased it.

The front door opened. "Hey, Shiloh—" Ramsey's words cut off, and he stopped mid-step. "What are you doing?"

"Yoga," I said as I moved into warrior two.

Kai lifted his head at Ramsey's presence but didn't make a move to leave his bed.

Ramsey moved in closer. I could feel his eyes on me, heating each place they touched. "I didn't know you did yoga."

"I don't—or didn't," I gritted out. "But Hadley said it's good for clearing your head."

He studied me for a moment. "Not today, though?"

"Too crowded." I'd take Sky out later and go for a good run. That usually helped.

Ramsey brushed his lips against my bare shoulder. "I'm sorry about the reporter."

"It's not the end of the world." There was so much worse than a stupid news article.

"You're still allowed to be pissed off."

"But I don't want to be."

He arched a brow in silent question.

I switched sides with my pose, facing away from Ramsey. "I don't want it to get to me. I want to forget my name was ever in a paper to begin with."

"That's what this is? A search for distraction?"

"It was supposed to be."

Ramsey stepped closer, his heat radiating into my back.

"I don't think tandem yoga is going to be any better," I muttered.

He chuckled, and the sound sent pleasant vibrations against my skin. "I don't think yoga's my thing."

"You never know if you don't try."

"I've got a better idea." His hand skimmed down my side, and my heart picked up speed.

"What's that?" My voice came out as more of a croak.

Ramsey's hand stilled. "Do you trust me?"

"More than anyone." The words were out before I'd even consciously thought them, but they were the unequivocal truth—and they likely revealed far too much.

His lips skimmed my shoulder then traveled to my neck. "Best gift you could ever give me, your trust."

I swallowed hard. "It's true."

"Shiloh?" He whispered my name, his breath cascading over my skin.

"Yes?"

"Can I touch you?"

I tensed but didn't let myself stay there. I breathed through it, letting each exhale loosen my muscles further. "Yes." I wanted more of having Ramsey's hands on me. His mouth. I wanted it all—with him and only him.

The one word was all he needed. Ramsey bent and picked me up bridal-style, carrying me into the room we'd spent the past two nights in. He laid me on the mattress gently as if I were made of the most delicate glass.

His gaze locked with mine. "Need you to talk to me through this. Tell me if we're good. If we need to slow down or stop altogether."

I nodded.

"Words, Shiloh."

"I can do that."

He grinned. "Good."

Ramsey's finger traced the strap of my sports tank. "I might not be a fan of yoga, but I'm a fan of the gear."

A small laugh escaped me, but I was soon swallowing it whole when his mouth landed on my skin. His lips skimmed the shell of my ear then traveled down to my neck.

"So damn smooth. So damn beautiful."

My breathing picked up.

"You good, Shiloh?"

"Good." I swallowed again. "I like feeling your mouth on me."

My face flamed as soon as the words slipped out, but Ramsey just smiled wider. "I'm glad."

His lips traced the strap of my tank the way his finger had, but this time, he kept going. His mouth found the swell of my breast, skimming across the surface and sending a riot of sensations ricocheting through me. I was hot and shivering all at once, like a fever had caught hold and wouldn't let go.

As Ramsey's mouth teased, his fingers slipped beneath my tank, playing across the skin there. It was like some sort of symphony that I never wanted to hear the last note of. Goosebumps pebbled my flesh as I arched into him, seeking more of something I wasn't sure how to name.

Ramsey's hands went to the hem of my tank as he pulled back from me. I felt the loss of his mouth instantly, ready to beg for more, but his burning, onyx eyes had me choking on the words.

"Can I take this off?" There was a rasp to the question that had me pressing my thighs together to alleviate the building pressure.

"Yes." The single syllable was part breath, part word.

Ramsey's knuckles grazed my sides as he lifted my tank. My back arched, moving on instinct, rising as if to seek more.

He tossed the tank to the floor and stared down at me. His fingers trailed across my stomach, slowly making their way up to my bare breasts. The rough pads of his thumbs skated under the swells. "You feel so good. It almost seems impossible for you to be real."

I looked up at him, his focus riveted on me.

Ramsey swept his thumb along the underside of my breast. "But I'd live forever in the dream."

I felt that rightness, too. There were also nerves in the mix, but there was no fear. "Touch me."

It was a simple plea. Yet, it was everything.

Ramsey's eyes flared. He palmed my breasts, his thumbs swiping across my nipples.

I sucked in air as sparks danced along my skin. They left a trail in their wake, traveling lower to the apex of my thighs. "Ramsey…"

"Tell me what you want."

"More."

His hands left my breasts and hooked into the band of my workout leggings. "Yes?"

"Yes." There was no hesitation, only the quest for more of the sensations that Ramsey gave to me.

He tugged my leggings and underwear free, and then I was completely bare to him. I thought I'd be frozen. Terrified. But I was liquid gold, that amber heat pooling in different spots of my body.

It was Ramsey who stilled. He stared raptly, reverence on his face. "Shiloh...everything about you is a wonder. So damn beautiful. Don't think I'll ever be able to stop staring."

Ramsey's fingers traced up my thighs, igniting more sparks. All I wanted was for those sparks to catch flame. His hands hooked under my legs, lifting them so nothing shielded me from his view.

His thumb traced closer as his eyes came to mine. I spoke before he had a chance to ask. "Yes."

Ramsey grinned. A moment later, his tongue was circling that bundle of nerves. I nearly bowed off the bed. The sparks inside me intensified, so many I lost track of where they landed.

A single finger slid inside me, and my hips shifted to meet it. Ramsey's tongue circled closer to exactly where I wanted him most as his finger moved in and out of me. But I wanted more. Some part of me knew that what I craved was fullness, a completeness—one that would only come with one thing.

Ramsey added a second finger. There was a slight stretch, but I barely noticed it in my search for more. My fingers dug into his shoulders. "Ramsey."

He seemed to read it all with just his name. His fingers moved faster as his tongue flicked over my clit. Light danced across my vision, and those sparks turned to flames—a wildfire that cascaded over my body in wave after wave. I lost track of everything around me until, finally, I slowly came back to myself.

Ramsey grinned down at me as his fingers slid from my body. "That a good enough distraction for you?"

A laugh bubbled out of me. "I don't think there's a single thought in my brain."

But that wasn't entirely true. There were words to the warmth that still swirled around me. Ones I was still too scared to give voice to. But I felt them. And I knew they were the forever kind.

I held my hand up to shield my eyes from the sun as I looked across the round pen. "All right, girl. I'm sure you've had bad experiences with this kind of thing before, but I promise, I'm not going to hurt you."

Onyx stared back at me, a look of challenge in her eyes.

We'd made tremendous progress over the past few weeks. She was wearing a halter now. I'd gotten her comfortable with the saddle blanket and the soft brush. But the lead rope was something else altogether. And I needed her good with it before we could move her to the pasture with some of the other horses.

"I want to make sure you have friends. You want that, too, don't you?"

She only blinked at me.

I sighed, staring down at the rope in my hands. "I bet he was cruel with this." I took the rope and wrapped it around my shoulders. "See? No pain."

Onyx shifted her weight from hoof to hoof.

I ran my hands up and down the synthetic fibers, trying to convince her. Nothing about Onyx's posture changed. In fact, it worsened. She pawed at the ground, making sounds of distress.

I instantly backed up, throwing the lead rope to the side. "Okay, no rope. That's okay. You'll let me know when you're ready."

"Should've known you were a weak-ass little bitch."

I whirled at the sound of Kenny Chambers' voice. But he'd already grabbed hold of my hair, yanking hard.

I tried to twist my body so I could use my knee and shoot for his groin.

But the sting of a blade pricked my neck.

"Don't fuckin' move. You think you can steal from me? My horses? My boys? And then *you* get a restraining order on *me*?!"

My ribs closed tightly around my lungs. I couldn't suck in air. I tried to think, to come up with a plan, but nothing came to mind.

Kenny gripped my hair tighter. "What? Got nothin' to say now?"

The bite of pain made my eyes water. "You hurt me, and you'll never see the outside of a prison cell."

His hand released my hair and went straight for my neck, squeezing. "You're a message. I'll leave your body for that halfwit of a boyfriend to find, and then I'm going to Mexico."

Darkness played at the corners of my vision as I struggled to breathe. Flashes of the shed and Howard Kemper's hand around my throat flared to life. I slammed my elbow back into Kenny's gut. He howled in pain, the knife dropping to the ground.

Onyx reared, letting out a whinny.

I whirled and kicked, landing a solid blow to his ribs. But it wasn't enough. Kenny was on me in a flash. He knocked me down and then clambered on top of me, his hands closing around my neck again.

There was no air as I thrashed. Flashes of sky caught my vision, but as my world went dark, I knew even they wouldn't be enough to save me.

Chapter Thirty-Six

Ramsey

KAI WHINED AT ME, AND I SENT HIM A POINTED LOOK. "You're the one who wanted to come with me."

Usually, he stuck close to Shiloh, but when he saw me pulling out the fencing gear this afternoon, he'd come straight to my side. He knew it meant that he'd have a chance to run in the woods while I repaired the fence line. But he'd soon gotten bored and had been whining at me to move back in the direction of the barn.

"You can go on your own. You know that, right?"

Kai barked.

He wanted all his people together. I didn't blame him. "One more rail, and we'll head back."

My phone buzzed, and I tugged it from my pocket. The app for my Halo system flashed an alert. I tapped on the screen. It was a motion sensor on one of the cameras. My gut tightened as I pulled up the feed.

Cain had warned me that we'd likely get some false alerts from wildlife in the area, but I didn't see a deer or an elk when the video came into view. Not even a damn cougar.

A man scaled the fence and climbed over—one I recognized.

I was running before I knew what was happening, as if my body had put the pieces together before my brain had. I pushed harder, my muscles burning. Kai was at my side in a flash.

The barn and the rest of the ranch were too far away. I strained harder, my lungs crying out. I didn't give a damn. All I could think about was Shiloh. All I saw in my mind was her face. The way her eyes danced when she laughed or sparked with wonder when I touched her. How she'd changed everything for me.

The barn came into view, but I still couldn't see the round pen. I pushed faster, rounding the building. The sight that met me had panic tearing through me. Shiloh was on the ground, not moving. Kenny straddled her, his hands at her throat.

Kai let out a growl and a bark and charged—faster than I ever could have.

Kenny's head snapped up, and he whirled around. His eyes widened for a moment, and then he fumbled on the ground for something.

Shiloh coughed and wheezed, writhing on her side as Kai jumped through the rails of the round pen. My heart lodged in my throat as silver glinted in the afternoon light—a knife.

My muscles seized as I forced them to work even faster. I launched myself over the fence just as Onyx reared up with a loud whinny. The motion had Kenny's focus jerking away from Shiloh, but it was too late.

The mare struck his shoulder with a swift blow. Kenny yowled in pain. He raised the knife to strike, but I was there.

I caught him with an uppercut to the jaw. His head snapped back, but his arm came down, the silver of the knife flashing in the sun. Sharp pain bloomed in my arm.

I landed a second punch and then a third.

"Ramsey, stop," Shiloh croaked.

Only her voice could've broken through my haze. But I couldn't take my eyes off Kenny. He mumbled something, trying to sit up, and I leveled a final hook to his cheek.

Shiloh's hand fisted in my flannel. "You got him."

Kai let out a growl, baring his teeth.

I snatched the knife from Kenny's hand and instantly moved back to Shiloh. My hands skimmed her face, down to her neck, hovering where red marks encircled it. "Where are you hurt? Can you breathe okay?"

Sirens sounded in the distance, and I realized I must've hit the emergency alert in the app. I had no memory of doing it. All that had filled my mind was Shiloh.

She rested her forehead against mine. "I'm okay."

I hauled her into my arms, cradling her against my chest. I wanted to believe those words, but I needed to feel their truth. To feel Shiloh's breaths come and go. To feel her heat. Her life. I needed to know that I wasn't going to lose her.

I hissed out a breath as Hadley cleaned the wound on my arm.

"Careful," Shiloh ordered in a harsh rasp.

Hadley arched a brow. "You want it to get infected?"

"No," she muttered.

I linked my fingers with Shiloh's, squeezing gently. "I'm fine."

She scowled at me. "That asshole got you with a knife."

"It's a shallow cut."

"I should've let you and Kai finish him off."

Hayes groaned as he walked up. "I'm going to pretend I didn't hear that."

Shiloh turned her scowl on her brother. "He could always have a little accident on his way to the station…"

Hadley chuckled. "I forget how vicious she can be when she's riled."

"Like a rabid dog," Hayes agreed. "But you'll have to settle for jail with no hope of release anytime soon."

It wasn't enough. Not because of me but because Kenny had almost taken Shiloh from me. Stolen the light I'd found. The one person who could clear away all the shadows.

"Where's Beckett?" I asked.

"Right here," he said, rounding the side of the ambulance. His gaze immediately went to his sister, settling on the marks on her neck. "Did you lose consciousness?"

"Not really. Maybe for a second or two."

He gently probed her neck, and I didn't miss her wince. He set his medical bag on the gurney next to me. "Does it hurt to swallow?"

"My throat's a little raw, that's all."

"Have you had anything to drink?"

"I gave her some apple juice," Hadley said as she dried my wound. "Can you help me glue this guy back together?"

"Let him finish with Shiloh first," I cut in.

Begrudging respect filled Beckett's gaze as he pulled a penlight from his bag. He flashed it over Shiloh's eyes. "I don't think you have a concussion this time."

"I didn't hit my head," Shiloh said. "I told you, I'm fine. Can you help Hadley with the glue?"

Beckett rolled his eyes. "You two are a pair of martyrs." But he snapped on gloves and got to work helping Hadley.

She hovered her hands over my arm on either side of the wound. "I need to hold things in place. It might hurt a bit."

"If I take you into the clinic, I can numb you up first," Beckett offered.

"Just do it." I didn't want to leave the ranch, and I wasn't stepping away from Shiloh for a single second.

Kai pushed in closer to Shiloh and me. Hayes smiled down at him. "You've got some damn protective animals around here." His gaze lifted to Onyx in the round pen. "Feel like I need to give that mare a medal."

Shiloh stroked Kai's head as she looked towards her protector.

"She'd probably settle for some treats." She lifted her gaze to mine. "Sure you don't want the drugs?"

"I'm sure."

"Here we go," Beckett said.

Pain, hot and intense, tore through my arm as Hadley held my cut together. It only took a matter of minutes for the glue to dry, but by the time it did, my breathing was ragged.

Shiloh glared at me. "You should've taken the dang drugs."

I leaned forward and kissed her softly. "It's all done now." As I straightened, I looked at Hayes. "What happens next?"

"Chambers' bail has been revoked. He'll go to trial for child abuse. Then he'll be tried for what happened here today. I doubt he'll see the outside of a cell before he leaves this Earth."

I turned to Shiloh. So damn strong and beautiful, even though she'd been through hell. The punishment Kenny would get wasn't nearly enough. But it *was* something.

Shiloh leaned forward, resting her forehead against mine. "We're safe. That's what matters. He's going to rot while we get to *live*."

And I was determined not to take a single moment with Shiloh for granted.

Chapter Thirty-Seven

Shiloh

I PULLED THE FLUFFY, WHITE ROBE TIGHTER AROUND MYSELF as I leaned back on the couch pillows. Ramsey lifted my legs and deposited my feet on his lap. The fuzzy socks with their polka dots looked ridiculous, but I couldn't find it in me to care. All I wanted was cozy comfort.

I'd been cold all day. Even as the sun had shone down on us while the deputies swarmed the property, I'd been freezing. It was the kind of cold that sank into your bones and was nearly impossible to get out.

The long bath had helped, and Ramsey had stayed by my side the whole time, running the bath and pouring the bubbles. He'd sat with me as I soaked, not saying a word, simply giving me the comfort of his presence.

His thumbs dug into the arch of my foot, and I let out a moan. "Feel good?"

I nodded. "Heaven."

"Want anything else to eat?" he asked hopefully.

My mouth curved. "If I have one more bite of anything, I'll burst."

Ramsey had made homemade macaroni and cheese for me, my parents, Beckett, Addie, and Ev. Hayes and Hadley would've stayed, too, but they were on duty. I think my mom had fallen a little in love with Ramsey tonight as they worked side by side in the kitchen.

"You didn't eat that much," Ramsey argued.

I arched a brow in his direction. "Do you need to get your eyes checked? That was a trough of mac and cheese, a plate of salad, and two brownies."

His lips thinned. "Just make sure you have a full breakfast tomorrow."

I sat up, leaning into him. "Ramsey, I'm not hungry, and I'm perfectly fine." I wasn't sure how many times I needed to say it before the shadows left his eyes.

He tipped his forehead against mine, resting it there.

My phone buzzed on the coffee table. I let out a growl of frustration but straightened, plucking it up. Hayes' name flashed across the screen. I hit accept.

"Hey, everything okay?"

"Everything's fine. You with Ramsey?"

"He's sitting next to me."

"Put me on speaker."

I did as he asked but not without thinking about how much things had changed. Hayes and Ramsey trusted each other, and I would never take that for granted.

I shifted the phone so it was between us. "Okay, you're on."

"I got a visit from one of Kenny's cronies tonight."

"Who?" Ramsey demanded in a gruff tone.

"Al Johnson. I guess word of what he did already made it around town."

"Great," I mumbled.

"In this case, it *is* a good thing," Hayes said. "When Al heard that Kenny attacked you, he decided to come forward with some additional information."

"What kind of information?" Ramsey pressed.

A squeak sounded over the line, and I knew Hayes was leaning back in his desk chair. "The night Shiloh was attacked in town, Kenny and Al were at the Bar & Grill."

"I didn't see him there."

"Probably because they were on the bar side. But Kenny got a good look at you and started spouting off about you and Ramsey ruining everything for him. Went on a real tear, I guess. Al bought him a beer and got him calmed down, but Kenny left right after you did, said he needed to get home to take care of some things."

Ramsey's knuckles bleached white as his hand clenched around the couch cushion. "He's the one who jumped Shiloh."

"I'd say it's a pretty good guess. He's not talking, so we don't know for sure." Hayes' chair squeaked again as he moved. "I don't think he's responsible for the letters, though. My guess is it's Ian trying to mess with you."

"You're probably right." And as much as the letters had scared me, I felt a sense of relief for the first time in weeks at knowing that the person who had tried to hurt me was behind bars.

Ramsey stared down at the phone. "Do you think Kenny's lawyer will let him talk?"

"There's not a lot in it for them. We aren't going to offer a deal for information—not unless he wants to plead guilty to attempted murder."

Ramsey's knuckles turned white again.

"Thanks, Hayes," I hurried to say. "I really appreciate you calling." But Ramsey didn't need us rehashing everything that had happened. Not tonight.

"No problem. I'll call you tomorrow morning with an update. Get some sleep."

"Goodnight." I hit end on the call and set the phone back on the coffee table. I leaned forward and placed my hands on Ramsey's face. "Talk to me."

His eyes burned with a mixture of so many things I didn't know where to start in identifying them.

"I could've lost you."

The words came out in a low rasp, a guttural admission that cost way too much to speak out loud.

I moved in even closer, resting my forehead against his. "I'm right here."

"You almost weren't."

Each syllable was tortured, and I felt powerless to stop Ramsey's pain. I didn't have the first idea what words to give him. Instead, I gave myself—my presence, my touch.

My mouth met his, tentative at first and then seeking more. My tongue parted his lips, searching, giving, trying to assure him that I was here and not going anywhere.

"Shiloh." Ramsey rasped my name, the syllables vibrating against my lips. He pulled back, searching for something. "I love you. That word isn't enough, not for what I feel for you, but it's a start."

My lungs burned with the kind of pain you got when you took your first breath after diving too deep in a lake. It was bliss and agony all at the same time. Joy and terror.

"I love you, too."

He was right. It wasn't nearly enough, but it was everything I had to give him.

My palm pressed against Ramsey's chest. I felt his heart beat in a rapid rhythm against it, and I looked into those fathomless, onyx eyes. "I want everything with you."

"Whatever you want, it's yours."

The words came so easily for Ramsey, and without a moment's hesitation.

My fingers moved to the hem of his t-shirt. I tugged it up and over his head, then sent it sailing to the floor.

"Shiloh…"

"Everything." I poured all I had into that one word. I didn't want to hold back. I wasn't scared—I couldn't be, not with Ramsey.

Those dark depths searched my face again. "You're sure?"

"Never been more sure of anything in my life."

He moved then, so fast the air rushed out of me as Ramsey lifted me into his arms. My legs encircled his waist as he stood and strode to the bedroom. As quickly as he'd made it in there, he lowered me to the bed so slowly it was almost painful.

But I couldn't find it in me to ask him to hurry, not when he had such reverence etched on his face. My hand lifted as if it had a mind of its own. I had to feel that tenderness with my fingertips.

They sifted through the thick stubble, feeling the emotion beneath. The love. The acceptance. The trust.

"Never knew I could feel this." The words came in a husky whisper, but they rang with truth.

Ramsey cupped my face, his fingers trailing down to my neck and the opening of my robe. "I thought this part of me was broken. That I'd never have this with anyone. You're a miracle. Made me truly live again."

Everything in me burned, and all for this man—his touch, his love, his very soul.

Ramsey's hand dipped lower, cupping my breast and swirling his roughened thumb around my nipple. The shiver that ran through me was nothing but pure pleasure—the knowledge that I was alive and, like Ramsey, somehow unbroken.

I arched into his touch. Into *him*. My mouth found his, seeking all of him. I lost myself in the kiss, knowing that everything we had been through had made us somehow perfect for each other.

My fingers found the button of his jeans, boldly seeking that *more* I knew I was ready for.

Ramsey stilled. "Condom. I need—"

"I'm on the pill," I said, cutting him off.

He blinked a few times.

"I've been on it to regulate my periods since I was fourteen."

Ramsey's eyes bored into mine. "There hasn't been anyone for me in a long time. You're sure?"

I swallowed hard as I nodded. "I don't want anything between us. I want to feel everything."

I didn't want to miss a second. A sensation. Nothing.

Ramsey shucked his jeans and boxers and stepped between my legs. One hand went to the tie on my robe while the other skimmed up my thigh.

As my robe fell open, Ramsey stared down at me. I could feel everything in that stare, and my nerve-endings came alive under it. My skin heated. My soul sang.

His fingers played a symphony over my skin again, skating in nonsensical patterns as if he just had to know what every place on my body felt like. My breaths came quicker, short pants that begged for more.

Ramsey's lips hovered over mine as his fingers dipped between my thighs. "Yes?"

"A thousand times, yes." I sucked in a breath as he slid two fingers inside me, moving slow and steady. It was a million different sensations, and I rode out every single one.

Ramsey shifted, and my eyes locked on his hardening length. I couldn't look anywhere else, fascinated as it grew and changed. The first flicker of apprehension passed through me.

"Look at me, Shiloh."

My eyes shot to Ramsey's.

"It's you and me. We go as fast or slow as you want. We can stop at any time."

His kindness, his understanding, they only made me want him more. My hips rose to meet the tiny thrusts of his fingers. That brief moment of anxiety melted away into nothing but heat. "I want you. This. I want our everything."

Ramsey lowered himself to the bed next to me as his fingers continued to stroke. "Love you."

That heat spread. It was different this time. There was a steadiness to it, one edged in desperation. There was nothing I wanted more than Ramsey.

"Please." It was the only thing I could think to say.

Ramsey's fingers were gone, and then he was rolling on top of me, one hand framing my face. "I'd give you the world if it was within my power."

"All I need is you."

His tip bumped my entrance as my legs wrapped around his hips. Ramsey looked down at me, nothing but love in his eyes. He slid in slowly, and my fingers dug into his shoulders as he moved. There was a flicker of pain, but it quickly melted into that golden heat.

"Heaven," he whispered in my ear. He pressed his lips to my temple, causing more of that heat to spread.

My hips moved in small, testing motions at first, sending sparks cascading across my skin and somewhere deeper. Ramsey met me exactly where I was, first with gentle thrusts and then deeper ones.

My back arched, welcoming him in, asking for more. He gave that to me. His hips angled in a way that had light dancing across my vision. Then, his thumb circled my clit, and I was drowning in sensation. So much that it had me fraying at the seams.

But I didn't care. Every last piece of me could unravel because I was here with Ramsey. He was mine, and I was his. And he would always own my soul.

Ramsey groaned and thrust deep, right where I needed him. I gasped as I spiraled, losing sight of the world around me. But none of that mattered because we were losing sight of the world together, even as we found something new—our everything.

Chapter Thirty-Eight

Ramsey

I PULLED SHILOH AGAINST MY SIDE AS WE SAT ON THE FRONT steps watching the sunrise. I couldn't stop touching her—my fingers tangling in her hair, my lips on her neck. Anything to have just a little more of her. I wanted her imprinted on every part of me.

Shiloh nuzzled in closer as Kai sniffed around the grass in front of the cabin. "I want to spend some time with Onyx today. Make sure she's all right."

"We can do that." The mare munched on her breakfast in the round pen across the way, but I didn't miss how she glanced around. She was on edge, waiting to see if Kenny would return. It would take time, but she'd feel safe again. And she'd reclaimed some of her power by taking him down as she had.

My lips ghosted over Shiloh's hair. "What do you want for breakfast?"

She grinned. "Whatever you're making. If I'm making it, it's going to be cereal or scrambled eggs."

I chuckled. "Fair enough."

My phone buzzed on the steps behind me. I felt around for it and picked it up. "Hello?"

"Ramsey? It's Sandy Miller."

A lead weight settled in my stomach. "Are the boys okay?"

Shiloh straightened, motioning for me to put the phone on speaker.

"They're perfectly safe and healthy, but I'm afraid Aidan heard about Shiloh's attack from one of the neighborhood kids. He's real torn up. Blaming himself."

I muttered a silent curse. "We can come over to see him today."

"I was hoping you'd say that. I think it might be good if you and he have some one-on-one time before Shiloh comes over. You can reassure him before he sees her."

I glanced at Shiloh. She nodded, but I didn't miss how her fingers dug into my thigh. She wanted to see Aidan, too, to reassure him herself and make sure that he was okay.

"I can be over by ten."

"I'll see you then. Thanks, Ramsey."

I hit end on the call and set my phone down.

Shiloh stared out at the horizon. "It makes me want to give Kenny another knee to the balls for putting Aidan through this."

I ran a hand up and down her arm. "Aidan's strong. He'll make it through. We'll make sure of it."

"He shouldn't have to. How many times has he taken his father's actions on his shoulders?"

"Probably more than he can count." And the thought made me sick. "But that'll ease with time and distance. Once Kenny's in prison for good, those boys will really start to heal."

Shiloh looked up at me. "They deserve a good home. The best. And not just a temporary foster placement."

"You're right about that." It was something I'd been thinking about. The Millers were great, but they weren't a permanent home for Aidan and Elliott. And finding someone who would take a teenager and a six-year-old together would likely be a challenge.

"We need to talk to Hayes and see what he says about making sure they end up somewhere amazing."

"We'll go this week."

Shiloh nuzzled my neck. "Love you."

My chest gave a painful squeeze. "It's more than that."

She smiled against my skin. "It's everything."

I headed down the wide trail, Aidan at my side. I'd thought it might help to get out and moving, take the focus away from the pressure of a heart-to-heart. I'd discovered in the prison program that the words came easier when you were working on another task.

Sandy had been right about leaving Shiloh back at the ranch. I'd seen the relief in Aidan's eyes when he'd seen that it was just me. But I hadn't wanted to leave Shiloh alone after everything that had happened, so after much grousing, she'd agreed to invite her mom and Hadley over for brunch but not before saying, "If I poison them, their deaths are on you."

I'd thrown together a breakfast casserole and told her that she wouldn't have to worry about killing her family. I smiled down at my feet at the thought. Hell, I missed Shiloh already. Something was wrong with me.

"What are you thinking about?" Aidan asked.

I sent up a few silent curses. I needed to get my head in the game. "Nothing."

"You were smiling this big, goofy smile."

I grimaced. "I was thinking about Shiloh." There was no sense in denying it. Aidan could read a lie from a million miles away.

"Is she okay?" he asked softly.

"She is. She has a few bruises, but that's it. And I know she really wants to see you."

Aidan's mouth pressed into a thin line. "I wouldn't want anything to do with me."

"We've talked about this, A. Shiloh doesn't blame you for anything your father did. You're nothing like him."

Aidan's eyes reddened, but he didn't say a word.

I grabbed his elbow gently, bringing us both to a stop. "Talk to me."

He stared down at the dirt path. "I can get angry like my dad does. When I heard what he did to Shiloh, I wanted to pummel him."

My gut twisted. This kid was so damn hard on himself. Held himself to standards no one could ever meet. Yet that was one of the reasons he'd never be like Kenny. "Anger's natural. It's what you do with it that counts."

"If he'd have been standing there, I would've hurt him."

"Because he hurt someone you care about. There's nothing wrong with wanting to protect the people around you, the ones who are important to you. And it's understandable to want some justice for all the times he hurt you, too."

Aidan kicked at a rock. "I hate feeling all that...rage swimming around inside me. It's like it's eating me alive."

God, I knew that feeling. So deeply—even if it had faded with time. "I hate it, too."

He looked up at me in question.

"I felt that way every day after I got out of prison. Every day after my stepdad was sentenced, I drowned in that anger."

"How did you stop it?"

"I needed an outlet. Somewhere to release it."

A thoughtfulness spread over Aidan's expression. "Like boxing or something?"

"Could be. For me, it was the horses. I couldn't work with them with that anger coursing through me. I had to expel it before I set foot in a ring. I ran it out of myself with hard work: stocking hay, cleaning stalls, feeding, fixing fences. I let it flow through me while I did all those things. Then, by each afternoon, I was ready to work with the horses, and they gave me back a sliver of peace. That grew day by day until the anger wasn't eating me alive anymore."

"I don't know what my outlet is. I like working with the horses, though."

I gripped Aidan's shoulder and squeezed. "You may need to try a few things on for size. We can get you signed up for a martial arts class. Maybe something creative, too, like art."

Aidan made a face.

"Don't knock it. I've seen some pretty badass art out there."

"Maybe…" he said begrudgingly.

"And we keep working with the horses at the ranch. And, most of all, we talk. This stuff only has power over us when the shadows fester."

"I don't want to live in the dark anymore."

I pulled Aidan into a tight hug. "You don't have to. And even if things look murky, you just have to remember that you're not alone. I've got your back. And that's never going to change."

Aidan let out a shuddering breath, and I knew he was trying to hold back tears. He pulled out of my hold. "Why would you want to help me?"

"Because I know what it feels like to feel powerless and out of control." My mind flashed to Lor and the gift she'd given me with the horses. "Someone helped me find my way. I'd like to help you, too. But only if you want me to." It had to be Aidan's choice, or it would never work.

He looked up and met my gaze dead-on. "Out of the dark?"

I gripped his hand in a half shake. "Out of the dark."

Chapter Thirty-nine

Shiloh

HADLEY'S EYES NARROWED ON ME AS I MOVED AROUND the kitchen, cleaning up. "You're glowing."

I froze for the briefest of moments before continuing to load plates into the dishwasher. "Must be that new skincare regimen I'm on."

She snorted. "Please. I can barely get you to use sunscreen."

I bit back my smile as I continued with my task. "I've actually become partial to bubble baths lately." But only when Ramsey was involved.

Hadley stared at me, blinking a few times. "Bubble baths?"

I shrugged. "They're relaxing."

"I know that, but you haven't taken one since you were like seven." She pinched my arm.

"Hey! What was that for?"

"Just checking to see if you're real. I was beginning to wonder if you were some AI that had replaced my sister."

I glared at her. "I'm very real, thank you very much. But if I were an AI, I'd take you out first for that pinch."

Hadley didn't laugh as I'd expected. "You were attacked yesterday, and this morning you were basically singing as you served brunch. You didn't get annoyed when Mom started probing. You agreed to host a bridal shower for Everly with me. Who are you, and what have you done with my prickly but beloved sister?"

I straightened, leaning back against the counter. "I'm happy."

It really was that simple. Ramsey had given me the kind of joy I'd never thought to have. And not simply because I was in a relationship, but because he'd opened my eyes to so much. He'd helped me find the bravery to step into the unknown, and what was on the other side of that was more beautiful than I ever could've imagined.

Hadley sucked in a breath as her eyes filled with tears.

Panic gripped me. "Shit, Hads. Don't cry."

"You're happy."

"Yes?" I said it like a question, unsure if that would make her dissolve further.

She launched herself at me, pulling me into a hard hug. "I've seen the changes in you, little by little, but I can see it all now. You're living again."

I hugged my sister back, relishing the fact that I felt no grating sensation across my skin, no desire to pull free. I could enjoy this closeness with Hadley. "I am. And there's no going back."

"I'm so glad," she whispered hoarsely.

"Love you, Hads."

"I love you, too. More than I can say."

She released me and stepped back, her gaze sweeping over me. Her eyes widened a fraction. "Did you sleep with him?"

Hadley's question came out as more of a shriek, and I clamped a hand over her mouth as my face flamed. "Will you be quiet? Mom is right outside." Kai had conned her into a never-ending game of fetch, but she could come in at any moment.

Hadley's eyes widened further. "You did!"

Thankfully, my hand muffled her words, but I still glared at her. "Are you thirteen?"

She pulled my hand away. "No, I'm not thirteen, but I am nosy as hell. Was it good? Ramsey seems like he's the strong, silent type. Or maybe he's a secret dirty talker."

I pressed my hands over my ears and started humming. "I can't hear you."

Hadley grinned. "So, it's the dirty talk."

"Will you *please* stop talking?"

"I thought you couldn't hear me."

I scowled at her. "Apparently, your voice could cut through soundproof walls."

Hadley's grin stretched into a smile. "I like to make sure I'm heard."

I groaned. "No one could ever miss a word."

She threw an arm over my shoulder. "I'm happy for you, Shy."

The heat in my face was back. "It feels weird to say thank you to that."

Hadley barked out a laugh. "You should always say thank you for good dick. That spirit of gratitude will only bring more into your life."

My nose scrunched up. "You just had to take it there, didn't you?"

She shrugged. "I'm nothing if not honest."

"A little *too* honest…"

"Calder's a beast. He does this thing—"

I clamped my hand over her mouth again. "Stop. Please, stop. I will literally give you anything you want if you just stop talking right now."

Hadley stuck out her tongue, the tip touching my palm, and I yanked my hand away. "Gross."

"Hey, sharing is caring."

"Not when it comes to this." The last thing I wanted was mental images of what my sister and Calder got up to behind closed doors. I gripped her shoulders, leaning down to meet her gaze. "For the love of all that's holy, can we please talk about something else?"

Her shoulders slumped in defeat. "Fine. Let's chat bridal shower. Laiken said we could do it at The Gallery. I thought that might be fun. We could do a high tea theme. Several kinds of tea, little finger sandwiches, petit fours."

I collapsed back against the counter. "I already said yes to that girly-ass bridesmaid dress. You're going to make me go to some fancy tea, too?"

Hadley pressed her lips together to keep from laughing. "The dresses are gorgeous."

I stared at my sister. "They're pale pink. And they have that floofy fabric."

"Floofy?"

"That's the technical term."

"I think *gauzy* would be more appropriate. They're whimsical and fun."

My jaw clenched. "They're evidence that I love Everly more than I should if I'm wearing that thing."

Hadley patted my shoulder. "You're a good future sister-in-law."

That melted the annoyance in me more than a fraction. I wanted to be a good sister. And Everly deserved the wedding of her dreams after everything she'd been through. "Oh, all right, I'll do the damn tea, too. Laiken and I can be in charge of decorations if you and Addie can do food." If I had Laiken helping me, I couldn't screw things up too badly.

"Deal." Hadley motioned me out of the kitchen. "Let's go for that ride. It's too nice to be cooped up today."

I sent up a silent thank you. A trail ride was much more in my wheelhouse than awkward conversations about sex or weddings. "You had me at ride."

Hadley chuckled. "I had a feeling."

We headed outside just as Kai dropped his tennis ball at my mom's feet, letting out a happy bark. She smiled, shaking her head. "I swear he could do this forever."

"He definitely could." I turned to the dog, who was in the midst of a full-body wag. "Want to go for a ride, Kai?"

He leapt in the air, sending up another bark and turning in circles.

"Trail ride?" my mom asked.

"If you're up for it."

"I'd love that. It's been too long since I've been out on the trails with my girls."

Far too long. Before my kidnapping, we'd gone all the time. But afterwards, those trips had been fewer and farther between, my mom's anxiety heightened by what might happen. To be back doing something we all loved felt more than right.

Hadley reached down and gave Kai a scratch. "Only if we can run."

"Always giving me gray hair." My mom laughed. "But don't forget who taught you to gallop. I'll leave you in the dust."

Hadley's eyes twinkled. "We'll just see about that…"

She started jogging towards the barn, my mom immediately running after her. Kai chased them both, barking as he went. I grinned and followed the circus.

Mom and Hadley made their way down the rows of stalls in the barn, trying to decide on their mounts for the day. I pointed out a few that I thought would be good matches for them as I grabbed a lead rope. "I'm going to grab Sky from the paddock."

They waved me off as they playfully bickered, setting a wager for their race. It made me happier than I could ever express, seeing the two of them getting along so well. It had been a long road to that closeness, and it only made us all appreciate it more.

I headed out the back of the barn towards the paddock where Sky grazed with a few of her pals. I pursed my lips to whistle, but no sound came out. A hand clamped over my mouth.

Shock slowed the world around me. I took in everything between heartbeats. Quick snapshots. The cloth over my face. The sickly-sweet taste in my mouth. The hulking form behind me.

"Hurry up! Before they realize she's gone."

That voice sent panic through me, but I was already fading, losing my grip on everything. All I could think as the sky blurred was that the voice sounded familiar…

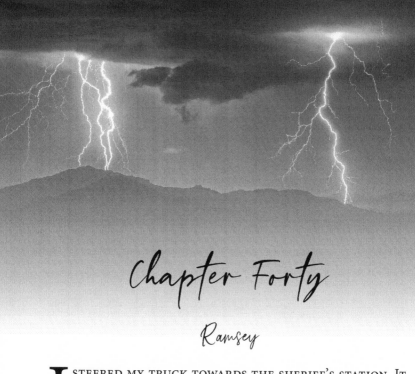

Chapter Forty

Ramsey

I STEERED MY TRUCK TOWARDS THE SHERIFF'S STATION. IT wasn't lost on me, the irony of this, that I was seeking out law enforcement headquarters without being forced into it. But Shiloh had changed everything for me. When she brought the light into my world, she'd illuminated everything around me. I no longer saw things in only black and white but all the shades of gray. And, more than that, she made things technicolor.

Pulling into an empty spot in the parking lot, I shut off my engine. I sat there for a moment, staring up at the building. I'd probably lost my mind given what I was about to do, but it felt right. The idea had been circling around in my head, but certainty had settled over me after my conversation with Aidan today. I just had to hope that Shiloh would be on board.

I pushed open my door and climbed out of my truck. The sun shone as I climbed up the stairs. It was the first truly warm day of the season. I was taking that as the Universe agreeing with my path.

Opening the door, a buzzer sounded as I stepped inside. An

officer I didn't recognize looked up from the counter. "Afternoon, sir. Can I help you?"

"I'm here to see Hayes."

"Who can I tell him is here?"

"Ramsey Bishop."

The officer picked up his phone. As he spoke in hushed tones, I looked around the space. I didn't feel the pull of anxiety like I had the last time I was here.

The officer hung up and nodded at me. "You can go on back."

"Thanks." I headed through the door that I knew led to Hayes' office. A few officers nodded at me as I made my way through the sea of desks. Deputy Young sent me a wave, and I returned it with a chin lift. Hell, if I weren't careful, I'd end up with friends here.

I stopped outside Hayes' office and knocked.

"Come in."

I stepped inside and closed the door behind me.

"Where's Shy?"

"At the ranch with your mom and sister. They were having brunch and going for a trail ride."

The tension in Hayes' shoulders eased. "They haven't been riding together in forever."

I lowered myself into the chair opposite his desk as I studied Hayes' face. "It's a good thing they're going then?"

I couched it as a question. I didn't want Shiloh in a situation that might bring up painful memories or start a fight.

Hayes shook his head as if trying to clear away fog. "It's really good. The three of them used to go all the time. After the kidnapping, it kind of all fell away."

That phantom tightening in my chest came back, a pain not just for Shiloh but also for the whole Easton family. "You all went through a lot."

Hayes leaned back in his chair. "It marked us all in different ways. I don't think any of us handled the aftermath well."

"It seems like you're finding your way now."

"We are. More and more. And it helps to see Shy doing so well." His gaze locked with mine. "You're a big part of that. Thank you."

I fought the urge to squirm. Direct compliments made me twitchy. "She's the one who's responsible. Took the steps to find her happiness."

"But you helped light the way."

Maybe Hayes was right. Maybe it wasn't just Shiloh who'd lit up my world. It was possible I had done the same for her. That balance made for a relationship that would stand the test of time.

I didn't look away from Hayes, wanting him to see the truth in my words. "She changed my life in a way I didn't think was possible."

A grin stretched across his face. "I'm damn happy for you both."

"Thanks, man."

"But I'm guessing you didn't come here for a heart-to-heart."

I chuckled. "That wasn't on the docket. I actually came by to talk to you about Aidan and Elliott."

Hayes sat up straighter. "Are they okay?"

His reaction had me realizing for the millionth time just how wrong I'd been about Hayes. I nodded. "They're good. Aidan and I had a long talk this morning. He heard about his father attacking Shiloh and was heaping a lot of that on his shoulders."

"Hell. None of this is his fault."

"I think he has glimmers of understanding that, but it's going to take time."

"What can I do?"

I drummed my fingers on the side of the chair. "With my history, how hard do you think it would be to get approved to be a foster parent?"

Hayes' eyes widened. "You want to take those boys home?"

"It's going to be a good while before they're eligible for adoption. Kenny will have to be stripped of his parental rights first. I want them to have a stable home and not have to move from place to place. The Millers are great, but they don't have the energy to keep up with Aidan and Elliott nonstop."

"And you have an understanding of what they've been through that the Millers never will."

"That, too. Aidan and I have developed a bond, one that lets him open up with me. And Elliott is in love with Shiloh."

A smile pulled at Hayes' mouth. "Have you talked to her about this?"

"About the boys' future, yes. Not about fostering to adopt. I didn't want to get her hopes up if it was impossible with my past. She loves them, and it would crush her if it didn't come through."

Hayes studied me for a moment. "Ramsey, your record was completely expunged. There's nothing that would hold you back from being a foster parent unless you've knocked over some banks I don't know about."

"Just because my charges were overturned doesn't mean that my history won't come up in a background check. Hell, they won't even need that. The media coverage was so intense that I bet anyone who picked up my file would know exactly what's in my past."

"And they'll see what I do. Someone uniquely qualified to empathize with children who have experienced trauma. The fact that you're willing to use your pain for good says exactly the kind of man you are."

"I'm good at using it with horses—"

"And with people," Hayes said, cutting me off. "You have this messed-up idea that you're only good with animals, but that couldn't be further from the truth. I've seen you reach people I wasn't sure could be reached. And I couldn't imagine a better foster parent."

I struggled to swallow, but it felt as if my throat had a boulder in it. "I want Aidan and Elliott to have the childhood they deserve."

"So do I. And we're going to make that happen."

I nodded, unable to get any more words out.

Hayes pulled out his cell phone and began tapping on the screen. "I'm reaching out to a contact in social services.

Certification can take anywhere from one month to four, but we'll do what we can to speed that up."

"I need to make sure Shiloh's on board." Because she was a part of my life, now and forever.

Hayes grinned at me. "You really think she's not going to be all over this?"

I chuckled. "You have a point there. She was already telling me that we needed to come and talk to you to make sure that Aidan and Elliott got the best possible placement."

"Now, she can make sure they do."

A sense of rightness settled deeper into my bones. This was a family I'd never expected, but one that was beyond perfect for me.

My phone buzzed in my pocket. I slid it out. An alert shone on the screen from my security system, but it wasn't one I'd seen before. I opened the app.

"What is it?" Hayes asked.

"The security system lost power."

"It has solar-powered backup power."

An invisible fist wrapped around my heart and squeezed. "Call Shiloh. See where they are."

I tapped through the app to get more information as Hayes hit a contact on his phone. They should be out on the trails by now. Not even on the ranch. Yet, I couldn't take a full breath. Not until I knew that Shiloh was safe.

Hayes' jaw tensed. "It went straight to voicemail."

"Call Hadley."

He did so immediately as I thumbed through my security app. When I finally reached the right screen, I sucked in air that felt as if it were made of barbed wire. *Line disconnected.*

"Hadl—" A stream of words I couldn't make out on the other end of the line cut him off. I watched as panic slowly set in. "She's gone. They can't find Shiloh anywhere."

I ROLLED OVER WITH A GROAN. EVERYTHING HURT. MY BODY felt as if I'd run a marathon with no training, and my head thrummed in a way that should've signaled the hangover from hell. I blinked a few times.

With each opening of my eyelids, light filled my vision, making me wince and cringe. But with each blast of light came glimpses of an unfamiliar space. The panic came in bursts, each blink bringing more and more until it had woven around my chest in a vise grip.

I forced my eyes fully open, taking in the room around me. I lay on a musty mattress on the floor, covered by a ratty blanket. There was nothing else in the tiny room, no furniture or even a lamp. The light came from the window, the single bulb overhead extinguished.

My breaths came quicker as I searched my mind, trying to grab hold of the last thing I remembered. Things came in flashes: my morning with Ramsey, Hadley and my mom, the barn.

I jerked upright as the memory of the hand clamping over

my mouth slammed into me. My heart railed against my ribs as if it were trying to break free. This wasn't happening. Not again.

Tears stung the backs of my eyes, but they weren't ones of despair or even fear. They were tears of pure fury.

I wouldn't be a victim. Not again. I'd fought too hard to get my life back.

Pain lanced through my chest at the thought. Images of that life filled my mind: Kai's rambunctious hilarity, Onyx's fragile trust, afternoons teaching Elliott about horses, seeing Aidan blossom under Ramsey's guidance, and truly reconnecting with my family for the first time, giving them a chance to know me.

Ramsey.

It was just one word, a single name, but it had come to mean everything to me, gently spurring on my bravery and helping me find the path that was mine and mine alone.

The burn behind my eyes intensified as more memories swirled. The way I felt completely safe with Ramsey, how my body came alive under his touch, and how I felt myself for the first time in my life.

A single tear slipped free, and I quickly wiped it away as if that would erase everything running through my head. It was impossible, but I didn't have the luxury of falling apart.

I pushed myself to stand, but my legs wobbled, and my head spun. Whoever had taken me had doused me with chloroform or something similar, and the drug had left behind one of the worst headaches of my life.

I shoved the pain aside and tried my best to focus. I ran over the events of the afternoon. Replaying them, I focused on every detail. I hadn't heard any unfamiliar sounds as I'd stepped outside. I hadn't seen anything out of place.

I pictured the horses in the paddock. They'd been grazing, but a few had been focused on a specific direction. They'd seen something. It was a detail I should've noticed, but I hadn't. I'd been too focused on the prospect of a trail ride with Hadley and Mom.

Pain lanced my sternum at the thought of them. They had to

be beside themselves. I moved to the window, studying the sun in the sky. It didn't look like much time had passed—an hour or two at the most.

Had they seen anything? I got another flash of memory—one man speaking to another, telling him to hurry. Something scratched at the back of my brain. I reached but couldn't quite grasp it.

I let out a soft growl of frustration and moved closer to the window. The lock was broken. It couldn't be that easy. I tried to open it, but the window didn't budge.

Studying the frame, I let out a silent curse. It was nailed shut, and the panes themselves were too small for me to fit through even if I broke one.

My stomach cramped as I thought about what this all meant. Someone had planned this. They'd prepared this place. They'd looked for all the potential exit points and cut them off.

Nausea swept through me, but I shoved it down, turning to study the rest of the room. It was a log cabin of some sort, the walls made of thick tree trunks, cut and spliced together. There were no planks that I might break free.

I still analyzed every single log, looking for points of weakness or anything that might help. When I reached the last one, my panic ratcheted up a notch. Instead of falling apart, I moved to the door.

Faint voices sounded from outside the room, and everything in me twisted. My breathing stuttered, each attempted inhale tripping over the exhale. Memories assaulted me in a barrage: Howard Kemper's rage-filled expression, the blow of his hand against my face, the fear that held me captive, and thoughts of never seeing my family again.

I stumbled back, leaning against the wall. I squeezed my eyes closed and focused on my breaths. Ramsey's voice echoed in my head, telling me to focus on one thing. I could see his eyes as if he were standing right in front of me, those glittering, onyx depths soothing away the worst of the panic. He was here with me because he was a part of me. Just like I was a part of him. Nothing could ever steal that away.

The door flew open, and a figure filled the space. His towering form had me pushing off the wall and bracing for an attack. He simply laughed.

"We meet again, Shiloh. I heard all about you for years and years. Howard wouldn't shut up about you. But hearing is different than seeing it in person."

It took a few moments to register that this was Howard's cellmate, August. And the single word slipped from my lips without me giving permission. "Why?"

It was all I really wanted to know. I needed to understand the reasoning behind him wanting to terrorize me.

August's mouth curved into an ugly smile. "I had to know if you were as special as he said you were."

My stomach cramped as nausea swirled through me. "Where's Ian?"

It had to be the two of them. The other voice had sounded so familiar—the one that sent shivers of fear through me. August might be morbidly curious about me, but Ian wanted to end me.

August chuckled, rubbing a thumb across his lower lip as his gaze tracked over me. "Oh, he'll be here before long. But someone else wants to say hello first."

The panic was back, a bolt of electricity running through me as I searched behind August's hulking frame. Footsteps sounded on the wood floor, a heavy, echoing thump that reverberated in my already thrumming head.

August stepped to the side, making room for whoever was coming. The hall was dark, and the only thing I could make out was shape and size. Yet something about the way the figure moved was familiar, recognizable in a way that had ice sliding through my veins.

He stepped into the room, his face twisted with a mixture of anger and something I couldn't identify. "Shiloh, you disappoint me. I thought you were different. Special." His head shook as if he were trying to clear it. "No, you *were* special. And I'll get you back there. Even if I have to take a switch to you every day for a year, you will return to what you were always supposed to be."

A trembling took over my body, intensifying with each word. I couldn't move. Couldn't speak. The only thing I could do was mouth a single word.

Howard.

Chapter Forty-Two

Ramsey

I PACED BACK AND FORTH AS A TECH WORKED ON THE SECURITY system. She was on the phone with one of the experts at Halo, trying to get all the data they could. But the lines hadn't just been disconnected. Someone had cut them.

Whoever had taken Shiloh had been watching for weeks. Long enough to see the new security going in and paying close enough attention to know exactly how to cut the power source. The thought had me fighting the urge to put a hole in the wall. Instead, I simply picked up my pacing.

Shiloh's family sat in the cabin's living room, her father's arm around his wife, trying to console her. Hadley held one of the twins on her lap, cradling Birdie to her chest as Calder held the other. Beckett rubbed Addie's back as she wrung her hands. Everly brewed a pot of tea in the kitchen, a faraway look in her eyes.

They were in hell. And, worse, they'd been there before, so they knew the depths of that landscape. Hayes held a hushed discussion with the officer he'd put in charge, Lieutenant Ruiz. He hadn't made some power play to remain in control; he'd simply asked to be involved with the search and decisions.

I moved closer to the two men, hoping to hear something. Ian's name caught my attention. "Did you find him?"

Ruiz scowled at me, but Hayes held up a hand to ward off whatever the man was about to say. "Not yet. He's not at the ranch he inherited from his uncle or any of his usual hangouts. But we have an all-points bulletin out on his truck, and his parole officer is looking, too. We'll find him."

But would it be soon enough? That question pinballed around in my brain. With each cycle through, horrible images appeared, each one worse than the one before. Was she cold? Was she terrified? Was she still breathing?

She had to be. If someone had wanted to kill her, they could've done that already. There would've been no point in taking her. But some things were worse than death.

I shoved that thought from my head and focused back on Hayes. "What about August Ernst? Have you located him yet?"

Kenny Chambers was still locked up, so it couldn't have been him. Even with everything Shiloh had been through these past few weeks, the possibilities were limited.

Hayes shook his head. "I talked to his parole officer. August isn't supposed to check in until tomorrow. He's made every other appointment. But he did call in sick from work today."

"Did someone go by his house?"

Ruiz let out a grunt as if to say, "*Do you think I'm an idiot?*"

Hayes sent him a sidelong look. "He wasn't home."

My gut gave a vicious twist. I knew August was off. I could tell it simply from looking at his mugshot. And Shiloh had gotten it right. There was a deadness in his eyes.

"You've got an A.P.B. out on him, too, right?"

"Of course, we do," Ruiz snapped. "But now, we're wasting time explaining things to you instead of making progress."

"Ruiz—"

"It's the truth."

"Guys," the computer tech called. "I've got something."

We all turned and hurried over to her screen.

She tapped on a few keys. "I've been searching all the cameras for the five minutes before they cut the power. I got two people on video. I don't think they knew the camera's angle could get them here."

The tech pulled a frozen image up onto the screen—two men, both in baseball caps, one closer to the camera. I recognized him instantly. August Ernst. I let loose a stream of curses.

"Get a warrant for Ernst," Hayes barked to Ruiz and then turned back to the screen. "Can you zoom in on the second guy?"

The tech nodded. "It gets a little pixelated, but I can try to clean it up."

Her hands flew over the keyboard, and she moved the mouse in tiny, expert motions. As she worked, a face came into focus.

All of us went dead-still behind her.

"It's not possible. He's dead," Ruiz muttered.

But there was Howard Kemper, standing right in the middle of the damn screen.

Everything in me went wired. There wasn't anything that would terrify Shiloh more than being faced with that man. The one who had written her every week for nine years. God only knew what plans he had for her. Revenge? Something more twisted?

Ruiz pulled out his phone and began dialing. I was able to make out snatches of conversation as he ordered warrants for August and Howard. Just hearing Howard's name again made me shake, and fury pulsed through me. It was almost too much for my body to handle.

Hayes spoke in quick, demanding sentences to someone on the phone. It took me a few minutes to realize it was the prison warden. As his voice rose, I knew heads would roll. "You find him, and you stick a guard on him. He doesn't make one damn phone call until my officers have picked him up for questioning."

Hayes paused for a moment, and then his expression hardened.

"Save your damn apology. Just do what I asked." He ended the call without another word.

"What?" I growled.

"Howard Kemper was a model prisoner. And with that, he got privileges—like his choice of work-detail assignments."

"Where did he work?" I prodded. I knew Hayes was leading to the how, but he wasn't getting there quickly enough.

"The prison's medical ward. The warden said the doctor on staff took Howard under his wing. Was mentoring him."

My back teeth ground together. "Or Howard was mentoring the doctor. Manipulating him into finding him a way out."

Hayes ran a hand through his hair, tugging on the strands. "That's what I'm guessing, too. Howard supposedly died from a seizure, but he never made it to the hospital. If a doctor was helping you, you could fake that."

"Holy hell. This is unreal," Ruiz muttered. "I'm going to pick up the doc myself."

"I'll go with you—"

"You can't, Hayes. Do you want to be the reason something gets thrown out as evidence? You have a conflict of interest. Let me handle this."

Hayes gritted his teeth. "Call me as soon as you question him."

"You know I will." Ruiz clapped him on the shoulder. "We'll find her."

I had to hold on to that. Hope. I'd given up on it years ago, but Shiloh had given it back to me. She'd shown me the light that hid within the shadows. Showed me that I could be more than I ever thought possible. And I would fight for her. Hell, I'd burn down the world to get her back. No one could stop me.

Chapter Forty-Three

Shiloh

I COULDN'T GET MY BODY TO STOP TREMBLING. IF ANYTHING, the shaking only intensified. I tried to get the image in front of me to compute, the face that had been burned into my nightmares. The one that was supposed to be buried six feet under.

"H-how?"

My voice carried the same reverberation that shot through my body in waves. I hated the sound. The proof that this man could still terrorize me.

August grinned. "Howard has a real way with people. He can convince them he's whatever he wants them to believe he is."

I didn't look at Howard's cellmate as he spoke, even with the crazy claims he was spouting. I couldn't take my eyes off Howard. It was too dangerous—as if he were a pacing predator, and I was bracing for an attack. *Ask another question.* I needed to keep them talking and get as much information as possible. Had to keep them at a distance.

"Who did he convince?"

Howard chuckled, but the sound didn't match up with the man

or the circumstances. It was jovial, like a Santa Claus laugh. "The doctor in the medical ward really was going through a hard time."

August joined in his laughter. "Ol' Doc Adams was at the end of his rope with his wife leaving him and taking the kids."

"Ripe to believe in evil women who can ruin your life." Howard's eyes narrowed in my direction. "And I know all about that. I was a comfort and a listening ear. I'd felt the level of betrayal that comes with trying to help someone and having them turn on you."

Help. My stomach roiled. He truly believed that, and nothing anyone said could convince him otherwise. And my challenging it would only bring pain.

"You faked your death."

August clapped his hands, rubbing them together. "It really was brilliant. Doc helps fake the seizure. One bribe of a mortuary employee later, and you've got yourself an escape."

"I had to be in that damn body bag for hours, though." Anger lit across Howard's features as his head swiveled in my direction. "That's on you, too. You'll pay for everything you've put me through. But by the time I'm done with you, you'll be the perfect wife for my son—minding your place, appreciating all we've done for you."

August's mouth twisted into a feral smile. "I'll be helping with that training, too. And we're gonna get started real soon."

A wave of dizziness swept over me, nausea intensifying with it. "I don't feel very well. I think the drugs you gave me messed with my system."

August snorted. "Don't try your manipulations on us."

Howard took a step forward, his eyes glinting in the afternoon sun. "You trying to twist us into pitying you? Attempting to use your weak, womanly status to make us feel bad for you?"

I didn't retreat, no matter how much I wanted to. I forced myself to stand firm. The rage pumping through me at his words helped. The last thing I would ever be was weak. But the only chance I had now was to outthink these two. To find an opening and run like hell. I'd have to wait until one of them left. I had no hope of getting free when it was two on one.

"I'm just telling you the truth. I'm shaky and dizzy."

Howard studied me more intently. "She does look a little pale."

August scoffed.

"Get her some juice from the fridge," Howard ordered.

August's jaw tightened. "You do it."

Howard's eyes narrowed on him. "This is my deal."

"But I'm not your servant."

"You work for me. I gave you that cash to get on your feet."

"And I've more than paid you back."

That anger was back in Howard's eyes, but it was no longer pointed at me. "You screwed up getting her the first time. Almost got caught."

A muscle in August's cheek fluttered wildly. "She kneed me in the fuckin' balls." His head snapped in my direction. "You'll pay for that, too."

Shock rocked through me at the knowledge that August had been the one to grab me outside the Bar & Grill. I couldn't help the shudder that followed. He could've taken me then and locked me in this cabin weeks ago. There would've been no stolen moments with Ramsey and all the firsts I got with him.

August turned back to Howard. "I got the letters to her. Hell, I found someone to take photos of her for years for you."

I stiffened. Photos? Seemed they'd been watching for who knew how long, infiltrating my life when I thought I was safe.

The tension in Howard eased a fraction. "The photos were good. You're right. You've helped more than a little."

"Damn straight."

Howard squeezed August's shoulder. "Will you please get some juice for Shiloh? I want to talk to her."

August's jaw was still tight, but he nodded. "Yeah, whatever."

The tension between the two was something I needed to use to my advantage. If I could sow more seeds of discontent, maybe one of them would bail. The thing I couldn't figure out was who would be worse to be alone with. The worst-case scenarios with each were vastly different.

I pressed my hands harder against the logs of the wall. Panic gripped me, and dark spots danced in my vision.

Breathe. Focus on one thing.

Ramsey's face flashed in my mind again. Those eyes were my touchstone. Dark like an endless night sky. But I knew sparks would come—pinpricks of light when he laughed. Or when we lost ourselves in each other. I wouldn't lose him. I wouldn't lose our everything.

"Shiloh?"

Howard's voice brought me back to the here and now, and I scooted away as he inched closer.

That tiny movement was a mistake. Rage filled his expression. "Don't you dare move away from me."

I froze. "I think I might throw up. I didn't want to do it on you."

"Liar. I can sense your lies when they fly from your mouth."

I shook my head vigorously, the movement making my head pound. "I'm not lying. When I'm sick, I don't like for anyone to touch me."

Howard's face turned a mottled red. "No one should be touching you. No one but me and Ian. But I saw those photos. You let that heathen put his hands on you. His mouth."

Everything in me twisted, my stomach spasming. "I love him."

I didn't know if that would make things better or worse, but it was true. And I wouldn't deny it for anything.

Howard moved in a flash, slamming me against the wall. My head snapped back into the logs, and spots danced across my vision. His hand tightened around my neck, digging into the bruises Kenny had left there. "You're a treasonous whore. You were promised to my son, and you do *this* to him? When I offered you everything?"

"He doesn't want me." The words barely escaped my throat.

Howard's grip on me loosened a fraction. "We'll just see about that."

He gave me one more hard shove and then released me. I couldn't manage to stay on my feet. I dropped to the floor as if all the strength had left me. My ears rang, and my vision tilted. I didn't know if I'd make it through a day with Howard, let alone the year he predicted.

The burn was back behind my eyes. I wanted home. Ramsey. Kai. Aidan and Elliott. Sky. Onyx. My nosy family butting into my life and telling me what they thought was best for me.

August strode into the room and threw a bottle at me. It landed at my feet. "Drink it."

I squinted through my double vision to take in the bottle. It was orange juice, one of those single-serving deals. My hand shook as I picked it up. It took three tries to open it, but I heard the pop of the seal and sighed in relief. I guzzled it down.

Howard scowled at me. "Now you drink what we give you?"

He hadn't forgotten all my refusals to eat or drink when I was ten. But things were different now. I knew they had nothing to gain by drugging me, and I desperately needed the sugar the juice would provide if I had any hope of fighting back.

A door slammed outside, and my gaze shot to the hallway. "Who is that?"

Howard grinned. "You'll just have to wait and see."

A door opened and closed. "August?" Footsteps echoed after Ian's voice. "Where are you?"

"Back here."

Those footsteps grew closer, and Ian's large frame filled the doorway. His face went deathly pale. "Dad?"

"Hey, son."

"Y-you died. They called me."

Howard scoffed. "Don't you know better than to trust a fuckin' pig? I thought I taught you better than that."

Ian simply stared at his father as if looking at a ghost.

Howard chuckled and gestured to me. "And I got you a present to apologize for not letting you in on the plan."

Ian scowled at the not-letting-him-in-on-the-plan piece,

sending a glare in August's direction. His gaze moved where his father had gestured, his eyes widening as he took me in. "Have you lost your fucking mind? You took her?"

His voice made the pulse in my head intensify, the pain like icepicks to my brain.

"Watch your tone, young man. I did this for you! You need to show me some respect."

"I don't want her. I've never wanted her. The cops are already on my ass, and you do *this*?"

Howard's hand shot out, slapping Ian across the face. Ian blinked a few times, stunned in a way that told me his father had never been physically violent with him before. But I'd known that Howard Kemper had it in him. Cruelty. And a paranoia that everything else was powerless against.

Ian gritted his teeth. "I'm worried they'll catch you because of this. Because of *her*."

Howard studied his son, a harshness in his gaze. "You need to trust that I know what's best for you. As soon as Shiloh's ready, you'll take her as your wife. We're going to build the life we should've always had."

"A nice compound in Canada." August shot me a lascivious grin. "We'll take all the wives we want."

Howard nodded. "Raise those children right. No traitors like your sisters," he spat at Ian and then turned back to me. "You'll birth me some righteous grandchildren."

"No." The single word slipped from my mouth without my permission.

Howard whirled on me. "You'll submit, or you'll die. Those are your choices."

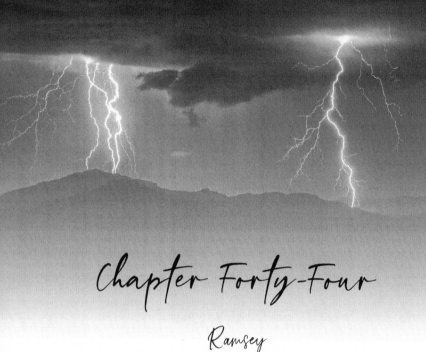

Chapter Forty-Four

Ramsey

I LEANED AGAINST THE FENCE OF THE ROUND PEN. ONYX WAS despondent in a way that said she knew something was wrong with Shiloh. She missed her friend and confidante. The only being she'd truly begun to trust.

My chest ached with the thought of it. The weight of it all tugged on the bones and organs as if it would rip it all apart, and I would bleed out on the ground. Somehow, Shiloh had become the glue that held it all together. Without her, I was only pieces.

Kai pressed into my leg, and I reached down to rub behind his ears. "We're gonna find her."

"We will."

I turned at Hayes' voice. "Anything?"

He shook his head. "Not yet."

My fists clenched, my fingernails piercing my palms in a way I knew would leave scars. But I didn't give a damn. I welcomed any pain that would distract me from the shredding feeling in my chest, the utter annihilation that was ripping me apart.

"Every minute is time she's being hurt. Terrified. Every second is a chance that something's happening to her that she might not come back from." The words tore from my throat, shredding that, too.

Hayes gripped my shoulder, squeezing to the point of pain. "Shy's strong. She's gonna fight. Hell, she'll probably find a way out of there before we get to her."

But I didn't want her to have to fight her way out. She'd done that for too much of her life. And I didn't think Howard Kemper would let her get away this time. "He's obsessed with her. He could do anything."

Hayes' jaw hardened. "We have to hope that means he's keeping her alive and unharmed."

But he'd harmed her before. Shiloh had just hidden how badly from her family. What he did to her now when she was a grown woman could be so much worse.

Hayes squeezed my shoulder again. "We have to hold on to hope."

"It's killing me. Ripping me apart," I rasped.

"I know."

"I love her so damn much. That hurts, too. But it's the kind of pain I could live with. I can't live in a world without Shiloh."

Hayes' grip on me loosened a fraction. "You won't have to. It's not going to happen."

He moved then, pulling me into a hard hug. No one had made a move to touch me other than Shiloh in years. Even Lor didn't try. The signals to stay far away were too strong.

This simple kindness almost broke me. Instead, I hugged Hayes back. We stood there for a count of ten, gripping each other's shoulders with a ferocity that bled with our need to get Shiloh back, a determination for only that outcome.

I clapped Hayes on the back and released him. "We're gonna find her."

"Damn straight."

"Is the doc talking?"

A muscle in Hayes' jaw ticked. "He folded the second Ruiz

picked him up. Wouldn't stop talking the whole ride back to the station."

I hoped that asshole fried. That he landed in a cell and never got to grace the outside again. "Were you right?"

Hayes nodded. "He helped Howard fake the seizure and then bribed a mortuary employee to put the tag from Howard's body bag on a John Doe."

"Tell me they got him, too."

"They did. He lawyered up, but his boss at the mortuary was only too happy to give all the corroboration Ruiz needed."

Kai butted my hand, and I gave him a scratch. "Does the doctor have any idea where Howard might be now?"

"Not a clue. He arranged for the mortuary employee to drop Howard off outside Wolf Gap, but he had no idea where he planned to go."

I muttered a curse. "What about August Ernst's bank records?"

"Nothing that points us to where they might be holed up."

I wanted to hit something. We had to catch a break. Somewhere. Something.

Hayes ran a hand through his hair, tugging on the ends of the strands. "We've got officers searching the area around Ian's ranch, another group searching around the cabin where August was staying, and more questioning every single person who has a tie to Howard, August, and Ian. Everyone who works for the department is out looking. Someone knows something. We just have to find them."

God, I hoped he was right. It was nearly impossible to disappear without a trace these days. Not with cell phones, security cameras, and social media. Too many people were watching. But we lived on the edge of civilization. Someone could vanish into the woods if they knew where they were going and had help. We had to find a trail to follow.

Hayes' phone rang, and he pulled it out of his pocket, answering it instantly. "Easton."

The volume was high enough that I could faintly hear the other side of the call.

"Hey, Sheriff. A weird call came through dispatch."

"What do you mean weird?"

"It's like someone dialed in but isn't talking. We can just hear the conversation happening around it."

Hayes' brows pulled together. "Does it sound like someone's in trouble?"

The woman was quiet for a moment. "I thought I heard Shiloh's name."

The air around us electrified. In a flash, Hayes had his phone on speaker. "Trace the call and patch me through to the caller but keep our end on mute."

"Yes, sir."

An instant later, the line crackled, and faraway voices came over the speaker.

"Dad, let's leave her for now. I want some time with you. I thought you were dead, for fuck's sake."

I instantly recognized Ian's voice but couldn't tell if he was the caller.

"You're trying to manipulate me. I thought you said you trusted my vision for your life."

The second voice had to be Howard's, but he sounded farther away.

"I do trust you. But I'm also worried about you. This cabin is only five miles from Ramsey Bishop's ranch. Anyone could figure out where you're staying."

I immediately pulled out my phone, tapping on my map app to search a five-mile radius around my place.

"You think I don't know what I'm doing, boy?" Howard demanded, his voice louder now.

"Of course, you know what you're doing. I just want you to be safe. Hayes has a hard-on for you, and he'll have every cop in a thousand-mile radius out looking for you."

Things were quiet for a moment, and then we heard a grunt and sounds of a struggle.

"Who the hell did you call?!" Howard screamed. "Traitor! My own damn son."

Another voice filled the speaker. "It's fuckin' 9-1-1."

"You're dead," Howard growled. "I'll kill you, and Shiloh will be mine. You never deserved her—"

The line went silent, and the call dropped. And we still had no idea where they were.

Chapter Forty-Five

Shiloh

HOWARD SLAMMED IAN INTO THE WALL AS AUGUST stomped on his phone with his boot. The little bit of hope that had flared to life in my chest as Ian had slipped his phone from his pocket extinguished in a single breath. It wasn't enough. Ian hadn't been able to tell Hayes exactly where we were.

But he'd given them something. Not a direction, but a range of miles—just five from home. I could run that in my sleep. Maybe even in the drug-induced haze I was currently in. But I had to get free first.

Howard's hand closed around Ian's throat, squeezing. "Why would you do this to me?"

Ian's eyes blazed, but he showed no sign of fighting back. "I'm so damn tired. You and Uncle Allen, your anger and paranoia, it's like a disease. I let it eat away at me, too. But I'm not going back to jail for you. I'm done."

Howard slammed him harder into the wall this time. "Yellow-bellied traitor. I should've known. You and that sister of yours aren't worth the dirt on my boots."

Ian's jaw hardened as if a fury had been lit deep inside him. He gave his father a hard shove, shocking the man, then hauled off and punched him in the jaw. "You can drown with Allen, but you're not taking me down with you."

August charged forward, landing an uppercut to Ian's ribs. I winced at what I knew likely broke bones.

"You're a fuckin' snitch," August bellowed, launching another punch that Ian dodged. "Nothing I hate worse than someone who turns on his own."

Ian lashed out with a palm strike to August's nose. I heard the crunch of cartilage from across the room.

"Bastard!" August keeled over, holding his nose as blood poured from it.

"Don't move," Howard growled.

My gaze jumped to him, zeroing in on the gun in his hands. It was pointed center mass on Ian.

Blood roared in my ears, and my gaze moved from the men to the door, trying to analyze the risk of making a run for it. Their positions had changed amidst all the fighting, and there was a narrow path to the door. If I could only move fast enough…

Howard spat a mouthful of blood onto the floor. "I was going to give you the world."

Ian swallowed hard, not looking away from his father. "The world is a shack that's falling apart with barely reliable power? Waking me up at all hours of the night to run drills for the impending *attacks*? Never letting me have normal friends or, God forbid, date? Nothing that would take me away from the fucked-up universe you created."

A flash of pity swept through me at his words. I'd known some of what Everly and Ian had experienced growing up, but not much. It was no wonder that Ian had turned into someone so full of hate. Between his father and his uncle, he'd experienced little but brainwashing and abuse. It only made me respect Everly more. She'd made it free of that place, and she hadn't let them warp her mind. She'd become nothing but goodness and light.

Howard's chest heaved with labored breaths, his arm shaking in an effort to hold the gun steady. "I gave you a life free of the sickness of the modern world. I made it so you would always be able to take care of yourself, no matter what came our way."

Ian scoffed. "What came our way? You were convinced that a roving group of bandits were going to try to steal Mom and Evie from our house, or the military's special forces were going to attack us for stores of canned foods."

Howard pressed the muzzle of the gun into Ian's chest. "The world has gotten to you. I see it now. Without Allen to hold you in line, you've been sickened by the influences in your orbit. I never thought I'd have to end you. But it's for your own good. I won't let you corrupt Shiloh."

My stomach cramped as Ian's gaze locked with mine. He moved in a flash. His knee came up, landing a shot to Howard's groin. "Run!"

The word reverberated in my ears, but I was already moving. The world slowed around me, and I swore I heard each beat of my heart as I dashed for the door.

August cursed, scrambling to his feet to run after me, but Ian punched him in the jaw, sending him sprawling. My legs shook as I pushed them harder. The door to the hall was so close. Freedom just past that.

"Shiloh!"

Howard bellowed my name with a force that I swore shook the walls. It only made me run harder, the jolt of adrenaline spurring me on.

A shot rang out. I glanced over my shoulder for the briefest of moments, only to see Ian collapsing to the floor, clutching his stomach. But I couldn't stop. I had to keep going. The only hope either of us had was if I could find help.

Sun streamed in from the open front door. I pushed harder as footsteps echoed behind me. I ran down the front steps of the cabin and towards the trees. I had no idea where I was. It was monumentally stupid to run in the forest with no sense of direction, but I had to get away. Once I put some distance between us, then I could get my bearings.

Branches slapped at my arms and my face as I ran. Howard yelled after me, nonsensical things I couldn't completely make out. I only caught every third or fourth word—my name, *stop*, *obey*.

All it did was make me go faster. My muscles trembled, the drugs in my system wreaking havoc on every part of me. But I had to keep going.

My head swiveled as I ran, looking for anything even vaguely familiar. I'd lost myself in these woods more times than I could count, searching for peace amidst the nightmares. I needed that now—a little of the hope I'd found in every incarnation of the sky above.

The breeze moved the trees, and sunlight lit a path up ahead—a trail. My eyes strained. There was an old, gnarled tree trunk. A pine that had been struck by lightning. One I knew.

Relief charged through me. I could follow that path. I knew where it would lead. Back to Ramsey. Back to my home.

A hand snatched out, grabbing my hair.

I screamed as Howard yanked me back against him. His chest heaved, his sour breath filling my lungs. "You can't run from me. You'll never escape. I should've seen it from the beginning. You were always meant to be mine. I'll break you and remake you into the perfect wife."

Chapter Forty-Six

Ramsey

"THEY'VE GOT A LOCATION." HAYES WAS ALREADY moving towards his sheriff's department SUV.

I jogged after him. There was no way I was letting him go without me.

"Where's your backup?" Calder called, hurrying behind us, the rest of the family on his heels.

"All our search parties are in the opposite directions. It'll take them at least thirty minutes to get there. We may not have that long." Hayes beeped the locks on his truck.

"I'm coming," Calder immediately said.

"Me, too," Hadley echoed.

Calder turned on his wife. "Hads…"

"Oh, so you can play cop, but I can't? Because I'm a woman?"

Calder framed Hadley's face with his hands. "Because I have firearms training, and you've never held a gun in your life."

I didn't miss the Glock holstered at Calder's hip as if he'd known he might need to step in.

"I'll come, too," Gabe offered.

"Dad, you're the only other person armed. We need someone to stay, just in case any trouble winds up back here," Hayes argued.

Gabe's face hardened, but he nodded. "Call me the second you get her."

"You know I will."

I slid into the passenger side of the SUV, and Calder climbed in the back. Hayes cranked the engine. Rocks flew as he sailed down the drive. "You know how to handle a weapon?"

I hit the button for the gate on my phone. "Had my own ranch since I was eighteen. What do you think?"

Hayes inclined his head to the glove box in front of me. "Got my personal backup in there. Take that. Code to the lockbox is 8-8-2-1."

I leaned forward, opening the glove box and entering the code. I made quick work of checking the weapon and then slid the holster onto the side of my jeans.

"Backup is twenty-five minutes out," Hayes said, obviously repeating something someone had shared through his phone's earpiece.

"How many?" Calder asked.

"Got about eight officers in this first group. Everyone else is on their way."

That was good. The more people looking, the quicker we'd find Shiloh. But all I could think about was what could happen to her in the time between now and then, and all the ways she could be hurt—or worse.

I gave my head a hard shake, trying to clear the images. Hayes took a sharp left, moving deeper into the forest. The trees towered above us, blocking out much of the sun as if the world around me knew that I was in danger of losing my light.

Hayes hung a right and screeched to a halt in front of a rundown cabin I'd had no idea was even in the area. We were all out of the SUV in a flash.

"I'm lead," Hayes clipped.

Calder and I fell into step behind him. Everything was quiet. Too quiet.

No birds called overhead. It was as if even the wind had gone completely still. From years of working with animals, I knew what that meant: a predator was near.

The door to the cabin was wide-open. Hayes raised his weapon. "Carson County Sheriff's Department. Announce yourselves."

"Back here," someone called. The voice was weak, barely audible.

Hayes picked up his pace but didn't drop his weapon. He cleared the living area we passed, then made his way down a short hallway.

As we stepped into a tiny bedroom, my gaze instantly moved to Ian Kemper sprawled on the floor. Calder immediately holstered his weapon and knelt beside him.

"Damned gut shot," Ian wheezed.

Calder lifted his shirt and winced. "We need EMTs."

"They're already en route in case of injuries," Hayes said.

On their way because he thought there was a good chance Shiloh could be hurt. I turned to Ian. "Where are they?"

"I gave her a chance. Told her to run. She took off for the woods. Looked like she was heading north. My dad was on her heels, though. August right behind them."

I started in that direction, not waiting.

"Hold your damn horses. I'm lead, remember?" Hayes barked.

I didn't say a word. If Hayes wanted to lead, he'd have to hurry the hell up.

We both went quiet as we moved through the trees, listening for any signs of movement. I pointed to a branch up ahead. I would've missed it if it weren't for the beam of light breaking through the brush—a few strands of long hair, that mixture of brown and gold. My chest seized.

I should've taken it as comfort. Shiloh was alive and running. But for how long?

"We look for the path," Hayes said quietly.

I saw it now. A broken branch here. Trampled brush there. We had a trail to follow.

A muttered curse had us both freezing. Hayes held up a hand, telling me to stay still. I listened harder.

"Goddamned bastard. My fuckin' nose."

My eyes narrowed as I pointed to my left. Hayes stepped off the makeshift path and moved towards the voice. I could just make out a figure through the trees. He was bent over, blood pouring out of his nose. He didn't even notice our approach.

Hayes lifted his weapon mere feet away. "Carson County Sheriff, don't move."

August jolted upright. For a moment, he looked as if he might run, but then his shoulders slumped, and he held his arm up to his nose in an attempt to stop the bleeding. "Bastard branch got my nose bleeding again."

He spoke as if he weren't caught red-handed as part of a kidnapping plot that would put him in prison for the rest of his life.

"August Ernst, you're under arrest for criminal trespass and kidnapping." Hayes began reading August his rights as the cuffs went on.

"Where is Shiloh?" I growled the words low, but they had August struggling to take a step back to get some distance from me. I let my feral edge show then. Let August see exactly who he was dealing with. I was more predator than man at the moment, and I didn't give a damn.

"I-I-I lost 'em, but they went that way."

I picked up to a run, headed back to the makeshift trail. Hayes called after me, but I didn't listen. I knew he had to secure August in the back of his vehicle before he could keep searching. I didn't have that kind of time to waste. Shiloh was close. I could feel it. I just had to get to her.

I ran faster, listening for any unusual sounds and looking for any signs of human presence. It was a flash of color that caught my attention—gold caught in the sunlight.

I came to a dead stop, squinting through the trees. I barely made out a form. My heart cramped and seized as Shiloh came into view. So damn beautiful. So damn strong.

Then my world went sideways as Howard Kemper lifted a knife to her throat.

Chapter Forty-Seven

Shiloh

THE BLADE PRESSED INTO THE SKIN OF MY NECK AS HOWARD held me against him, my back to his front. "I told you not to move."

"I'm gonna pass out." It wasn't a lie. Spots danced in my vision as I struggled to stay upright. "You'll slice my neck without meaning to."

Howard moved the knife lower, right over my chest. "Don't think I can't do damage here."

I wasn't an idiot; I knew he could. But at least this way, I could take a full breath. With each inhale, my lungs burned. I couldn't help but wonder if I'd broken a rib at some point. Or maybe that run through the woods had been more than my body could take.

Everything in me hurt, but my soul most of all. Because I didn't know if I had much fight left in me. All I wanted was Ramsey. To feel his arms around me in the safety of our haven in this world. I swore I could feel it even now, that glimpse of our everything. I would've given anything to have just a single moment of it now. Of him.

Howard shook me, the blade biting into my chest. "Got nothing to say for yourself? There'll be punishment for this. We'll have to live in the woods for a while until the heat calms down."

He said "*we*" as if I were a part of this grand plan, like we were on the run together. Nausea rolled through me as he pressed himself harder against my back. I could feel him hardening even now.

Howard chuckled. "Good thing you can do your wifely duties anywhere."

Bile surged in my throat, and fear locked my muscles, but I found my fight again. I would never be Howard's victim, not again, especially not in an even sicker way than before. I just had to find my next opening—and it would come.

"Where are we going?" The words were barely audible, spoken through gritted teeth. It took everything in me to hold back my screams of fury. I'd rather him end me than know what it was like to have his hands on my skin.

Howard urged me forward, moving the knife to my ribs. "We'll find a cave. You'll be able to rely on me. Unlike my son, I take pride in being able to live off the land. I'll provide for you and our children."

The bile was back, burning my throat and cutting off my air. I coughed, struggling to get a good breath.

"You won't trick me into thinking you're weak. I know you'll just run again. You'll have to stick close until you can prove yourself trustworthy."

I bit the inside of my cheek to keep from throwing some choice curses in his direction. Instead, I put one foot in front of the other, looking for my next opportunity to run. The trees here were thick, not making escape easy. I prayed for a river that I could jump into and be carried downstream without having to run, but there was no such luck.

My breathing became more labored as we walked, and I slowed my pace and then stopped altogether. "I just need a minute. Those drugs—"

"Were necessary. Because of *you*." Howard pressed the knife harder into my ribs.

I cried out as the blade pierced my skin.

"Lower the knife and step back."

My head snapped up at the voice, one so sweet to my ears that I swore I was hallucinating. Ramsey stepped out from between the trees. "It's over. Lower the weapon."

Howard grabbed hold of my hair with one hand as he pointed the knife directly at my stomach. "Y-you're not supposed to be here. She doesn't belong to you. She's mine."

"She belongs to herself," Ramsey said calmly, moving closer. "And you have to let her go."

"Stop! Stay where you are, or I'll gut her right here."

Ramsey froze. His gaze jumped from the knife to me, and I saw so much pain in those eyes. There was nothing he could do. He had a gun but no shot. Howard was too close. Any direction he came from could end with a bullet in me, too.

"Love you, Ramsey. Love our everything." I didn't know if I would get another opportunity to give him those words, and I wasn't taking the chance.

Howard's hand fisted tighter in my hair, shaking me hard. "Shut up! You don't speak to him."

The knife slipped a fraction in his anger. That blade was the only power Howard had. The only control.

"Let her go, Howard."

"She's mine!" he screamed.

"I'll never be yours. You're worthless. Not even a man. Who has to steal a wife? Is it because you know that no one in their right mind would ever agree to marry you? Because you're sick and twisted and can only get it up when you know you're hurting someone—"

Howard slammed the blade into my stomach.

The pain stole my breath. White light danced across my vision, but I didn't stop. I knew I only had moments. I staggered forward, trying to give Ramsey the shot.

One. Two. Three. The pops echoed in my brain. Then, I was crumpling to the ground.

My ears rang, my vision blurring. Ramsey's face appeared.

"Shiloh." My name tore from his throat as his hands hovered over me. "Why?"

"I had to get the knife," I croaked. "Had to take his power." I let out a wheezing breath. "Love you always."

His hands went to my face. "Don't talk like that."

My lips tried to smile, to give him the words again, but I couldn't get them out.

"Help's coming. Just hold on. We're gonna get you to the hospital and get you all fixed up."

Wetness hit my cheeks, but it wasn't from me. It was from Ramsey. My strong, fierce Ramsey was crying. For me. "Love you."

The words barely passed my lips. His face swirled in my vision, melding with the sky around him, and together, there truly was nothing more beautiful: my sky and my soul. I watched them become one and then faded into them both.

Chapter Forty-Eight

Ramsey

I SCRUBBED AT MY FINGERS. A NURSE HAD GIVEN ME A BRUSH and said it would help. It didn't seem like it was making a damn bit of difference. The blood was scoured into my skin, tattooed there, permanent and unwavering. That only made me scrub harder.

Images ran through my mind on repeat: the rage and delusion on Howard's face, and the look of utter belief in me on Shiloh's, as if she thought that simply because I was there, it would all work out.

But there was no guarantee. I should've known that nothing was guaranteed. Instead, Shiloh was in surgery. She'd lost so much damn blood—way too much.

"Use this."

Hayes stepped up beside me and squirted soap onto my hands. My nose wrinkled at the scent, clearly full of chemicals and whatever killed super germs. But it cleared away the worst of the blood.

Blood that had gotten on me while trying to stop the flow as I waited for help. I swore I could still feel Shiloh's pulse beneath my hands. I felt every heartbeat. Knew the moment they had started to slow and feel sluggish.

Hayes gripped my shoulder and squeezed hard. "You're gonna take your skin off."

I let the brush drop to the bottom of the sink and rinsed my hands. What difference did it make if I flayed myself on the spot? I wouldn't be any sort of human if I lost Shiloh.

"Come on."

Hayes gave me a light shove in the direction of the private waiting room while I dried my hands. It was the last place I wanted to go. I didn't want to be surrounded by all that grief and fear. It would only amplify mine. It would send me back to drowning in the darkness, only this time, I didn't have the light to brighten the shadows.

I went anyway. Because that was where Shiloh would want me to be—with the people who loved her the most.

That vise tightened around my chest. I could barely suck in air as I stepped into the room. Gabe had an arm around his wife, holding her close as she wept silently. Birdie and Sage were both pale and far too still for girls their age. Hadley and Calder kept a close eye on them, Calder linking his fingers with Hadley's.

The gesture was second nature, but it sent an ice pick of pain to my chest. Would I get to feel Shiloh's hand in mine again? The juxtaposition of silky and smooth, dotted with calluses. That hand was a mirror of her: tough yet tender. And everything I loved.

Everly stood, crossing to us and wrapping her arms around Hayes. "Anything?"

"Not yet." Hayes rubbed a hand up and down her back.

Ev's face was mottled red from crying. Her brother was a few floors up in recovery. I couldn't imagine the war raging inside her. The father who'd come back to try to ruin everyone again, but the brother she'd never been close to trying to do the right thing for once.

I sent a look her way, testing the waters. I'd been the one to end Howard. And I'd never regret it. I'd only regret not being able to do it sooner. She looked up at me, blinking away tears. "I'm so sorry, Ramsey."

I jerked back a fraction, but she pressed on. "I'm sorry he made you kill him. I'm so sorry—" Her voice hitched. "I'm so sorry he hurt Shy. Again."

Hayes pressed a kiss to her forehead. "His actions aren't on you."

A grimace swept over Everly's face.

"He's right," I told her. "You can't hold his weight. You'll drown under it."

She let out a shuddered breath but nodded. "I know that. I just...I wish I could've somehow seen..."

Addie reached out from the chair she was sitting in and squeezed her cousin's hand. "You're not psychic. No one could've predicted this."

Not a single soul. But I wished I'd had a little bit of clairvoyance.

"I'm going to go check in with the team again," Beckett said, pushing to his feet.

Laiken stood then, taking her fiancé's hand and pulling Boden to his feet. "We're going to get everyone some food. Any requests?"

No one said a word. I doubted anyone would taste whatever they forced down.

Boden turned to Birdie and Sage. "How about burgers and milkshakes?"

Birdie stared down at her hands. "Can I have strawberry?"

"You sure can. Sage?"

"Whatever you get is fine," she mumbled.

Hadley leaned over, hugging her close and whispering something in her ear. Sage nodded, then sniffled. "Chocolate, please. That's Aunt Shy's favorite. I want chocolate for her."

"I want chocolate, too," Birdie said, changing her order.

Laiken gripped Boden's hand. "We'll get everyone chocolate in honor of Shy."

"Thanks," Hayes said as they passed.

"Call us if you think of anything else you might need," Boden returned.

Hayes nodded.

My chest ached with the weight in the air. How this family, one of blood and choice, came together when the chips were down. How they'd do anything for each other. Shiloh had to live so she could experience more of that, more of the knowledge that she was so deeply cared for.

Quick footsteps sounded on the linoleum. Beckett skidded to a stop in the doorway. "She's out of surgery."

Everyone stood, throwing out questions all at once.

Beckett held up his hands to quiet us. "They're taking her up to ICU now."

Intensive care. That wasn't the news I'd wanted. I'd wanted to hear that she was awake and talking and fine.

"She lost a lot of blood. Her heart slowed to dangerous levels during surgery so they're watching her carefully, but they're optimistic," he explained.

"We need to go to her," Julia croaked.

Beckett grimaced. "They only want one visitor at a time for now."

"Send Ramsey," Hayes said. "That's who she'd want with her."

My throat constricted as everyone in the room looked at me. "I'll watch over her." Hell, I'd breathe for her if I had to.

"Come on." Beckett motioned me forward. It was the most acceptance I'd received from the man. I wouldn't hesitate.

Blood roared in my ears as we made our way down the hall and into a waiting elevator. Beckett pressed a button for a floor I didn't register and, seconds later, the doors opened again. He led the way to a set of double doors and picked up a phone. After a few mumbled words, the doors opened. He nodded to something on the wall. "Sanitize your hands before you go in. You don't want to risk infection."

I obeyed, rubbing the cold gel between my palms. A man

in scrubs stepped forward and nodded at me. "Follow me, Mr. Bishop."

He led me past a sea of rooms, the beeping grating on my ears. He pointed to an open door. "Ms. Easton is through there. She is breathing on her own, which is a great sign, but she has several tubes in place to give her the support she needs, and she's getting another transfusion, as well."

I didn't nod or say a word. I simply stepped inside. I had to be with her. Needed to watch her chest rise and fall and tell her that I was there.

My steps faltered as I walked towards the bed. I'd never seen Shiloh so pale. As if there was no blood in her at all.

I strode to her side, easing down into the chair by her bed. My hand found hers, only an oxygen monitor on one finger. I lifted it, pressing a kiss to her palm. "Shiloh…"

I broke on her name, two syllables bringing me to my knees. My shoulders shook in silent sobs. "I'm so sorry. Please. Come back to me."

Chapter Forty-Nine

Shiloh

FAINT BEEPING PULLED AT ME, AND MY MOUTH TWISTED into a grimace. "Quiet."

A hand squeezed mine. "Come on, Shiloh. Open those eyes. Let me see those ice-blues."

I wanted that. Wanted to see the owner of that husky voice. I struggled to lift my lids, but they were so damn heavy.

Lips pressed to my forehead as a hand squeezed mine. "You've got this."

My eyes fluttered, bursts of low light filling my vision, and then onyx eyes were staring back at me. Ones I thought I'd never see again. "You're here."

"Where else would I be? My place is with you."

My throat burned, my eyes following as tears slid down my cheeks.

Ramsey instantly framed my face with his hands, worry filling his expression. "Hey, hey. You're okay. You're safe. I've got you."

"I thought I was losing you."

"Never." The single word was an uttered vow. "You've got a

shadow for life, I'm afraid. You won't be able to kick me to the curb even if you try."

A small laugh escaped me, but I instantly regretted it. Hot-white pain surged in my belly.

"Don't laugh. You've got a world of stitches in your stomach."

I nodded, swallowing hard.

"Want some water?"

"Please."

Ramsey held a straw to my lips. "Nice and easy."

I took a few sips and then released the straw. The cool water was heaven on my throat. I reached out for Ramsey. My hand shook, the weakness surprising me. "How long have I been asleep?"

"A little over twelve hours, but you lost a lot of blood. It's going to take some time to recover." Ramsey wove our fingers together, stroking the back of my hand.

"Howard?"

Storms swirled in Ramsey's eyes. "Dead."

"Good." I only wished it could've been me who'd ended him.

Ramsey leaned forward, pressing his forehead to mine. "I'm so sorry. I never should've left you alone. I should've found an-other way to get the drop on Howard—"

I squeezed Ramsey's hand as hard as I could. "You came for me. And when I needed to be strong, it was your face I called on."

He let out a shaky breath. "I almost lost you."

"You should know by now I'm stronger than that."

His mouth curved the slightest amount. "I should. Bravest soul I've ever known."

"I missed you." I knew it had only been hours, but it felt like a lifetime.

"Could barely breathe without you," Ramsey whispered against my lips. "Every time I inhaled, it felt like breathing in shards of glass."

"I'm sorry."

"Don't make me go through that again." His lips brushed against mine. "Stay with me."

"I'm here. Always."

Ramsey pulled back a fraction. "Will you move into the main house with me? Make things official?"

I frowned at him.

"What?"

"I like the guest cabin. It's cozy."

He barked out a laugh. "Only you would want the tiny-ass cabin instead of the mountain lodge."

I scowled at him. "I like what I like."

Ramsey brushed his thumb across my cheek. "There's a hell of a bathtub in the main house."

My brows lifted. "I have found myself partial to baths lately."

"You and me both."

A knock sounded at the door. "Hey, Ramsey, do you want—?" Beckett halted mid-stride. "She's awake."

"Hey, big brother."

"You're awake." He rushed towards the bed and immediately started listing off questions.

I held up a hand. "Slow down. I'm okay. The pain isn't too bad, and Ramsey already gave me some water."

He let out a shaky breath and ran a hand through his hair. "You scared the hell out of us."

"I'm sorry. I didn't mean to."

Beckett leaned down and pressed a kiss to the top of my head. "Thanks for coming back to us."

"Always."

Beckett shot Ramsey a grin. "It's a good thing, too. This guy has been an insufferable mess."

Ramsey glared at him. "I thought we had a pact."

"That was to not tell Shy that you were crying like a baby and snotting all over her."

My mouth dropped open. "Beckett."

He shrugged. "Oops."

Ramsey shook his head and leaned forward to press his mouth to mine gently. "Not ashamed for you to know how much I love you."

Beckett made a gagging noise.

"Beckett Easton, you are not making ugly sounds like that," my mother said as she moved into the room. Her eyes shone as she crossed to the bed. "My girl."

"Hi, Mom."

She shoved Beckett aside and pressed a kiss to my cheek. "So strong."

"I'm sorry if I worried you."

She brushed the hair away from my face. "I've had too many moments with my girls in this hospital. But if there's one thing I know, it's that they're fighters. They'll always make it through."

Pride surged in my chest. My mom wasn't letting this level her. She was standing strong. Believing in me.

I squeezed her hand. "Love you."

"Love you, too. More than you'll ever know."

Voices sounded in the hallway and, seconds later, chaos descended on my room. I could barely keep up with the gentle hugs and I-love-yous. But one person hovered in the background.

Everly wrung her hands as she watched everyone milling about. I motioned her forward, and she swallowed hard. The crowd parted as she moved towards me.

I sent her my sternest expression. "Ev, if you blame yourself for any of this, it's really going to piss me off."

Her lips twitched, but I still saw strain around her eyes. "Can I at least say that I'm so sorry this happened?"

"You can." I pulled her into a hug, ignoring the pull on my stitches. "Couldn't ask for a better sister to bring into the family."

"I heard that," Hadley called.

"My *favorite* sister," I said in a stage whisper.

Everly couldn't hold in her laughter as she held me tighter. "I love you, Shy. I couldn't be prouder to be a part of this family."

"Even if we bring chaos wherever we go?" Hadley asked.

Everly grinned as she straightened. "Even then."

Beckett chuckled, pointing at me. "But this one takes it to a whole new level. Pissing someone off so they'll stab you?"

I shrugged. "I had to get the knife somehow."

Everyone groaned.

I looked up into those onyx eyes that were the beginning of everything. "And I knew he'd catch me when I fell."

Addie sniffled. "Don't you dare make me cry. If I start, I won't stop."

Beckett chuckled and wrapped an arm around his wife. "Such a tender heart."

"It's the hormones." She wiped at her eyes.

Beckett nuzzled her neck. "Sure, it is."

My dad moved through the crowded room to my side. "Love you. Don't you dare do that to me again."

I leaned over to kiss his cheek. "Ramsey said something similar."

"I knew I liked him."

Warmth spread through me at that. Ramsey had become a part of our ragtag family, even if he hadn't wanted to. And it was exactly what he needed.

My dad reached out a hand to him. "Thank you for doing everything in your power to save her."

Ramsey swallowed hard. "I'd do anything for her."

"I know it. That's why I like you."

"Hey, guys," Hayes called.

Everyone looked over at him. "Think we could clear out for a few minutes? There are two boys who really want to see Shiloh and Ramsey."

My heart clenched. "Aidan and Elliott are here?"

Hayes smiled at me. "Came first thing this morning. Refused to let the Millers take them home until you woke up."

Tears filled my eyes again. Ramsey leaned over, wiping them away. "Don't let them see you crying."

"It's okay if they see. Then they'll know how much I've missed them." They were the one piece of the puzzle that was missing.

"We'll be back," my mom whispered, giving me another kiss.

My family filed out one by one, and I practically bounced in my bed. Ramsey growled at me. "Don't pull at your stitches."

I stuck my tongue out at him. "I'm happy."

He shook his head but kissed me soundly. "Love you."

"Love you more."

A throat cleared in the doorway, and I pulled away from Ramsey. Hayes stood there with Aidan and Elliott.

Aidan bumped Elliott's shoulder. "See, El? Told ya. If he's kissing her, she's just fine."

Elliott flew at the bed. Thankfully, Ramsey caught him as he launched himself and deposited him gently beside me. "Careful. She's got some stitches in her stomach, so we have to be really gentle."

Elliott bobbed his head up and down. "Does it hurt?"

"A little. But it helps to see you and Aidan." I figured going with a watered-down version of the truth couldn't hurt.

"But you're gonna be okay, right?"

"I'll be chasing you around the barn before you know it."

Elliott puffed up his chest. "I'll take care of Sky and Onyx for you until you're better."

The burning behind my eyes was back. "I can't imagine a better caregiver." I looked up at Aidan, who stood at the foot of my bed. "Think you'd be up for helping?"

He nodded. "Of course. Whatever you need."

I motioned Aidan closer. When he was just a step away, his hand found mine, and he squeezed. "I'm so glad you're okay. I…" He swallowed thickly. "I was so scared."

I squeezed his hand back and then pulled him down for a hug, not giving a damn that my stomach felt like it was on fire. "I'm right here, and I'm not going anywhere."

Elliott lay down next to me, burrowing into my side. "Love you, Shiloh."

Aidan released me, wiping under his eyes. "Me, too," he whispered.

Everything burned now, but it was the good kind—a fire that blazed because so much love surrounded me that I was drowning in it. My gaze lifted to Ramsey's over Elliott's head. "Never thought I'd get this lucky. I couldn't love you all more."

Chapter Fifty

Ramsey

TWO WEEKS LATER

I LEANED BACK AGAINST THE STEPS AS I TOOK IN THE SHOW in the round pen. I might have moved Shiloh into the main house, but the cabin steps were still the perfect vantage point to watch her do what she did best: make miracles.

The sun dipped lower in the sky, casting the landscape in a rosy glow. It made Onyx's coat take on a gleam, or maybe it was just the pride the horse had in herself shining through.

I'd never seen anything like the moment those two had been reunited. Shiloh had made me pull over right next to the round pen, refusing to get into bed until she'd seen Onyx and Sky. Onyx had let out a whinny that cracked my damn heart. The two of them had stood forehead to forehead for…I didn't know how long. I hadn't had the heart to pull them apart.

Something about being without Shiloh for a week had broken through Onyx's walls. In the past few days, she and Shiloh had made massive strides.

Movement flickered out of the corner of my eye as Lor approached, lowering herself to the step next to me. She was quiet for a moment, watching Shiloh guide Onyx around the pen on a lead rope. "Should she be up and around this much?"

"Probably not, but you try telling her that."

The doctors had said that walking and movement were good, all part of the healing process. But I wasn't sure they'd say the same if they saw just how much Shiloh was trying to take on.

Lor let out a snorted laugh. "She's got steel in her veins."

I sent a sidelong glance my friend's way.

She leaned back, letting out a sigh. "I was wrong."

My brow lifted at that. "Did the *w*-word just pass your lips?"

"Oh, shut up."

I chuckled.

A shadow passed over Lor's eyes, making her seem older than her years. "Didn't want any trouble finding you. I worry about my boy, even though you're a man now. Always will. But I tried to talk you out of a life that's made you happier than I've ever seen."

My ribs constricted around my lungs. "Lor—"

"No, let me say my piece. I've never seen you like this. There's a peace in you that's more than I could've hoped for. She healed you."

I laid my hand over Lor's, squeezing her fingers. "We healed each other."

She stared down at the contact. "I'll love her forever for that."

"Good. Because I'm gonna make a family with her."

Lor's eyes flew to mine. "She know that?"

I choked on a laugh. "I'm just getting around to talking to her about it."

"Men," Lor huffed. "Always assuming."

I grinned. "Sometimes, it pays to be confident."

She shook her head as she rose. "I'll be back tomorrow to check on your new arrival. Hopefully, Shiloh won't have kicked your ugly mug to the curb overnight."

I pushed to my feet, Kai rising with me. "Love you, Lor. Need you to know that. You saved me, too."

She swallowed hard, her eyes misting over. "Love you like my own. That'll never change."

"Glad to hear it."

Lor waved me off. "Go kiss your girl and stop making an old woman cry."

The corner of my mouth twitched. "You could never be old."

"Sweet-talker," she muttered as she headed for her truck.

I made my way towards the round pen, Kai on my heels. Onyx's ears twitched at our approach, but she didn't tense. "What do you think? Is she ready to meet the welcome wagon?"

Shiloh's mouth curved into a smile that hit me right in the gut. "I think she's ready." She patted Onyx's neck. "What do you think, girl? Want to make some friends?"

The mare quivered as if she understood every word.

"I'm gonna unlatch the gate, and we'll walk her over, nice and easy."

"Sounds like a plan."

I unlatched the chain and walked the gate open, motioning for Kai to heel. Onyx's head lifted as Shiloh guided her towards the exit. I didn't miss how Shiloh guarded her movements. She was still hurting more than she wanted to let on. Flickers of anger and fear rose in me, along with the memories, but I did my best to let them pass through on a breeze.

It would take time for the scars to fade for all of us. All we could do was breathe through it and look for the good—like this moment right here.

I fell into step next to Shiloh and Onyx, Kai keeping pace but giving the mare her space. "Push it a little too much today?"

Shiloh sent a glance my way. "It's annoying how perceptive you are."

I chuckled. "Get used to it because you're stuck with me now."

She leaned into me, her warmth and life seeping into my muscles and bones. "I kinda like being stuck with you."

"Glad to hear it."

We walked in silence to the pasture, enjoying the comfortable quiet that Shiloh and I preferred. So often, what passed between us didn't need words but said everything.

I unlatched the gate, and Shiloh led Onyx inside. She leaned forward, pressing her cheek to the mare's. "This is a new beginning for you. There's a whole beautiful world waiting. You just have to take the first step."

My throat tightened, emotion clogging it as Shiloh unhooked the lead rope. Onyx didn't move at first, simply stayed close. Shiloh gave her a pat on the neck. "Just one step."

The mare seemed to hear her. She lifted her front hoof, then her back. Soon, she was walking, slowly approaching the group of horses waiting for her. Pep lifted his head and let out a whinny. Onyx picked up to a trot at his call, jogging towards them. They sniffed and nosed each other in greeting before they all settled in to munch on the lush grass.

I moved in behind Shiloh, wrapping my arms around her. "You did that. You gave her a miracle."

"*We* did it. You and me. I think I could do anything when I know you're with me."

The burn was back. The one I relished because it was from Shiloh. "How would you feel about another miracle?"

She twisted in my arms so she could take in my face. "What did you have in mind?"

"I talked to your brother about what it would entail to become a foster parent."

Shiloh's hands fisted in my shirt. "Aidan and Elliott?"

I nodded. "I want to give them the home they deserve. I want to give them the family they deserve. You want to do that with me?"

Tears glistened in those pale blue eyes. "I can't imagine a better miracle than building a home with you and those boys."

"It's a bigger everything."

Shiloh smiled up at me. "I think we're up for the challenge."

"Love you, Shiloh."

She nuzzled into me, breathing deeply. "You're my sky."

I stilled. "Your sky?"

"My pinpricks of hope on the darkest nights. You are that in living form for me. You always will be. And I think we can be that for the boys, too."

The burn had caught fire, lighting everything inside me aflame. I welcomed it all. "Just when I think I can't love you more."

Shiloh grinned up at me. "I like to keep you on your toes."

My lips met hers in a long, slow kiss. One that told her I'd never tire of that until the day they put me six feet under.

Epilogue

Shiloh

TWO MONTHS LATER

"I LOOK RIDICULOUS," I MUTTERED AS HADLEY RELEASED my hair from the curling iron.

She sent me a look through the mirror. "Just trust my vision, would you?"

I stuck out my tongue at her, and she laughed.

Addie groaned, leaning back in her chair. "Just take comfort in the fact that you couldn't possibly look as ridiculous as me. I just had to get knocked up before Ev's wedding."

Laiken snapped a photo of the three of us as her hand went to her own slightly rounded bump. "You all look beautiful."

Addie glared at her and pointed. "You keep that lens pointed away from me today."

Laiken pressed her lips into a firm line to keep from laughing, but it only worked for so long before a giggle escaped. "I don't think I've ever seen you look that stern."

Addie rubbed her swollen belly. "That's because I mean business."

"Don't listen to her, Laiken. I want lots of photos of my glowing cousin. And she can't even yell at me for it because I'm the bride," Ev said, brushing invisible wrinkles out of her dress.

I would never have thought that Everly would go over-the-top whimsical for her wedding, but she had, and it worked somehow. Lanterns hung from the trees outside and lined a makeshift aisle through the garden she and Hayes had made for themselves. The entire event was drowning in flowers of every type and pastels of every shade. But Everly herself was the most amazing vision I'd ever seen.

I swore she would float down the aisle. She'd asked my father to escort her. While she'd thanked Ian for what he'd done for me, and there was more peace there, the two would never truly be brother and sister. She could forgive him for the past, but she'd never forget. The best she could do was move on into her new life, and my dad was only too happy to help lead her there. We'd all given him more than a little ribbing when he'd dissolved into tears at her asking. The two shared a special bond, and it warmed all our hearts to see.

Addie opened her mouth to argue with Ev and then snapped it closed. "She's right, dang her. I can't say anything."

Everly burst into laughter and squeezed her cousin's shoulders. "You'll be happy to have these photos one day."

Addie laid her hands on top of Everly's. "What I am is over the moon for you. I can't think of anyone who deserves a world of happiness more."

Everly sniffed as she looked around at the women in the room. "We all deserve it."

Hadley made a tsking noise. "Don't start crying. If you ruin my makeup job, I'm going to be pissed."

Everly fanned her face. "No tears. Raccoon eyes just aren't appropriate for saying 'I do.'"

I snorted and ran my fingers through my hair, loosening the

curls. I stood and nearly tripped over my dress. "Everly Easton, if I trip and fall on my face, I will never forgive you."

Ev snorted, and then her eyes filled again. "Everly Easton. It's my first time hearing it out loud."

"Hell," Hadley cursed. "You're determined to ruin my makeup."

The door opened, and Mom stepped inside. "Shy, Ramsey and the boys are looking for you."

"Everything okay?"

Mom gave me that gentle smile that she only had for one person. "I think Elliott wants to go over his *job* one more time."

My mom and El had become best pals. He spent more than his share of afternoons learning to garden and cook with her. I think it was his innocence, unmarred by everything he'd been through, that had drawn my mother in. He reminded her of all the hope there was in the world.

"I'll be back," I called, heading out the door and down the hall.

"I just want to show her how I'm going to hold it one more time." Elliott's voice sounded from around the corner.

Aidan sighed. "You've practiced like a hundred times."

I grinned at the bickering tone. Most people wouldn't revel in that sound, but I did because it was a brotherly one. For so long, Aidan had been forced to play the role of father to Elliott, but now, a month after the boys had come to live with Ramsey and me, they were finally settling into a true brotherly dynamic.

I rounded the corner, and three heads turned in my direction. All of their jaws dropped.

"Lolo, you look like a fairy," Elliott said in a reverent tone.

I tried not to scowl at that. The blush dresses Everly had chosen for the bridesmaids were beautiful, but so not me. The only thing that made the garment feel like it *fit* were the embroidered specks on the fabric that made it look as if I were clothed in a twilight sky.

Aidan coughed to hide his laugh. "He's right. You look beautiful, Lolo."

The use of the boys' nickname for me had me softening. "Thanks, but I don't think you should get used to it."

Ramsey's onyx eyes blazed as he moved in close. "Most beautiful sight I've ever laid eyes on."

My heart skipped a beat. It didn't matter how often those eyes met mine; I could still get lost in them. "You don't look so bad yourself."

Ramsey wore a white dress shirt and black jeans that fit him just right. While Hayes had given Everly her every heart's desire when it came to the wedding, he'd put his foot down when it came to the groomsmen. Black jeans, white button-downs, and boots. It somehow worked.

Ramsey leaned in close and whispered in my ear. "Your parents are taking the boys tonight, right?"

I shivered as his hand skated over my bare back. "Yup, they're going camping this weekend."

"There is a God in Heaven."

I couldn't hold in my laughter. Alone time had been a little harder to get this month.

"Lolo, look. Like this, right?"

I turned in Ramsey's arms to take in Elliott. He held the ring-bearer's pillow with focused attention.

"I think that's perfect. You've got this. You could do it backwards and in your sleep."

He scrunched up his face. "But I don't have to, do I?"

Ramsey patted him on the shoulder. "Just one forward-facing trip down the aisle, wide-awake."

He relaxed. "Thank God. I'm already gonna sleep for a week after this. It's a lot of pressure."

None of us could hold in our laughter at that. It was the release we all needed on a day that was a lot more than any of us were used to. But come Monday, we'd be back to life as normal.

Our simple existence with Kai and the horses. The one that all of us loved more than words.

⌐

"Dance with me."

I looked over at Ramsey. "You dance?"

He frowned in my direction. "You don't think I have rhythm?"

My cheeks heated. "Oh, I know you have that."

Ramsey chuckled and got to his feet, holding out a hand. "Come on."

I placed my hand in his and followed him to the dance floor. "I'll probably step on your feet."

"Worth it." Ramsey pulled me into his arms and glided us back and forth to the slower tune the band played.

I couldn't help but look around the tent at all the people I loved. Boden had Laiken's legs in his lap as he rubbed her feet. She lifted her camera, taking a quick shot of her fiancé, and I didn't miss how he reached out to rub her belly next.

Beckett twisted Addie in a spin, and her laughter caught in the air as she kicked up one bare foot, such joy on her face. Hadley had Birdie's hands, while Calder had Sage's, the four of them dancing to the beat of a song that absolutely wasn't this.

The bride and groom were completely lost in each other. Hayes brushed the hair back from Everly's face and leaned in for a kiss as they danced. As he pulled back, he mouthed, *I love you.*

Ramsey nuzzled my neck. "Happy?"

I let myself get lost in his heat. "It was a good day."

"The best."

"Even if I had to wear a dress."

He chuckled. "You want one of these one day?"

I pulled back so I could take in Ramsey's face. There was only curiosity there. A genuine question. "With you, maybe."

Ramsey's mouth curved. "Before or after we adopt the boys?"

"Before," I said in a hushed whisper.

"That means we need to do it soon."

I reached up, my hand pressed to his stubbled cheek. "I'd marry you tomorrow. Bind myself to you in any way I could."

Ramsey's onyx eyes shone in the low light, those glittering specks appearing in their depths. His hand dipped into his pocket, and he pulled out something that caught the light. He slid the band onto my finger—a scattering of black and clear diamonds that reminded me of the night sky. So perfectly me.

His eyes collided with mine. "Next week. You, me, the family."

My heart nearly burst at his claiming of my family as his own. "I can't imagine anything more perfect."

"Because it's you and me. Our everything."

I pressed my forehead to his. "It's our sky. It just keeps getting bigger."

Bonus Scene

Shiloh

I STROKED ONE HAND OVER SKY'S FACE AS I USED THE OTHER to scratch under Onyx's chin. My girls had become quite the pair. Bonded in a way that made my chest squeeze every time I saw them race across the pasture or push their heads together as they munched on grass.

Pressing a kiss to Sky's nose and then to Onyx's, I straightened and turned back towards the house. The front door flew open, and Elliott charged out, flying down the steps towards me. He hit my middle with an *oomph*. "Mom, what time is it now?"

The single word hit me like it did every time. With the best kind of ache. One that spoke of the hardship that both Elliott and I had been through to get to this place. Somewhere I'd earned the best title I'd ever have. Aidan had never grown comfortable using it, but I felt just as much love when his nickname for me slipped from his lips.

I grinned as I glanced down at my watch. "We don't need to be there for another forty-five minutes."

Elliott danced back and forth on the new shoes Ramsey and I

had gotten him for this occasion. He'd grown out of his last pair way too fast. "I want to get a good seat, though."

I pressed my lips together to keep from laughing. "We'll get a good seat. Promise."

He wrapped his hands around my arm, tugging me towards the house. "But, just in case, let's leave early."

"All right. Where are the twins?"

"Dad's braiding their hair, but they're almost ready."

My grin was back. Ramsey's fingers had proven far more adept at handling the girls' hair than my own. They'd been wary of him when they came to live with us six months ago, but now Clary and Sarah looked at Ramsey as if he were their personal superhero.

And, in so many ways, he was. It had been Ramsey's idea to continue fostering, opening our home to children who needed a safe place for however long they needed it. We'd had pairings for only a couple of days, and others that lasted months, but I had a feeling that Clary and Sarah would forever be a part of our brood.

The front door opened, and a little girl with red hair leapt over the threshold. "Look how pretty my hair is, Lolo."

I beamed both at her use of Aidan's nickname for me and at the joy on her face. "You look beautiful, Clary."

Ramsey strode out of the house with Sarah on his hip, her hair in pigtail braids that matched her sister's. My heart skipped a beat as his onyx gaze cut to me. So much passed between us in that moment. We hadn't lost the ability to speak without words. And right now, he was promising that we'd get some alone time later.

"You look gorgeous," he rasped.

My cheeks heated as my hands skimmed over my dress. "You know I hate this stuff."

He chuckled. "It's only for a few hours."

"Thank God," I muttered.

Elliott tugged my hand again. "Can we go *now*?"

My gaze flicked back to Ramsey. "He wants to make sure we get good seats."

Ramsey's expression softened. "Let's hit the road."

We got the girls into their booster seats as Elliott climbed into the third row of the SUV. Once we were all settled, Ramsey took my hand in his as he drove away from the ranch.

My stomach twisted and flipped as we got closer to the high school. I squeezed Ramsey's fingers, trying to ground myself.

He glanced in my direction. "You okay?"

"Not really."

Worry creased his brow.

"This came way too fast."

The concern melted from Ramsey's expression, and he lifted my hand to his mouth, kissing it. "He's not disappearing from our lives."

"I know. I just…I'm gonna miss him."

"The University of Oregon is only a day's drive, and you have all summer with him first."

I needed to remember that. To hold on to the here and now. And I was so proud of Aidan I thought my heart would burst. After he'd come to live with Ramsey and me, he'd studied hard and was finishing out his senior year strong in the top ten percent of his class.

But even then, Aidan had been unsure about college. He'd played the role of Elliott's father for so long, the idea of leaving him behind to pursue his education had seemed wrong to him. But after some long conversations with me, Ramsey, and finally, Elliott, Aidan had come around to the idea. But it wouldn't be easy for any of us.

Ramsey pulled into a parking spot, and Elliott was out of the SUV in a flash. I threw open my door, calling out to him. "Wait!"

Luckily, my dad was right there, waiting, catching Elliott around the waist with a laugh. "Where do you think you're going?"

"I gotta get good seats," Elliott said with an exasperated sigh.

My dad wrapped his arm around Elliott's shoulders. "You've got nothing to worry about. Your grandma made us get here two hours ago to save seats."

Not only had Ramsey and I become Dad and Mom, but my

parents had become Grandma and Grandpa. And they couldn't have been happier about it.

Ramsey appeared, holding Clary's and Sarah's hands. "What have you been doing for the past two hours then?"

My dad chuckled. "Just going stir-crazy. But you don't mess with Julia on a mission."

Ramsey grunted. "Understatement."

"And how are my girls?" Dad asked, grinning at them.

Sarah grabbed for my hand, ducking behind me as she did. But Clary beamed at him. "Ramsey braided our hair."

"I can see that." Dad's eyes sparkled as he glanced at Ramsey. "Your skills only improve with time."

Ramsey merely grunted and started guiding us all towards the football field where the graduation ceremony was being held. I couldn't hold in my laugh.

We made our way through the sea of people towards the front two rows, where my mom had saved us all seats. The second Clary and Sarah saw Birdie and Sage, they took off running. They had something like hero worship for Calder and Hadley's twins. And the girls had taken Clary and Sarah under their wings.

The other little ones were back at my parents' ranch being watched by babysitters until we got back there for Aidan's party. My heart gave a squeeze as I took in the rest of our loved ones. Everly and Hayes. Hadley and Calder. Addie and Beckett. Laiken and Boden. My mom. They'd all shown up today to make sure Aidan knew just how loved he was.

Hayes extended a hand to Ramsey and pulled him into a back-slapping hug, and then pressed a kiss to the top of my head. "How are you two holding up?"

Ramsey wrapped an arm around me. "Shiloh lost it on the ride over."

I smacked his stomach with the back of my hand. "I did not."

He pressed a kiss to my temple. "Whatever makes you feel better."

"Ladies and gentlemen," a voice called over the loudspeaker. "Please take your seats."

We quickly found ours, and I gripped Ramsey's hand in one of mine, Elliott's in the other, as the ceremony began. A girl I recognized gave a valedictorian speech about friendship. The principal recounted the class's many accomplishments. And then the students started parading across the stage.

The thing I loved most about graduations in a small town was that they were personal. They gave each student a chance to say something after receiving their diploma. Some were funny. Some ribbed their friends. Others were heartfelt and emotional.

As they called Aidan's name, our section leapt to its feet and let out deafening cheers. Aidan couldn't hold in his laugh as he took us all in, shaking his head. But I saw the pride in his eyes. The love.

"He's the best kid ever," I said to Ramsey.

"Gonna miss the hell out of him," Ramsey said hoarsely.

Aidan shook the principal's hand as he took his diploma, pausing for a photo. Then he moved to the microphone. He swallowed hard as he looked out over the crowd. "Wouldn't have made it here without two people in this audience."

He looked at Ramsey and me, and my fingers dug into Ramsey's hand. "Dad, Mom, thank you for giving me the most beautiful life. One I never thought I would have. I'll never be able to repay you, but I'll do everything I can to be the man you've taught me to be."

I didn't even try to hold back the tears. I let them fall freely down my face because they were a mark of how much I loved the son of my heart. And when I glanced up at Ramsey, I saw tears tracking down his cheeks, as well.

I pressed my face into his. "It's you. You're the magic that gave us all this beautiful life."

Ramsey pulled me close. "It's all of us. What we've made together."

I pressed in closer, feeling the love swirling around us. "It's our sky."

Acknowledgments

So much life happens while books are written. The happy. The sad. And everything in between. During the writing of this book, there was a lot of hard. I got leveled with one thing after another, and it was truly the love of amazing people that got me through.

So many kindnesses were heaped on me during the season, I honestly couldn't fit every person at the end of this book. But if you sent a card, a gift, a Facebook message, or an email, THANK YOU. Love and kindness can truly change someone's world.

There are some folks I'd like to say a special thanks to. First, in my writerly world.

Sam. For holding my hand from across the ocean. Cheering me on to finish this book when I thought there was no way in hell it would happen…and helping me find the love for it again. Your friendship is a true gift. Just remember you promised half the year in Oregon…

Laura and Willow. For letting me snot-cry when my heart was in pieces and life was one hit after another. And for somehow managing to make me cackle-laugh in the midst of it all. Thank you for sprinting and cheering and making sure I crossed that finish line. #LoveChainForever.

Emma. Your kindness in the midst of your own struggles just shows what an amazing heart you have. I'm so lucky to have you in my life. Thank goodness for the wormhole and that random thread in Inkers!

My Slackers: Amy, Kristy, & Rebecca. I love you all to pieces. Thank you for rallying around me every single day while I was writing this book. And during the *many* editing passes, too. This little corner of the internet has brought me such joy, laughter, and incredible support.

Second, in my non-writer world.

My STS soul sisters: Hollis, Jael, and Paige. Your love never wavers. Nor your support. In the hardest moments and the happiest. It is such an honor to do life with you. I love you so very much.

The Lex Vegas Ladies. Thank you for your kindness and check-ins and for making me feel so loved, even when we're so far away.

And to all my family and friends near and far. Thank you for supporting me on this crazy journey, even if you don't read "kissing books." But you get extra-special bonus points if you picked up one of mine, even if that makes me turn the shade of a tomato when you tell me.

To my fearless beta readers: Crystal, Kelly, and Trisha, thank you for reading this book in its roughest form and helping me to make it the best it could possibly be!

The crew that helps bring my words to life and gets them out into the world is pretty darn epic. Thank you to Susan, Margo, Chelle, Jaime, Julie, Hang, Stacey, Jenn, and the rest of my team at Social Butterfly. Your hard work is so appreciated!

To all the bloggers who have taken a chance on my words... THANK YOU! Your championing of my stories means more than I can say. And to my launch and ARC teams, thank you for your kindness, support, and sharing my books with the world. An extra-special thank you to Crystal, who sails that ship so I can focus on the words.

Ladies of Catherine Cowles Reader Group, you're my favorite place to hang out on the internet! Thank you for your support, encouragement, and willingness to always dish about your latest book boyfriends. You're the freaking best!

Lastly, thank YOU! Yes, YOU. I'm so grateful you're reading this book and making my author dreams come true. I love you for that. A whole lot!

Also Available from
CATHERINE COWLES

The Tattered & Torn Series
Tattered Stars
Falling Embers
Hidden Waters
Shattered Sea
Fractured Sky

The Wrecked Series
Reckless Memories
Perfect Wreckage
Wrecked Palace
Reckless Refuge
Beneath the Wreckage

The Sutter Lake Series
Beautifully Broken Pieces
Beautifully Broken Life
Beautifully Broken Spirit
Beautifully Broken Control
Beautifully Broken Redemption

Stand-alone Novels
Further To Fall

For a full list of up-to-date Catherine Cowles titles,
please visit www.catherinecowles.com.

About

CATHERINE COWLES

Writer of words. Drinker of Diet Cokes. Lover of all things cute and furry, especially her dog. Catherine has had her nose in a book since the time she could read and finally decided to write down some of her own stories. When she's not writing, she can be found exploring her home state of Oregon, listening to true crime podcasts, or searching for her next book boyfriend.

Stay Connected

You can find Catherine in all the usual bookish places…

Website: catherinecowles.com

Facebook: facebook.com/catherinecowlesauthor

Catherine Cowles Facebook Reader Group: www.facebook.com/groups/CatherineCowlesReaderGroup

Instagram: instagram.com/catherinecowlesauthor

Goodreads: goodreads.com/catherinecowlesauthor

BookBub: bookbub.com/profile/catherine-cowles

Amazon: www.amazon.com/author/catherinecowles

Twitter: twitter.com/catherinecowles

Pinterest: pinterest.com/catherinecowlesauthor